A GIFT for GUILE

ALISSA JOHNSON

Cover art by Judy York

Published by Sourcebooks Casablanca, an imprint of Sourcebooks, Inc.
P.O. Box 4410, Naperville, Illinois 60567-4410
(630) 961-3900
Fax: (630) 961-2168
www.sourcebooks.com

Printed and bound in Canada.
MBP 10 9 8 7 6 5 4 3 2 1

For Jon Eric Nelson

One

1872

"Hello."

Hello. Quite possibly the single most innocuous word in the whole of the English language. It was difficult to take exception to the word *hello* under nearly any circumstance. Unless, of course, it happened to be uttered in the wrong place, at the wrong time, by the wrong man—in which case that one simple word spelled disaster.

Esther Walker-Bales stood amid the bustling crowd of Paddington station. For several long seconds, she did nothing but stare through the thick crepe of her weeping veil at Sir Samuel Brass. All six feet three and a half enormous inches of him.

He smiled at her, full lips spreading beneath a thick, dark beard. It wasn't a cheerful smile, though. It wasn't even a friendly smile. It was an *I am seriously put out with you, but we will discuss it later* smile. The sort a child misbehaving in public might expect from a father, if one's father happened to be a seriously put out giant.

"I said"—Samuel leaned forward to tower over her, his deep voice edging toward a growl—"hello, Esther."

His misguided attempt at intimidation goaded her into action. "What are you *doing* here?" she demanded, then shook her head once. "No, never mind. It doesn't matter. You have to go. Right now. Go." She gave him a discreet push.

He didn't budge an inch.

"No." Straightening, he flicked the edge of her veil with his fingers. "Who died? A husband? Cousin?"

No one had died, and he damn well knew it. "An interfering acquaintance of mine. A woman threw him on the tracks at"—she looked pointedly at the station clock behind him—"eight minutes past six."

"You've taken the death to heart, I see. I'm touched."

She was tempted to "touch" him with the dagger she had strapped to her ankle. "You have to leave."

"No. What are you doing in London?"

"Standing on platform number one in Paddington station."

His smile grew a little more strained. "Why are you standing in Paddington station?"

"I like trains." A locomotive began its laboring journey out of the station as if on cue, sending a billow of smoke and steam to the ornate ironwork above. Just the sight of it made her throat itch and her eyes water. She didn't like trains especially.

"Right." Samuel threw a quick look over his shoulder at a noisy group of passengers. "We're leaving."

"No, I can't."

"Why not?"

She gathered her meager supply of patience.

"Samuel, listen to me. I will tell you everything you wish to know." Some of it, anyway. "But not right now. Please, if you won't leave entirely, then at least go"—she waved her hand in the direction of an empty, and distant, alcove—"stand over there. Pretend you don't know me."

"God, if only," he muttered. "Esther, you will tell me what is going on, or I will haul you out of here. Over my shoulder if necessary."

He could probably get away with it. Samuel had been a police officer once. He'd gained considerable fame nine years ago for his part in rescuing a kidnapped duchess, not to mention bringing her captor—the notorious gang leader Horatio Gage—to justice in the process.

He was a mere private investigator now, but he still retained some notoriety, in large part because he had survived being shot on multiple occasions. *The Thief Taker Almighty*. That's what the papers had dubbed him.

It was fairly ridiculous.

It meant he could be recognized, though. No one in the station's crowd would move to stop his departure, however unorthodox, with an unknown woman.

Still, he wasn't likely to risk the attention, for the same reason she wouldn't risk leaving her hotel without the veil. She couldn't afford to be seen; his threat was empty. "You'll not make a scene."

"I will take a thirty second scene over arguing with you in here indefinitely." There was a short pause, then he lowered his voice. "Do you doubt me?"

Yes. Or maybe no. Damn it, she couldn't tell if he was bluffing. "I'm waiting for someone."

"Who?"

"None of your concern." She half turned away, giving him her shoulder and, hopefully, giving the impression to passing travelers that the two of them were not together. As Samuel was staring right at her, however, she feared it was a futile gesture. "*Please*. Go away."

"Are you waiting on a mark?" he guessed. "An accomplice?"

"What? No. I'm not a criminal." Not anymore. Not for a long time.

"Then you've no reason for secrecy. For whom are you waiting?"

"My lover."

"Try again."

She honestly didn't know if she was pleased or insulted by how quickly he dismissed the idea. "I don't know. And I'll not find out if you stay here. *Go. Away*."

This last she punctuated by turning her back on him completely.

And that was when she saw him—a scrawny young man of maybe sixteen, with a long face, sallow complexion, sharp chin, and filthy blond hair peeking out from under a ragged cap. He stood ten yards away and was staring at her as if he'd known her all his life. Only he didn't. Esther had never seen him before. And he couldn't possibly see her clearly behind the veil.

She sensed Samuel tense behind her. "Is that him?" he asked.

"I don't know."

The boy's gaze flew to Samuel, then he spun about and bolted in the opposite direction.

"Damn it," Esther hissed.

Samuel brushed past her with a curt, "Stay here."

The ensuing chase was oddly subdued, with the young man's escape hampered by the crowd and Samuel slowed by his apparent unwillingness to draw attention to himself. Esther knew him to be quick and agile. He would have no trouble running the boy down under normal circumstances. Today, he strode after his prey in long, unhurried strides, neatly sidestepping people and luggage alike.

Esther lost sight of them several times as the groups of travelers shifted and reformed. A large family with a small mountain of trunks blocked her view for several seconds before they moved on and Esther spotted Samuel through the clearing. He was at the far end of the station, only steps behind the young man.

Grab him, she thought, heart racing. *Grab him!*

Samuel stretched out an arm, but the young man dodged left, dashed to the edge of the platform, and leaped into the path of an oncoming engine. Nearby onlookers sent up a cry of alarm, but the young man was over the tracks and out of danger in the blink of an eye. Samuel, on the other hand, was trapped on her side of the station, his path blocked by the long line of passenger carriages that followed.

For a moment, Esther thought he might hop on the moving train and pass through the other side to continue the pursuit. In fact, she rather hoped he would. She'd not wanted him there, but since he'd been the one to scare the young man off, the least he could do was bring him back.

Samuel casually turned away from the platform edge

instead, as if he'd merely been a curious bystander, and began a leisurely stroll back to her.

The young man was gone.

Esther balled her hands at her sides. Oh, this was awful. This was a dreadful, dreadful mess. Seething, she waited for Samuel's return and wholeheartedly wished he could see her look of derision through the veil. "I *knew* you would ruin this."

His gray eyes narrowed dangerously, but he didn't respond other than to say, in the stiffest manner possible, "Shall we, Miss Bales?"

He offered his arm.

She glowered at it.

Samuel leaned in again. "Do you think to run?" he inquired in a soft voice laced with menace.

Of course she didn't intend to run, not while encumbered by a thick veil, heavy skirts, and a bustle. Still, she took some satisfaction in making him wait for an answer.

"Not yet," she replied. Then she headed for the exit on her own.

Samuel fell into step beside her. His large hand came up to settle lightly at the small of her back, much to her chagrin, herding her out of the station and toward a public hackney.

"I've rooms at the Anthem Hotel," she told him.

He didn't comment but simply assisted her inside the carriage, spoke to the driver briefly, then climbed in after her.

The instant the door was closed and the curtains drawn, Esther lifted the stifling crepe veil and scowled at him. "How the devil did you find me?"

"I followed you."

"What? All the way from Derbyshire?"

"No, I tracked you from Derbyshire." The carriage started with a soft jolt, and he pulled back the edge of a curtain for a glimpse outside. "I followed you from your hotel."

"How did you know where I was staying?" It might have been easy for him to find out that she'd boarded a train headed for London the day before yesterday, but he couldn't have known where she'd gone after that.

"London has a finite number of hotels."

As *finite* didn't necessarily mean *small*, she decided not to ask how long he'd been looking. "You shouldn't have come after me."

"I had no choice." He let the curtain fall back into place. "You snuck away in the dead of night."

"What rot. I departed from my own home at half past five in the morning in full view of my staff." That wasn't anywhere near the same thing as sneaking.

"You sent no word to your family."

"Nor was I obligated to do so." Her brother, Peter, was sixteen years old and away at school, and her older sister, Lottie, was traveling with her husband, Viscount Renderwell, in Scotland. It wasn't as if they might pay an unexpected call upon her little cottage and be shocked to find her missing.

"They'll worry," Samuel pointed out. "London isn't safe for you."

She didn't need him to point it out. "Of course they would worry. That's why I didn't send word. And neither will you. You'll keep this to yourself."

He lifted a brow at that. "Will I?"

"There is nothing to be gained from troubling them."

"Lottie has a right to know."

"She does not. Lottie is my sister, not my mother. I am twenty-eight years of age. I keep my own house, and I may take leave of it any time I please." She gave him a taunting smile. "I may even sneak out of it if I so choose."

Samuel studied the small woman sitting across from him. The flaxen hair, heart-shaped face, ivory skin, and wide blue eyes lent her an air of angelic innocence, but that was an impression otherwise wholly undeserved.

Miss Esther Bales, formerly Walker, was the youngest daughter of the late William Walker, one of England's most infamous criminals. He'd been a thief, burglar, confidence man, and all-around blackguard. Highly intelligent, monstrously manipulative, and shrouded in mystery, Walker had been alternately feared and idolized—at least, until Samuel and his fellow police officers had tracked him down some thirteen years ago. Confronted with evidence of his crimes, Walker had agreed to turn informant in exchange for his freedom and a chance at redemption. In the four years before his death, the man had aided them in their work, specializing in deciphering encryptions employed by gangs in and around London.

Only he'd not given up his old life. Will Walker had kept up his criminal activities in secret, and Esther had helped him.

Though he suspected she'd be surprised to hear it, Samuel didn't hold it against her. She'd been hardly more than a girl at the time. He didn't fault her for foolishly trying to help her bastard of a father. Moreover, he believed she regretted it.

Samuel had been foolish enough to try to help his mother once. He was familiar with that particular brand of regret.

No, it wasn't Esther's past as Will Walker's daughter that drew his ire—it was her stubborn refusal to move forward. It was the tenacity with which she clung to the old habits of manipulation and deceit. There was kindness in Esther. There was unfailing devotion to those she loved. And when it mattered most, there was honesty. Time and again, Samuel had caught glimpses of those traits. He saw the remarkable woman who had, against all odds, managed to resist her father's best efforts to carve out everything that was good and generous in her. Those brief moments fascinated him. But the glimpses were just that—temporary flashes that disappeared as quickly as they arrived. Esther never set aside the Walker customs of trickery and guile for long. And for some reason, that bothered him to an unreasonable degree.

Esther cocked her head at him. "If you think to unnerve me by staring at me for the whole of our trip, you are bound for disappointment."

He rather doubted she'd have mentioned his staring if it didn't unnerve her. To test his theory, he sat back against the thin cushions of the bench and went right on staring.

She folded her arms across her chest and stared right back.

She had spine; he'd give her that.

It was tempting to see how long she could hold out, but a battle of wills fought in silence wasn't in his best interest. He wanted answers. "Who was the man at the station?"

She matched his clipped tone. "I honestly do not know."

"Why did you come to London?"

"I've already answered that."

"No, you refused to answer."

"No, my answer did not meet with your satisfaction, but that is your misfortune, not mine."

Samuel was not a man given to speeches, even small ones. He preferred economy of words over lengthy discourse. Sometimes a simple grunt was sufficient to get one's point across. But there were times when nothing short of a lecture would do.

"You wish to speak of misfortune, Esther? Then let us speak of the misfortunes you court by coming to London. Nine years ago, your family was forced to leave town under assumed names in order to hide from men who might strike at you in revenge against your father. It was only last year that one of those men found you, nearly killed you and your sister in a stable fire, shot me in the shoulder, and kidnapped your brother."

Esther did not appear to appreciate his oratory efforts.

"Heavens, I'd quite forgotten," she drawled in a voice that could only be described as sweetly caustic. "Thank *goodness* you are here to remind me of all the little details of my life."

God, she was infuriating. "Esther—"

"You're rather like my very own talking diary."

Truly, truly infuriating. "If you don't wish to be spoken to like a fool, don't act like one."

She rolled her eyes at that and half stood in the carriage as if to knock on the ceiling. "Oh, this is all quite pointless. I'm leaving."

Leaning forward, he caught her fist before it could connect. "Sit down."

She went utterly still but for a gentle sway in time with the rolling carriage. She didn't struggle, shout, or try to pull her hand away. She didn't so much as bat an eyelash. She simply remained as she was, so close he could smell the rose-scented soap on her skin, watching him through cool blue eyes.

"Let go of me."

There wasn't a trace of anger or fear in her voice. It was low and steady and, like the rest of her, perfectly calm. Unnaturally calm. Like the eerie quiet before a storm.

Samuel risked a quick glance at the hem of her skirts. She likely had at least one dagger strapped to her ankle. Her father's favorite role for her had been that of henchman. She was slight of build, hardly his match in strength, but she was skilled with her blades, and she was damned quick.

When she didn't immediately reach for her weapons, he looked up again. Although her expression remained devoid of any emotion, an unsettling shadow had fallen over her pretty blue eyes.

"I am not going to stab you," she said quietly.

He wasn't sure why he felt like a brute all of a sudden, as if he'd bruised her somehow.

It was the difference in their sizes, he decided.

Her hand felt small and fragile enveloped in his. He released it with more care than was probably necessary. "Take your seat. We're almost there."

She sat down slowly and with a subdued air about her that he found as unsettling as the shadow in her gaze. "My hotel is at least another ten minutes away. I would prefer to procure my own transport."

"We're not going to your hotel."

That announcement perked her up a little. "You cannot mean to take me all the way to Derbyshire in a public hackney."

"We're not going to Derbyshire. My house is in Belgravia." On the very, very uttermost edge of it, which was the only slice of Belgravia he could afford without begrudging the cost. He'd just as soon live elsewhere, frankly. But his work sometimes required he entertain clientele at his home, and his clientele were the sort of men and women who expected to be entertained in homes with fashionable addresses.

"Why are we going to your house?"

"I imagine you can figure that out. I'll send someone to the hotel for your things."

Now she looked quite like her bristly self again. "No. Absolutely not. I am not staying with you. It isn't decent."

"Isn't *decent*?" Of all the arguments an unmarried woman dressed in widow's weeds might produce "it isn't decent" had to be among the most absurd. "You cannot be serious."

"I'll not be a source of gossip for your staff."

"We'll tell them you're my cousin."

"People marry their cousins."

"Then we'll tell them you're a client." She wouldn't be the first individual with an assumed name to spend time under his roof. Granted, she'd be the first woman to do so, but his servants were accustomed to the peculiar necessities of his work. Not one of them would bat an eye at her presence, nor breathe a word of it outside of the house. He had chosen each member of his staff with extraordinary care.

"Do your female clients often spend the night?"

He almost told her yes, just to put an end to the argument. And he very much wanted this argument to end, as the carriage was already rolling to a stop in front of his house. But the lie would probably bring him more grief than it was worth.

"What does it matter what my staff thinks?" he asked. "You'll never see them again."

"It isn't just your staff. Lottie will find out. And so will Peter. Lord knows you'll tell Renderwell and Gabriel. And Renderwell's sisters might hear of it, which means his mother certainly will, and she'll tell everyone in the village and—"

"All right, all right." Bloody hell. "I'll take you to the hotel after I'm done here."

He imagined that, given the circumstances, Esther's immediate family wouldn't much care that she'd spent the night under his roof, but he couldn't be absolutely certain. And damned if he had to haul the woman all the way back to Derbyshire, only to be subjected to a lecture on decorum from the Walkers, of all people, for his troubles.

Resigned, he threw open the carriage door, hopped down, and offered Esther his hand.

She wouldn't take it. "I am not going in with you."

"Fine. Keep the doors shut and the curtains drawn. If you attempt to run off, I will return you to your family trussed up like a duck."

She gave him a pretty smile. "What if I've a mind to run off to Derbyshire?" Then she reached out, grabbed the handle, and closed the door in his face.

Samuel growled at the carriage door. Sometimes, when it came to Esther, a grunt simply wouldn't suffice.

He wasn't particularly worried that Esther might try to run away. If she wanted to escape, she'd have tried at the station. Still, he thought it prudent to flip the driver an extra coin.

"Wait here." He thought about it, then added another coin. "Ignore everything the lady tells you."

Two

There had been a time, not so very long ago, when Samuel could expect to be greeted at his door by one of his maids. She would take his coat and hat, make polite inquiries after his day, and inform him that all was well in the house. Then he'd be left alone to go about his business in peace.

Oh, how he missed those times.

There was no one waiting for him in the foyer that evening. He tossed his hat and gloves on a side table and winced when a great crash arose from the other end of the house. It was followed by a feminine shriek, another crash, and then a cacophony of angry voices, slamming doors, and pounding footsteps.

Within seconds, a shaggy gray beast, its teeth bared and gleaming white, tore into the foyer. It reared up and planted two hulking paws on Samuel's chest, knocking him back a solid foot. Samuel stumbled to the left. The beast slipped, stumbled to the right, and slammed into the side table, sending the hat and gloves toppling to the floor, along with an expensive vase that shattered against the tiles.

Undeterred, the beast gathered itself and launched a second attack.

"Off, you sodding beast! Off—" Samuel was forced to snap his mouth shut when a great, wet plank of a tongue lapped at his face.

Swearing silently, he threw an arm around the animal's shoulders and managed to wrestle it to the ground just as a young maid came hurrying into the room carrying a lead. "I'm sorry, sir. I'm sorry. He got away from me."

Samuel scrubbed his sleeve over his face as the girl struggled to slip the lead around what was, at best guess, an ill-advised cross between an average Irish wolfhound and an exuberant hippopotamus. "Quite all right, Sarah."

Sarah dodged a series of desperately happy tongue laps. "Gor, it's like wrestling a ship of the line." She dipped her hand in her apron pocket and pulled out a sizable chunk of bread. "Here now, beastie. Look what I have. Look. Wouldn't you like a taste of this?"

The beastie would, indeed. He ceased his squirming and gobbled up the treat while Sarah attached the lead. "There we are, nothing to it."

Brushing off his trousers, Samuel gained his feet and discovered his stout, silver-haired housekeeper, Mrs. Lanchor, glaring at him from across the foyer. "Sir Samuel, this animal is out of control."

He spat out a piece of dog hair as discreetly as possible. "He's just excitable."

"A Pekingese is excitable. This dog is deranged."

Samuel glanced down at the wild, gleeful amber eyes and lolling tongue. A thick glob of food-laden slobber gathered at the edge of the dog's mouth, then made a slow but steady descent toward the floor. Mrs. Lanchor could be right. "He's young, and this is all new to him yet."

"He has been here two weeks."

Was that all? He looked at the jagged remains of the vase. The second in four days. "He'll calm with age. Take him into the garden."

"With age?" Mrs. Lanchor planted her hands on her hips. "We cannot have this sort of nonsense going on for years. What if you'd had a guest with you? What if he leaps upon a young lady? What if—?"

"I'll continue to work with him. The garden, please, Mrs. Lanchor," he repeated as he headed for the stairs. "I'm in a hurry."

He pretended not to hear Mrs. Lanchor's final, dire warnings on the perils of keeping dangerous animals in one's home.

The dog was undisciplined, not a danger. Well, not the sort of danger she was implying. Besides, this wasn't his home. It was merely a house Renderwell had insisted he buy six years ago and pay a decorator a small (and in Samuel's opinion, wasted) fortune to outfit in the manner befitting a fashionable gentleman. It was where he ate, slept, and sometimes worked, but it was not his home.

Home was his modest country house in Cheshire, decorated in the comfortable style he preferred—lots of dark colors and solid furniture. It had a generous garden and plenty of land on which to roam. That was where he felt most at peace, and where he had been spending more and more of his time lately.

Particularly since Renderwell had taken up permanent residence at Greenly House in Derbyshire, a mere twenty miles away.

Maybe he'd retire, as Renderwell had last year. He had more than enough funds to live on comfortably for the rest of his life. Gabriel could buy out his portion of the business, if he liked. The idea had its merits. Mrs. Lanchor was fond of the area. She'd grown up in a nearby village. And the beast would enjoy the space, the freedom. It wasn't fair to confine a dog of that size to a garden with the diameter of a dinner plate.

Yes, maybe he would retire.

If he survived the next twelve hours with Esther Walker-Bales.

Five minutes later, Samuel tossed a valise onto the carriage floor and took his seat across from Esther.

Eleven hours, fifty-five minutes to go.

She scowled at the bag at her feet. "What is that?"

Assuming the question was rhetorical—anyone could see it was a valise—he didn't bother with an answer.

She rolled her eyes and huffed. "Where are you going, Samuel?"

"To your hotel."

"To…? No. You cannot stay with me. That is worse than me staying with you."

"I'll obtain my own rooms." Next to hers, if he could manage it. He wondered if he should try for adjoining rooms, or if that would be *indecent*.

"People will see if you come knocking on my door."

He shrugged. "People will assume I desire a word with my sister."

"You cannot tell the hotel I'm your sister. You don't have a sister."

"I do tonight."

She cast her gaze up as if to beg for patience. "Samuel, be reasonable. Everyone in London knows who you are, and everyone knows you do not have a sister."

"I'm not as famous as you seem to think."

"Yes, you are. Lottie said you and Gabriel and Renderwell became tremendous sensations for rescuing Lady Strale."

Samuel considered his next words carefully. That rescue was a sensitive, even volatile, subject for the Walker family. He, along with Gabriel and Renderwell, had received accolades for their roles in saving the kidnapped duchess, but it had been Will Walker who had gone into a thieves' den and carried the unconscious woman to freedom. And it had been Will Walker who had gotten himself mortally wounded in the process. Presumably he'd played the hero to atone for the fact that he had also played a part in the duchess's kidnapping, however unknowing. He'd only meant to steal the Strale diamonds off her person at a ball, but his accomplice had run off with the woman herself.

Their accomplice, he corrected. Esther had been at that ball. She'd helped her father.

Whatever his reasons had been for sacrificing himself, however, Will Walker had saved the woman in the end. Unfortunately, the police couldn't admit to having worked with a known criminal, and the ensuing fame would have put the Walker children at risk. It had been decided that Will Walker should be buried in an unmarked grave in Brookwood Cemetery. His last, and likely only, heroic deed would remain a secret to all but a handful of people.

The Walker children had not been happy with the decision. They'd changed their name to Bales, moved to Norfolk, and cut off all contact with Samuel and his friends until last year. "It was a decade ago," he said now. It had scarcely been more than nine years, but a decade sounded better.

"People still recognize you, I'm sure."

"I'm not being stopped in the street by strangers." Not anymore, thank God.

"The concierge will recognize your name at the very least."

"I'll use an alias."

"And if he recognizes you on sight?" she asked. "He'll know you're lying."

"He will assume I've either taken on a widow who prefers to conduct business in secrecy as a client, or…"

"Or what?" she asked warily.

He probably shouldn't have mentioned the "or." "Or he will assume I have taken on a widow who prefers to conduct a different sort of business in secrecy."

"Oh *God*."

"It's a hotel. It won't shock him. And your family will be satisfied if we have separate rooms." They had damned well better be.

"It will draw attention to me."

"You drew attention to yourself in coming to London."

"I am aware of the risks," she snapped. "I have taken every precaution—"

"The best precaution would have been to stay out of London altogether."

She pressed her lips together in frustration. "We will not agree on this."

"No."

He didn't expect that to stop her. Esther struck him as the kind of woman who would argue with an empty room until she was blue in the face. He was a little surprised, then, when she sat back against the bench cushions, crossed her arms over her chest, and flatly refused to say another word.

Very well—if she wanted to pout for the duration of their carriage ride, she could pout. They'd discuss her trip to London, and her immediate return to Derbyshire, once they reached the hotel.

Esther wasn't pouting. She was thinking. And also ignoring Samuel, but only because that made it easier to think.

More than anything right now, she needed to be sensible. She had planned the trip to London with extraordinary care, paying meticulous attention to every detail. If she let her temper get the better of her now, all that hard work and preparation might come to nothing.

Yes, Samuel was a presumptuous, maddening, dictatorial arse.

No, she would not boot him from a moving carriage. Or, more realistically, give him the slip when they reached the hotel.

It would be tantamount to cutting off her nose to spite her face. Because despite all that careful planning, things had spiraled out of control rather quickly since she'd come to London. And Samuel might be just the presumptuous arse she needed to set things right again.

For all his many, many unfavorable qualities, he remained a clever, well-connected gentleman accustomed to working in secrecy. And he was a man she could trust. Not unequivocally—she didn't trust any man unequivocally—but she was fairly confident that he was, in a general sense, a reasonably decent human being. It was more than could be said of most people.

Furthermore, she was stuck with him. She simply didn't have the time or resources to engage in a game of cat and mouse with the man. Trustworthy or not, welcome or not, Samuel was staying. That being the case, he might as well be of some use.

She was putting the finishing touches on her plans of how best to utilize his presence when they reached the hotel. Esther allowed Samuel to assist her from the carriage but left him to secure rooms on his own. She had no interest in being subjected to the staff's knowing smirks.

Inside her own rooms, she yanked off the loathsome mourning bonnet and tossed it aside. She wished she could change out of the itchy crepe dress as well and into her soft cotton nightgown. It wasn't quite seven, but she would have given nearly anything just then to crawl into bed and sleep for a week.

Instead, she used the few moments of solitude to practice what she wanted to say to Samuel, then took a series of deep, steadying breaths to settle what remained of her temper. When Samuel knocked softly on her door a few minutes later, she was ready to have a civil, rational conversation with the man.

"It's open," she called out.

Samuel locked the door behind him and gave her a look of reproof. "It shouldn't have been open."

"I knew you were coming."

He removed his hat and tossed it on a chair. "So you're talking to me now?"

"I wasn't being quiet to punish you." That had merely been a happy coincidence. "I needed to think."

"Fine. Now I need you to talk."

"Very well," she said but offered no other response. She would let him talk first. It would give him a sense of control, which every man desired, and it would give her a sense of what cards he might be holding.

He gestured toward the door. "I've ordered a meal for us."

Not a promising hand, Sir Samuel. "Thank you."

Then he gestured toward a set of armchairs. "Will you sit?"

"Thank you, no." If she sat, and he didn't, it would put him in a position of power. He already towered over her by a solid foot—no point in making it three. "But you may sit, if you like."

"No." He caught his hands behind his back, the dark fabric of his coat pulling across broad, muscular shoulders. "To business, then. I've a compromise to offer, Esther."

Well, it appeared he had been making plans of his own. "I am all ears."

"If you will agree to leave London first thing

tomorrow, I will promise to keep this little excursion a secret from your family."

And that, she thought, was why she trusted Samuel and even liked him on occasion. Another man would continue to demand to know, first and foremost, what she was doing in London. Samuel sought first to secure her safety, and through compromise no less. His approach did not meet her needs, unfortunately, but she appreciated his choice of priorities nonetheless.

"That is a reasonable offer," she returned, "but I'm afraid there is no benefit in it for me. I have every intention of informing Lottie of my trip upon my return."

"Have you?"

"Of course. The purpose of my secrecy is not to deceive my family. It is to keep them from worry, which they'll not do once I am safely back in Derbyshire." She held up a hand when it looked as if he might argue. "I have another suggestion. I will allow you to aid me in my purpose in coming to London, thereby speeding its conclusion. In exchange, you will promise not to send word to my family—or Sir Gabriel or Lord Renderwell."

"Gabriel will be back in town in a little over two days."

"Well, with any luck, my business will be done by then." Oh, she hoped she would be that lucky. She liked Samuel's fellow private investigator Gabriel even more than she liked Samuel, but she trusted him far less.

"What is your business?"

"Promise first."

He shook his head. "Tell me what you are doing in London, and who that young man we saw today is, and I will consider keeping your confidence whilst you're here."

"That is not—"

"I'll make no promises until I know what sort of danger you're facing."

Damn it, she would have to compromise on the compromise. "I don't know who he is. I don't," she insisted when he growled at her. Again. "I've no idea. I… Here. Look." She retrieved her chatelaine bag from the bed and pulled out a small, torn piece of paper, which she handed to Samuel.

He read the short note in silence.

I know who you are. Meet Wed. Pddy sta. 6:00 p.m.
Come alone. Bring 10p.

It was rather funny to watch his expression jump from grim to befuddled. "Ten pence? Ten *pence*?"

"It is most odd," she agreed.

"What sort of blackmail is ten pence?"

"Perhaps he meant pounds," she ventured, then shrugged when he gave her a dubious look. "It is as good a theory as any you've offered."

He held up the note. "Was this sent to you in Derbyshire?"

"No, it was handed to me yesterday by a young boy in Spitalfields."

"Spitalfields?" He dropped his hand. "You went to *Spitalfields*? You idiot."

Oh, he did make it hard to be civil. "I am not an idiot."

"You went to Spitalfields," he repeated, very

slowly. “Realm of rookeries and flash houses. Home to footpads and cutthroats and—”

“And people like me,” she finished for him.

“You are not—”

“I was born in Spitalfields.”

That seemed to bring him up short, but only briefly. “You may have been born there, but—”

“But I grew up in boardinghouses in places like Bethnal Green. Quite an improvement over the common lodging house of my infancy, I’m sure. We had a room, sometimes two to ourselves. Such luxury.”

“I don’t—”

“And when I was six, my father took us to Bath, where he swindled a small fortune from a young woman and used those ill-gotten gains to rent an entire house. We lived there for three months, until the young woman’s brother came home from abroad, broke into our house, beat my father senseless, shot him in the leg, and gave Lottie three pounds to see the lot of us out of town. We came back to Spitalfields.”

She paused, but he didn’t try to speak, which was a little disappointing. She rather liked interrupting him. “It was several more years before my father became a proficient criminal. I was ten the last time we paid for lodgings in the East End.”

And she’d been nineteen the last time she’d worked there with her father, but she didn’t mention it.

She gave him a look of reproach. “How quick you are to remind me of my filthy origins when it suits your purpose, and how easily you forget when it does not.”

“I didn’t mention your origins. You did.”

“I…” Oh. Right. She had. She was, perhaps, a

mite touchy about her sordid past. Particularly in the company of someone like Samuel, whose pristine beginnings made her own seem even shabbier by comparison. But Samuel was not wholly without blame.

"You assumed I was waiting for a mark or an accomplice at the station," she pointed out. And he'd been worried she might stab him in the carriage. That had cut to the quick. Years ago, she had flashed her blades at a few of her father's more unpredictable cohorts because her father had asked it of her. She'd been a foolish young woman then. She wasn't a monster now.

"I didn't assume," Samuel retorted. "I merely asked. And for what it's worth, I didn't know of your origins."

Frowning, she retrieved the note from his hand. "How could you not?"

"Your father's early career and whereabouts were always a mystery."

"Renderwell must know by now." As far as Esther could tell, Lottie told her husband every damned thing.

"Probably. He's never mentioned it." He studied her a moment, his expression one of idle curiosity. "You have the speech and manners of a lady of breeding."

She didn't mind curiosity, so long as it wasn't a precursor for judgment and disdain. "My father's doing. It's difficult to swindle a class of people with whom you can't converse. Father was a great mimic, and he taught us well. He wouldn't allow anything but fine manners and speech under his roof. When we had one."

"It's an act?"

"No. I suppose it must have been, once," she

admitted. "But by the time we went to Bath, the fine accent and manners were natural to me."

"Didn't your friends wonder at both?"

"I didn't have friends," she replied, a little surprised at the question. "Father kept us isolated regardless of our neighborhood. He had too many enemies. When interaction could not be avoided, we used an alias." And had learned early how to remember a fabricated family history. They had been the Oxleys, the Farrows, the Gutierrez family. Her father had quite enjoyed being Hernando Gutierrez, the dashing Spaniard who'd taken in his orphaned nieces and infant nephew. Lottie and Esther had been forced to call him Uncle Hernan for months. "I thought you knew all this as well."

"I knew that to be the case when your father worked for us." He tipped his head at her. "I didn't know you'd always been alone."

"I wasn't alone. I had Lottie. And later Peter." And she didn't like the way he was looking at her. As if he pitied her. What was that but another kind of insult? "We are quite off topic. I am not an idiot for having gone to Spitalfields."

"Anyone who goes into places like Spitalfields when they have a choice otherwise is an idiot."

"That is unfair. There are decent, honest, hardworking people who live there."

"A great many. But their combined innocence does not render the cutthroats less vicious. What were you doing there?"

She shook her head. A compromise went both ways. "I'll have your promise first."

Samuel scratched his bearded chin in a thoughtful manner. "If I agree to help you with your business, then you must agree that I am responsible for that business, and your safety, for as long as you are in London."

"No." *Good Lord, no.* She couldn't believe he'd even suggest such a thing. Either he was jesting, he was testing her, or she had significantly overestimated his intelligence.

"Esther—"

"I'll not take orders from you." She didn't take orders from anyone. "You may give orders, if you like, but I'll not promise to follow them."

"Orders that don't have to be followed are called suggestions," he replied in a bland tone.

"Then I shall agree to take your suggestions under advisement."

His gaze traveled over her in an assessing manner that made her pulse quicken. "I could take you home in shackles."

"And I could take myself back to London the next day. Or do you mean to play my gaoler for the rest of your life?"

He didn't reply except to produce an angry humming noise in the back of his throat, which she very much hoped was not an indication that he was giving the gaoler idea serious consideration.

"Samuel, you cannot stop me from finishing my tasks in town. All I am asking is that you not make the process more difficult than it needs to be. For me, or my family."

The humming noise stopped, but his hands opened and closed into fists at his sides. Imagining themselves curved about her throat, no doubt.

"Fine," he bit off at last. "I'll help you and keep your secret for the duration of your visit."

"Excellent." Oh, *excellent*. Esther hadn't wanted to admit it, even to herself, but once she'd decided on making use of Samuel, she'd quickly become enthusiastic about the idea. For the last few days, she had been alone in London. Alone and, at times, a little frightened. With Samuel at her side—

"*Provided*—" Samuel added, holding up a single finger. "You are not in town for reasons that are monstrously stupid."

She should have known he wasn't finished. "Define 'monstrously stupid.'"

He dropped his hand. "*Define* it?"

"'Stupid' is a relative term."

"No," he replied. "It really isn't."

"It certainly is. I believe my reasons are sound, but you might very well think them stupid." She rather assumed he would, in fact. He'd already declared her an idiot for going to Spitalfields.

"I didn't say stupid, I said *monstrously* stupid. If you've come to town to tread the boards, I am going to wire Scotland and haul you home, promise or no promise."

Treading the boards wouldn't be stupid, it would be suicide. If that was the sort of behavior that worried him, she was probably safe. "Very well. But if you break your promise over what I am about to tell you, I warn you—I will make your life a living hell."

"No change for me, then," he said dryly and made a prompting motion with his hand. "Tell me why you're in London and why you went to Spitalfields, then."

"I have come to town to find someone."

"Someone from your youth? You know better," he chided. "Your father kept you isolated for good reason."

"Not someone I knew. Someone…" Oh, this was going to be an uncomfortable conversation. "I was looking for… That is, I am looking for my father."

Sympathy and a fair amount of trepidation passed over his face. "Esther," he said in a tone usually reserved for calming overexcited children and raving lunatics. "Your father is dead."

"No, not Will Walker," she replied impatiently. "My natural father. The man my mother ran off with when Lottie was two and abandoned to return to Will Walker a few months before I was born."

He appeared perplexed rather than surprised. Evidently her illegitimacy was something Renderwell had seen fit to tell him. "Why?"

"Why did my mother leave him?" she asked, knowing full well that wasn't his question. "Because that was what the woman did. She arrived, she charmed, she took money, she left. Eventually, and to the regret of all, she came back again."

"No, why do you want to find this man?"

She bit her lip and shook her head. "You wouldn't understand."

"I certainly don't at present."

And he never would. She couldn't claim to know every detail of his early youth, but Lottie had mentioned once that Samuel's father was a vicar somewhere in the south. How could she possibly explain to the son of a vicar what it meant to wish for a better father and a better life? "It doesn't matter why. I do, that's all."

"He lives in Spitalfields?"

"He did nine years ago."

"How do you know?"

She reached into her bag again and produced a second torn piece of paper. "Last year, when Lottie and I were arranging to have our things moved from Willowbend to Greenly House, I found a portion of a letter that had fallen behind a drawer in an old desk. It was from my father. Mr. George Smith."

She gave him the scrap of paper but didn't wait for him to read it. "There isn't much to it. Mr. Smith asks after my mother's health. He hopes she is well. He assures her he is well, and the rest is missing. But look." She tapped the other side of the letter, where a date and part of the address remained intact. *Mr. George Smith, No 58, Commercial Street, London.* "I'm told it used to be a grocers, but it was lost to a fire some years ago. I was also told that Mr. Smith survived, but no one knows for certain what happened to him after the fire. A few people did seem to think he moved to either Rostrime Lane in Bow or to a street in Bethnal Green with 'apple' in its name. Or possibly 'pear.'"

That wasn't strictly true. One person had mentioned a fruit-themed street in Bethnal Green. She knew for entirely different reasons that her father had lived on Rostrime Lane the year *before* he'd sent the letter from Spitalfields.

Samuel frowned at the note. "This couldn't have been meant for your mother. It was written well after her death."

"Five years after," she agreed. "He must not have known. I don't know how else to explain it. Perhaps there had been no contact between them after my birth. Perhaps the letter was an attempt to reestablish that connection." Though how the man had known where to send the letter remained a mystery. "I can't imagine he kept up a correspondence with Will Walker."

"How do you know Mr. Smith is your father? There is no mention of a child in this note."

"My mother told me." The lie slipped off her tongue without thought. She regretted it immediately but couldn't find it in herself to take it back. The truth required a long and painful explanation, and she'd quite had her fill of explanations today. "Before her death, she told me his name."

Samuel handed the letter back to her. "Did you wear your veil in Spitalfields?"

"Yes, of course. Only..." She winced. "I lifted it to speak to an elderly woman. She had difficulty hearing. It helped her to see my lips. It was only the once."

"Once was enough. Someone recognized you."

She blew out a short, aggravated breath. "It would seem so."

Three

Rather than put the loathsome mourning bonnet back on, Esther hid behind a folding screen while their meal was brought in the room and set out on a small table before the fireplace.

Sometimes, it felt as if she'd spent the whole of her life hiding. From the police, from her neighbors, from her father's friends and his enemies alike. And now from a trio of silly young maids who giggled nervously at Samuel's every request.

She couldn't judge them harshly for it. Samuel cut an imposing figure. In part because there was just so much of him but mostly because *so much of him* was undeniably appealing. His muscular physique and rough-hewn features were hardly fashionable, but fashionable wasn't always what a lady desired in a man. Some women might sigh over a pretty prince, but others preferred the captain of the guard.

It was Samuel's eyes, however, that compelled a lady to take a second look. They were such an unusual shade of gray, very nearly the color of steel, but sprinkled with warm flecks of gold about the irises.

And on the rare occasions that he smiled, they crinkled nicely at the corners. He looked cheerful then, kind and approachable, like a man who welcomed your company and conversation.

She could count on one hand the number of times she'd seen him smile like that. Not one of those smiles had been meant for her.

"Leave the lids," Samuel said. "You may go, thank you."

Esther rolled her eyes at the ensuing round of giggles. However understandable their admiration, she wished the maids would hurry about their chore and be gone. Her mouth watered at the aroma of warm bread and roasted meat. Riddled with nerves, she'd not eaten since the day before. She was famished.

As soon as the door shut on the last giggle, she darted out from behind the screen and pulled the lid off one of the platters.

Oh, asparagus. She adored asparagus.

Samuel gestured for her to take a seat. "You're fond of asparagus, I believe."

"Yes. How did you know?"

He pulled out his own chair and began removing the other lids. "You mentioned it."

"Did I? When?"

"Last year. On the twenty-eighth of June."

She stopped midreach for her napkin. "That is very specific."

"I've a keen memory."

He remembered the exact date she'd made an offhand comment about asparagus. That wasn't keen. That was... Well, she didn't know what that was, except disconcerting. "Can you recall everything I've ever said?"

He frowned a little as he transferred a thick slice of ham to his plate. "Good God, why would I want to?"

For your own improvement, she thought but kept the put-down to herself. Lord knew he could use both the improvement and the put-down, but she was in no hurry to ruin the tentative truce they seemed to have formed.

She smiled at him instead, a thin, tight-lipped smile she was quite certain did not make her eyes crinkle nicely at the corners.

Samuel took in Esther's strained smile and paused in the act of cutting his ham. "Something the matter?"

"Not at all. I am merely"—she tilted her head a little and pursed her lips—"taking the moral high ground," she decided, and then smiled in earnest, evidently pleased by the notion.

He set down his knife and fork. He hated when people took the moral high ground. By default, that meant everyone else was on the low ground. "Why am I on the low ground?"

"It's nothing. You were insulting, that's all. I am trying to let it pass."

She wasn't doing a very good job of it. Also, he couldn't see that she had any right to this particular patch of high ground. "You've insulted me. Repeatedly."

"Yes, but not since..." She shook her head. "It doesn't matter. Might we agree to both make an effort to be civil going forward?"

He grunted in assent. It was doubtful that they would manage civility for long. But he wasn't opposed to the effort.

He did wonder, however, which insult she'd been thinking of when she'd offered that first smile. Maybe it was when he'd called her an idiot. He'd called her that once before, last summer. Actually, he'd called her an imbecile, but that was close enough. And now that he thought on it, he'd called her a fool in the carriage, and that was essentially the same thing. The sting of a single barb could generally be brushed off, but when that same barb was delivered time and time again, it had the potential to stick and fester. He was personally susceptible to slights referencing Frankenstein's monster.

Samuel made a mental note to refrain from belittling her intellect in any future sparring and returned his attention to his meal.

"I assume you have a plan in mind for tomorrow?" he asked after a time. She'd want to go into Bethnal Green and Bow probably. He wondered if he could convince her to let him go in her stead.

"I need to go back to Spitalfields. I need to find the little boy who gave me the note."

"No." And he wasn't going to be civil about it.

"Yes."

"The man who sent that note knows who you are, Esther."

"He thinks he does. That is why I must find the little boy," she replied reasonably. "He can tell me who gave him the note, and I can find out what, exactly, is known."

"I saw the man at the station. I can look for him in Spitalfields. Alone."

"That man knows he was seen. He might avoid Spitalfields." She pointed the tines of her fork at him. "He'll certainly be avoiding you. But a small boy is unlikely to have the wherewithal to leave his neighborhood, and he'll not be actively hiding from you. It would be faster and smarter to look for him than to look for the young man."

"It would be safer and wiser for you to leave London immediately," he grumbled.

"We've already discussed this. I'll not go home until my business is concluded. Besides, I'll not be in immediate danger going back to Spitalfields. If the man wished to attack me on the street in broad daylight, he'd have done so already. It is very unlikely he will attempt to do tomorrow, in front of you, what he would not attempt yesterday when I was alone."

"Describe the boy to me. I'll go to Spitalfields and find him."

"I can't describe him. Not well. He gave me the note and dashed down a side street before I could ask him a single question. I would recognize him, but I couldn't tell you what he looked like, other than to say he was a small boy, possibly near eight years of age, with very large eyes and hair that was nearly black." Her face screwed up in thought. "I might be imagining the eyes. He may have just had long lashes."

"Sketch him for me. You've some skill as an artist."

"I have every skill as an artist," she corrected. "But I can't do it. I can't sketch well from memory, even if I know the subject well. I need to see it before me."

"Damn it, Esther."

"I don't see why this should be a point of contention," she said, reaching for her wine. "You walk about London openly every day. There must be dozens of men who would like your head on a platter. Why is it you are allowed to thumb your nose at danger, but I am not?"

"It's different."

She took a long sip of her drink and set the goblet down slowly. "Is that a euphemism for 'because you are a woman'?"

"No." Possibly. He might give it some thought later. "You have family, Esther. They care about what happens to you."

"And yours do not?"

He said nothing and hoped she would assume she had won the argument. He wasn't going to discuss his family.

"My family," Esther continued, "is the reason I will wear that miserable veil when I leave this room and the reason I will leave London and never return—*after* I have found the boy, the person who wrote the note, and my father." She cocked her head at him. "Are you going to break your promise to help me?"

"I promised to help you with your business. I did not promise to help you put yourself in unnecessary danger."

"It isn't unnecessary," she returned. "Not to me. Are you going to break your promise, then?"

She repeated the question almost casually, as if it was of no consequence to her one way or the other. But that eerie stillness had returned. She held herself stiffly, and her expression was shuttered tight.

She didn't want him to break his promise, he realized. But she expected it. A woman like Esther, who had been raised by a man like Will Walker, would always expect to be betrayed. And she would guard herself accordingly.

He wished he could prove her right in this instance, but refusing to keep his word would do neither of them any good. She would find a way to Spitalfields with or without him. "I'll not break my promise."

This time when she smiled, it didn't look as if she'd swallowed bad meat.

"Excellent," she chimed and went back to her meal.

Samuel pushed his own plate away, his appetite lost. He shouldn't have made the promise, but there'd been nothing else for it. If Esther was determined to be in London, she would be in London. Frankly, it was a miracle the contrary woman wasn't dead set on remaining in London alone.

It had been a mistake, however, to offer his promise before he'd secured her agreement to follow his orders. Then again, some errors were easily got around. Most, in fact. Which made him wonder…

"Esther?"

"Hmm?"

"Why didn't you simply agree to take orders from me and then find a way around the agreement?"

She glanced up at him. "Why didn't I lie, you mean?" She shrugged. "I didn't want to. Why didn't you agree to help me and simply plan to make me follow your orders whether or not I cared for the idea?"

Again, he said nothing.

"Oh, that *is* what you've planned, isn't it?" She

made a disgusted sound. "I told you, I'll not follow your orders."

"And if the orders are sensible?"

"I don't need you to tell me how to be sensible." She pointed her fork at him again. "And don't you *dare* contradict me on that point, Samuel Brass. We agreed to be civil."

"Is *that* an order?"

Rather than answer, she jabbed her fork into an asparagus stalk and bit the tip off in a most uncivilized manner.

He decided to take that as a yes.

The remainder of the meal passed in relative peace, primarily as neither party felt it necessary to speak. Esther supposed silence was as good a route to civility as any.

At least Samuel didn't look quite so put out as he had earlier. He didn't look particularly pleased, mind you, but he never really did around her. She imagined that, with her, he would always be something of a curmudgeon. Sir Samuel Brass, the curmudgeonly giant. Yes, that fit him quite well.

She finished her meal as quickly as she could without making a spectacle of herself and sent up a small prayer of thanks when the maids who came for the dishes turned out to be older and faster than the first three.

Samuel glanced at the clock as she stepped out from behind the screen. "You haven't any plans to leave the hotel tonight, I presume?"

"No." In fact, she was very much looking forward

to finally crawling into bed. She pulled her chair out from the table and took a seat. "But if that should change, I'll come to you directly."

You see? Sensible.

"You'll stay in this room."

She decided in the interest of their truce that he was asking a question, not delivering an order. "Yes. And I'll not answer the door for anyone except you." Sensible again. "Do you mean to stay inside as well?"

"Yes."

"Well then, good night."

"Good night."

She frowned after him as he walked to the door. Something had been niggling at her all evening: a doubt, or a question she'd not been able to place. Suddenly, she realized what it was.

"Samuel?" She waited for him to turn around again. "Why are you here?"

"I don't understand the question."

She scooted so she could see him properly over the back of her chair. "You sought me out in Derbyshire because Lottie and Renderwell asked you to check in on me whilst they were away, didn't you?"

There was a small pause before he answered. "Yes."

"I thought so. When you discovered I'd left, why didn't you simply wire Renderwell in Edinburgh and be done with it? You weren't obligated to track me down. Nor are you required to help me now."

She wasn't his sister or even his friend. She wasn't his responsibility. So why trouble himself over her safety?

"Renderwell is my friend," he replied. "Your sister is his wife."

"And word of my disappearance would have upset her, thereby upsetting him," she guessed.

"Essentially."

She didn't know why she should find that explanation a little disappointing. "Well then, thank you for thinking of my sister, however indirectly."

His only response was a single grunt. Then he left. This didn't surprise her particularly. He always grunted when she thanked him for something. Like when he'd rescued her from the stable fire, and when he'd rescued her brother from the kidnapper. She'd not yet figured out whether the grunt meant *You're welcome* or *I don't wish to discuss it* or *Devil take your gratitude, troublesome wench*, but she rather thought it might be the last.

She told herself it didn't matter. It simply did not matter what Sir Samuel Brass thought of her.

All her life, she had twisted herself into knots worrying over the good opinion of others. Not an unusual predicament, really, else there'd be a sight fewer women running about in itchy crepe. Nearly everyone gave some thought to what their friends and neighbors thought of them. Most people, however, sought acceptance through conformity.

She had stolen it through deceit.

Esther had learned at a very young age that she would never be able to compete with her sister's cleverness nor Lottie's natural bond with their father. She would always be the second-best daughter in Will Walker's eyes. But she'd had talents and gifts of her own. She was nimble of finger and sharp of eye. She could throw a blade with pinpoint accuracy and draw a pencil or brush over paper with enviable skill.

And she could act. Brilliantly. Give her a role, any role, and she could fill it with aplomb. Cunning thief? Simpering flirt? Proper lady? Obedient daughter? She could play any one of them at the drop of a hat.

And she had. She'd played them all and dozens of others over the years. Until that had become all that she was—a woman who played at being someone else.

I can be whatever you like. I am exactly who you want me to be. Just tell me who that is.

It wasn't who she wanted to be now.

She would not play the chastised child for Samuel. She would be herself, and that would have to be good enough.

Four

Commercial Street was a broad thoroughfare lined with tall, thin brick buildings pressed together like matchsticks stood on end. Most of the buildings had shops or warehouses on the ground floor and offices or rooms to let above. It was normally a bustling street, crowded with vendors, pedestrians, and street traffic, but a hard early morning rain had kept most people indoors. When Esther and Samuel arrived at midday, the residents were just beginning to emerge from their shelters to sweep the sidewalks or set out their wares.

"His shop was somewhere about here," Esther said, motioning at a building of relatively new construction. "It was torn down two years ago to make room for the new building."

"Where were you when the boy came with the note?" Samuel inquired.

"There." She pointed down the street. "At the old clothes shop next to the booksellers on the corner."

Though it was generally regarded as ungentlemanly to allow a lady to walk nearest the curb, Samuel put himself between Esther and the shops as they walked down the street. It wasn't Commercial Street that worried him. It was the peripheral maze of winding, twisting alleys and lanes that broke away from the thoroughfare that posed the greater threat. It was in the crumbling old Huguenot mansions with people crammed inside like livestock, where misery, deprivation, and disease culminated in the desperation that too often bred violence.

A desperate man could slip in and out of the maze in the blink of an eye.

"We might have better luck looking for the boy at one of the markets," he commented. "Better spot to nick a watch or purse."

She stopped and turned to face him, and though he couldn't see her features clearly beneath the veil, he was fairly certain she was scowling at him again. "That is a terrible thing to say. You don't know he's a thief. You don't know the first thing about him other than that he had the misfortune to be born into poverty. He could be a perfectly honest, perfectly lovely little boy. You should be ashamed of yourself, insulting a child."

"I didn't think you'd consider 'thief' to be an insult." Not in this particular instance.

"You don't know the first thing about me either," she said softly and turned away to resume her walk up the street in stony silence.

Samuel fell into step beside her.

He wasn't going to apologize. He'd not said anything wrong.

He'd made a reasonable assumption about the boy, and about Esther. A hungry child might reasonably be expected to pick a pocket if it was the surest way of putting food in his mouth. Samuel didn't condone the theft, but neither did he blame the child. He had assumed Esther would agree.

He looked down the next alleyway and spotted a pair of very small girls laboring over a washbasin set on the cobblestones. Even the youngest children worked in neighborhoods like this. They ran errands or took in laundry to earn a few coins. A few honest coins.

Uneasy, Samuel looked away. Maybe he hadn't been completely reasonable in his assumptions. Maybe he was, on occasion, a bit hasty in his judgments.

Very well, he was routinely hasty.

"You're right," he admitted. "He might not be a thief."

Esther nodded once but said nothing.

"I should not have prejudged him," he admitted.

When she remained silent, he gently caught her arm and brought them both to a stop. He didn't know why it was suddenly so important that he explain himself to her—it just was.

"I've spent years chasing the worst sort of men through slums like this. And years ferreting out people's darkest, ugliest secrets." Vice, infidelities, betrayals of every imaginable variety. And before that had been the war. Since the age of seventeen, he had been swamped in the worst humanity had to offer. "It has made me suspicious. And hard."

"Suspicious, certainly." She tilted her head at him. "But you're not such a hard man, I think."

"I am." He wasn't apologizing for it—he was merely stating a fact.

"Hard men aren't nearly so quick to admit the

flaw," she countered, and a hint of a smile entered her voice. "Or chase a woman they don't like across an entire country because her disappearance might interfere with the happiness of a friend."

"I didn't chase you. I tracked you." And he hadn't done either strictly for Renderwell's sake. The truth was, he'd checked in on Esther at her cottage because he'd wanted to. He'd followed her to London because he'd been worried.

She snorted at his comment, then twirled her lacy black parasol against her shoulder. "It occurs to me that if this boy tries to pick your pocket, I'm going to feel like a fool."

"You shouldn't." He offered his arm and was absurdly gratified when she took it. "There is nothing shameful in assuming the best of someone."

"Shameful, no. Foolish, yes. It is surely wiser to hope for the best, rather than expect it, but it feels wrong not to give people, especially children, the benefit of the doubt."

Samuel agreed with her, but he still searched the last alley they passed before the old clothes shop with a sharp eye.

The woman at the shop remembered speaking with Esther but had no recollection of a small boy with dark hair and large eyes carrying a note. Might be little Jim Hanning or Michael Landsworth or Sean Jennings. Could be any one of dozens of children who passed by her shop every day.

They tried the neighboring shops next, then several shops across the street, but no one remembered seeing the lad.

"We'll just have to walk the street," Esther decided as she maneuvered around a shoe shiner. "See what we can find. We can speak with everyone I visited on Tuesday."

To Samuel's dismay, it appeared as if Esther had visited nearly everyone in Spitalfields on Tuesday. They stopped in a cobbler shop, a butcher's shop, two apothecaries, a draper's shop, and several emporiums of useless bric-a-brac. They even stopped to talk to a man selling peppermints from a cart.

"Why would you speak with a street vendor?" Samuel demanded as they stepped away. "Did you honestly imagine he was selling his goods in that very spot over a decade ago?"

"No. I just wanted a peppermint. No harm in asking him about Mr. Smith whilst I was at it. I thought perhaps the vendor might have lived here all his life."

He lifted a brow in question.

"He's from Leeds," she admitted with a shrug and moved on.

Esther wrinkled her nose as she veered around a puddle with a suspicious layer of foam on its surface. In the country a soaking rain left everything fresh and renewed, but London was like a filthy dog: you could dump a bucket of water on it, but that didn't make it clean. It just made it wet.

On the whole, however, the excursion down Commercial Street was a far more pleasant endeavor than it had been when she'd come on Tuesday. People had looked at her askance then. Those she had spoken with had leaned close, trying to peer through the veil. She'd been nervous, wary of everyone she met, every person she passed. After she'd read the note, she'd been afraid.

Although she wasn't inclined to mention it aloud, she understood why Samuel questioned the risk she took in coming to town. It was dangerous for her here. And having spent the last nine years rusticating in the country, she was a little out of practice when it came to facing danger—a fact she'd been acutely conscious of when she'd been alone.

She drew plenty of attention today, of course. Some people gawked at Samuel, either because they recognized him or simply because of his size. Others seemed to find the sight of a woman in deep mourning out for a stroll with a fashionable gentleman in Spitalfields simply an interesting spectacle. But those extra looks didn't bother her today. With Samuel at her side, she felt safe. Cautious still, but emboldened.

They came to a stop outside a tavern. Samuel frowned at the sizable group of men visible through the window, then turned and studied the bustling street.

She knew exactly what he was thinking. Was it better to leave her outside alone or expose her to the sort of men who drank in the middle of the day?

"I'll wait here," she offered, not because she was particularly afraid of the men inside, but because the scent of tobacco smoke and ale never failed to bring up memories that made her queasy.

"Stay close," Samuel instructed. "I'll only be a minute."

When he left, she turned and watched the passing pedestrians, hoping for a glimpse of the boy or young man they sought.

"Spare a coin, mum?"

She looked over her shoulder at the unexpected question and discovered a man lounging against the wall not ten feet away. He stood in the shadow of a neighboring shop blind, and his head was bowed low. All she could see of his features beneath the brim of his hat was a bullish chin.

Her skin prickled with nerves. He'd not been there a moment ago. She was certain of it. And people who hid their faces couldn't be trusted.

She ought to know. "I'm afraid I—"

"Have a heart. I only need enough for a crust of bread."

It didn't look as if he was in immediate need of feeding. He looked hale and strong, and his workman's clothes, while worn, were free of patches and frayed ends. She glanced at his feet. Beneath several layers of caked-on dirt was a very fine pair of boots.

She wondered what poor sod had been forced to relinquish them.

This man didn't need her coin, and she was tempted to deny him just on principle. But if he decided to press the matter...

She dug into her bag and retrieved a coin, which she held out for him. Better she waste a little money and be rid of him quickly.

The stranger stepped to the edge of the shadows and reached for the coin. His fingers closed over her own and lingered.

She snatched her hand back. "That's plenty for something to eat. Now—"

"You can't do better?" He cocked his head, as if

studying her, and she noticed a small, indented scar on the side of his chin. "You look as if you could. Looks as if someone set you up proper."

Something in his tone made the hair on the back of her neck stand on end. She shifted the grip on her parasol.

It was dangerous for her here.

"That is all I have for you, sir. Be on your way."

"Oh, I think you've—"

The shop door opened behind her. A second later, Samuel was at her side. He took one look at thc man and moved to stand in front of her. "Problem?"

The man hunched his shoulders, bent at the waist, and bobbed his head like a serf genuflecting to his master. "None, sir. Not a bit of it." He held the coin up and began to back away, bowing all the while. "The lady showed me a kindness, is all. Bless her. Sir. Mum. Fair day to you both."

Samuel took a step forward, but Esther stopped him with a touch on the arm and a shake of her head. They had quite enough on their hands without bothering with a false beggar.

As the stranger turned a corner and disappeared, uneasiness gave way to annoyance. "Oh, he was all deference and good manners with *you*, wasn't he?" she grumbled.

Samuel looked down at her. "What did he say to you?"

"He wanted coin, that's all." He'd been aggressive about it, and he'd been strange. But this was London. Aggressive and strange were to be expected.

"He was hiding his face."

"I noticed." Transferring her parasol to the other hand, she wiggled the tension out of her fingers. "I also noticed, as I'm sure you did, that he was considerably too large to have been the man from the station."

"Men don't hide their faces unless they have a reason."

"I suspect someone wants him for something." The fine boots, like as not. "But he's not the man we're looking for, and if we start chasing after every suspicious, overzealous beggar in the city, we'll never get around to doing anything else."

Samuel considered this a moment before agreeing with a single nod. Taking her arm, he ushered her away from the tavern.

"Did you learn anything inside?" she asked as they crossed the street.

"No."

"Pity, but—oh, look there." She pointed toward a trio of young girls sitting on the curb and industriously arranging the small piles of flowers at their feet into nosegays they placed in baskets.

"The flower girl in the green dress was here on Tuesday. I didn't speak with her, but she might remember the boy."

All three girls scrambled to their feet as Esther and Samuel approached.

The girl in green held out her half-filled basket. "Flowers for the lady, sir?"

"Thank you, no. I'm looking for a boy. Somewhere near to eight years of age, dark hair, large eyes. He was on this street on Tuesday, possibly carrying a note."

"Big eyes and dark hair?" the girl in green repeated.

"You know him?" Samuel asked.

The girl looked him over with a shrewd expression, then tapped her basket. "I've carnations, violets, roses, and lavender, sir. Sweetest you'll find anywhere. And only two pennies a bunch."

Samuel heaved a sigh. "Right."

He purchased a nosegay of violets and lavender and shoved it at Esther without any ceremony whatsoever. Without so much as looking at her, in fact.

"Thank you, kind sir," she muttered under her breath and plucked the flowers from his fist before he could damage the blooms. She carefully inserted the small stems into the belt at her waist next to her chatelaine bag. "You're quite the most romantic automaton I know."

"What'd she call you?" one of the girls asked. "Auto-what?"

"Ignore her. What do you remember?"

Rather than answer Samuel directly, the flower girl gave her friends a knowing bob of the head. "Could be Lizzy's boy."

The youngest of the girls made a face. "Lizzy Hopkins?"

"No, not Hopkins," the third girl retorted with the impatience of an older sister. "Causer. Her with all them pretty-eyed lads."

"Do you have a name?" Samuel inquired.

The girl in the green dress shook her head. "Just Lizzy Causer's lads." She pointed down the street. "Peerpoint Alley. Mind you, I won't be having them flowers back if it ain't him."

"Thank you," Esther called out as Samuel took her by the elbow and hurried her off.

In the wrong direction.

"Where are we going?" she demanded. They'd just come down this stretch of road. One would think a man with a keen memory might recall that sort of detail.

"Not we," Samuel replied. "You. You are not going down that alley."

She didn't want to go down any alley, particularly. While she very much hoped the denizens of Peerpoint Alley were all the very best of people, she wasn't eager to risk her neck on it. "I don't see how it can be avoided. You can't find him without me. You've never seen him."

"I have a surname, an approximate age, and a description. If he's there, I'll find him. And you"—he stopped outside a milliner's shop they'd already visited—"will wait in this shop until I come for you."

"But I want to speak with this boy." She also wanted to be of use. She had her daggers strapped to her ankles. Where was the sense in Samuel risking his neck all alone?

"I'll bring the boy to you."

She pulled her arm away. "That is ridiculous. You heard the flower girl. Lizzy Causer has *all them boys*. What if she has a dozen of them? You can't haul them all out one by one."

"How could she have a dozen boys near eight years of age?"

She didn't really think there would be a dozen. She'd been thinking more along the lines of three or four and indulging in a bit of hyperbole. But if he really wanted an answer, she'd give him one. "She might have stepchildren, or she might have several sets of twins between the ages of six and eleven, which might easily be confused with eight years of age. Or she might have both and—"

"Get in the shop, Esther."

She wished she could cross her arms, but the blasted parasol was in the way. She closed it with a smart snap instead. "That sounds like an order, Samuel."

He took a long, deep breath through his nose. "One order," he ground out. "I want to be able to give you one order a day whilst you are here. And I want you to follow it without question and without complaint. That is not an unreasonable request."

"You're trying to change the rules." She didn't have any objections to that. She liked her rules a little flexible. "Very well. But in return, you must follow one order a day from me."

"Get in the shop."

"I am not"—she reached out and pulled down the arm he'd thrown up so imperiously to indicate the shop's door—"getting in the—"

"Is that him?"

"What?" Esther followed his gaze, turning around. "Where?"

Samuel nodded toward a small dark-haired, big-eyed boy sitting at the entrance of a completely different alleyway across the street. Not picking pockets, thank God. He was shaving kindling from a small stump of wood with an ax blade that looked far too big and unwieldy for his small hands.

"It is," she said, dropping her hand. "That's him. How did you know?"

"Big eyes, dark hair, roughly eight years of age, not far from Peerpoint Alley."

As Samuel and Esther neared, the boy pushed aside overlong bangs and looked up, and up. His big brown eyes widened. "Afternoon, guv."

"What is your name, lad?"

"Henry, sir. Henry Causer."

Esther nudged Samuel aside—honestly, did the man have to approach every situation with intimidation?—and leaned down a little, hoping to put the child at ease.

"Do you remember me, Henry? You brought a note to me on Tuesday." She pointed down the street. "At the old clothes shop."

The boy's expression turned wary as he squinted for a clear look at her face. "Maybe. I brought a note to a widow Tuesday."

Samuel nudged her back. "Do you know where to find the man who gave you the note?"

"Maybe."

"Two bob if you take us to him."

Henry shook his head. "Not worth me skin, sir."

"Is the man not to be trusted, then?" Samuel asked.

"He's not a bad sort. But his friends..." Henry finished the thought with a hitch of one bony shoulder.

"Would you lead us to him for a half crown?" Esther offered.

Henry thought about it. "I got a name."

A false one, no doubt. Esther suspected he wouldn't offer the real one for a fortune. Not if it meant putting himself at risk.

"I've an idea. I need..." She dug through the bag at her waist and found her small notepad and pencil.

She tore out a sheet of paper, scribbled out a hasty note, and showed it to Samuel.

Pddy station. 5:00 p.m. Wed. I will be alone.

He snatched it out of her hand. "No."

She snatched it right back. "Yes."

"No." He reached for the note again.

She lifted the note up high, realized how ridiculous that was, and stuck it behind her back instead. "Yes. We can discuss the particulars of it"—she bobbed her head sideways at the boy—"*later.*"

"There will be no discussion."

She hitched up a shoulder. She was going. And so was he, with any luck, but if he didn't wish to discuss it, all the better for her.

Turning to the boy, she folded the note in quarters. "How does this sound, Henry? I will give you a crown to deliver this note to the man. If he follows the instructions inside, either I or this gentleman will meet you here one week from today at three o'clock in the afternoon and pay you an additional sovereign."

The boy's mouth dropped open at the exorbitant bribe, but he quickly snapped it shut again. "I can't make him do nothing. And how do I know you'll make good on your promise?"

"You can't, and you don't. But you'll have a crown regardless." And a much better chance at an entire sovereign if he delivered the note. All at little to no risk to himself.

The boy took a quick nervous look down both ends of the street, then held out a grubby hand. "Let's have it, then."

She handed him the note and reached into her bag

for the coin, but Samuel stopped her with a shake of his head.

"Wait." He dug into his pocket and pulled out four shillings. "Do you have one more?"

"Whatever for?"

"Just..." He wiggled his fingers.

She gave him a shilling, which he passed off with the others to the boy.

Henry tucked the note and coins away, gathered up his wood and blade, and dashed down the alleyway.

Next to her, Samuel shifted his feet restlessly.

"You want to follow him," she guessed.

He grunted, which, on this occasion, she took to mean yes. She had half a mind to follow him as well, but a boy like that would slip through a window or door the moment he suspected he was being followed.

"Why did you do that?" she asked Samuel as they turned to leave. "Give him five shillings instead of a crown?"

"Because there's likely someone with whom he is obligated to share some portion of his income for the day, if not all of it."

"Oh, I see." By giving the boy several coins instead of just one, Samuel had given him a chance to keep at least some of the money for himself. "I told you," she said, smiling at him as they turned to leave. "Not such a hard man."

"You are not meeting that man at Paddington station, Esther."

"Very well, I take it back," she grumbled as they steered around a set of carts. "You're like a stodgy, disapproving older brother, you know." She thought about that. "Worse, you're like the best friend of an older brother. You assume all the overbearing familiarity without having any right to it."

He looked at her with disbelief. "You'd not spend a night at my house, but you would accuse me of being stodgy?"

"It isn't the same."

"How is that not the same?"

"Being stodgy and overbearing makes you a bother. Being an unmarried, unchaperoned woman under your roof makes me…less."

"Less what?"

Less respectable. Less of a lady. Less than him. "Just *less*."

He digested this in silence as they made their way back toward the carriage, staying quiet for so long, she began to wonder if he'd heard her at all.

"It was not my intention to make you feel less," he said at last. "It is not how I see you."

"Isn't it?" She'd meant to level an accusation, not ask a question, but it had come out all wrong. She sounded uncertain and wary, maybe even a little bit hopeful. Embarrassed, she turned away to stare at the fruit and vegetable vendors across the street as if they were the most fascinating things in the world. "Don't answer that."

Please don't answer that.

"I don't mind answering."

She might very well mind the answer, no matter how hard she tried not to care. "It's not important. I didn't mean—"

"You're not less. Therefore I do not see you as less. Simple as that."

She'd not say thank you. It wasn't really a compliment, no matter how good it felt. "I am trying, you know, to be more."

Why, oh why, could she not bite her tongue?

Samuel looked at her thoughtfully. "I believe you might be."

She certainly wasn't going to thank him for *that*. Might be, indeed.

Five

She was not going to Paddington station.

Samuel understood, even appreciated, that Esther was quick-witted, courageous, and skilled with her blades. He accepted that he couldn't send her home, or even leave her behind at the hotel. But she was not, under any circumstances, going to meet the strange young man at the station alone. It was ludicrous, and he would not allow it.

Convincing her of the wisdom of his decision, however, was going to be tricky.

"You do realize," he began casually, "that even if I agree to let you go to Paddington—"

"It is not your decision to make."

"Even if you go to Paddington," which she would not do, "it will be after Gabriel returns. He'll be back day after tomorrow."

She gave a disgruntled sigh. "Yes, I did consider that. I don't suppose you'd be willing to lie to Gabriel? Keep my presence in London a secret?"

"No."

"I thought not," she replied without any sign of

resentment. "Well, it can't be helped. I had to give the young man time to make arrangements."

"Arrangements?"

"Yes, of course," she said, as if all made perfect sense. "If he is a resident of Spitalfields, then it is highly unlikely he is a gentleman of leisure. If he has employment, he'll need time to make arrangements so as not to lose his position. I assume he wished to meet me on a Wednesday for a reason. It might be because that is the only day he is free of his responsibilities."

"If he knows who you are, there is every chance he knew you when you worked for your father. It is doubtful he has reputable employment."

"Even thieves have responsibilities."

"Certainly," he drawled. "We wouldn't want to jeopardize the man's criminal prospects."

"I didn't do it to help him. I did it to increase the odds of meeting him at Paddington station."

Which she was not going to do. "You are not going to meet this man alone. It would be reckless."

She sighed again, but this one had a hint of a groan. "I don't want to meet him alone. I should like you to be there with me."

He would be there all right. Alone. "It's too dangerous."

"I'll be there to protect you." She gave a small huff of defeat when he failed to laugh. "It isn't unreasonably dangerous. We have already determined that the man does not wish to do me immediate harm."

No, she had theorized. Anything could be theorized. "He may have refrained from confronting you on the street because he is aware of your particular talents with knives. He has friends, evidently. He might have thought it wise to have them along when he approached you."

"He was alone at the station."

"As far as we know."

"And as far as he'll know, I will be alone next Wednesday as well. You will be..." She turned to him and her bonneted head bobbed up, then down as she looked him over. "Well, I don't suppose you blend very well. You'll have to hide."

He bloody well wasn't going to hide while she faced an unknown danger, but there didn't seem to be any point in arguing the matter at present. Esther was determined in her plan. It would be easier if he let her scheme today and simply find the man himself before Wednesday. "We'll leave the meeting at Paddington station as an option for now."

She tucked her parasol under her arm and rubbed her hands together with glee. "Wonderful."

He stared at her, appalled. "Are you...*enjoying* this?"

"Of course not." She glanced down at her hands. "Perhaps a little."

"Esther, you are in danger."

"As you very often are," she returned. "Do you mean to tell me you don't enjoy the occasional spot of danger?"

"It's different," he said and wondered if she was as tired of hearing that as he was of saying it.

She cocked her head at him. "Do you think because I am a woman, I don't wish for adventure? For something more than a quiet life of reading and needlepoint?"

"No."

"Do you think I shouldn't?"

He thought it best not to comment. He had no philosophical objections to a woman pursuing a life of adventure, or even danger. In theory. He just didn't want to encourage Esther specifically.

"Well, I do want more," Esther continued, her enthusiasm building as they resumed their walk down the street. "I want excitement. I want to outwit that young man. I want to explore London and travel the world. I want to go to lectures and museums, shops and theaters. I want to see the Louvre and ride an elephant in India. I want a challenge. I want purpose, something more than mere survival."

All things that had been denied her. And would always be denied her. He couldn't imagine what that was like, to yearn for the world and be given an isolated cottage in Derbyshire instead. Even if he retired to a life in the country, he'd never be trapped as she was. He could hop on the rail on a whim and be back in the swirl and excitement of London in a matter of hours.

Perhaps that was why she had worked for her father—because it had been her only opportunity for excitement, her only chance to have a sense of purpose.

"Do you miss working with William?" he asked and immediately wished he'd kept his mouth shut. Just like that, her shoulders slumped, all the lively enthusiasm drained out of her.

"No." She tapped the tip of her parasol absently against the curb as they walked along. "That wasn't exciting."

"What was it?"

He didn't expect her to answer and was surprised when she shrugged and said, rather quietly, "Pitiful."

He stared at the top of her dark bonnet. "You are a great many things, Esther. Pitiful is not one of them."

"Not now." She stopped again, a few feet from the back of the carriage, and looked up at him. "Haven't you ever done something you're not proud of, Samuel?"

"I'm not proud of being a hard man."

"You're not—" She broke off and shook her head. "Doesn't matter. Are you trying to be a better man?"

"Yes."

She nodded firmly once as if to say *There you are.*

He wasn't entirely clear on what that meant, but he wasn't given the chance to ask.

A large gig came careening around the corner. Its young and obviously inebriated occupants tossed a bottle from the vehicle and laughed wildly at the pedestrians who scrambled out of the way of bottle, horse, vehicle, and the spray of puddles sent up by the carriage wheels.

Samuel grabbed Esther and shoved her behind him just as the gig raced by, launching a great wall of ditch water over the curb and onto him.

It soaked him through to the skin, and there was nothing he could do but drag a hand down his face and flick the excess moisture from his fingers.

Esther snickered. Actually, she coughed, but it was a hide-the-snicker sort of cough. It didn't fool anyone.

He glowered at her.

She snickered again.

"Get in the carriage, Esther."

For once, she complied without argument. She clambered inside, one hand covering her mouth. The moment the door was closed, her laughter filled the carriage.

"Oh. Oh, Lord." She flipped up her veil. "I'm sorry. I'm terribly sorry. But the *state* of you. Good heavens." She calmed herself a bit and reached over to pat his knee. "My hero."

Then she laughed some more.

He ought to be offended, really. Annoyed at the very least. But he couldn't seem to move beyond amazed.

He'd never heard her laugh before. Not like this. Not with her head tipped back and the sound just flowing from her.

Samuel wracked his brain for a single memory of Esther laughing, *really* laughing, and came up blank. Years ago, when she'd been little more than a girl, she had giggled. Once or twice, she may have chuckled. Certainly, he'd heard her snicker. But he hadn't heard her laugh. Not as a child, and not since he'd known her as an adult.

The woman simply didn't laugh in front of him.

It seemed an odd thing not to have noticed before now. Stranger still that he should find an ordinary sound so extraordinarily appealing. There was a sweet, clear tone to it that made him think of wind chimes. Not the tinny sort Mrs. Lanchor had hung in the garden two years ago (and the beast had mauled into oblivion three days ago) but the solid sort that put one to mind of woodwinds.

Her laugh reminded him of wind chimes that reminded him of woodwinds. By God, he was England's finest poet.

"You've changed," he murmured. There used to be a brittleness about her, a deep unhappiness she kept hidden away along with her kindness and honesty, all buried beneath a layer of cool indifference. He couldn't see that brittleness anymore.

"Beg your pardon?" Her laugh tapered off slowly, and she looked at him uncertainly. "I didn't mean to cause offense." A spark of mischievousness lit in her blue eyes. "Well, maybe a little offense, but—"

"I'm not offended... Maybe a little offended," he corrected with humor. "But I wasn't implying that you've changed for the worse. It's for the better."

"Oh." Her lips curved in a small, hesitant smile. "Thank you."

"You're happier, aren't you?"

"I am," she agreed, and so readily that he could only assume she'd given the matter some thought recently. "I am starting to be."

"It is nice to see." It was more than nice. It was something else, something more.

Here, he thought, was the woman he'd caught glimpses of before. The remarkable one who amazed and fascinated him. Only it wasn't just a glimpse. He remembered her insistence that he wasn't a hard man and her defense of the little boy. And he wondered now if the traits he admired in her had never been quite as buried or transient as he imagined. Anything could seem like a glimpse, he realized, if one looked away too quickly.

He was finding it hard to look away from her at present. A light, very pretty blush had formed high on her cheeks at his comment.

"Thank you," she said softly.

He grunted, which, for some reason, she seemed to find amusing.

Laughing softly, she loosened the ribbons of her bonnet. "Are we going straight back to the hotel?"

His gaze followed her pale fingers as they slid through the black velvet strips. For some reason, he found the sight absolutely mesmerizing. "Er…Yes. Unless you've other ideas?"

She shook her head. "We need to get you out of those wet clothes." Her smile froze and her eyes went round. "Not we. I didn't mean *we*, as in you and me. It was more the royal we. I… That is…" She cleared her throat, set her bonnet carefully in her lap, and then stared at the drapes as if she could see straight through them. "You'll catch a cold."

Something cold was exactly what he needed at present. Something cold and very distant. Far, far away from the temptation that had suddenly and most unexpectedly presented itself.

Because he could picture what Esther had suggested. He could picture it *perfectly*. Her small hands working the buttons on his coat. Those agile fingers loosening the knot of his necktie. The slide of her palms beneath his coat.

Samuel shifted uncomfortably. Strictly speaking, this wasn't the first unseemly thought he'd had about Esther. She was a pretty woman, and he was a man with a pulse. It was only natural that he'd thought of her in that manner before. Rather frequently, truth be told.

But this was different than a passing fantasy any man might have about any attractive woman.

He wasn't any man. She wasn't any woman. And this wasn't about her beauty.

It was about *her.*

He, Sir Samuel Brass, very suddenly, and rather desperately, wanted Esther Walker-Bales.

And he bloody well knew better.

She was his friend's wife's younger sister. Which made her no relation to him whatsoever, but still the closest thing to a sister he'd ever had. More importantly, she was a menace. She was fascinating and beguiling and an absolute *world* of trouble, an ocean of aggravation. Every moment he spent in her company was a moment spent tempting disaster.

At that particular moment, he simply didn't care.

He leaned across the carriage, slipped a hand around her neck, and brought her forward for a kiss.

It was Esther's first kiss.

And for the rest of her life, she would lament the fact that she somehow managed to miss the first two seconds of it.

It was just so unexpected. One minute she'd been sitting there, wishing she could pull her veil down to hide her blush, and the next minute, Samuel was kissing her. It took a moment for her brain to catch up, and then another for her to decide if she cared for the sudden turn of events.

At the three second mark, she decided she did. She liked it very much indeed.

She'd never been so deliciously aware of someone before, of every breath and every movement. Samuel's form filled her vision. When she closed her eyes, the sensation of his mouth moving over hers crowded her mind.

He kissed her gently, slowly, as if testing her response, and she followed suit, matching his movements and pace. Without experience to draw from, she used him as a guide, being careful when he was careful, turning her head when he turned his. The kiss took on a lovely dreamlike quality, a hazy and decadent game of follow the leader. And she was only too happy to play along, to enjoy the slow chase.

It was exciting and magical and perfectly wonderful.

Until Samuel pulled away and looked at her as if she was someone he'd never seen before. "You've never done this," he murmured.

She gaped at him. Simply gaped. Of all the things that might have been said in the moment, she could not imagine a less flattering, less romantic bit of commentary. Except maybe, *Drat. I thought you were someone else.*

She leaned away from him. "I apologize for my lack of skill."

"Don't apologize. Nothing wrong with it."

That was an improvement by only the slimmest of very slim margins.

He leaned toward her again, but she put her hand on his chest and pushed him back.

"Have *you* not kissed a woman before?" Because if this was the way he went about it, there couldn't be a woman in England who'd let him kiss her more than once.

A crease formed between his brows as he studied her. "I didn't mean to wound your feelings. I am surprised, that's all. You are a beautiful woman in possession of a unique, even flexible sense of morality. I assumed you had indulged yourself at some time."

Flexible. She knew what that meant.

"I am not my mother. I don't go about dallying with men who are not my husband." She may have been an accomplished flirt in Norfolk, but she'd not been a trollop. She'd never done anything that could jeopardize her family's respectability in the village. She had smiled and giggled and batted her lashes, enjoying the innocent appreciation of many gentlemen. All of whom she had promptly sent on their way the second they gave any indication of real attachment.

Not once had she let a man take liberties.

"A string of dalliances was not the sort of indulgence to which I was referring," Samuel replied. "I was thinking of a kiss. Nothing wrong with a kiss or two. Renderwell gave me the impression that your sister had a brief romance with the village butcher."

"And now she has Renderwell. Perhaps you'd prefer her more tutored favors."

A line of annoyance appeared across his brow. "I don't want your sister. And I told you, it was not my intention to wound your feelings. I made an observation, that's all."

He hadn't wounded her feelings. He had stepped on her pride, or possibly her vanity. Either way, the insult demanded retaliation.

"Well, if we are making observations about our partner's inadequacies, I should like to note that your beard is scratchy. And you smell like wet pavement."

He reached up to rub the offending beard. "I see. If the experience was so unpleasant for you, why did you participate?"

She gave him a tight smile. "I didn't want to wound your feelings."

He lowered his hand slowly. "This was a mistake."

"Oh, *clearly*."

Well done, Samuel. Brilliant job.

This was the downside of being stingy with one's words. The less one said, the more out of practice one became at speaking at all, and the more out of practice one became, the less likely it was that one would manage to say the right thing. Which led a man right back to keeping his mouth shut.

As he was doing now.

Samuel sat back in his seat while Esther turned to stare at the curtains. Not for the first time, he wished he had Gabriel's gift with words. Gabriel was the talker, the charmer. He was the man Renderwell sent to extract information from witnesses and informants.

Renderwell sent Samuel to speak with victims or the families of victims. They didn't need someone to talk to them; they needed someone to listen. He was adept at listening.

Fat lot of good it did him now. Esther wasn't talking. And he didn't know what to say to make things right again.

He really hadn't meant to insult her. The evident lack of experience had been a surprise, that was all. And a pleasant surprise at that. It was probably small of him, but he could admit he took jealous pleasure in knowing he was the only man she had kissed.

And what was wrong with remarking on something he liked?

Where was the offense in commenting on a lady's lack of experience with men?

God help him, he didn't know. He didn't see it.

I can tell you've been generous with your favors.

That seemed like the sort of thing a lady might find offensive.

But either his statement had not been the entirely harmless observation he imagined it to be or Esther was a prickly, contrary woman who was far too quick to find fault and toss insults.

After some deliberation he concluded that the truth probably fell somewhere in between.

Then she shot him a hard, narrow-eyed glance designed to draw blood, and he decided that "in between" fell just a hair more on the prickly side.

He doubted she'd accept an apology from him at that moment even if he did manage to stumble through one. In fact, she looked half-ready to slice off a portion of his tongue if he so much as tried it.

Better all around, he thought, if he just kept his mouth shut.

Six

After changing into dry clothes, Samuel left the hotel to see to a few items of his own business about town. He didn't like leaving Esther alone, but she was safe enough in her rooms. Besides, he'd seen Esther use her blades. She wasn't what one might call entirely helpless.

She also wasn't what one might call entirely predictable. Keeping this in mind, he completed his errands and was back at the hotel in just over an hour—and was more than a little surprised when he discovered one item of business lounging against the door to his rooms.

Sir Gabriel Arkwright straightened his tall, lean frame and held up a familiar note. "This was unexpected."

"As are you." Samuel unlocked his door and let them both in. Suddenly, the day seemed much improved. "I left that note with your housekeeper not an hour ago."

"Then we missed each other by thirty minutes."

Samuel tossed his hat and gloves on the bed and grinned at his oldest friend. "Have you been waiting outside my door like a lost pup for long?"

"Two minutes at most," Gabriel replied and smirked. "Were you in Miss Bales's company for long before you came running to me for help like a frightened child?"

"It's been nearly a full twenty-four hours."

"And neither of you mortally wounded?" Gabriel gave an appreciative bob of his blond head. "Impressive."

Samuel certainly thought so, but it was always nice to have one's accomplishments recognized by a friend. Or family, in this case. Gabriel was a brother to him in all but blood.

Renderwell was family as well, but he'd been a baron when Samuel had met him, as well as Samuel's commanding officer in the military and later with the police. When they'd left the police to become private investigators, Renderwell had naturally stepped into a leadership role. He'd been Viscount Renderwell, the Gentleman Thief Taker. Samuel and Gabriel had been his men.

Gabriel, on the other hand, had never been Samuel's superior. They were equals, as brothers should be.

"I'd be glad of your assistance in this, Gabriel."

"You'll have it." Gabriel smiled pleasantly as he removed his own coat and laid it over the back of an overstuffed chair with the meticulous care of a valet. "For the next sixteen hours. I'm for Scotland in the morning. Mr. Cobb of Park Lane fears his son has set up house outside Edinburgh with an actress."

All of Samuel's notions of putting a bit of space between himself and the prickly woman across the hall went up in smoke. "Put him off a week."

"Can't be done." Always impeccably groomed, Gabriel took a moment to smooth down his windblown blond hair. "He has heard talk of marriage."

"Hell."

"Do you expect Esther to be in London a week, then?"

Not if he could help it. "That is her intention."

"What is she doing here?"

"I can't tell you." Feeling unaccountably embarrassed, Samuel rubbed the back of his neck when Gabriel lifted his brows. "I promised."

"God, you and your morals," Gabriel muttered. "Is she in some sort of trouble?"

"Not the sort you're imagining."

"Are you certain of that?"

"I am. But you may ask her yourself, if you like." Esther meant to tell her family the truth once she returned to Derbyshire. It was possible she could be convinced to tell Gabriel the truth a few days early. "Before you do, I should warn you that she'll ask you not to send word of this to Renderwell."

"She expects me to lie to him?"

"No, just keep her stay in London a secret until she returns to Derbyshire. She'll tell him herself."

"I see." Gabriel leaned against the back of the chair. "Have you agreed to this?"

"I have." He wasn't given much choice in the matter but wasn't going to admit to that. "Will you?"

"If you think it's for the best," Gabriel decided after a moment's consideration. "Renderwell won't thank us for keeping her secret."

"No." Samuel pictured Renderwell's reaction to the news. "You might want to take your time finding Mr. Cobb's son."

Esther soaked away her irritation in an enormous cast-iron tub. She had paid extra for a private bathing room and had decided upon her first day, and first bath, that it was coin well spent. The Anthem Hotel was not particularly new or luxurious, but it had been partially renovated a year ago, and some clever soul had thought to add a water heating system to the list of improvements.

All she need do to scrub away the stench of London was turn a knob in the wall, and out piped hot water. It was wonderful. The tub in her little cottage used an attached furnace that took nearly half an hour to heat the water. That was the sort of tub Samuel had in his room. She knew this for a fact, because that room had been offered to her upon arrival.

He had to wait for hot water. She did not. Funny how much pleasure could be found in the little things.

Smiling to herself, she reached over the edge of the tub to retrieve the dagger she'd left sitting on a stool. She idly turned the blade over in her hand, then tested the tip with her finger.

She had come by her talent almost accidently at the age of ten. After reading about a knife-throwing act in the paper, she'd taken a scrap of wood and a kitchen knife and, on a whim, given the exercise a go. To her astonishment, and her father's delight, she'd shown considerable aptitude. He'd brought her a cheap set of daggers the very next day.

In truth, she would have continued her practice with or without his encouragement. She loved throwing daggers. She loved the weight of them in her hand, the glint of steel as a blade sailed through the air, and the way her arm ached after long hours of practice.

She liked knowing she had the means to defend herself. It made her feel strong and powerful.

But most of all, she liked the moment just before the weapon left her hand.

In that second, that one beat of the heart, time slowed, the world went still and dim, and all her worries fell away. There was no fear, or shame, or anger. There was no thought at all. There was only her blade, a single spot in the distance and a tremendous sense of peace.

Those fleeting seconds were one of her greatest joys. And she'd very nearly let Will Walker take it all away.

What a fool she'd been to play the henchman in the hopes of earning his affection. There was satisfaction in seeing her dagger hit the center of a target. There was no satisfaction in seeing fear in a man's eyes. Unless one counted the time she'd stabbed one of her brother's kidnappers in the shoulder, but that was different. That had been necessary. It hadn't been necessary for her to work with her father. And it hadn't made her feel powerful. It had made her feel desperate and pitiful, just as she'd told Samuel.

After the disastrous diamond theft and her father's death, she'd put her blades away for a time, afraid and ashamed of what she had become.

Then she had seen this dagger in the back of a shop in her village, and she had purchased it as an act of defiance, a way to take back something that belonged to her. Something that would always belong to her.

Feeling much improved, she gave the dagger another twirl and set it aside.

"Esther?" There were three quick raps on her door. "Sir Gabriel is here."

Esther froze. Sir Gabriel? But he wasn't supposed to be back so soon. She hadn't yet figured out how best to deal with him, how to explain, how to—

"Esther?"

She scrambled out of the tub. "A moment," she called out, grabbing a towel on her way out of the bathing room. "Just a moment."

She dried herself as quickly as she could, threw on her undergarments, and pulled out a pale blue tea gown, the only concession to comfort she'd made aside from her nightgown—and the only item of dress she had that didn't require a bustle and corset.

"Esther?"

"Yes. Coming." She struggled into the gown, buttoned it in a hurry, grabbed a handful of pins, and piled her damp hair atop her head in a fashion she was sure she wouldn't care to see in the mirror.

Samuel's hand was lifted for another knock when she opened the door.

"Gentlemen." She motioned them inside and closed the door behind them.

The men stopped just inside the room. Four eyebrows lifted, and two pairs of eyes tracked a bead of water that slipped down the side of her face. She wiped it away as discreetly as possible. Which, frankly, wasn't all that discreet.

"It is good to see you, Sir Gabriel." Only it wasn't, really.

Laughing blue eyes met hers. "And you, Miss Bales."

"Would you care for a drink?" She gestured at the bottle of wine on the table.

"Wouldn't mind it. Don't trouble yourself," he said, stepping around her. "I'll see to it. Samuel?"

"Thank you, no."

While Gabriel busied himself at the table, Samuel leaned down and whispered in her ear, "You might have said you were indisposed."

"Yes, well..." She'd not thought of it. "You caught me unawares."

"I can see that." He tapped a finger against her back. "You've buttoned your gown wrong."

She reached behind her. Drat, she had. She'd missed a button somewhere and now the whole thing was pulled askew.

How was she to convince the eternally well-dressed Sir Gabriel Arkwright that she was a competent woman capable of making her own decisions while standing in an incompetently buttoned gown? *With increasingly wet shoulders*, she added, swiping away another trickle of water.

It was ridiculous.

Deciding that what he couldn't see wouldn't embarrass her, she sidled over to a set of armchairs in front of the hearth (ignoring Samuel's snort of amusement) and took a seat as Gabriel returned with the drinks.

She accepted her glass with a polite smile. "You were not expected back so soon, sir."

"I would have made it a point to come earlier"—he lifted his glass in a small toast—"had I known the pleasure of your company was to be found in town."

Such a charmer, Sir Gabriel. When he wanted to be. She'd seen him play other roles as well—the gentleman, the rake, even the simpleton when it suited his purposes. Perhaps that was why she liked him but didn't trust him. They were too much alike.

Gabriel settled in the seat across from her. "Would you like to tell me *why* the pleasure of your company is to be had in town, Miss Bales?"

"Hasn't Samuel told you?"

She looked to the man in question, but he didn't appear inclined to explain himself. He'd pulled up a chair from the table and was now staring at the carpet near her feet. No, not near her feet. At her feet. Her bare feet.

She drew them back under her skirts and wondered why wet hair and bare toes should make her feel so exposed, as if she'd just stepped out of the bath and was still naked instead of swathed in several layers of linen, cotton, and taffeta.

Gabriel took a sip of his drink. "Samuel thought you might prefer to tell me yourself."

"I see." She debated how much to tell him, then decided it probably didn't matter what she told him. Samuel would likely fill in whatever information she chose to leave out. "I assume you are aware that I am illegitimate?"

"I am."

"I've come to London to find my natural father."

"May I ask why?"

"I would rather not discuss the particulars." If Samuel saw fit to share her secrets, she couldn't stop him, but she'd not tell them herself.

"Should I be worried about the particulars?"

"No." She didn't expect him to believe her, so she gestured at Samuel with her glass. "He'll worry about them for the both of us."

"He will at that," Gabriel conceded with a small laugh. He quickly grew pensive, however. He swirled his drink lightly a moment, then set the glass aside without taking another sip. "I feel compelled to mention the obvious, Miss Bales."

"And that is?"

"Some people don't wish to be found."

"That has occurred to me." How could it not, when she spent so much of her own life trying not to be found?

"Some people also don't deserve it," he said and shrugged when she frowned at him. "He left you in the care of a criminal. Is such a man worth your bother?"

"I don't know." She didn't know the first thing about Mr. George Smith, other than that he might have been a grocer some years ago. "He may not have been aware that Will was a criminal. He could have thought I would have a better life with my mother."

Besides, it didn't matter if her father deserved to be found or not. She wasn't doing it for him, not entirely. She was doing it for herself.

"There is another matter of concern," Samuel said. "Give him the note from the young man."

She started to rise, then remembered her dress. "Er…"

Her gaze shot to Samuel.

He smiled at her. It was a perfectly ordinary, perfectly bland smile. But his gray eyes danced with unholy glee. The arse.

She sat back down. "It is just behind you, Sir Gabriel, in the bag on the table? If you would be so kind… Thank you."

She retrieved the note and handed it to Gabriel. He read it over while Samuel filled him in on the events of the previous two days.

At the end of the telling, Gabriel shook his head at Samuel. "Renderwell is going to kill you." He swore and set the note aside. "And me."

"Why you?" Esther inquired.

Samuel answered for him. "I asked Gabriel not to send word to your family."

Esther stared at him as a lovely warmth filled her chest. If he had come to her with flowers, chocolates, and an apology delivered in the form of a sonnet, she would not have been more shocked. Nor so touched.

He'd asked on her behalf, knowing Gabriel would be more inclined to accept a request from a friend. He had spared her the trouble of asking, possibly the indignity of begging, for Gabriel's silence. It had not been required of him. She had not expected it of him. He had done it of his own accord.

The anger and wounded feelings she'd been nursing since the kiss in the carriage drained away.

"Thank you, Samuel."

Pink toes peeking out from under pale blue skirts.

Samuel shoved the image aside and tried to concentrate on what his friend was saying. Something about his trip to the continent and... He had no idea. Not the foggiest notion. The man had been talking about his trip since they'd left Esther's rooms almost a quarter hour ago, and Samuel couldn't recall a single specific detail of what had been said.

Because he couldn't stop thinking about Esther's feet. Her *feet* for Christ's sake. The pink skin, the graceful arch of her foot, the hidden ankle just above, the smooth expanse of skin leading up to the hollow behind her knee. He'd always liked that spot. Soft and sensitive—

"Hell, you have that look about you."

"Sorry? What?" He blinked at his friend. "What look?"

"The same look Renderwell had when he was sniffing at Lottie's heels."

"I'm not in love with Esther." He was, at most, in annoyed lust with her. And it was a deviant lust at that. Feet, indeed.

"As you like," Gabriel replied with a smirk. He glanced at the clock. "I've some time to do a bit of digging tonight. I might look into this man at the station."

Samuel shook his head. His friend had just returned from a monthlong trip to the continent and was leaving for Scotland on the morrow. He could have one night between jobs to relax. "I'll see to it in the morning. Let's have a meal."

They got drunk instead. Well, technically, Gabriel got drunk. Samuel stopped after the second glass. He didn't mind the dulling effects of a little drink (or a lot, when the occasion called for it), but there was Esther's safety to consider. It was unlikely she'd be attacked in the hotel, but should the unthinkable happen, he'd just as soon not pass out on her attacker's feet.

Wouldn't mind so much if it was her feet... *No.* No. He was not going to think about her feet.

What was the point? It was unlikely he'd get another look at them. Unless she had a mind to take off her slippers before she kicked him.

It was possible he deserved a kick. It was possible he'd been hasty in his decision not to put the blame of their disagreement solely on his shoulders. He did have a tendency to make hasty judgments.

"You've that look again," Gabriel said to him—or slurred at him, really. The man was truly sotted, slouched like a half-filled sack of potatoes in his seat.

Samuel started to deny the accusation, then decided against it. What was the good of having a brother, after all, if one couldn't confide in him?

"I kissed Esther," he admitted and frowned at his empty glass. "She didn't care for it."

"Women..." Gabriel began knowingly. He swung his glass around, looking as if he meant to follow up that comment with a poignant observation or two on the more aggravating qualities of the fairer sex. Somewhere after the third or fourth swing, he appeared to have forgotten what he was on about. "They smell like sugar biscuits sometimes. Quite like that."

Something of a non sequitur, but Samuel couldn't argue with fact. He liked the smell of sugar biscuits, too. "Esther smells like roses."

He liked that even better.

"Isn't roses. Pa'onies."

"Ponies?" He sincerely hoped the man wasn't implying that Esther smelled like a horse. He wasn't drunk, but he was exceedingly comfortable in his chair. He didn't feel like standing up to punch his friend.

"Not ponies. *Peonies*," Gabriel corrected, over-enunciating the word. "The flower."

"What the devil are you talking about?"

"You've seen them. Enormous, fluffy things." He

made an indecipherable shape with his hands. "Like puffed up roses. She smells like those."

"Like puffy roses?"

"Not roses. Peonies. Different species, man." He frowned drunkenly into his glass. "Is it species with flowers? Or breeds. Maybe it's family."

"Species, I think. Could be subspecies." Neither of them had excelled in biology. "Doesn't matter. Esther smells like roses."

"Peonies."

"Roses."

"Wager on it?"

He'd wager that this was one of the most ridiculous conversations he'd ever had. "What do you suggest?"

"I win, you go to Scotland for me. Bloody hate the cold."

"It's August."

"Still bloody colder'n it has any right to be," Gabriel muttered.

"If I went to Scotland for you, you would have to remain here with Esther."

Gabriel gave this some thought. "Five pounds. Winner takes five pounds."

"Done."

Esther snuggled deeper into her blankets as Samuel and Gabriel's muffled laughter floated into her room from across the hall. There was something wonderfully reassuring about the sound.

Years ago, when she'd been very little, her father had rented rooms from a woman with an enormous old Rottweiler named Champ. On the nights her father would take Lottie out until the small hours of the morning, Esther would sneak downstairs, lonely and afraid, and curl up with Champ next to the kitchen stove. The dog was too old and too docile to serve as any sort of guard, but that wasn't why she'd sought him out. She'd liked the sound of his snoring. When she closed her eyes, she could imagine it was the rumble and puff of a mighty dragon watching over her as she slept.

In her bed at the hotel, she listened to another low rumble of laughter and smiled to herself. It was like having two pet dragons, she supposed. She'd not gone looking for them, and she was going to have the devil's own time managing them. But, still, it was nice to know they were there.

Pity the sound wasn't soothing her to sleep like Champ's snoring. Frustrated, she tried adjusting her blankets, but it didn't help. Her body was eager to give in to exhaustion, but her mind reeled and spun like a top. And it kept coming back around to the same thing.

Why had Samuel kissed her?

Earlier, the question had been buried beneath a mountain of anger and insult. Now the latter had melted away and the question was left standing all on its own, demanding her attention.

Why had he done it?

Samuel had never shown that sort of interest in her before. He'd never sought out her company or flirted with her. He'd never stared at her longingly from across the room. And she was dead certain of this, because she'd spent more time than she cared to admit staring at him.

Not that she'd been mooning over him. He just always seemed to be catching her eye, always piquing her interest. She'd known so few men like him—honest and courageous and trustworthy. And completely, utterly, out of her reach.

The fact was, she thought better of Samuel than Samuel did of her. And it wasn't just a matter of him being oblivious to her charms. He was simply too familiar with her flaws. He knew her secrets, her every fault, her worst attributes, her most humiliating mistakes. Well, perhaps not the worst. But he knew most of her mistakes, enough to judge her and find her lacking.

And he did. *Oh*, he did.

One way or another, Samuel had always made his opinion of her perfectly clear.

He didn't like her. He didn't respect her. He would never trust her.

So why had he kissed her today?

Certainly, they'd come to a slightly better understanding of each other over the course of the morning, but that couldn't possibly be sufficient to cause a radical change of opinion on his part. Was it just curiosity? Had he simply been looking for a way to keep her quiet? Had he accidently swallowed a bit of toxic ditchwater?

She scrubbed her hands over her face with a groan. Guessing was pointless. She would never know the true answer unless she asked Samuel, which was obviously out of the question.

"Curiosity," she whispered into the room. If she couldn't guess, and she couldn't ask, she'd just decide what was true for herself. "It was just curiosity. Nothing more."

Seven

ESTHER WONDERED WHAT THE LONDON PRESS WOULD have to say about the two pitiful creatures who shuffled into her rooms to take breakfast. Samuel appeared to have changed at least, but Gabriel was wearing the same clothes, his hair was askew, and his handsome countenance was dulled by a sickly pallor. They both looked as if they'd not slept.

"Oh, how the mighty have fallen." She leaned over and sniffed as Gabriel took a seat next to her. "You smell like a distillery, sir."

He gave her a smile that managed to charm despite his unhealthy complexion. "You smell like peonies."

"It's roses," she corrected.

"Damn."

She didn't know why Gabriel should be disappointed or why Samuel should find his friend's disappointment so amusing. "Do I want to know why—?"

"No." This from both men.

She decided to take them at their word. "Fine pair of guards I had for the night. Drunk as lords, the both of them."

"Samuel wasn't drunk," Gabriel replied. "And you, Miss Bales, are not in need of a guard."

She beamed at him. "Thank you, Sir Gabriel."

"Don't put ideas in her head," Samuel muttered.

"She doesn't need me for that either."

Samuel made a face at the table of food. "Did you wear your veil when this arrived?"

"No, of course not," she chimed sweetly. "I was quite as you see me now, and before the maids left, I gave them each a portrait of me with my full name, address, and family tree printed on the back. I encouraged them to share the information amongst their friends."

Gabriel took a cautious sip of his tea. "I think probably she wore the veil."

She sent Samuel a teasing grin and was gratified to see his mouth curve with begrudging humor. She hoped his willingness to smile meant he wasn't still brooding over their argument in the carriage. To begin with, he hadn't any right to act the injured party. More importantly, she didn't want to fight with him.

He'd kissed her out of curiosity, and obviously, the kiss had been more enjoyable for her than for him. That stung, but Samuel had made up for his callousness by being so thoughtful last night. Her pride would mend, as pride always did. Particularly when one made certain not to repeat the same humiliation twice.

She would not kiss Samuel again. He would not point out her lack of skill. She wouldn't have to wonder why he'd kissed her in the first place. And that would be that. They could get on as they had before.

It was all quite sensible. Strange that it should leave her feeling so dissatisfied.

Next to her, Gabriel grimaced at his plate and pushed it away. "I can't eat this."

Esther pulled herself away from her woolgathering and tsked sympathetically. "Have a little of the eggs, at least." She nudged the plate back. It was strange to see Gabriel so out of sorts. He was usually so careful to appear fit and well groomed. "You'll feel the better for eating something."

Samuel shook his head at Gabriel. "Don't. Don't let her nurse you. You'll be dead in an hour."

"I nursed you." She laughed. She'd taken good care of him after he'd been shot last year. "You're still here."

"I've a stronger constitution. Gabriel doesn't hold up well under torture."

"Torture?" What drivel. But she was as happy to hear the teasing note in his voice as she had been to see the smile. "I was mercy itself. Florence Nightingale might take lessons from me."

"You hit me on the nose."

"I flicked you on the nose." She demonstrated with her fingers. "Delicately." And so might the lady with the lamp do as well if her patient tried to stand up for a drink ten minutes after being shot. "You were a terrible patient. That was the trouble."

"Agreed," Gabriel said and shrugged at Samuel. "You've always been a terrible patient." He gave Esther an apologetic look. "So have I been, I'm afraid. I'm not eating the eggs."

"But—"

"I've a long ride to Scotland," he interrupted and rose from his seat. "I'll find something more appealing along the way."

Samuel pushed back from the table. "We'll see you to the station."

"No need. I have to stop off at home first for my things." He rolled his shoulders, as if suddenly a little uncomfortable in his own skin. "And I intend to burn these clothes. Have your breakfast. I'll send word when I arrive." He took Esther's hand and kissed the back of it like a proper, old-fashioned gentleman. Or a charming rogue, as was really the case. "Miss Bales. A pleasure, as always."

"Sir Gabriel."

Esther waited until Gabriel left before turning to Samuel. "Does he often drink to excess?"

"No," Samuel replied, but he continued to stare at the door, a crease between his eyes. "Very rarely."

"Are you worried about him?"

"He works too much. He needs a proper rest."

"You care for him like a brother." Or a mother, but she didn't think he'd appreciate that comparison.

"He is the nearest thing I have to a brother. I've known him since childhood."

"You went to school together, didn't you?"

Samuel nodded. "Flintwood Academy."

"Flintwood?" That was new information. "I've heard of that institution." She leaned forward to whisper dramatically. "They say it is where the wicked boys are sent."

"Not wicked," he corrected, one corner of his mouth hooking up. "Merely the unruly."

"I find it difficult to imagine you unruly," she replied, sitting back.

There was a moment's pause before he said, "I was a brawler."

"Were you really? I cannot picture it." He was such a contained man. She'd never seen him lose his temper completely. It was difficult to imagine him as a wild young man, eager for a fight. "With whom did you brawl? The local boys I suppose—"

"With my father."

Amusement vanished, and she swallowed against a lump in her throat.

"Oh. Oh, I see." She didn't, of course. She couldn't begin to imagine what that must have been like. Her father had been many things—many terrible, unforgivable things—but he'd never raised a hand to his children. "I'm sorry."

He lifted a shoulder in a careless shrug. "My father liked to drink, and when he drank, he liked to hit things. My mother, in particular."

"How old were you?" she inquired.

"Twelve."

"*Twelve?*" For God's sake, that wasn't brawling. Children brawled with other children. A grown man brawled with other grown men. A grown man didn't brawl with a child. That wasn't a fight. That was a beating. "I'm so sorry."

"He wasn't a large man. I owe my size to my maternal grandfather, I'm told. By the time I was twelve, I fancied myself big enough to stand up to him. And so I might have been, had my father not picked up the fire poker."

"Oh my God."

He shook his head at her, as if dismissing the memory. "It was a long time ago, and it worked out well in the end. I was sent to Flintwood, where

I received a decent education and lived without a moment's fear of my father. And I met Gabriel there, though you'd not recognize the man in the child. He was the scrawniest eleven-year-old I've ever seen, and one of the cleverest. And meanest."

"Gabriel?" She found it difficult to reconcile that description with the carefully charming man who'd only just left. There was more to Gabriel than met the eye, certainly, but she'd never suspected meanness.

"He settled down in a few months."

"What happened to your mother?"

"She left my father nine years ago, when I was knighted and the papers recounted all the unhappy details of my early childhood. Even the most loyal of friends and servants will talk for the right price." He shook his head again. "She lives with my aunt now. Doesn't matter."

It did matter. She wanted to ask him more about his childhood and his parents. Did he ever wonder what his life might have been like if his family had been different? Did he ever wonder if *he* might have been different? Maybe even better? Did he believe one could become a better person if one really put her mind to it?

Oh, she had so many questions and a sudden urge to share her own thoughts, her own experiences, even her real reason for coming to London.

He was eager to change the subject, though. She could see it in his eyes, which had grown distant and shuttered. If she tried to push him for more information now, it would be an awkward and one-sided conversation.

She forced a casual smile. "Friends and servants

from your childhood? You really were a sensation, weren't you?"

"We were." He tapped his fork absently against the table. "You look as if my history has surprised you. Didn't you read the papers nine years ago?"

"Not for a time," she replied. "We left London just days after Lady Strale's rescue, you'll recall. We were trying to start a new life in Norfolk. There was so much to do, I simply didn't have time for reading. And we kept our distance from the neighbors at first, so there was no one to tell us the latest gossip."

"Do you resent me for it? I know your sister did for a time."

"For our banishment to Norfolk? No." On the contrary, she'd been grateful. She wanted to tell him that but couldn't think of a way to explain her feelings without opening the Pandora's box that was her past. "I quite liked life at Willowbend."

"I should have thought it too dull for you."

"It was, eventually, but I enjoyed it at first. It was something new, after all."

"I suppose it was. But what of the decision to keep your father's role in Lady Stale's rescue a secret? You must have been angry about that."

"Not at all." Unlike her sister, she'd never been under the mistaken impression that Will Walker had become a reformed man. She'd always known him to be a blackguard. He'd earned his ignominious end. But even if he had sought redemption, it would have made little difference for the Walker children. "Lottie says that, had our father been given his due credit for the rescue, we'd have become sensations as well."

"Yes."

"Making it an easy thing for our father's enemies to find us." There was no escaping the past. No matter how much one might wish it. "It was all done for the best, and I suspect you've earned that knighthood a dozen times over, with or without my father's help."

That seemed to cheer him up rather nicely. "I like to think so."

"I heard you were all given very dramatic names and descriptions by the papers. Renderwell was the Gentleman Thief Taker, Gabriel was the Thief Taker most likely to seduce his prey, and you were—"

"Don't say it."

"Thief Taker Almighty," she said and laughed when he groaned. "Oh, come now, it isn't so terrible a name. I should think you'd be flattered."

"Flattered?" He made a face at his plate. "No one wants to be remembered for having been shot an inordinate number of times."

"Only four," she replied and bit the inside of her cheek to keep from laughing again.

"Only four?"

"Just the three when you'd earned the name."

His expression turned baleful. "Just three."

"Indeed. It should be at least six to warrant 'Almighty.'"

"Six? Why *six*?"

"I don't know. It can't be counted on just the one hand. That's something."

He gave a short bark of laughter. "Why not make it eleven so it can't be counted on the hands at all?"

"That seems a trifle excessive."

"A trifle...? Esther, *one* is excessive."

She agreed wholeheartedly, but she was enjoying the silly disagreement. Even better, so was he. "But not all that impressive, is it? Anyone might stumble into the path of a single stray bullet." She shook her head at him. "No, I think six is a reasonable threshold."

"I see. Well, I shall endeavor to increase the pace of my stumbling, as it appears I have some way to go."

Suddenly, the conversation no longer felt quite so silly. The humor took on a dark, even macabre cast. It was one thing to argue over the number of shots in the abstract; it was another entirely to look at the man and remember him ashen faced and in pain, a bullet hole in his shoulder.

"Samuel?" She waited for him to meet her gaze. She knew he didn't fully trust her. She accepted that he would probably never believe half of what came out of her mouth. But for reasons she didn't fully understand herself, she wanted him to believe her now. She wanted it desperately. "I am very glad it has not been six."

He smiled at her then, that wonderful, cheerful, friendly smile she'd never had from him before.

"So am I, Esther."

For the life of him, Samuel could not figure out what had possessed him to share his ugly childhood memory with Esther.

It wasn't that his father's penchant for drink and violence was any sort of secret. But what was general knowledge and what one brought up as breakfast conversation were two different animals entirely.

Furthermore, the incident with the fire poker wasn't general knowledge. By some miracle, it had never made the papers, and he'd never spoken of it to anyone but Gabriel and Renderwell. He'd never intended to speak of it to anyone else. He wasn't ashamed of the fight—he'd not done a damn thing wrong that night. But it was an uncomfortable business, laying out one's personal pain for someone else's perusal.

So why the devil had he blurted the thing out over eggs and toast?

Maybe it was some sort of attempt to repair whatever damage had been done by the kiss. Or maybe it was to repay her for that kiss.

No, not repay her. He didn't like the sound of that, as if he'd purchased her favors. She'd not sold her touch. Rather, she had given him a part of herself she'd never given anyone else. And she'd told him of her longing for adventure and excitement. He'd wager that wasn't something she shared with many.

Maybe he'd simply wanted to give her some part of himself in return.

Or maybe he had a bit of the drink left in his system. Never mind that he'd not imbibed enough to be feeling the effects hours later. The drink would explain his odd behavior. It would also explain the equally strange fact that he didn't feel at all embarrassed by it. He wasn't the least bit uncomfortable.

Before, with his friends, recounting the fight with his father had left him feeling drained, even a little sick.

Now, he felt…a bit cheerful, really.

There'd been a sick moment or two in the retelling, but then Esther had teased him about his ridiculous moniker and engaged him in a ludicrous discussion about the minimum number of bullets required to earn it, and now he felt quite like his usual self.

She had cheered him up, he realized with no small amount of surprise.

Esther Walker-Bales, that prickly, unpredictable, infuriating woman, had cheered him up.

Eight

"SOMETHING OF A STEP UP FROM ROOMS OVER A grocer on Commercial Street," Samuel commented.

Esther peeked out the carriage curtains at the long line of houses on Apton Street. Bethnal Green was hardly a desirable section of town, but this particular street was located a fair distance from the notorious Old Nichol Street rookery and appeared to be solidly middle class, with modest but well-tended homes. Which made it more of a leap than a step.

"Perhaps he wasn't a grocer," she ventured. "Perhaps he owned the building in Spitalfields and the grocer was his tenant. It was some time ago. People confuse details. Or we could have the wrong street." This last was unlikely. *Apton* was the closest thing to *Apple* or any fruit-based street name they'd found in the area.

"Why would he have used the Spitalfields address on the letter he sent to your mother?"

"I don't know." She motioned at the door. "Let's see if we can find out, shall we?"

"There is something we need to discuss before we begin this search in earnest." He reached over and took her hand in his. "Esther, we don't know anything about this man other than that he had an affair with your mother, the wife of Will Walker."

She looked down at their joined hands. His was warm and strong and nearly swallowed her own. "You think they all moved in the same circles," she guessed. "That he might be a criminal and a threat."

"I wouldn't wager on it." He gave her hand a quick squeeze before letting go. "If George Smith always knew of you, then he knew Will Walker was the man raising you. If he had any desire to betray either of you, he could have managed it years ago."

"Yes, that was my thought as well."

"But the possibility of betrayal still remains."

She nodded and suddenly wished he'd not released her hand so quickly. "He might be a different man now."

"Yes."

George Smith's circumstances might have changed over the years. Or he may have always been the sort of man who wouldn't stoop to betraying a child but could live with betraying a grown woman. Or he may have remained unaware of her existence all these years.

"Are you prepared for such a possibility?" Samuel asked.

"Yes. I mean to lie to him," she admitted. "At least initially. It's been my plan from the start. I'll tell him my siblings died in an outbreak of influenza and I married and moved to Boston years ago. Now I am widowed and only in London for a short visit." She made a face, annoyed with the circumstances. "All this time and effort, all this worry and work to meet my father, and I'm going to lie to him."

"It can't be helped."

"Yes, I know." She tipped her head at him, curious. "Why are you only now mentioning this? Why didn't you bring this up at the hotel or in Spitalfields?"

"We weren't looking for your father in Spitalfields; we were looking for the boy. We certainly weren't going to find him at the hotel. You might meet him today."

That didn't explain why he'd waited to speak up. Unless… "What if I'd not thought to lie to him, or agreed to do it?"

"You're already here," he pointed out. "Why argue with a reasonable suggestion when you're so close?"

"And if I refused to be reasonable?"

He gave her a thin smile. "This isn't a public hackney."

"I thought as much." He could take her back to Derbyshire, forgoing the trouble of getting her out of the hotel and into the carriage.

She could hardly fault him for the plan. It would be the only sensible response to what would have been a terrific act of stupidity on her part. The idea that the plan had been needed at all, however, was a little insulting. "I'm really not an idiot, you know."

"I know," he said simply. "With any luck, we'll know what sort of man your father is by the end of the day." He opened the carriage door and hopped down, then turned and frowned at her when she moved to follow. "What are you doing?"

"I'm coming with you."

"No, you're not."

"Well, I'm not waiting in the carriage."

"Yes, you are."

"That is ridiculous." She threw her hands up in annoyance. "Why did I come along at all if it was only to sit in here?"

"I assume if we find him, you'll want to speak with him?"

"I want to speak with whomever answers the door."

Samuel shook his head. "A young widow asking questions is an oddity. People don't like oddities."

"Of course they do. That's why we have circuses and curiosity shops."

"People don't like oddities showing up at their front doors unannounced at nine in the morning. They do, however"—he pulled a calling card out of his pocket and handed it to her—"like a bit of excitement."

Esther read the card with a sigh.

Sir Samuel Brass, Private Investigator.

Yes, being handed a card such as this would be exciting. Even if the name wasn't recognized, the profession certainly would be. People would want to help Sir Samuel Brass, Private Investigator. They would likely want to help him even if he brought along an odd widow, but they might feel more constrained in her company.

"Oh, very well," she muttered. She gave him back the card and sagged back against her seat after he closed the door and ran off to have all the fun.

She might as well have stayed in Derbyshire and hired Samuel to find her father. One might argue that it would have been the safer course of action, but her purpose in coming to London hadn't been simply to meet her father; it had been to *find* him. The search was an important step on the path of setting things right.

She wasn't finding him now; she was waiting for someone else to find him for her. And she wasn't even paying him for the trouble.

She felt like one of those indolent country gentlemen who went hunting but didn't do anything but stand in a field and shoot. It was their servants who carried the weapons, flushed out the pheasants, retrieved the carcasses, carried them home, then cleaned, cooked, and served the birds. She didn't want to stand in the field and shoot. She wanted the work.

Esther pushed aside a corner of the drapes to peek outside as Samuel climbed the front steps to the first house.

This wasn't atonement. It was atonement by proxy.

Samuel, on the other hand, didn't seem to mind the arrangement at all. Over the next few hours, he appeared quite content to go from house to house alone, staying only briefly in some but disappearing for fifteen minutes or more in others. He returned to the carriage every so often to inform Esther of his progress, or lack thereof. No one on the street had heard of Mr. George Smith, but the neighborhood was filled with let houses. Few of the inhabitants had lived in the area for more than three years.

Esther's small store of patience began to wane.

After his fourth visit to the carriage, she was feeling completely useless and decidedly grumpy. It didn't help matters that he returned smelling suspiciously of tea and pastries.

"Are these people feeding you?" she demanded.

Samuel looked down at his lapel and brushed away a crumb. "Maybe a little."

"Was that a biscuit crumb?"

"Banbury cake."

"Banbury cake?" Who served Banbury cakes at eleven in the morning? For that matter, who ate Banbury cakes at eleven in the morning? "We only just had breakfast."

He shrugged and said, "It was a Banbury cake." As if that explained everything.

After a moment's consideration, she had to admit that it did. Banbury cakes were delicious. She slumped farther into her seat, now grumpy *and* hungry. "Well, bring some back with you next time."

"I'll see what I can manage."

He didn't manage Banbury cakes, but after another hour, he managed to procure useful information at last.

"We may have something," he told her, taking his seat across from her. "According to Miss Latimer—who was born, raised, and intends to die in the house at the end of the street—a Mr. and Mrs. George Smith occupied number fourteen Apton Street for thirty-seven years. Mrs. Smith passed on five years ago and Mr. Smith moved away to parts unknown. They had one son, Arnie, who left for school at a young age and rarely came home for visits."

"Thirty-seven years?" That couldn't be right. She knew for a fact that George Smith had lived in Bow more recently than that. "Was she certain?"

"Quite. She didn't know Mr. Smith well. He had a reputation for being a haughty and snobbish man who held himself apart from his neighbors. Considered himself superior. She also mentioned that, if he is still alive, his age would be somewhere in the midseventies."

"It's the wrong George Smith." Now she was grumpy, hungry, and disappointed.

"Not necessarily. Men sire children in their fifties."

"Not with my mother. She ran off with dashing young men who amused and adored her, not pompous gentlemen who would look down on her. Besides, she ran off to Brighton that year, not Bethnal Green." And there was the matter of her father having lived elsewhere during that thirty-five-year time span. "It's the wrong George Smith."

Samuel rubbed his chin. "I'm inclined to agree, which means either there is another George Smith in the area, or you were given false information."

"There are bound to be others in the area." With a name like George Smith, there could be dozens.

As it turned out, there was exactly one. Two hours later, and three streets over, Samuel found a Mr. George Albert Smith, age twelve.

"It's no good," Esther decided upon hearing the news. "The information I was given must have been wrong."

Samuel nodded in agreement then tilted his head a bit to study her. "You look as though you've lost heart."

"I've not lost heart. I'm disappointed, that's all." And it wasn't the temporary setback that bothered her so much. It was the inaction. Failure by proxy was even worse than atonement by proxy.

"We've places to look yet," Samuel said, "and there's more to a search than going door-to-door. There are records to be gone through as well. Deeds to the old building in Spitalfields. Birth registries, census records. If your father is in London, we'll find him."

Good Lord, how did one go about searching

records for a George Smith, exact age, location, and marital status unknown? "And if he isn't in London?"

"Then we'll find him outside of London. Should we try our luck in Bow first?"

Oh, she had so hoped they wouldn't really need to visit Rostrime Lane.

"Are you opposed to luncheon beforehand?" If it was cowardly to put off the inevitable for another hour or two, then cowardly she would be. She wasn't up to facing her past just yet.

"Not at all." Samuel stuck his head out to give orders to the driver.

Back to the hotel, she thought. Back to her rooms. Then, if she was very lucky, back to the carriage. Such an adventure.

"I'm going to look out the window," she grumbled. "Are you going to make a fuss about it?"

"Not if you put down your veil."

She obliged him without complaint and found that the view lifted her spirits a little. It was difficult to maintain a sour mood while London itself passed before her eyes.

The day had not gone as she had hoped, but it was only one day. One morning, really. She needn't assume she would have to be inactive for the rest of her trip. There were plenty of things she might do yet. She could search through the paperwork. Maybe she could convince Samuel to let her join him at one or two houses on Rostrime Lane.

Certainly, she was going into number twenty-three. Given the choice, she'd rather stroll through the gates of hell and invite the devil to tea, but that wasn't an option. Someone had to go into number twenty-three, and she would be that someone. She had to be.

Also, there was still the mystery of the young man at the station to solve. She was needed for that.

Esther grimaced a little as she became aware of the tenor of her thoughts. Had her life truly become so dull, so unbearably monotonous, that the possibility of physical danger was now a welcome relief? Was the chance to sort through papers, or view London through a moving window, really the most exciting thing she could hope for?

She found herself craning her neck for a glimpse at an intriguing roofline in the distance and realized that, yes, her life had become just that dull and, yes, this was likely the most she could expect.

She sighed, and with sufficient volume for Samuel to take note.

"Do you know the worst part about being a police officer?" he asked her. "And being a private investigator?"

Esther flicked a glance at him. "Not the lack of pastries, evidently."

"The waiting," he informed her. "Waiting in court, waiting to speak to a witness or a suspect. Waiting to talk to a magistrate or a judge. Waiting for someone to come forward with information. There is an abominable amount of waiting in the work."

"You didn't have to wait this morning."

"Of course I did," he replied. "At every house. How many people do you imagine are up and about prepared to greet visitors first thing in the morning?"

"It isn't first thing."

"In town, anything before one in the afternoon

is first thing in the morning." He pulled the curtain nearest him back another inch for a quick glance out the window. "For every minute of conversation I had in those houses, I spent ten minutes waiting alone in a parlor or sitting room."

She wasn't sure she believed him. Certainly, the early visits might have roused a few people unexpectedly, but it was nearly one in the afternoon now. The neighborhood was middle class, not aristocratic, and it was only the aristocrats who felt it was their duty to sleep past noon every day.

He was trying to make her feel better, she realized. His approach was obvious, awkward, and not at all effective. It didn't matter in the end. Where the tactic failed, the effort succeeded.

She found herself smiling simply because Samuel Brass was trying to make her smile.

Samuel watched Esther as she stared out the window. He couldn't see her features clearly through the veil, but he didn't need to. He had the keen memory.

Without any effort at all, he could bring up every detail of her face in his mind's eye. Right down to the tiny freckle at the corner of her mouth.

He'd been thinking about that freckle quite a lot. He'd been remembering the taste of her skin at that very spot. He'd been imagining sampling it again more than he cared to admit.

By tacit agreement, neither of them had mentioned their kiss the day before.

As he watched her, the delectable freckle so clear in

his mind, Samuel realized that he *wanted* to mention the kiss.

If it wasn't mentioned, then they couldn't discuss it. If they didn't discuss it, then he couldn't be absolutely certain things were right between them again. They *felt* right to him. It seemed as if the anger and awkwardness had passed. He was not, however, a consistently good judge of such matters. And Esther was remarkably skilled at hiding her true thoughts and feelings. He didn't want her to hide them now. If she was still angry…if she was hurt, he wanted to know. He wanted to fix it.

He cleared his throat, uncomfortable with the task before him. "Esther."

She didn't so much as flick him a glance. "Hmm?"

"I want it to be understood."

"Yes?"

"I liked kissing you." There, that was clear. In no way could that be misconstrued as an insult.

She looked away from the window at that, and there was a long pause before she spoke.

"I see," she said at last. She closed the curtains, lifted her veil, and stared at him some more. Finally, she looked away and asked, "Then why did you insult me?"

"I did not insult you." He grimaced at his defensiveness. "That is…that was not my intention, and—"

"You implied I did something wrong."

The devil he had. "There is nothing wrong with what we did." He would *never* imply otherwise.

"No, not with what—" She made a small frustrated noise. "Your comment implied that I did the thing badly."

"I don't see how. I merely observed that you were unpracticed but—"

"Yes," she cut in again. "Unpracticed. People who engage in activities they've not practiced, perform *badly*."

"It isn't a performance, Esther."

"Then why did you feel it necessary to offer a critique?"

"It was not a critique."

"It certainly wasn't a compliment," she muttered.

"I told you I liked it. How is that not a compliment? I *meant* it as a compliment." Surely that counted for something.

"One can like something awful," she returned and began digging through the bag at her waist.

"I find that hard to believe. No one likes something awful, else it wouldn't be—"

He broke off when she pulled out a miniature picture frame and held it up for him to see.

He had no idea what he was looking at. It appeared to be some manner of pond captured from a view aloft. There were two enormous lily pads at the top, what could be a lopsided boat stretched across the entire bottom half of the water, and what were either overlong blades of grass or very small trees scattered about the banks. "What the devil is that?"

"Peter's self-portrait at the age of six."

Ah. Eyes, mouth, and hair on a head. "It's…um…"

"It's atrocious. And I like it." She tucked the frame back into her bag. "And when he gave it to me, I did not embarrass him by remarking upon his obvious lack of artistic skill."

And she was embarrassed, he realized. He'd not

noticed that at first. For obvious reasons, he'd noticed her anger before all else. Now he saw the faint blush in her cheeks and her determination to avoid his gaze.

Suddenly, he remembered his first kiss. The nerves, the eagerness, the pride. And yes, afterward, the awkward embarrassment. How much worse would it have been had the young lady remarked upon his lack of experience? And then insisted they hold a conversation on the subject the next day?

That wouldn't have been embarrassing, he decided. It would have been mortifying.

He swore and rubbed the back of his neck. He had chosen his words, and his timing, very poorly.

"Esther." Leaning over, he took one of her hands in his. "There is absolutely no reason for you to feel embarrassed. There is nothing embarrassing in a woman—or a man—being inexperienced in these matters." Nor should there be anything embarrassing in discussing them, but he rather doubted she could be convinced of that at present. He sat back and pointed at her bag instead. "You say that portrait is atrocious, but you don't mean it. It is only when viewed from the wrong perspective that it becomes less than it is."

"And what is it through the correct perspective?"

"Beautiful. If Peter gave you a thousand more just like it, they would all be equally beautiful. Equally cherished."

"And equally unskilled," she said, but she was softening. He could see it.

She fiddled with the clasp of her bag a moment, her mouth turned down in a thoughtful frown. "You made me feel as if I'd done it all wrong."

"God." He'd been a damned oaf. "I'm sorry for

that. I didn't mean to... You didn't do it wrong. Honestly, there *isn't* a right or wrong way to kiss." He reconsidered this. "Apart from a few obviously ill-advised techniques, but—"

"Such as?"

Bloody hell, he should have known she would ask.

"I don't know," he muttered and wracked his brain for an example. Any example. "Don't recite the alphabet. Don't hop on one foot. Don't spit."

"Don't hop on one foot and *spit*?" Gone was the blush of embarrassment, the averted gaze. She goggled at him, all astonished amusement. "You've found this to be a common mistake amongst the kissing population, have you?"

"Of course not—"

"Because if that is the sort of kissing you've been experiencing, you really ought to have given me a standing ovation."

"It is not—"

"All the way back to the hotel."

"I haven't—"

"Three curtain calls worth at least."

He pinched the bridge of his nose.

"And tossed roses at my feet," she continued.

In the ensuing silence, he dropped his hand and eyed her warily. "Are you quite finished?"

Her mouth trembled with contained laughter. "Thornless ones. So that I might partake of their scent without pricking my unspitting lips."

"For God's sake," he laughed. He was amused, frustrated, and unable to tear his gaze away from those very lips. "I should have done all those things. I should have..." He searched for the right thing to say. "I can be very clumsy with words."

She considered this before offering him a hesitant smile. "I am sometimes quick to perceive a slight where none was intended."

"These are not complementary flaws."

Her gaze dipped to his mouth. "Not very complementary, no."

"We are not compatible people," he said and began to lean forward.

She shook her head slowly and leaned toward him as well. "Not at all compatible."

"We probably shouldn't—" he began, drawing closer.

"Oh, we absolutely shouldn't—" she agreed.

They met halfway, their lips coming together softly in the center of the carriage.

He curled his fingers into the edge of the seat to stop himself from reaching for her. He would not control what happened between them this time. If she wanted a change, wanted something more or something different, she would have to lead them both in a new direction. He wanted her to take that risk, to experiment, to discover for herself what he hadn't been able to put into words. There was no right or wrong, no good or bad way to enjoy a kiss. Even mistakes could be part of the fun if one was kissing the right person.

There were quite a few mistakes he'd like to make with Esther Walker-Bales.

He sensed her impatience at his reserve. She scooted closer and grasped the front of his coat in her small hands. After a moment, she pulled away to look at him through hooded lids. "Why won't you kiss me?"

"I want you to kiss me. Do whatever you like, Esther. It won't be wrong. I promise."

"Is this a lesson?"

"For both of us." He pressed a kiss to the beguiling freckle above her lip. "How am I to know what pleases you," he whispered, "if you don't know what pleases you?"

Her pretty blue eyes lowered to his mouth. "Anything I like?"

"Anything." *Everything.*

She hesitated only a moment, then lightly pressed her lips to his and held still, as if absorbing the sensation for the first time. It was the sweetest of touches, and his body responded by going hard as stone.

Pulling away a little, she ran her finger over his mouth, tracing the edges. After a moment, she leaned in again and kissed his bottom lip, a small, gentle movement that made him shiver. She lifted her head once more, and her tongue darted out to catch his taste on her lips. He had to close his eyes at the sight of it, his fingers digging harder into the seat.

He'd often thought of kissing in terms of eating—tasting and sampling. Esther nibbled at him like he was an entire table of exotic culinary delights. She sampled lightly, retreated to savor each flavor, then came back again and again for another test, another bite, another kiss.

He did his best to sit still through her delicate onslaught. Desire raced through his blood. His muscles ached from the need to reach for her.

When he felt her mouth part over his, he felt his control slipping away.

That was the trouble with handing Esther the reins. She had too much courage, too much curiosity. She'd drive them both straight over a cliff. And, God help him, all he could think was that he wanted to go faster.

An apology formed on his lips, but he wasn't sure if it came out as a mumble or a growl, and didn't much care. He let go of the seat, slid his hand around the nape of her neck, and pulled her close so he could devour her.

Somehow he managed to remove her bonnet and delve his fingers into the silken locks of her hair. Still it wasn't enough. He hauled her into his lap, her skirts dragging against his legs.

With one arm bound tight around her waist, he used his free hand to press lightly against her chin. "Open for me."

She obeyed with a small moan and he slid his tongue inside the warmth of her mouth, tasting her deeply for the first time.

Suddenly he was torn between the sharp pleasure of the kiss and the pressing need to go faster, do more, take everything. Even as he lost himself in the moment, his mind raced forward to the next, to how quickly he could remove the layers of fabric between them, how it would feel to have her naked and willing beneath him, how his name would sound spilling from her lips as she took her pleasure.

She tensed against him and shifted, and he realized that his hand had found the hem of her skirts. He'd bunched them up to her calf, his knuckles brushing along her leg.

No, not like this. Not in a carriage. Not with Esther.

He wanted a bed of down for her. He wanted to give her moonlight and candlelight, flowers and soft words. His hand fisted in the material of her gown briefly before he released it.

Determined to do the right thing, he began to soften the kiss in stages, relaxing his hold, returning to the light tease of his lips over hers. He pressed a kiss to her jaw, her cheek, her temple, then pulled away.

She blinked at him owlishly. Her lips were swollen, her skin flushed. She looked unbearably sweet. It took everything he had not to pull her close again.

Not in a bloody carriage.

"The carriage is stopped," she whispered.

It had been stopped for some time.

Wordlessly, and with enormous regret, he lifted her by her hips and set her on the seat next to him. He retrieved her bonnet from the floor and settled it back on her head, tying the black ribbons carefully beneath her chin.

She returned the favor by straightening his tie. For reasons he couldn't name, the simple gesture made his chest tighten with pleasure.

"It would appear we did it right this time," she said quietly.

He curled his finger under her chin and tormented himself with one last taste of her lips. "Both times."

She gave a small nod in agreement. "About that..." She cleared her throat. "Your beard isn't really scratchy. I'm sorry I said so before."

"Forgiven."

A corner of her mouth hooked up. "Did smell wet, though."

He laughed at the small, silly barb as he opened the carriage door. It would always be this way with Esther, he supposed. There would always be a bite with the sweet.

She surprised him by reaching past him to shut the door again.

Then she stared at him, worrying her bottom lip.

"What is it?" he asked. "What's the matter?"

"Nothing. I just..." She looked away and back again. "I like kissing you, too," she said at last, and quickly, as if it was a little difficult to get the words out, or maybe she just found them hard to say while they were looking eye to eye.

She smiled hesitantly once, then pulled her veil down, swung the door open, and hopped out on her own.

He watched her walk toward the front door of the hotel. Yes, there would always be the bite and the sweet with Esther, he thought. And there would always be surprise.

He was finding he liked the combination more than he had realized.

Not curiosity, then.

Esther bit into her apple and scrunched up her face in thought as she stared out her hotel window.

Her assessment of Samuel's reason for kissing her had been wrong. A man didn't kiss a woman twice out of curiosity, not when the first kiss ended so badly.

And Samuel had not kissed her like a man scratching at the itch of curiosity. *Her* kiss had been curious.

His had been…elemental, devastating, a little bit dangerous. Absolutely wonderful.

She sighed and smiled at the memory. Perhaps she'd been wrong about his feelings toward her all along.

Then she winced a little, remembering his angry words less than a year earlier.

Selfish imbecile.

No, his feelings for her had been clear.

So what had changed? She supposed *she* had to some degree. Certainly, she was happier than she'd been in the past, and she was determined to improve herself in a way she never had been before. But she was still a Walker, illegitimate or not. She was still the woman who'd played henchman for her criminal father, still the woman who'd spent years as a liar and a thief, and she would always be that woman. There was no escaping it, no rewriting the past.

Samuel hadn't cared for that woman. Not one jot. And yet… She ran her finger along her lip, smiling at the delicious memory of Samuel's mouth moving strongly over hers.

You're a temporary diversion, a nasty little voice in her head said. *A passing amusement. He'll replace you when something better comes along.*

She ignored the voice, long since accustomed to the fear that she wasn't really wanted, wasn't quite good enough for anyone. That fear had been at the heart of her determination to work with her father and her terrible need to seek out the approval of others. She'd been so desperate to prove the nasty little voice wrong.

Those days were past. She might not be able to rid herself of the old insecurity entirely, but she could choose how to respond to it, and she chose to acknowledge it and set it aside.

She didn't have to prove a damned thing.

Taking another bite of her apple, she wondered if she was simply overthinking the matter. Maybe she didn't need to worry over the why and how of it all. Perhaps she should just accept and enjoy the experience without questioning every little detail.

She could do that, couldn't she? She could be the kind of person who simply appreciated a spot of good fortune without looking for strings, or a trick, or a trap.

No, probably not, she conceded and took another bite.

Second- and even third-guessing the intentions and motives of others was too ingrained a habit.

Only...

She frowned down at her half-eaten apple.

She truly did *trust* Samuel. She didn't suspect him of toying with her emotions or playing her for a fool. She wasn't searching for the trick or trap.

For all that they argued like a pair of warring generals, she felt remarkably at ease in his company.

Perversely, she was remarkably ill at ease with that idea.

It wouldn't do to become too comfortable with Samuel. Comfort could lead to things like affection and expectations. Which, in her experience, too often led to rejection and disappointment. And regrets.

It would be better, and much safer, if she remained... merely curious.

Samuel left Esther at the hotel under the guise of seeing to a few more items of personal business about town.

He wanted to stay. In fact, he stood in the hall outside her rooms for a considerable amount of time, debating the merits of going back inside to continue what they had started in the carriage.

It would have been the wrong choice.

He'd managed to do everything right today. He'd said the right words before and after the kiss. And now he'd made the right choice by walking away from Esther before things got out of hand.

It could be argued that the best option would have been to keep his hands off Esther entirely. Samuel was of the opinion that such a choice wasn't so much right as it was ideal, and therefore unrealistic and unreasonable. A man really ought to make a point of keeping reasonable expectations lest he consign himself to perpetual failure.

He would take things slowly, move forward carefully. He would give them both the time and space needed to decide what came next.

Feeling pleased with himself, with Esther, and with the world in general, he returned to Spitalfields on his own. He had several days to discover the identity of the mystery man from the station. He meant to have the job done in half that time.

Until proven otherwise, the man was a threat to Esther, and Samuel couldn't let that stand. It was his responsibility to remove the danger he posed. It was his office to protect. Not simply because Esther was a woman, not as a matter of pride, but because safeguarding those important to him was what a man *did*.

He thought of his father then, reeking of gin and hate. And he remembered his mother with her bruised face and bitter tears.

Safeguarding, he amended, was what a *good* man did.

Nine

Samuel's fine mood wore off slowly. The back lanes and alleyways chipped it away in small increments like a fine chisel working against marble. Every narrow, cluttered alley he entered, every fetid common boardinghouse, every informant he bribed or browbeat for information left him feeling a little angrier, a little harder.

Honest, hardworking boys might outnumber the thieves and liars of the world. As a rule, however, honest boys didn't have access to the secrets of criminals. For that, one had to spend time and effort and money on the criminals themselves. So much time and so much effort on those sorts of men—men who were willing to snitch on their friends for a few coins—that it became difficult to remember, or perhaps easier to forget, that boys like little Henry even existed.

By the time Samuel returned to the hotel four hours later, his general outlook on the world had soured considerably, and there was a painful knot throbbing between his shoulders.

Finding the door to Esther's rooms unlocked only cemented his temper.

He shut and locked the door behind him, then turned to scowl at Esther. "Why is the door not locked?"

She looked up from the book she was reading in one of the chairs by the hearth. "Where have you been? I thought we were going to Rostrime Lane."

"We'll have to go tomorrow. Why wasn't the door locked, Esther?"

"It was locked."

"It was not." He gestured at the door. "I just walked through it."

"Well, it isn't locked *now*. Or rather it is, but it wasn't." She pointed at the window. "I saw you come into the hotel. I assumed you would want a word and so I unlocked the door. Are you going to tell me why you've been gone all afternoon?"

Rubbing at a new ache that had spread from his shoulders to the back of his neck, he took a seat across from her. "I called on a few informants in and around Spitalfields, looking for your man at Paddington. I have three names."

"You went looking for him?" She snapped her book shut. "You told me you were attending to personal business."

"I take all my work personally."

Her eyes narrowed to slits. "And we were getting on so well."

"I was in that part of town. I asked a few questions whilst I was about." It was only a half lie. He had been in that part of town, just not for any other reason than to ask after the man.

"You should have taken me with you."

"I didn't intend to be gone for long. Someone gave me the name of a sailor they thought might have useful information. I had to track him down before he left port tomorrow. It took more time than I anticipated."

"I see." She tapped the cover of her book absently. "Did the sailor have useful information?"

"No."

"If you had time to run about asking questions and tracking sailors, then you had time to fetch me. I might have helped."

"Your help wasn't necessary."

"Necessary and useful are not the same thing. I could have been of use."

He had several arguments at hand capable of disputing that assertion, and sufficient common sense not to use any of them. "Yes, you could have been."

"Then why didn't you take me with you?"

"Because it was dangerous, and I'll not place you in danger, no matter how useful you might be."

She picked up her book and shook it lightly. "Better I should sit here and read poetry while you face danger alone and on my behalf?"

"Yes." By God, yes.

"No, it is not better. Not for either of us. Samuel, be fair—"

"Fair?" he snapped and jabbed a finger in her direction. "If you were another woman, any other woman of my acquaintance, I would have hauled you back to Derbyshire by now."

"I'd only come back."

"Yes, because you are you. And because you are

you, I have refrained from posting guards outside your door every time I leave. And I want to, Esther." He jabbed his finger again, for no other reason than that he found the gesture satisfying. "I *very* much want to."

She appeared singularly unimpressed. "You are in a peculiar mood."

"I am in a foul mood," he muttered and dropped his hand.

"I was being polite." She studied him a moment, her expression unreadable. "Would you like to tell me why your mood is foul?"

"No."

"Is it something I've done?"

He winced at the hint of uncertainty in her voice and scrubbed his hands over his face. "No. Esther, no. I'm just—"

"You're certain? You're not still upset about the door being unlocked?"

"No. Well, yes. Don't unlock it until I've knocked next time. And put your veil on if you're going to be peeking out the windows." He almost smiled when she rolled her eyes. "But no, it's not the cause of my poor temper. And neither are you."

"All right." She set the book aside and frowned at him thoughtfully. "Out of curiosity, why haven't you stationed guards outside my door?"

"Do you think you need them?"

She shook her head. "Do you?"

It wasn't so much that she needed them as that he wanted them for his own peace of mind.

She shrugged when he didn't immediately answer. "I wouldn't make a fuss over it."

"I beg your pardon?"

"If it would make you feel…I don't know"—she began to wave one hand around as she searched for the right words—"like a properly responsible gentleman, seeing to the safety of the helpless lady"—she waved her hand some more—"or what have you, then, by all means, hire a guard or two."

"You wouldn't complain?"

"I might complain a little," she admitted. "But I promise not to produce a proper fuss. Why are you looking at me as if I've grown a second head?"

"*You* wouldn't produce a fuss?"

"Not a proper one," she clarified. "Why should I? There's no harm in being overly cautious. Of course we could run into trouble if those guards start asking questions. Start poking about."

"Yes." There were several men he could trust to guard Esther with their lives, but even the most loyal of men were not immune to curiosity. The possibility of discovery was another reason he'd not sought out those men straightaway.

"It might be worth the risk," Esther continued, "if you mean to go flitting off about town without me on a regular basis."

"I don't flit." Grown men did not *flit.*

"What if something should happen whilst you're away?" she asked with a touch of drama. "What if I forget to take out my daggers, and forget to lock the door, and also forget that a cry for help would be heard by any number of guests or staff in this hotel? However would you live with yourself if I, unarmed, unguarded, and mute, fell prey to a villain?"

"That is not amusing."

"It is a little amusing," she countered and offered an inviting smile. She sighed when he didn't smile back. "I am capable of taking care of myself. And, if I am not, I am quite capable of screaming for help."

Everything inside him revolted at the image of Esther in danger and screaming for help. Neither the image, nor their argument, was improving his mood. He needed to change the subject.

"Is that why you left Greenly House and your family?" he asked. "To prove you could take care of yourself?"

"I..." She broke off and frowned at the sudden jump in topic. "No. Not exclusively."

"But it played some part?"

"I thought we were discussing the possibility of my demise due to your lack of gentlemanly care."

"I don't want to discuss your possible demise. How large a part?"

"A small one. I didn't leave to prove I can take care of myself. I know I can, and that's quite enough for me. Lottie and I ran Willowbend for years without assistance, you'll recall." She bobbed her head back and forth twice. "Well, Lottie took on most of the responsibility, to be honest."

"She is the eldest."

"And a natural leader," she said with more than a hint of pride. "But she didn't lead alone. We raised Peter together, and there were responsibilities that were entirely my own. At any rate, we had no one to answer to at the end of the day but ourselves. I quite liked that. I didn't like having to answer to Renderwell at Greenly House. My life is sufficiently restrictive. It does not require a man intruding on what little freedom remains."

"I thought you were fond of Renderwell."

"I adore him. He makes my sister exceedingly happy." She shrugged. "I've simply no desire to live in a house run by a man, that's all."

Any man? Or just a brother-in-law? Or just a brother-in-law who happened to be peer of the realm accustomed to issuing orders? Would she live in a house run by her own husband? A lover? A presumptuous butler? He wanted to ask but wasn't sure how to go about it without sounding as if he were seeking a particular answer. And wouldn't that be a pretty trick, when he didn't know what sort of answer he'd care to hear?

"If your freedom was only a small part of the reason you left, then what was a larger one?" he asked.

She shook her head at him and looked away. "You wouldn't understand."

"You've said that to me before. I think you're wrong."

Her gaze moved to his, sharp and assessing. It made him uneasy. Not that she should stare at him so intently, but that she might not find what she needed to see. It unnerved him, how badly he wanted to be what Esther needed, even if only in this small way.

"If I tell you," she said quietly, "will you promise not to speak of it to your friends?"

"I give you my word."

She nodded once and he felt a moment's pleasure at that small sign of acceptance. It was no mean feat to gain the trust of Esther Walker-Bales.

"I was too comfortable," she said at last.

He considered this at length, until he was forced to admit that her original assertion had been correct. "Very well, you're not wrong. I don't understand."

She made a sound that was half laugh and half sigh. "I am very good…generally…at making people like me. I can't read a person so well as Lottie, but I can often tell what a person hopes to gain from a new acquaintance, and I provide it." She paused to pick at an invisible thread on her skirts—a sign of nerves he rarely saw from her. "I can be lively and witty, or serious and sedate, or a gossip, or a bookworm. I can be quite conservative in my political views or a revolutionist. I can be whatever they want."

"But not what you are?"

"I don't know what I am. Not entirely. That was part of the problem." She clenched her hand against her leg. "I didn't ingratiate myself to Renderwell's sisters in an attempt to manipulate or deceive them. I just needed them to like me."

"Why?"

"Because I don't know what I am," she repeated. "But if people like me, then it follows that what I am can't be all bad." She laughed a little at his dubious expression. "It is not sound reasoning, I know."

"It makes a kind of sense. Aren't you yourself with Lottie and Peter?" The Walker-Bales siblings had always struck him as being uncommonly close.

"More than anyone else. But I fear it is still less than I would like. Or it was." She went back to picking at her gown. "I wasn't even aware of what I was doing until somewhat recently. And then we moved to Greenly House and I found myself putting on an act, as it were, for Renderwell's sisters. And his mother, and I don't even like his mother."

"No one likes Renderwell's mother."

"True." She stopped plucking at her skirts to give him a pert smile. "You're part of why I moved as well, you know."

"Me?" Horrified at the very idea, he sat up straight in his chair. "What the devil did I do?"

"Oh, you are worried," she laughed.

"I'm not in the habit of running women out of their homes. What did I do?"

"It isn't what you did," she replied, apparently taking pity on him. "It's what I couldn't do. I could never make you like me. It drove me to distraction, trying to find the role I thought you wanted me to fill. But it never seemed to work with you. You hated me even after I nursed you back to health—"

"You did not nurse—"

"—like Florence Nightingale," she finished, loud enough to drown out his dissent.

He relaxed in his seat and caught her gaze. "I've never hated you, Esther."

"I thought you did," she admitted, looking away for a moment. "And that bothered me. But more than that, it bothered me that I should be so bloody bothered. No one person's good opinion should mean so much that another person should feel compelled to change who they are to obtain it."

"Did my opinion matter so much?" he asked, both curious and worried. Had Esther hoped for a friendship with him all this time? The notion appealed to him, but he was equally appalled by the idea that their antagonistic relationship had wounded her in ways he'd failed to recognize.

"Everyone's did," she replied and continued on before he could request clarification. "It is working, you know."

"Is it?"

"Yes." She tapped her finger against the armrest. "Do you remember last year when the stables were set on fire and I went in after Mr. Nips?"

"I'm not likely to forget it." His jaw tightened at the memory, forcing him to speak through clenched teeth. "It nearly killed you and your sister."

"Yes, you were very angry. I apologized to you. Twice, as I recall. I told you I was very sorry for having put the life of an old pony above my own."

"You did."

"I take it back."

Well, that was unexpected. "I beg your pardon?"

"I'm not sorry I did it. I am very sorry that Lottie ran in after me and was injured. That will haunt me, I think, for the rest of my life. And I am sorry that I frightened the people who love me. And I am exceedingly grateful to you and Renderwell, and always will be, for rescuing us. But I am not sorry I went in after Mr. Nips. I'm not sorry he was saved. He deserved better than to be abandoned to the fire."

"You would have died for him."

"Not intentionally. It certainly wasn't my expectation when I ran into the stables. I never imagined I would find his stall door wedged shut or that the fire would spread so rapidly. But I did knowingly risk my life for him, and I would do it again. I love

Mr. Nips. He has been a loyal friend for nearly fourteen years."

"He bites."

"He doesn't bite me," she countered pertly. "I should think it all makes very little difference to you, either way. You never accepted my apology."

No, he never had, and for good reason. "You apologized for going after Mr. Nips."

"Yes, I know."

"I wasn't angry with you for that."

"What rubbish," she countered. "My memory might not be as fine as yours, but I remember your anger perfectly well. You called me a selfish imbecile."

"And so you were, for not calling for help first."

"But I did. I yelled, 'Fire.'"

"You didn't. Lottie saw you running across the lawn. You weren't yelling."

"Well, not then. There was a man in the woods with a gun. I'd rather hoped he wouldn't notice me. I yelled before I opened the door." She lifted her shoulders. "It's not my fault if no one heard."

"You should have made certain someone heard."

"And by that you mean I should have shouted until you or one of your friends came and took care of the problem for me?"

"Ideally, yes. But—"

"But you wouldn't have gone into the stable for Mr. Nips."

His voice lowered of its own accord. "I would have. If you'd asked it of me."

"Oh." Her expression went a little soft. "That's tremendously sweet of you. Thank you. Truly. But I wouldn't have asked it of you. I wouldn't expect you to risk your life for my pony while I waited comfortably in my parlor."

"Esther—"

"But I could have asked for your assistance," she broke in. "We could have done it together. It would have been the smart thing to do." She nodded thoughtfully. "I should have secured help before I went outside."

"I shouldn't have called you a selfish imbecile."

Her eyes widened in mock surprise. "I wish I could paint this moment. Preserve it for posterity. Sir Samuel Brass very nearly apologizes twice in one day."

He smiled, but mostly because she so clearly wanted him to smile. Apparently, it looked as obligatory as it felt, because she sagged in her seat a bit, then studied him with a sharp eye.

"Enough talk of the past," she decided after the moment. "Do you know what you need, Sir Samuel?"

He felt it best not to hazard a guess. Esther had a look about her all of a sudden—a little eager, a little thoughtful, and too mischievous by half. He didn't trust that look.

"You need to have fun," she announced.

He'd been right to be wary. "Fun."

"Yes. Surely you've heard of it," she drawled. "Amusement? Divertissement? A rollick? A lark?"

"Rings a dim bell."

"We are in London, the most exciting city in the world. Well, in England anyway."

He knew he was going to regret his next question before he even asked. "What did you have in mind?"

She rubbed her hands together as she'd done in Spitalfields. Another bad sign. "I purchased something at the shop down the street. I shouldn't have," she admitted before he could chastise her. "It wasn't safe. But it is done now, so there's no point in you wasting your breath on a lecture."

"What did you purchase?"

"Come and see," she urged, jumping out of her chair.

He followed her to the other side of the room, where she knelt down to dig through a small trunk. After a moment, she produced two small racquets and a shuttlecock.

He lifted a brow. "Battledore and shuttlecock?"

He was not playing battledore and shuttlecock.

"No." Setting aside the racquets and shuttlecock, she reached into the trunk and pulled out a considerable length of thin, frayed rope. "Badminton. The man at the shop said it is all the rage in India. You see, rather than attempt to keep the shuttlecock in play as long as possible, one must hit it over the rope and past an opponent, rather like tennis, only without so many rules." She frowned at the rope. "Actually, I'm not sure there are any rules."

"So, it's battledore and shuttlecock with a rope."

"No, it's badminton. It's competitive."

It was competitive battledore and shuttlecock with a rope. "Is it a special sort of rope?" he asked, taking it from her. It didn't look special. It didn't look like it could hold a flag on a breezy day. "Did you pay extra for it?"

"It is an average rope. It was given to me free of charge due to its condition." She pressed her lips together a moment, then gave him a sheepish look. "And because the shopkeeper might have been under the impression that I was a recently widowed woman purchasing a gift for a fatherless child."

"Good Lord, Esther."

"I wasn't attempting to swindle the man," she replied defensively. "He made the assumption, and I could hardly stand there in widow's weeds and correct him, could I? I tried to pay for the rope. He wouldn't take it." She snatched the rope back. "Do you wish to play or not?"

As she likely overpaid for the "badminton" set several dozen times over what the rope (and possibly the set) was worth, Samuel didn't see the point in pursuing the matter. "This hotel doesn't have a garden."

"I know. We are going to play in Hyde Park."

"No, we are not."

"But we've an hour or two of light left yet and—"

"You can play this game in Derbyshire."

"But I can't play in Hyde Park in Derbyshire." She sat back on her heels and looked up at him. "I am in London for the first time in nine years, and once I leave, I will likely never have the opportunity to return. I'll never be able to go to the opera, or the theater, or a ball, or do any of the exciting things I spoke of before. But I can play badminton in a secluded spot in an enormous park where no one will see and bother us." She gave him a pleading look. "Please, come play with me."

Please, come play with me.

How could a man, any man, hear those five words from a beautiful woman and say no?

A man should say no. A properly responsible gentleman would say no. Only a fool would say yes.

"Fetch your bonnet."

Twenty minutes later, Samuel found himself with Esther in Hyde Park. He chose their spot with great care. Leaving Michael, the driver, to wait on the road, he led Esther through a thick stand of trees to a relatively open area that was sufficiently far from the road to shield them from view.

"We can't play here," Esther said when they stopped. "There are too many trees."

"We'll play around them. We can't be in the open, Esther."

"But… Oh, I suppose you're right." She patted the trunk of an ancient oak with one hand while she lifted her veil with the other. "They'll add challenge."

"Put your veil down."

"I can't play with the veil. I can't see properly." She looked around at their surroundings. "We're nowhere near a road or path, Samuel. I'm no more likely to be seen here than I am sitting in the hotel, where some forgetful maid might waltz in without knocking. But…" She pulled the sides of the veil down along the wide brim of her bonnet, leaving only the very front tucked up. "How's this?"

He considered it. The veil fell around her like a curtain, effectively obscuring her face from almost every angle. A person would have to be directly in front of her, and as near to her as he was now, to make out her features. She could easily pull the rest of the crepe down long before someone got that close. It would do.

She pointed a finger at him before he could agree, however. "I compromised on the trees. You can compromise on the veil."

He grunted.

"And you can do it a bit more cheerfully." She gave a little sniff. "*I* compromised quite gracefully."

He ignored this, because some comments weren't even worth the effort of a grunt, and turned his attention to setting up the game. With Esther's rather exacting guidance, two trees were selected and the rope strung between them, creating a line about five feet off the ground and seven feet across.

Esther handed him a racquet and took her place on the other side of the rope. "Ready?"

He felt perfectly ridiculous, standing in the woods in front of a rope, as if he were a child engaging in an invented game. But it was worth the discomfort to see the smile of anticipation on Esther's face. She looked relaxed and happy, and utterly beautiful. The late sunlight wove strands of deep gold in her hair and caught flecks of amber in her blue eyes. A breeze caught a lock of hair and slipped it free of its pins. Her dark widow's weeds might look out of place among the lush green of the woods, but Esther didn't. She belonged here, he realized. For all that she might enjoy visiting a city like London, at the end of the day, she belonged in the country, out-of-doors, in the fresh air, and far away from the prying eyes and strict rules of British society.

There was loneliness and boredom in isolation, but there was freedom as well. A woman like Esther needed that freedom. Just as he did.

"Everything all right?" she called out.

"What? Yes. Quite." He shook off his musings and motioned for her to start the game. "Ready."

She tossed the shuttlecock into the air, hopped up, and gave it a solid whack, sending it over the top edge of the rope and right past Samuel into the ground.

"Oh, point for me," she cried. "I *like* this game."

"Are there points?"

"I've no idea. There must be, I should think. Else the game would go on forever." She scrunched her face up in thought. "Shall we play to twenty?"

"Fifteen." He retrieved the shuttlecock and passed it under the rope. "We haven't much light left."

"You'll change your mind once I've arrived at fifteen without you. At this rate, it shouldn't take more than a minute," she teased, tossing the shuttlecock in the air for another volley.

He was ready this time. One quick step to the left and he sent the shuttlecock back over the net in a high arc. It went sailing a good six feet over Esther's head and landed a solid ten yards behind her.

"Point for me." He shrugged at her shocked expression and decided he might just enjoy this game. "You said there were no rules."

"You play dirty, Sir Samuel." A smile of unholy delight spread slowly across her pretty features. "Excellent. So do I."

~

Esther ceded the point but insisted they mark out a rudimentary field of play before continuing the game. They used trees as boundary markers and decided to make up any additional rules as needed.

Additional rules were most definitely needed. They started out relatively sensible, but as the game progressed, they grew increasingly creative, then a bit silly, and finally, utterly absurd.

One point for a hit over the net and past an opponent within the set boundaries, two points if one used a hand instead of the racquet. An additional half point was granted if one managed to score by hitting the shuttlecock after it bounced off a tree. One point was subtracted for bouncing the shuttlecock off an opponent. This she successfully argued down to three quarters of a point in her case, as he was by far the larger target. But they both agreed that two and a half points should be subtracted if either one of them jumped in front of the projectile on purpose.

And still, they played dirty. She feigned a twisted ankle and leaped up from her injury to deliver a scoring hit when he rushed to help. He feigned a hard hit, then scored himself after she ran off into the bramble in search of the shuttlecock he'd palmed.

They argued good-naturedly over boundary lines, stumbled over roots, had several near collisions with the trees, and nearly brought the rope down on several occasions after it was agreed that he could reach over it, so long as she could reach under.

The game was, by any standard, a complete disaster.

And Esther loved every minute of it. Every preposterous, ridiculous minute. She couldn't remember ever laughing so hard, couldn't remember the last time she had felt so carefree, so unguarded in someone else's presence.

She ought to feel a fool, lunging about in the

woods, swinging wildly, and missing more than half the time. But she didn't feel the least bit embarrassed.

That was Samuel's doing. When she'd suggested the trip to the park, it had been with the intention of coaxing Samuel out of his temper. He was such a reserved man, so proud and stodgy, she assumed the process would be akin to prying out a bad tooth.

To her astonishment, Samuel engaged himself in the exercise without resistance. He played with a disarming balance of childlike abandonment and adult perspective. He played with just enough competitiveness to keep the game challenging but didn't seem to care who actually won. He ceded points she didn't deserve and argued for points he didn't need. He lunged and dove and swung without any apparent self-consciousness. He laughed at himself freely and at her without spite. Not once did she feel as if he was judging either of them for their foolishness, not even when they had to stop the game to disentangle the top of her bonnet from a low branch of an evergreen.

He simply enjoyed himself in the moment, and that gave her the confidence and freedom to set aside old inhibitions, old fears of being judged and found lacking, and do the same.

She lost track of the points and time. They played until the golden light of late afternoon dimmed into the blue light of dusk and then the grainy gray of early evening. Until they could no longer see the rope between them. And she hoped it would never end.

"Enough." Samuel raised both hands before Esther could launch her next serve. "Enough. We're done."

"One more round."

He shook his head and squinted across the rope. "We've lost too much light. I can scarcely see you in that damned black dress."

"Oh, but—"

"We'll play another time."

In Derbyshire, he decided. He'd like that. He'd like to see Esther wearing a cheerful gown, laughing and playing in a grassy field in the bright light of day.

"Promise?"

"Gladly."

"All right then." She twirled her racquet as he headed to the knotted rope. "I knew these would be fun. That's why I went in the shop when I knew I shouldn't. I just knew they were worth it. I wanted to go into a shop farther down the street as well. There was the prettiest emerald green bonnet with matching velvet ribbons in the window. It was perfect. Just perfect. But I thought I shouldn't—"

Samuel heard the crack of brush beneath feet a split second before the attack. Three men rushed them, barging in from the darkened woods with their heads down like charging bulls. The first caught Samuel around the shoulders and knocked him back.

They staggered into the rope, snapping it in half. Samuel used the momentum to his advantage, twisting around, planting his feet, and bending at the waist to throw the man up and over his shoulder.

He straightened in time to see one of Esther's daggers streak past him, the steel blade glinting in a shaft of light. Samuel heard a shriek of pain and saw one man stumble back.

"Ahhh! Me leg!"

As the wounded man retreated back into the woods, Samuel turned to find Esther but didn't immediately see her. "Esther, run!"

He reached for the gun at his waist, but the extra second he'd taken to look for Esther was all the time his opponent needed to regain his feet. He threw a hard right jab and Samuel blocked it, caught the man's wrist, and did a quick side step. He twisted his assailant's arm around his back, yanked up, and heard the audible pop of bone separating from socket.

Screaming, the man kicked out behind him, forcing Samuel to release him and jump back.

Desperate to find Esther, Samuel looked away again and saw the dim outline of two forms struggling on the ground a few yards away.

Fury washed over him. When the man advanced on him again, swinging wildly with his good arm, Samuel knocked the attack away, balled up his fist, and let fly. The force of the blow snapped his opponent's head back and sent him reeling, but Samuel caught him by the lapels of his coat, jerked him forward again, and brought his own head down for a quick but efficient head butt. The man crumpled to the ground and stayed there.

Samuel didn't spare him another thought. He turned to Esther in time to see her attacker roll off of her, his hands covering his groin. "You *bitch*!"

Esther scrambled to her feet and lifted her skirts to reach for her second dagger, but the man recovered and reached into his coat at the same time.

The man was close enough for Samuel to charge, but Esther was closer. He lunged for her, putting himself between her and the assailant. Throwing an arm around her waist, he lifted her off her feet just as the sharp retort of gunfire rent the air. He ignored a sharp sting at his cheek and half carried, half dragged Esther to the nearest large tree. He shoved her behind it and pinned her to the bark, using his larger frame as a shield.

"My blade." Esther twisted against him. "I have another blade. If I can—"

"I have a gun." He covered her head with his arm. "Stay still."

Samuel pulled out his pistol, aimed around the tree without looking, and fired off a shot before the man got it in his head to flank them.

The man swore, out of anger rather than injury by the sound of it.

"This ain't over! You hear me, bitch? This ain't over!" There was more swearing, then a groan. "Get up. Come on. Get up!"

Carefully, Samuel risked a peek around the tree. He could just make out the form of the gunman hauling his fallen companion to his feet. Wishing he had Gabriel's perfect aim, he lifted his pistol again but was forced to duck for cover once more when his adversary shot blindly toward the trees, as he dragged his friend into the darkness.

Leaves and bramble crunched loudly underfoot then faded, leaving only the sound of Esther's ragged breathing mingled with his own.

He pulled back a little so he could run his hands over her, searching for injuries. "Are you hurt? Esther, are you hurt anywhere?"

"No. No." Her own hands came up to his shoulders. "You?"

"No. You're certain?"

"Yes, I—"

He grabbed her arm and pulled her away from their shelter, hauling her through the trees at a run. He'd rather track the men, but getting Esther to safety was his first priority.

Michael met them at the edge of the woods, a pistol in his hands. "Sir Samuel? Are you injured? I heard shots."

"Up top. Now. Go, man."

He yanked open the carriage door and shoved Esther inside. "Keep your head down."

"I don't think they're following—"

"Keep it down," he snapped and slammed the door shut.

Atop the carriage, Michael handed him the reins without a word.

Samuel drove them away from the park. Keeping to wide, well-lit streets, he wound the carriage around Mayfair, while Michael kept his pistol handy and an eye out for any sign they were being followed.

When he was absolutely certain there was no one trailing them, Samuel stopped the carriage, gave the reins back to Michael, and joined Esther inside.

He took a seat across from her, then lighted the lamp and took careful stock of her condition. Her bonnet was gone, her blond hair was slipping from its pins, and her gown was torn and muddy, but she looked otherwise unharmed. Except, there was something amiss with her eyes. They latched on to his and grew abnormally round.

"Oh my," she chirped.

Alarmed, he leaned forward. "What? What's the matter?"

They grew rounder still. "Oh dear."

"What is it?" His heart beat out a hard, angry rhythm. "Are you injured?" Had they missed a wound or…

"No. It's only… Your… Er…" She waved her hand over the bottom half of her face. "Your beard is… Um…" A nervous giggle emerged. Then another. "I think it's been shot."

He reached up and felt the damaged skin and hair.

It bloody well had been.

"You're bleeding," Esther said. "Is it serious?"

Disgusted, he sat back again. "No, it's a damned scratch."

"You're certain?" She reached out with a trembling hand and used one finger to gently turn his head. "So it is." Her nervous giggle returned, the sound at odds with her ashen complexion.

"Are you all right, Esther?"

"Yes, quite." Her lips trembled. "I was just wondering…" Another giggle as she pointed at his cheek. "Do we count that as number five?"

"This is not amusing."

"No. No, it isn't," she agreed and burst into laughter. But there was a jumpy, ragged quality to the sound. "I'm sorry," she gasped. "I'm so sorry. I don't know why I'm laughing. It's not at all funny. You might have been killed." A shiver passed over her form, followed by another short bout of laughter. "I can't seem to stop. I don't know why."

"I do." Shock, fear, relief, and the lingering need to

fight or run were all battling for supremacy. He knew the feeling well. She'd be cold soon, maybe nauseated, certainly exhausted. "Come here."

Before she could argue, he hauled her out of her seat and onto his lap.

She went still in his arms, her laughter stopping abruptly. "You don't have to—"

"Shall I let you go?"

After a moment's hesitation, she wrapped her arms around him and rested her cheek against his shoulder with a trembling sigh.

"It's all right." He pressed his lips to the top of her head. "It's over. You're safe now."

"I know," she whispered, but her arms tightened and the shivers remained. "I know we are."

For a long time, he kept her close, stroking her hair and murmuring the odd endearment he hoped she would find reassuring. This manner of comforting was new to him. He'd patted the hands of strangers and wiped away the tears of lovers, but he'd never simply held on, nor let himself be held in return. He quite liked the latter. The warm weight of her, the tight embrace, the whisper of breath against his neck, each sensation settled over him like a blanket, easing the chill of fear and smothering the heat of anger.

He held on until her shivers subsided and she pulled away, pushing a loose lock of hair out of her face. "I'm sorry, I didn't mean to make such a fuss."

"Don't apologize. It happens sometimes when—"

"I know. It used to happen with my father. He'd have a bad night and come home in such a state. Giddy and anxious." She shook her head, as if shaking free of an old memory. "But it's never happened to me before." She blew out a long breath and sat up properly. "I suppose I've never been exposed to that sort of violence. Not even when I worked with my father. Some of Gage's men liked to posture and threaten a bit, but none of them ever tried to strangle me. I suppose that's—"

"What did you say?"

"I… Which part?"

He didn't answer. He just pulled down the collar of her gown to reveal the red, swollen skin beneath. "Jesus God."

"Yes, my thoughts at the time were much the same."

Carefully, he ran his fingers beneath the injury as rage returned, boiling under his skin. Until now, he'd never understood the need of some men to seek vengeance. He'd suffered all manner of injuries at the hands of others in his line of work, but he'd never answered those insults with more violence than was necessary to subdue his attacker and bring him to justice. That had always been enough for him.

It wasn't enough now. It wasn't anywhere near sufficient to appease his rage. He wanted blood.

"You look very fierce," Esther said softly.

"He hurt you."

"And you." She drew his hand away from her neck, but he kept hold of her fingers when she would have pulled away completely.

"Did you punch your attacker?" he asked, studying the reddened knuckles.

"I did." She flexed her fingers experimentally. "Hurt me more than it hurt him, I'm afraid. I'm quite out of practice."

Cautiously, he bent her thumb this way and that, searching for signs of damage.

"I know how to make a proper fist." She pulled free and demonstrated, placing her thumb on the outside. "I didn't break anything."

"So I see. Did Will teach you how to fight?"

"A little. A person can only carry so many daggers. At some point, you've thrown them all, and then where are you?"

Throwing punches at men twice your size, he thought. The image did nothing to settle the roiling fury. "Did you often have to put the practice to use?"

"No. Never, thank God. I don't care for it, particularly." A hint of smile emerged. "I did a fair job of it tonight, though."

He thought of the man with the dagger in his leg, the other man groaning on the ground. She damn well had done a fair job of it. "You sent a man off limping and—"

"Limping. Oh. Oh, I just realized..." She shifted awkwardly and bent down to pull up the hem of her skirts to her ankles. "My dagger. He took my dagger. That *rotter*."

Her indignation surprised a laugh out of him. "I don't think it was intentional."

"It's not funny," she grumbled, her shoulders slumping. "It was my favorite one. My absolute favorite one." She slumped even farther. "And he broke my rope."

Ten

Esther would have been content to pass the night in the carriage. Everything she wanted was there. Safety, comfort, privacy. Samuel. She wished she had the nerve to wrap her arms around him once more, lay her head down again, and let the sound of his steady heartbeat soothe away the shadows of fear that remained.

All too soon, the carriage came to a stop outside Samuel's house. She thought longingly of her rooms at the hotel and her wonderful bath but said nothing as Samuel escorted her up the front steps.

For all they knew, the men at the park had followed them from the hotel. Samuel's home was closer, and safer.

She was a little surprised, then, when he motioned her to stay behind him as he cautiously stepped into the foyer.

"Do you think they might have come here?" she whispered as laughter, muffled but lively, floated up from downstairs. She glanced around his shoulder for a peek into a lavishly decorated parlor that looked undisturbed. "It doesn't appear as if there's anything wrong."

He cocked his head, listening. "Must be in the garden."

"Who? The men from the park?" She reached down for her second dagger.

"No." Samuel pulled her upright again. "No, it's all right. We're safe. I was only—"

His explanation was cut short by the appearance of a stout elderly woman. The housekeeper, by the looks of the perfectly enormous chatelaine attached to her belt. Stopping two feet inside the foyer, she took in their disheveled appearances with an air of great disapproval. "What was it this time?"

"We were accosted in the park," Samuel supplied.

The woman didn't so much as bat an eyelash at the news that her employer had been cavorting with a strange woman in Hyde Park after dark. "Are you injured?"

"He's been..." Unwilling to say shot and possibly incite panic, Esther waggled her fingers at her own cheek and nodded at Samuel.

Though the woman was nearly as short as Esther, she still managed to somehow look down her nose at Samuel's wound. "It doesn't appear to be serious."

"It isn't," Samuel returned. "Mrs. Ellison, however, has sustained an injury to her neck."

Ah, Mrs. Ellison—the name she'd used at the hotel. "I'm quite all right."

"Her neck?" the woman echoed, one brow winging up. "Shall I send for the physician?"

Esther took a quick step closer to Samuel. "Certainly not. I assure you, there is no need."

Samuel's hand came up to move in a soothing circle

at the small of her back. "At least let Mrs. Lanchor have a look at it. She's a fair judge of these things."

Esther hesitated. She knew the damage to her neck was minor, but it was tender and sore. It made her feel vulnerable and more than a little defensive. Any injury, no matter how small, was a weakness. She wasn't in the habit of exposing weaknesses to strangers.

She glanced at Samuel, who gave her a gentle, reassuring smile. "It's all right," he said softly. "You can trust her."

Esther didn't trust her. She didn't know her.

But she trusted Samuel. Reluctantly, she pulled her collar down.

To her relief, Mrs. Lanchor didn't poke and prod at the spot. She kept her hands to herself and inspected the injury with the cool detachment of a surgeon. "Any difficulty breathing or swallowing?"

"No."

"Then a cold compress should be sufficient," she announced and stepped away, giving Esther some much desired space.

Esther looked to Samuel and found his eyes were still focused on her neck. His expression darkened a second before his gaze snapped away.

"Right," he said a bit hoarsely. "Right. See to it please, Mrs. Lanchor." He nodded toward the woman, who took Esther's hand in a firm grip and led her upstairs.

Sitting on the foot of his bed, Samuel studied his injury in a hand mirror. He was going to have the devil's own time explaining the damage to the curious and nosy.

He deserved it, both the injury and any discomfort that followed. He'd earned it and more. What the devil had he been thinking, taking Esther to Hyde Park? Indulging in a child's game at the expense of Esther's safety?

He should have heard the men coming sooner. He should have paid closer attention, taken better care. He should have protected her.

"Has the mirror done something to incur your wrath?"

Esther's voice pulled him from his thoughts. Turning, he found her standing in the doorway.

"You should be resting. Where is your cold compress?"

"Sitting, warm and useless, next to a bed. I used it, and now I'm better. Why are you scowling at the mirror?" She came toward him, frowning at his cheek. "Is it the injury? Does it pain you?"

"You shouldn't be in here."

"Bit late for that, I'm afraid," she replied pragmatically. "Unfortunately, there will be talk now no matter what I do." She stood in front of him, her skirts brushing his legs. "Why haven't you taken care of that yet?"

"I was busy."

"Doing what?"

Berating himself, primarily. But also cursing their attackers, Will Walker, and the world at large.

He set the mirror down and said nothing.

"Well, we'll see to it now." Leaning down, she ran a dainty finger beneath the injury. "The rest of the beard will have to come off."

"No. Absolutely not."

She straightened and went to the bellpull, giving it a firm tug. "It will grow back, Samuel."

"I said no."

"And you lot accuse women of vanity." Returning to the bed, she grabbed the hand mirror and held it up to him. "Look at yourself. You cannot walk around with only part of a beard. You look as if you've…I don't know…half a dead monkey on your face."

Despite everything, despite the anger and fear, amusement bubbled to the surface. He reached up to scratch at the offending facial hair. "I've had this beard for nearly fifteen years." He felt his lips curve into a smile. "A *monkey*?"

She tossed the mirror on the bed. "It sprang to mind."

"But *half* a monkey?"

"Well, some monkeys are quite large." She hitched up her shoulders. "A baboon, for example."

He was fairly certain half a baboon would make several full beards. "Does this mean that before the bullet, it looked as if I'd an entire dead monkey on my face?"

"No, of course not. And to be fair"—she gripped his chin and turned his head for a closer look—"it doesn't look quite so much like half a dead monkey as it does an injured monkey. Or a cat, if the monkey bothers you. Or a ferret. Or a pair of small squirrels. Or—"

"Must we use animal imagery?"

"No," she replied and released him with a grin, "but I am enjoying the exercise."

He was as well, admittedly, but he still didn't want the shave. In a matter of moments, however, Sarah was sent off in search of the necessary tools. She returned in short order, carrying a tray filled with everything they would need to get the job done. "Here you are. Shall I fetch a footman or one of the grooms to assist?"

Esther picked up a pair of scissors off the tray. "I'll do it. I shaved my father a time or two."

Panic flared, and he caught her wrist when she stepped near and lifted the scissors to begin.

"Don't worry." She gave him a teasing smile. "I'm quite good with blades."

"That's not it." He flicked a glance at Sarah. "Thank you. That will be all."

"Yes, sir."

Esther wiggled her caught wrist lightly as Sarah left. "You've nothing to fear from me. In truth, I assisted my father quite regularly, and someone had to teach Peter how to go about it. I am perfectly capable—"

"I have a scar," he blurted out. In part because he wasn't certain how long she might go on reassuring him, but mostly because it was easier to say it quickly.

"I'll be careful of it. Where is it?"

He drew the line of it with his finger, an inch below the injury, all the way from ear to chin, and watched her eyes widen. He couldn't help but wonder if those wide eyes would fill with revulsion once she saw the scar itself.

"That is quite large," she said softly. "How did you acquire it?"

"My father."

"Your...?" Realization and horror dawned on her face. "The fire poker?"

"Yes."

"I see." She set the scissors aside and regarded him

through warm, thoughtful eyes. "Are you embarrassed, Samuel?"

"No." Only he was a little. Worse, he was embarrassed to be embarrassed by the scar. It was an old anxiety, rooted in a few ugly childhood memories. He should have outgrown it years ago.

"Is that why you grew the beard?"

Initially, yes. He'd been young and insecure, desperate to escape the taunts of his peers and eager to please the pretty young ladies. But he'd kept the beard because it suited him. He'd not given the scar much thought in recent years. He'd probably not give it a second thought now if it was anyone other than Esther standing before him.

She was so lovely. Surely, there wasn't a man in England who wouldn't take a second look at Esther Bales.

Strange how the beauty of one person could make him feel the lack of his own so much more powerfully.

"Samuel?"

"Beards are fashionable."

She twisted her lips at that nonanswer. "Is it the reason you don't want the shave?"

He didn't feel like answering that either.

"If you've had the beard for fifteen years," she said, "then you've not seen the scar for fifteen years. It might not be quite as awful as you remember it."

"I have a keen memory," he reminded her.

"I suppose you do." She gave him a sympathetic smile. "I'm sorry, but the beard must come off. Would you prefer to do it yourself? I could hold the mirror for you. Or I could fetch someone else."

"No. No, that won't be necessary." He wasn't

a child anymore. And Esther was not one of the young, shallow, spoiled sisters of his friends. She was the beautiful, fascinating younger sister of his friend's wife, which was entirely different. "Let's just get on with it."

She nodded and reached for the supplies.

Five minutes later, he couldn't decide if allowing Esther to shave him was the best or worst idea he'd ever had.

It all began in a perfectly unremarkable, even mundane, fashion, with Samuel trimming the excess beard himself while Esther sharpened the blade and worked the soap into a lather. But then she was standing over him, applying the first brush of the soap, and everything changed.

Her fingers rested lightly against his jaw, keeping him still while she applied the lather. Her face loomed close to his as she worked around his injury, and her breath passed over his lips, soft and sweet. He caught a hint of roses and woods through the soap.

She was close enough to touch, near enough to reach out and pull into his arms. All he had to do was turn his head and lean, just an inch or two, and their lips would meet. He *wanted* to turn his head, and he might have, if he'd not been certain it would break the spell.

It was one of the most sensual experiences of his life. Every touch, every breath, every brush of her skirts against his legs warmed his blood and heated his skin. It was bliss. He wanted to draw out the moment, tease every sensation out as long as possible.

But eventually, she stepped away and traded the soap for the blade.

He knew a moment's fear. It wasn't the blade that worried him—it was what the shave would reveal. It was an irrational and juvenile fear, but he was powerless to stop it.

His hesitation must have shown, because Esther paused before him and offered a gentle smile.

"I won't hurt you, Samuel."

It was impossible to know if she was aware of his thoughts. More than likely, she meant to assure him that she'd not do him a physical injury. But he liked to think that she understood the nature of his fear. He liked to think that she understood *him*.

"I know you won't." Rationally, he *did* know it. Believing it was another matter.

"Close your eyes," she suggested. "It might help."

"I don't need to close my eyes," he muttered, mostly because pride demanded he at least make a cursory show of courage.

"Try it anyway. It will help me. It makes me nervous, your staring."

"Liar."

She held up the blade and feigned a tremor in her hand. "You don't want me doing this, do you?"

The woman had hurled a knife in near darkness in the midst of an attack and hit her mark. Next to Gabriel, she had the steadiest hands of anyone he'd ever met. Still...

He eyed the sharp edge of steel aglow in the lamplight. It couldn't hurt to be cautious.

"I'll try it."

"Excellent."

He took a mental picture of that lovely smile to

hold in his mind, then closed his eyes and motioned her to begin.

Not surprisingly, having a blade passed over one's face proved to be slightly less arousing than being lathered with soap. While it may have been less of a sensual delight, however, it felt infinitely more intimate. It was the trust involved. His throat was exposed to Esther Walker-Bales and her blade, and she was being extraordinarily careful.

Her small, clever fingers tipped and turned his face, searching for just the right angle. The blade scraped softly against his skin in evenly pressured strokes, over and over again.

He held perfectly still under her ministrations, moving only at her command.

The entire experience made him feel like a green boy, caught between arousal, wonder, and the terrible certainty that, any second now, things would go horribly, horribly wrong. She would be repulsed by his appearance. He'd say the wrong thing or make the wrong move. Someone would barge in and break the spell. Her fingers would slip.

He was sixteen again, struggling with the buttons of a woman's gown for the first time. Only this was worse, so much worse. It wasn't some sweet country lass who had offered an afternoon of her time for her own pleasure. It wasn't just any pretty woman touching him now. It wasn't just any woman he was trusting. It was Esther.

"Nearly done."

Esther's voice floated above him as a warm, wet towel was applied to his cheeks and jaw. The sensation sent pleasant shivers across his skin.

"There we are."

Reluctantly, he opened his eyes and watched as she stood back to appraise her work.

"You'll not have a second scar, I think," she commented. "The injury is mostly superficial."

"Good. That's good." Devil take the recent injury. What did she make of the scar?

"As for the other, it isn't nearly as terrible as you made it out to be." She tilted her head to the side. "Quite dashing, really. Pity it doesn't come down over the eye. You'd be quite piratical."

"I..." For a moment, his brain struggled to accept the obvious. Esther wasn't repulsed. She didn't appear to be even vaguely put off. The rational part of him had expected as much. The greater part of him was relieved. "That appeals to you, does it? Pirates?"

"I've some romance in me, you know."

"Pirates aren't romantic."

"Not real ones, no." She tossed aside the damp towel and handed him the mirror. "Is it as you remembered?"

"Yes." He remembered it perfectly, every raised and jagged inch. And yet it was different. Somehow it was different. "And no."

"Perhaps the scar is the same," she ventured. "But the man is not."

He made a second, closer inspection. The last time he'd looked at himself clean-shaven he'd been an angry young man, ashamed of his past, furious with the world, and tormented by the nickname he'd earned on his first day at Flintwood. Frankenstein's monster. The wound had been fresh then, the mark of stitches still visible along the puckered skin. It had healed over time but the name stuck, and that was what he remembered—the taunting, the averted gazes in the local village, the barely concealed disgust.

He remembered the boy with the scar. Now he saw the man.

"Perhaps it is not as significant as I remembered," he murmured.

"You see?" She grinned at him. "You should leave it uncovered and devise some preposterous story to go along with it. You can tell people you acquired it fighting off a bear."

He lowered the mirror. "In England?"

"We have a zoo."

"I fought off a bear at the zoo."

"Yes." She wiggled her eyebrows dramatically. "After a rival pirate forced you into its enclosure at knifepoint."

"You're an imaginative soul, Esther."

"The best liars always are," she replied with a wink.

Just now, he preferred to think of her as a gifted storyteller.

Tipping his chin up, he inspected the underside of his jaw in the mirror. "It's strange seeing myself clean-shaven again after so many years."

"It suits you, I think. But if you like the beard, there's no reason you shouldn't grow it back."

He thought about it. "Do you like the beard?"

He meant to pose the question as if he was mildly curious, but he sounded uncertain even to his ears, as if he was seeking her guidance.

Embarrassed, he cleared his throat, then took a quick, furtive look in the mirror to make certain his cheeks had not become prone to blushing since last he'd seen them. They had not. Thank God.

"I do. And I like this." She wiggled her fingers at his chin, then turned away to retrieve the discarded towel. "I like you, Samuel," she said softly. "Just as you are."

Well, now he was glad he asked.

He liked her as well. He was beginning to think it might be more than that. Not love, surely. It was too soon for love, wasn't it? But it wasn't just affection or attraction he was experiencing. He'd had both for that delightful country lass. Esther meant more.

His gaze drifted over her profile, taking in the disheveled golden locks, the rose of her cheeks, the long, elegant neck... Where a man had wrapped his hands around the delicate skin and squeezed.

All because he had not taken enough care.

"I can't let you go back to the hotel," he heard himself say. "It isn't safe."

Esther turned her back on Samuel and busied herself with the shaving materials to hide her disappointment.

I can't let you go back to the hotel.

What sort of response was that?

The *I am eager to change the subject* sort, she supposed. Although, honestly, Samuel might have at least tried to be a little subtle about it. For the sake of his own pride, if not for hers. Who the devil panicked at "I like you"? It wasn't exactly a confession laden with promises and responsibilities.

She liked him. That was all. She also liked asparagus. For all he knew, she liked them in equal measure.

So why couldn't he like her back in the same manner? Say, as much as he liked clotted cream? She wasn't aware that he had a particular fondness for clotted cream, but most everyone had some level of fondness for it—

"Esther?"

"No. Yes. I know. I can't go back to the hotel."

"Your family will understand."

"They'll have to, won't they?" She tried to sound chipper, or at least indifferent, but for once, her acting skills failed her.

"Is something wrong? Aside from the obvious," he added when she gave him a pointed look over her shoulder.

"Why would there be?"

"I honestly do not know," he replied carefully. "Are you cross with me?"

"No." It wouldn't be fair for her to be cross, really.

"I think you are. That's the third time you've moved the soap on the tray. Will you set it down and look at me, please?"

She did as he asked, more confused than embarrassed. If he was eager to change the subject, why was he pressing her to speak?

"Have I been clumsy again?" he asked.

She was beginning to wonder. "Maybe."

"Ah." He scratched his jaw and eyed her cautiously. "Are you perhaps taking offense where none was intended?"

"Possibly." That was *always* a possibility.

"Right. And do you suppose you could tell me what I might have done wrong so we can decide together if I need to fix it?"

Not without humiliating herself. But she couldn't see any way around it.

"You've not done anything wrong, necessarily." He wasn't required to like her, after all. "It's just..." She felt her cheeks grow warm. "I said I liked you and I'd rather hoped you would say it back."

His dark brows drew together. "I did say it back."

"No, you didn't."

"Well, not in those exact words, but the sentiment was clear."

"It really wasn't." But if the sentiment had been intended, that was good enough for now. She started to smile at him.

"Of course I like you," he said. "That's why you can't go back to the hotel."

The smile fell. Not because she was offended, but because she was utterly confounded by the comment. "I beg your pardon?"

He grimaced. "It all sounded less clumsy in my head."

"One might hope."

"Let me try this again." His brow furrowed in concentration. "You're important to me. You can't go back to the hotel, because I want you safe. And I want you safe because you're important to me."

"Oh." Oh, that was *lovely*. Quite a lot better than asparagus and clotted cream. "Thank you. You're important to me as well."

His mouth curved into a silly, inviting grin. "Because you like me."

"Yes," she laughed. "Yes, I do. Clumsiness and all."

What an odd pair they were, she thought. He was right when he'd said that their flaws weren't complementary, but she'd been wrong to agree that they were not compatible people. They were well matched, really. They might take the long way around to understanding each other, but they got there eventually.

Not everyone managed that. They were too impatient, or too disinterested, or they were too unwilling to admit fault, or let go of anger.

Or they were dishonest with each other.

Suddenly uncomfortable, she busied herself with rinsing and wringing out the towel in a basin. She had lied to Samuel. She had lied to him about something important, and she didn't know how to fix it.

"What are you thinking about?" Samuel asked softly.

"Beg your pardon?"

"You look very serious all of a sudden."

"Do I? Concentration, I suppose." So much for her skills as a liar. How much concentration did a wet towel require?

He patted the bed next to him. "Come here for a moment."

She felt a little thrill of excitement despite her current discomfort. "Why?"

"I want to see your neck."

"Oh." She rather hoped he was being coy, but she doubted it. "It's quite all right. I can barely feel it now."

"Are you experiencing numbness? Come here."

"It's not numb. I meant it doesn't pain me." She dried her hands and pulled down the neckline of her gown to oblige him with a look. "You see? Much improved."

"Sit down. I want a closer look."

She shot a quick glance at the door. "I'm not sure that would be wise."

"The damage is done, as you said."

"I'm not sure there's a finite amount of damage a lady might do to her reputation." She was, however, quite certain the existing damage would not be improved should she be discovered sitting next to Samuel on his bed.

He gave her a curious look. "You will stand in a man's bedchamber and shave him, but you won't take a seat next to him?"

"Apparently so," she replied, amused at both of them. "Strange, isn't it, where one feels compelled to draw one's lines? On the surface it seems rather arbitrary. Maybe even ridiculous in my case."

"It *is* arbitrary and ridiculous," he grumbled.

"It isn't." It really was, but he looked so adorably disgruntled, she couldn't resist keeping up the pretense of protesting. "I may not have been raised to follow the rules, but I was raised with knowledge of them, and I've been required to live by them for a very long time now. Furthermore, I am quite aware of the consequences of breaking the rules—or at least of being caught breaking the rules—and I've no desire to pay the price—"

He cut off her rambling speech by catching her wrist and giving it a gentle but quick tug. Caught off guard, she stumbled forward and only just managed to spin about and sit on the bed rather than tumble onto the mattress face first.

She sniffed, smoothed her skirts, and bit back a laugh. "That was very ungentlemanly of you."

"It was." His thumb gently caressed the inside of her wrist a moment before he released her. "Do you want to get up?"

Not in the least. "I probably should. Your staff..."

"The floorboards in the hallway creak. We'll hear anyone approaching."

He leaned in, his gaze settling on her mouth. If his original intention had been to inspect her injury, he seemed to have forgotten it.

Just for the pleasure of teasing him, she leaned back an equal distance and pulled down the neckline of her gown. "You wished to see my neck, I believe?"

His lips twitched as he pulled her hand away to look for himself. "So I did."

Suddenly, all humor disappeared from his face. He ran his fingers above the injury and his eyes darkened, his expression turning cold. Before she could speak, he bent his head to her neck and gently touched his lips to the injury in a feather-soft kiss.

"I want to kill him for this."

His words were barely more than a whisper, but they were hard and filled with rage.

"It wouldn't heal me, or help you."

"No, and it won't come to that if I can help it." He cupped the side of her face and laid his warm lips against her temple. "But I want to."

She thought of the man with the gun and the bullet he'd sent skimming across Samuel's face. Carefully, she leaned forward and kissed his cheek.

"I understand."

She would have pulled away then, but his hand slipped around the back of her head, keeping her still. He turned to catch her mouth with his own, and for one brief moment their lips met and all the anxiety of earlier slipped away. Like the moment before the knife left her hand, she thought. Only better. So much better.

She wanted to stay like that, stay caught in that wonderful, magical moment, but the sound of footsteps and creaking floorboards broke the spell.

She leaped off the bed and was on the other side of the room by the time Mrs. Lanchor arrived. To his credit, Samuel didn't so much as smirk at her admittedly ridiculous reaction.

"You're just in time, Mrs. Lanchor," he remarked casually. "Mrs. Ellison could use some assistance."

She could? With what?

Confused, and feeling increasingly awkward now that the shaving was done and she had no excuse for being in the room, she looked to Samuel for direction. He nodded discretely at the tray on the chest of drawers.

"Right," she chirped. "The tray. And the bowl. And the towel. Please." Oh, brilliant. She couldn't have sounded less nonchalant if she'd tried. Honestly, what was it about being around Samuel that turned her into such an abominable liar? It was absurd.

Mrs. Lanchor would have to be an idiot not to suspect something was afoot, but she gave every indication of being perfectly oblivious. "I'll see to them. Will you be dining downstairs this evening, Mrs. Ellison?"

"Thank you, no." It was time to make herself scarce for a little while. She'd supplied the staff with enough gossip for one night. "I'll dine in my chambers, if it's not an inconvenience."

"None at all."

"Well, then. I'll just..." Do what, exactly? She

began edging toward the door without any clear idea of what she meant to do once she reached it. "I'll...go and have a lie down, shall I?"

Mrs. Lanchor inclined her head. "Very good. I shall instruct Sarah to bring you another cold compress directly."

"Thank you. That's very kind. Well, good night then. Sir Samuel. Mrs. Lanchor."

Samuel's low voice followed her to the door. "Good night, Mrs. Ellison."

Eleven

SAMUEL STEPPED INTO HIS PARLOR WITH HIS CHEEKS damp from the unseasonably cool and wet morning air. Transferring the small box he carried under his left arm, he rubbed the newly exposed skin and tried to figure out if he liked the sensation.

"Does it feel strange?"

He turned at the sound of Esther's voice and found her standing at the open door leading to the library. She wore a lavender tea gown clearly tailored to fit a larger woman. It sagged at the waist and drooped at the neck, and several inches of velvet-trimmed hem dragged on the floor. She looked a bit silly, really. And utterly beautiful.

Suddenly, he wished he'd waited to fetch Esther's things from the hotel. She didn't belong in widow's weeds. They were too severe, too sedate. Esther was neither. Maybe he'd wait a little while before bringing her trunk inside.

"A bit. Good morning, Esther."

"Good morning. What do you think of my new gown?" She grinned at him and lifted her arms out from the sides. The cuffs fell well over her fingers.

I think you're beautiful. "I think you'd make a fine scarecrow."

Laughing, she dropped her arms. "I would at that. But I quite like the color. Your lady friend has very good taste."

"Beg your pardon? Lady friend?"

"Mrs. Lanchor said the gown was left behind by a former houseguest." She emphasized *houseguest* as if it were a euphemism for something far more tawdry.

It wasn't a euphemism for anything. "I have house parties. And houseguests."

"Mmm hmm."

"I'm a gentleman. It's expected." Was she jealous? She didn't look it, particularly. Her color was high, but that might well be amusement.

"Certainly, it is," she agreed.

It was amusement, without question. Her lips were twitching.

A small part of him found that disappointing. A small, but evidently rather influential, part of him.

He shrugged with an affected carelessness. "A gentleman is expected to entertain all manner of...individuals."

The twitching stopped. Her brows lowered.

That was better.

"Do you know," he began conversationally, "I think I remember the owner of that gown."

"You *think* you remember?"

"It's been a week at least," he replied defensively and watched with pleasure as her expression turned to one of outrage. "Caroline. No, Cassandra... No..." He tipped his head back and squinted his eyes. "Clarice? That might ring a bell."

She crossed her arms in front of her chest. "Are you enjoying yourself?"

Quite a lot. "A little."

She gave a snort of disbelief. "You don't forget names."

"Provided I bother to learn them first."

Her mouth fell open in shock a split second before she burst into laughter. Wind chimes, he thought again. He could listen to the sound all day.

"I don't believe it. Not a word of it," she managed after a time. "I might believe it of Gabriel. Maybe even Renderwell before he married Lottie, but not you."

She was wrong about Gabriel and Renderwell, but if she wished to have a higher opinion of him than she did of his friends, who was he to argue?

"Are you questioning my reputation as a rake?"

"You don't have a reputation as a rake." Her eyes grew round. "Do you?"

It was difficult to tell by her expression if she was fascinated by the idea or merely skeptical. Probably a bit of both. "What do you think?"

"You don't."

Well, that was a bit quick. "How can you be so certain?"

"Because you're—" Esther's explanation was cut short by a loud crash and what sounded like an elephant galloping through the library. She spun about and took several steps back from the door just as the beast appeared. "What on earth…?"

The dog slid to a stop in the open door, momentarily distracted by the appearance of someone new.

Esther went still, the beast went still, and Samuel

slowly and carefully set the box aside and began moving forward.

"It's all right, Esther." He kept his voice calm and steady. If they both remained calm, if neither of them made any sudden moves, catastrophe might still be averted. "He doesn't—"

"Oh, aren't you beautiful," she cut in, her voice breathy with delighted wonder. "Aren't you *glorious*?"

Taking that as encouragement, the beast launched all thirteen glorious stones of himself right at her.

Samuel leaped forward, but he needn't have bothered. Esther sidestepped the animal, quick as you please.

"Here now, none of that," she chided. "Sit down."

Not surprisingly, the beast did not immediately comply. He turned about and gathered himself for another charge. But this Esther averted by making a fist and holding it over his head, so that he had to stretch his neck up and back for a proper sniff at the suddenly fascinating appendage. She reached farther back, forcing him to lean back as well...back and back until, finally, he had no other choice but to plop his rump on the carpet to keep his balance.

"There you are," she cooed. "What a good dog."

Samuel watched in astonishment as Esther knelt down and gave the dog a rub. "You're not afraid of him."

"Of course not. I might have been, I suppose, if he'd come in slinking or with his teeth bared. He looks as if he could take my head off with a nip." She ruffled the dog's shaggy ears. "But you were quite happy to see me, weren't you? What a darling you are." She glanced over her shoulder at Samuel. "What is his name?"

"He hasn't one at present. I've only had him a fortnight or so. We call him the beast for now."

She threw him an offended look. "You can't call him the beast. He needs a proper name."

"Lucifer would be fitting. Mephistopheles. Doom. Mount Vesuvius."

"Don't listen to him," she said to the dog. "What shall I call you, you great hairy Goliath. Ooh! Harry. I quite like that."

"I am not calling him Harry." Goliath had a nice ring to it, though. So did Vesuvius now that he thought on it.

"What's wrong with Harry?"

"I know men named Harry. Give me your hand." He pulled her to her feet when she obliged. "How is your neck?"

"Much improved, thank you."

He brushed away a loose curl to see for himself. There was no sign of bruising or swelling, and the angry red had dulled to a faint pink.

She ducked away and pointed at the box he'd set aside. "What do you have there?"

"I... It's... Er..." He didn't know why he was suddenly stumbling over his own tongue. Retrieving the box, he shoved it at her. "It's a present."

She looked mildly confused. "For me?"

"No, I merely wished for your opinion on the wrapping."

She snatched it out of his hands with a laugh. "Thank you."

"You're welcome."

She shook it gently. "It's rather light. Is it breakable? Should I be careful?"

"No. Are you going to open it?"

"In a moment. I've not had a present from a gentleman since my father gave me Mr. Nips. Well, I've had presents from Peter, but young boys don't count. I want to make it last."

"Will was alive for years after he gave you Mr. Nips."

She shrugged and began pulling at the knotted twine. "He forgot most of my birthdays."

Samuel made no comment but he silently wished he could go back in time, to when he'd known her as a young girl in London, and bring her a birthday present or two. What might have been different, he wondered, if she'd not been forgotten on those days?

Esther lifted the lid off the box and gasped when she saw the contents. She pulled out a long, thick rope with a series of dangling bright white ribbons tied along its length.

Samuel gave one of the ribbons a flick with his fingers. "So you can play more easily in the evenings."

"Oh, Samuel. This is wonderful. Thank you."

He grunted.

She grinned at the rope. "Peter will love it."

"Beg your pardon? Peter?" What did Peter have to do with it?

She laughed and gave one of the ribbons a tug. "I never would have thought to add these. I'm going to tell him they were my idea."

"Tell Peter?"

"Yes. Oh, he *will* be pleased. And impressed. As will his friends at school, I should think. Not so much about my fictitious cleverness, but with the set as a whole."

His friends at school.

She'd bought the damn badminton set for Peter. Which meant *he'd* bought the damn rope, and spent a good half hour in the store tying ribbons to it like a girl tying ribbons to a damn braid, for Peter.

He felt like an idiot.

But she was smiling. Actually, she was beaming at him as if he'd brought her a king's ransom in jewels. That wasn't so bad.

"This was very thoughtful of you, Samuel. And uncommonly creative." Hugging the rope close to her chest, she stepped forward and cupped his cheek in her free hand. Then she pressed a kiss to his cheek that lingered a hair too long to qualify as chaste. "Thank you."

Maybe he wasn't such an idiot.

"My pleasure," he replied and balled his hands into fists to stop himself from reaching for her again when she stepped away.

She was still smiling as she replaced the rope in the box. "Have you been out for long this morning?"

"Not very. An hour or two."

She shot him a speculative look. "Did you—?"

"I went in search of the rope. Nothing more." He'd needed something to occupy his time while she slept and he waited for breakfast. Which reminded him. "Have you eaten?"

"Not yet. Your housekeeper has set breakfast out for us. Shall we?" She patted her leg as she headed for the door. "Come along, Harry."

"We are not naming him Harry," he called out after her.

Samuel followed the sound of her laughter, then stifled a groan when she stepped into the breakfast room instead of the dining room. He loathed the breakfast room. It was too small, the furniture was too delicate, the colors were too bright, and everything in it was too feminine. There wasn't one square inch in the room that wasn't covered in flowers, lace, bows, fringe, or a combination of all four.

"This room is very dainty," Esther commented after they'd filled their plates at the sideboard. She took a seat at the small table and glanced about at the fringed purple drapes, vivid floral wallpaper, and contrasting wainscoting. "And complicated. How long have you lived here?"

Samuel took his own seat carefully. He didn't use the flimsy little chairs with their spindly, tapered legs if he could possibly help it. "Six years."

"And you've not changed it?"

He tried and failed to think of a way to answer that without sounding responsible for the purple drapes.

Esther's eyes widened at his silence. "This"—she twirled her finger in the air to indicate the room—"was *your* doing?"

"Not exactly. Renderwell suggested I hire a decorator."

"Was this decorator under the impression that only ladies eat breakfast in breakfast rooms?"

That had been his very assumption upon seeing the room for the first time. "He might have been." Amused, he pasted on a surprised expression. "You don't like it?"

"I..." She blinked rapidly several times and began to sputter. "I... That is... I apologize. I've been very rude. You've a lovely home, and I shouldn't have—Why are you laughing?"

He'd never seen her so flustered. He'd seen her angry, embarrassed, hurt, and amused but not ruffled to the point of tripping over her own tongue. It was so contrary to the confident woman he knew, he couldn't help but find it funny.

"Why are you laughing?" she demanded again. "I've insulted you."

"You've insulted me before," he pointed out.

"Yes, but this was out of carelessness, which is quite different."

"You've not insulted me."

"I have," she replied with a wince. "You've invited me into your home and I've disparaged it. It was wrong of me—"

He threw up a hand. "Esther, stop. You've not disparaged my home. You disparaged this room. This perfectly hideous room."

"It isn't..." She trailed off as her eyes meandered back to the wallpaper. "Well, it does make one a bit dizzy."

"Like a ride on a centrifugal railway."

She leaned forward, fascinated. "Have you done that?"

"Been thrown in a loop at a tremendous speed? No, thank you."

She sighed wistfully. "Oh, I should like to try it."

"Why am I not surprised?"

"Why haven't you changed this," she asked, indicating the room with her fork again, "if you don't care for it?"

"I don't give the room much thought, to be honest. I generally take breakfast in the kitchen."

"I see. Was it also redecorated?"

"No. Mrs. Lanchor insisted it be kept as it was."

"I see," she repeated and glanced toward the door. "Might we...?"

He was out of his spindly seat and tugging the bellpull before she could finish the sentence.

Samuel felt better the moment he stepped into the kitchen.

This was how a home should feel. Warm and inviting and lived in. It should smell of cut herbs and flowers and baking bread. It should be a little messy, a little bit scuffed at the edges. It should be a place where a man could move about without fear of damaging something.

He felt at ease moving about here. It didn't matter if his boots scraped the kitchen table leg; it was already pitted and scarred from years of use.

"What a lovely kitchen," Esther commented. "It reminds me of our old kitchen at Willowbend, the way the morning light comes through the windows." She took a seat at the table and sighed happily when the beast settled himself next to her with a tremendous groan. "I wish more rooms were like kitchens. They're so comfortably unpretentious."

He'd expected her to be comfortable enough in the kitchen; he hadn't expected her to truly appreciate it. "I thought you preferred finery."

"Something can be fine without being pretentious: soft taffeta, a pretty bonnet, a cozy chair, a well-appointed kitchen with good morning light."

"Fine company."

"Exactly so," she replied, but she grew quiet when his staff entered and set out their meal on the table.

Mrs. Lanchor and Sarah smiled at Esther. She smiled back but looked a little wary of the friendliness. The moment the staff left, she leaned across the table and whispered, "Your staff is being very kind to me."

"I should hope so. I don't pay them to be rude." He picked up his fork and decided that the lukewarm eggs were worth the move to the kitchen. "You don't have to whisper. They don't eavesdrop."

"That's not what I meant. What did you tell them?"

"About you? Mostly the truth. I told them you are a client in danger and therefore in need of my protection."

"That's not the truth." She sat back again. "That's not even a half-truth."

She was in danger and she needed his protection. Two-thirds of the truth as he saw it. "It doesn't matter. After last night, they are disposed to feel kindly toward you."

"They must think I'm hiding from a brutal husband or father." She leaned a little in her chair to glance at the open door. "I feel as if I've won their sympathies out of deceit. I don't like it."

"This from a woman who won a rope from a shopkeeper out of deceit."

"That was an accident."

"Esther, you *are* in danger. You were attacked. Their sympathy is not unwarranted."

"I suppose." She broke off a bit of bread and slipped it to the beast. Her eyes flicked to his as the dog's loud smacking filled the room. "I beg your pardon. I should have asked if I could feed him from the table."

"I don't mind." He might eventually, if the beast took the treats as a sign he could start helping himself, but he'd worry about that possibility later. Both the woman and the dog looked pleased with the arrangement. Why spoil their fun?

"Why is it you haven't a dog?" he inquired. "You're fond of animals. Dogs in particular."

"I mean to have one, after I return to Derbyshire. I couldn't before. Peter has a sensitivity to dogs and cats. Horses as well, though he won't admit to it."

"Why won't he admit to it?"

She hitched up one shoulder and was immediately obliged to tug the loose neckline back into place. "I suspect he thinks it detracts from the fact that he's a far more accomplished equestrian than his sisters," she said. "He's quite proud of it."

"I could give you riding lessons, if you like."

"I should like that, thank you. Next time we are in Derbyshire, then?"

"Next time."

What would that next time look like? He wondered. The last time they had seen each other in Derbyshire, they had been… What, exactly? He didn't know how to qualify the relationship he'd once held with Esther. Longtime acquaintances? It was odd to have known someone for years, and to have kept their greatest secret for all that time, and still not be certain if that individual counted as a friend. He had saved her life once. She had (arguably) nursed him back to health from a serious wound. Surely what they'd had was a kind of friendship. It was just a wary, begrudging kind of friendship.

And now they were something more than friends.

Would they still be something more once she returned to her little cottage? Could they still be more once she left the freedom and anonymity afforded her in London?

Suddenly, Derbyshire seemed a world away, and her return home seemed much too imminent.

He watched her break off another piece of toast and slip the small morsel into her mouth. She chewed slowly, lost in thought, and he forgot all about Derbyshire and riding lessons. He was captivated by the subtle movement of her lips, remembering how they felt opening beneath his own. Her tongue darted out to catch a tiny crumb at the corner of her mouth, and fascination turned to uncomfortable arousal. He wondered when breakfast had become such a sensual activity. When she licked her lips again, he wondered how long his staff was apt to leave them unattended and whether Esther would object if he hauled her over the table and into his lap.

She probably would. Still, he gave into the temptation to reach over and run the pad of this thumb once across her bottom lip.

Esther blinked and touched her fingers to her mouth. "Oh, did I have a bit of toast?"

"Yes." No. He'd just wanted to touch her.

"Well, thank you."

He gave her a smile designed to charm, and seduce. If all he had with Esther was a week, then he was going to make the most of it. "It was my pleasure."

A faint rose lit her cheeks, and he knew a moment's masculine pride that he could make Esther Walker-Bales blush like a schoolgirl.

He decided then and there that it would have to be more than a week.

She cleared her throat delicately. "Shall we go to Bow today? Or the General Register Office?"

Surprised by the question, he dragged his eyes away from her mouth. "Neither. You'll stay here. You need to rest."

She looked appalled at the very notion. "I do not."

"You were injured."

"Only mildly."

"Mildly *strangled*."

"You were mildly shot," she pointed out. "Will you be staying in as well?"

"There are a few matters I need to attend—"

"Don't you dare," she warned with a quick jab of her fork in his direction. "Don't you *dare* tell me you'll be attending to other business if you mean to attend to mine."

"I do have other business, you know. You're not my only client."

"I'm not a client at all. I'm not paying you." She sat up a little straighter in her chair. "Perhaps I should. That would make me your employer, would it not? What is your rate?"

He named a perfectly outrageous figure.

"You lie," she scoffed. "There aren't half a dozen people in England who could afford such a fee."

"The fee varies depending on individuals and circumstances."

"What on earth makes you suspect my circumstances would allow for such an expense?"

"Nothing at all."

She set down her silverware and crossed her arms over her chest in a huff. "You could just say you're not willing to take me on as a client."

"I believe I just did."

Her eyes narrowed, but it was more thoughtful than it was angry. She was hatching a plan of attack. Or escape. He was sure of it.

"Very well," she replied at last. "You are not in my employ."

He was fairly certain capitulation was not the plan. "No, I am not."

"And I am not in yours. Therefore, I suggest you attend to your business today, and I shall attend to mine."

Closer, but not quite it. "No."

She gave him a taunting smile. "Are you intending to extend an offer of employment to *me*?"

And there it was. "I—"

"Because I can't imagine any other reason for your presumption that I will follow your orders." She tilted her head. "What say you, Sir Samuel?"

"I say yes."

She uncrossed her arms, and the smile disappeared. "I beg your pardon?"

"Yes, I am extending an offer of employment." Hell, he should have thought of the plan himself. "I will pay you to follow every one of my orders. To the letter. Agreed?"

She tapped her finger against the table twice, then replied, "Certainly."

"Truly?" He'd hoped to convince her that the plan had real merit. He hadn't expected it to be easy.

"Yes. However, I require payment in advance." She held out her hand and waggled her fingers. "My rate is double your own."

Damn it. "I'll give you twenty pounds."

"Twenty pounds?" she echoed on a laugh. "That is a fraction of what it would take—"

"Forty." Half was a fraction.

She shook her head.

"Eighty," he tried.

"Will this number continue to grow exponentially until I say yes? How fortuitous that I have so much free time on my hands."

"Five hundred."

"You're not serious." Her mouth dropped open when he said nothing. "Good Lord, you *are* serious. You would pay me five hundred pounds to follow your orders?"

He'd pay twice that and more if it meant keeping her safe. "Yes. Do we have a deal?"

She wanted to accept the offer. He could see it. A line of concentration appeared across her brow and she was quiet for a long time. She tore off several bites of bread, eating half herself and tossing the other half to the beast in an absent manner.

Esther didn't need the money, but she wanted it. She had been poor once, and that sort of insecurity had a tendency to linger. The scars of hunger, that's what Gabriel called it. They couldn't be seen, but neither were they forgotten.

He felt guilty using that against her, but he'd live with the discomfort for the sake of her safety.

It wasn't to be, however. After struggling with the decision for a while longer, Esther shook her head. "I'm sorry, Samuel, but I'll not be under a man's thumb for any price."

"Why do you presume I would put you under my thumb?"

"Because it's what men do," she replied without heat. "And you do it, I suppose, because you can. You're allowed."

"I worked for Renderwell for years. I was never under his thumb."

"Because you're a man. You are expected to work, and you expect to be given work. I've seen you and Gabriel work with Renderwell. You functioned as a partnership, or a team. Renderwell's responsibility was to assign tasks and goals according to each man's strengths, but you fulfilled your duties as you saw fit. You participated. You made your own choices and had the pleasure of seeing your combined labors culminate in the successful completion of a challenge. Is that what you're offering me?" she asked in a skeptical tone. "Or would you ignore my strengths, my ability to make choices on my own, and simply order me to stay tucked up here out of your way?"

"You can't deny you'd find the order challenging."

"No," she replied with a small laugh. "I can't."

"I don't want you out of my way, Esther. I just want you safe."

"I know. I want the same for you. Strange, isn't it? We would each feel better if the other stayed tucked up safe and sound, but that would make the other miserable." She thought about that for a second as she chewed another bite of bread. "Does that make the desire to see the other safe a selfish one?"

Selfish desires weren't problematic by themselves. It was acting on them that wreaked havoc. Pity, that.

"A compromise, then. We'll stay in for the morning and visit Rostrime Lane this afternoon for"—he nearly said "three hours" before thinking better of it—"an hour."

"That's not nearly enough time. Four hours."

"Two."

"Three."

Perfect. "Three it is."

"And I'll not wait in the carriage."

He shook his head. "We've discussed this. The approach works best if I'm alone."

"You're presuming you'll think to ask every question *I* might think to ask."

"You're presuming I won't think to ask the right questions."

"Are you implying that I would ask the wrong ones?"

God, it was like having breakfast with a barrister. "It's beside the point. You can't risk being recognized."

"I'll keep my veil down, as had been my intention when I decided to come knocking on doors in London on my own."

Her original intention had likely been to knock and simply ask whoever answered if a Mr. George Smith was in residence. That was quite a bit different from being invited inside. She was going to find the curious looks of strangers discomforting and their willingness to confide, limited.

Some lessons, however, could only be learned through experience. Lord knew he'd made his share of missteps in his early days as a police officer and private investigator.

Not that she was embarking on a career in either.

It was just a lesson. One lesson. That was all. "We'll try it your way for one house, then revisit the matter."

"We have a deal."

There was something to be said for a quiet morning in Samuel's company. They had shared them before, of course, but always in the company of others. It was just the two of them now, settled comfortably in the parlor at the front of the house.

Esther fiddled with the corner of her book while she watched Samuel. He was what she thought of as a planter, like her sister. He took a book, took a seat, and stayed there, still as a statue. She had never been able to do that. She could lose herself in a book or her art for hours, but she couldn't sit still for all that time. Every ten minutes or so, she had to get up and move about.

Already she had taken several turns about the room. Unlike her sister, however, Samuel didn't appear to mind the distraction. He simply glanced up once, smiled absently, and went back to his book.

She watched as Samuel's brows lowered in response to something he read, then lifted a moment later as his lips slowly curved into a smile.

If she were a braver woman, she might set aside her own reading and see for herself what had captured his fancy. It wasn't but half a room between them. She could meander over and lean down for a closer look at his book. Maybe lean down a little farther. Maybe far enough to catch his scent. Perhaps, if she leaned far enough, he might take it as a hint or a suggestion to reach for her. Or she might need to be a bit more obvious in her intentions.

How bold could she be with Samuel? She could fake that sort of confidence when the occasion called for it. She'd pretended to be a bold woman in the past, but she'd never tried to be that forward as herself. Was she capable of it? Could she saunter over, slide the book from his fingers, and slip herself onto his lap? Could she twine her arms around his neck and kiss him? Just imagining it had her heart beating faster and a pleasant warmth humming through her veins.

Oh, it would be fun. He'd be shocked of course. And pleased, one should hope.

They needn't worry they'd be bothered unexpectedly. Mrs. Lanchor and two of the maids had gone out. The rest of the staff was either downstairs, upstairs, or outside.

She could do anything she liked. For as long as she liked.

To her own shock, Esther discovered she had already closed her book and set it on a side table without realizing.

She snatched it back.

What on earth was she thinking? For that matter, what on earth was she *doing*?

Kissing Samuel in carriages and even bedchambers. Imagining she could hop in his lap and kiss him in his own parlor. It was reckless, even for her, and she wasn't at all sure of her own motivations.

She liked Samuel. God help her, that was the only certainty she could claim. She liked Samuel Brass in a manner she'd never experienced with another man.

Was it love?

She believed in love. Not merely attraction or infatuation, but true romantic love. She'd always believed in it, even before she'd watched her sister hand her heart to Renderwell.

Believing in the existence of love, however, was quite a bit different than believing one might experience it for oneself.

She'd never hoped to fall in love. In the most fanciful moments of her early youth, she'd entertained a daydream or two of what it might be like to meet her fairy-tale prince, but they'd been only daydreams, like those of faraway lands she'd read about in books. Boston and China and the Himalayas. She knew they were real, just as she'd always known they were out of her reach.

Perhaps that was why it had been so easy for her to set the daydreams of her fairy-tale prince aside. What was the point of a dream without hope?

Or maybe it had been easy to set those dreams aside because she'd never been particularly interested in them.

Perhaps she was incapable of love. She'd long suspected that to be the case with her mother. The woman had been endlessly charming but devoid of all proper feeling, even for her own children. What if she had inherited some sort of moral deficiency…?

Esther acknowledged the fear and set it aside. Of course she was capable. She loved Peter and Lottie, and even their father at times, though he scarcely deserved it.

What if she was capable of love but incapable of

recognizing that she was *in* love? To hear the poets and playwrights tell it, falling in love was like being struck by a thunderbolt, but Lottie had once said that she'd been in love with Renderwell for years without realizing how she felt. It seemed unlikely one could fail to notice being struck by lightning.

Esther certainly didn't feel as if she'd been struck. Pricked perhaps, or nudged, or sideswiped, but not struck.

Then it probably wasn't love. And, considering the lies she'd told, that was for the best.

She really wasn't fairy-tale material.

Twelve

ESTHER GREW INCREASINGLY NERVOUS AS THEY MADE their way down Rostrime Lane. Samuel had offered to take her inside the first houses they visited that afternoon, but she'd declined. There was little point in asking questions to which she already knew the answer. She'd wait until they reached number twenty-three.

Surprise, and even a hint of relief, mingled with her nerves when that one house finally came into view. She pulled up her veil for a better view out the window. It didn't look nearly as foreboding as she remembered. The result of seeing it in daylight, no doubt. Eleven years ago, she had come at night, and the street lamps had cast long, malevolent shadows over the brick and turned the portico pillars into a set of glowing fangs.

The old brick building looked rather cheerful now. The shutters had been painted a deep blue recently, the walk was swept clean, and there were vibrant pots of flowers on either side of the front door.

Still, when the carriage pulled up in front, her heart began to race, and her stomach rolled.

She hated this house. Cheerful or not, merely looking at it made her feel ashamed and afraid.

Samuel hopped out and held out his hand. "Will you join me?"

Yes. Say yes. Take his hand and go inside. "I'll wait, thank you."

"Are you all right? You look a bit pale. Is it your throat? Are you—?"

"I'm perfectly well." She was a perfect coward. "Go inside. There is nothing amiss with me, I assure you."

"If you're certain..." Clearly, *he* wasn't certain. His keen eyes searched her face a moment longer before he reached out and carefully pulled down her veil. "We'll take a rest after this house."

Might as well, she thought. They likely wouldn't need to go into the next house after Samuel spoke with the occupants of number twenty-three. "If you like. Go on, Samuel."

A part of her hoped he would ignore her and hop back into the carriage. Maybe if he stalled a bit she would, in time, gather enough courage to join him.

It was too late. Samuel took one last look at her and closed the door. Moments later, he disappeared inside the house alone. There was nothing left for her to do but wait, and berate herself.

This is why she had come—to confront her past and atone for this mistake. She'd planned this for months. Yet here she was, hiding away in a carriage.

How could she hope to face her father if she couldn't even face an old house he'd owned years ago?

"Coward," she whispered into the empty carriage.

It didn't disagree.

Sick at heart, she turned away from the window and waited for Samuel's return.

Twenty minutes later, he climbed into the carriage looking rather pleased with himself. She lifted her veil and did her best to paste on an eager expression. Difficult, when she already knew what he was going to say. Mr. George Smith did not live at number twenty-three Rostrime Lane. He'd not lived there in over a decade.

"A Mr. George Smith lived here some ten or eleven years ago," Samuel informed her, settling into his seat. "He wasn't a grocer. He was in shipping."

"Shipping?" She hadn't expected that. She had a father in shipping. How strange and wonderful. "He must have owned the building in Spitalfields as we thought."

Samuel signaled to the driver with a quick rap on the roof. "Doesn't explain why he would address the letter from there."

"He might have wished to keep his address from my mother."

"And his child?"

"I said I was going to find my father. I didn't say I was going to like him." She shrugged and hoped it came off as careless. "Do they know where he might have gone?"

"The current occupants are a Mr. and Mrs. Thornhill. Mrs. Thornhill was out, but Mr. Thornhill claims they never met Mr. Smith. They learned of him from the previous owner of the property, a Mr. Brumly. He let the house to a number of individuals over the years, including your father. The Thornhills have no idea where that gentleman is to be found at present."

"My father didn't own the house?"

"No, in fact, he is remembered for having spent less than three months in residence. It was rumored that Mr. Smith suffered a sudden reversal of fortune."

Guilt settled heavily in her stomach, making her queasy. What she had done all those years ago would not have caused a reversal of fortune, but it wouldn't have helped either. "Might we find this Mr. Brumly?"

"We can try." He frowned at her. "You still look pale."

"Perhaps I do. Perhaps it is nervous excitement." She tried to smile at him. "I suspect a cup of tea will set me to rights."

An ocean of tea wouldn't be sufficient. She knew it, and from the suspicious look on Samuel's face, he knew it, too.

He kept his peace on the matter, however, saying nothing as they returned to his home and the chairs in the parlor.

For the space of an hour, Esther sipped hot tea liberally doused with milk and willed away the chill of old guilt. After the third cup, she was forced to accept that the tea was not going to help. Because it wasn't *old* guilt that made her fingers want to shake every time she caught Samuel looking at her from across the room.

It was *new* guilt.

After all her pretty talk of changing, of becoming a better version of herself, she'd both taken the coward's way out of a difficult situation and lied about it to the one person whose trust she desperately wanted to earn. She'd lied to the one man who deserved the truth.

She was failing. Failing Samuel, and failing herself.

She set her teacup down on its saucer so hard it was a wonder the fine china didn't crack.

"I lied to you before," she blurted out before she lost her small claim to courage. "I lied about how I learned Mr. Smith was my father, and why I want to find him."

Samuel looked up from his paper, his expression unreadable. "I beg your pardon?"

"I lied to you. I shouldn't have, and I'm sorry for it."

His expression didn't change as he carefully folded his paper and set it aside. "Would you care to elaborate?"

"I…um…" Her hands trembled as she set her cup and saucer on a small side table. "I don't know where to start, really."

"Try the beginning."

Her nerves jumped at the first hint of anger in his voice.

This was a mistake. She should have kept her mouth shut. He was already angry with her. What if he *stayed* angry with her? What if he didn't accept her apology? What if—?

"Esther."

"Just a moment," she snapped back. "This isn't easy for me. Not with you looking at me like…" She wasn't sure how to describe his current expression, so she just gestured toward his face and added, "That."

"How am I meant to look at you? You tell me you've been lying to me since you came to London—"

"Not the entire time. Not about everything. Honestly." *Honestly*. What a ridiculous word to use at the moment. "I've not been… That is… I don't want you to think that I've been lying to you about anything other than this. I've not done anything or planned to do anything you might find objectionable." She made a face at her choice of words. "Well, that's not entirely true, is it? You object to most everything I want to do. What I'm trying to say is that I… I've not…"

Oh, why was this so hard?

"Tell me this," Samuel said calmly. "Did you make the trip to London for any unlawful or immoral purpose?"

She wasn't surprised that he asked, but it still hurt to hear the question. It hurt that he should *have* to ask. "No. I swear it."

"I believe you," he replied, so quickly and easily that she knew he hadn't really considered it a possibility.

"If you didn't think I had, why did you ask?"

"Do you feel better for having denied it?"

"I suppose." Quite a bit, in fact. It was essentially the point she'd been trying to express in her inarticulate ramble. *Please don't mistake my current dishonesty with the sort of dishonesty I displayed in the past.* It was an absurd request but one she felt compelled to make. "Thank you."

"Sometimes it helps to acknowledge a sore spot before moving on." He made a prompting motion with his hand. "If we could move on."

"Right." She cleared her throat and fixed her eyes on the carpet in front of her feet. "When I was seventeen, my father…that is, Will Walker, came to me with a plan to burglarize a house on Rostrime Lane."

"I see."

No doubt he did. She risked a glance at him and relaxed a little when she still saw neither anger nor judgment. "At the time, I thought it odd. He'd given up climbing in and out of windows years ago. Too much risk and not enough profit, he said. But he was adamant we should go through with the job, and I was eager to please."

"He was your father."

He offered that as a kind of excuse, and she wished she could accept it. Some mistakes, however, could never be excused. "I kept watch outside whilst he slipped inside and out again with a satchel full of trinkets. Candlesticks, silverware, that sort of thing. We pawned them that night."

"Through Horatio Gage?"

The brutal gang leader she and her father had worked with during their last few years in London. Gage had been the one to turn a diamond theft into the kidnapping of a duchess and the one to shoot her father in the back. Gage and several of his gang members had eventually wound up on the gallows.

"Yes. Gage offered a third of their worth, six pounds. Father didn't even bother haggling. He was in such a fine mood. I'd never seen him look so pleased with himself. So smug." She could still see that bright, bright smile on his face. "He insisted we celebrate with drinks at the tavern."

"Doesn't sound like him."

"No. I thought it strange, too." Will Walker couldn't hold his liquor, and he knew it. As a rule, he'd avoided all but the occasional glass of wine. "But, as I said, he was happy, and I was delighted to be a part of that happiness. Three drinks in, he handed me the six pounds, less the cost of our drinks, and told me it was my inheritance. Courtesy of my real father, Mr. George Smith of Rostrime Lane."

Then he'd laughed and laughed while she'd sat there staring at her pieces of silver.

"I'm sorry," Samuel said softly.

Though she didn't want it, she picked up her cup again and sipped the last, cold bit of tea. "I stole from my own father."

"Did you come to London to apologize?"

"I don't know." She stared at the soggy bits of tea leaves at the bottom of her cup. "I never spent what was left of the six pounds. It's been sitting at the bottom of my hope chest for eleven years, waiting for me to… I don't know. Make a decision, I suppose." And she'd made a decision when she'd moved out of Greenly House. "I want to give it back. I want to give back every shilling I helped take from him."

"I think that's commendable."

She managed a small smile at the encouragement but wondered if he'd feel the same once she finished. "Do you know the worst part?" she asked in a voice barely above a whisper. "I kept going. I hated Will Walker after that night, but I kept helping him. I helped him every time he asked."

"He was your father," he offered again.

"He was Lottie's as well. She stopped." There were times she wondered if Will Walker's preference for Lottie's company had less to do with parentage and more to do with the fact that Lottie was simply a better, more likable person.

"As I recall, your father had a different sort of relationship with your sister."

"He adored her. Or gave a very good impression of it. Difficult to say with Will." Nothing about Will

Walker could be trusted. Charismatic, brilliant, and unpredictable, he'd been the center of their isolated world. The sun and moon revolved around that one man. With a single look, he could make a young girl feel like she was the most important thing in the universe. He could make her feel invisible and worthless just as easily.

She shook her head at the memory of how significant that one small man had been to her. "I told you I wasn't angry about how things turned out all those years ago, and I'm not. But I was angry with you at first for inserting yourselves into our lives. I was angry because your presence diminished his. There you were, the three of you, so strong and righteous in your pursuit of justice." The stuff of fairy tales. "And there was my father, sneaking about the shadows like a weasel. He was terribly small and petty by comparison. And that made me even smaller, my desperation to please him even more pathetic."

"It was never pathetic."

"It was. It *was*," she repeated with more force before he could object again. "And eventually that might have been enough to turn me from the life he wanted me to lead, but he died before I drummed up the courage to tell him to go to the devil." She let out a small sigh. "I lost the chance."

"I'm sorry."

"But that's the problem," she whispered. "I wasn't. I wasn't sorry he was dead, and I wasn't sorry I'd lost the chance. I was relieved." She set the cup down again and briefly pressed the heels of her hands against her eyes. "God help me, I was just so relieved to have the decision taken out of my hands. I was free of him, free of all of it, and I didn't have to lift a finger to see it done." She dropped her hands. "The decision was made for me. No courage required."

"There's no shame in experiencing a spot of luck."

"It was the coward's way out, even if it wasn't of my own choosing. I didn't want to be that girl again, and now I don't want to be the woman who hides in the shadows and hopes all the hard decisions are made for her."

"You're not."

She had been today. "I didn't go in that house with you. I was supposed to go in. But I got so scared, and you were there. I let you do it for me."

There was a pause before he said, "And?"

"What do you mean, 'and?'" Wasn't he listening? She'd been a coward.

His broad shoulders lifted in a shrug. "What's wrong with letting a friend help?"

"It's not help when it's doing all of the work. Besides, it was important I do this for myself."

"And so you would have done," he replied with confidence. "Had I not been there."

"You don't know that." *She* didn't know that.

"You wouldn't have come all the way to London only to give up on Rostrime Lane. You might have stood outside arguing with yourself for a good long while but, eventually, you would have knocked on the door."

"But I didn't." That was the salient point.

"You didn't have the good long while to argue, did you?"

"No, but—"

"Were you relieved that I went in your stead?"

"No," she replied, a little surprised to realize it. "No, I wasn't."

"There you have it."

"I—" She wanted to argue with him. Yes, she'd not been relieved to take the coward's way out, but that hardly excused her lack of bravery. There came a point in a conversation such as this, however, where continued objections began to sound like frantic bids for reassurance, even compliments.

Tell me again how blameless I am. Convince me.

That wasn't fair to Samuel and wouldn't be good for her.

She gave him an appreciative smile. "Perhaps you're right. I'll think on it some. Thank you."

He made a face and rose from his chair. "Right. Fetch your veil. We're going back."

"What? Back to the house? Today?"

"Right now," he replied, coming to stand in front of her.

"But we can't. You only just left. What reasons could I possibly give for coming back?"

"You're a clever woman. You'll think of something on the way." He held out his hand to assist her from the seat and sighed when she didn't immediately take it. "Esther, if you don't go back and see this done, you'll always regret it. Clearly, nothing I can say will change that."

He was right. If she didn't fix this now, she could very well find herself back in London a decade from now, once again trying to free herself of old regret.

She gave him a sheepish smile. "Once we arrive… I might need to argue with myself a bit first."

"I've the afternoon free, as it happens. Take all the time you like."

This time when he offered his hand, she accepted it.

Esther went into number twenty-three alone. She didn't need to argue with herself first, as she'd feared, and Samuel didn't insist he come along, as she'd expected.

The master of the house, Mr. Thornhill, was a harmless old gentleman, he assured her. She'd be safe so long as she kept to the story Samuel had given and kept her veil down.

The staff greeted her with friendly, if slightly confused, smiles and ushered her into the front parlor. She took in the small room with its comfortably worn furniture and tried not to picture Will Walker sneaking about the place in the dark, slipping items into his bag. They'd not stolen from this couple. Her father had never laid eyes on these things, and yet she felt guilty all the same, because he would have. He would have stolen the lovely little clock on the mantel without a moment's thought, and she would have helped him.

She shouldn't be here.

Mr. Thornhill didn't appear to begrudge the unexpected visit. An older man with a protruding belly and a puff of white hair, he smiled broadly at her as they took their seats.

"You are Sir Samuel's client, then?" Mr. Thornhill inquired. "He mentioned a widow in search of a lost uncle. Or was it your uncle's lost friend? I do apologize. My memory is not what it once was."

"My uncle's lost friend," she replied. "My uncle would search for Mr. Smith himself, but his health is failing. He wants very much to reestablish a correspondence with his childhood friend whilst he is still able. I know Sir Samuel has already made inquiries on my behalf, but I had rather hoped to find your wife at home. I understand she was unavailable this morning."

It was not the most creative of excuses for her visit, but it was believable.

"Mrs. Thornhill left a half hour ago, I'm afraid. She'll be disappointed to have missed both visitors today."

"I'm sorry to hear it." It might have been helpful to speak with the woman. As it was, she was left searching for any inquiry Samuel may have neglected to make in his earlier visit. "I was wondering, Mr. Thornhill, might Mr. Smith have left behind an item or two? A personal token such as a letter or—"

"Funny you should ask. Sir Samuel inquired after the same this morning and I told him there was nothing about the house, but then Mrs. Thornhill reminded me of this." He hefted himself out of his seat and retrieved a pocket watch and fob from the drawer of a nearby desk. "Found it when we first took possession of the house from Mr. Brumly. He didn't recognize it. Said it must have belonged to a previous tenant. We put it away in a cupboard thinking its owner might come back for it. That must have been…oh, many, many years ago. Quite forgot about it."

She accepted the watch from him and stared at the

large, elaborate letter *B* engraved on the case. "It's the wrong initial, I'm afraid."

"And so I told my wife. But she says, sometimes, the initial isn't that of the owner's, but of someone important to the owner. A gift from a wife, a son, or a daughter." He gave her a playful wink she imagined he'd not have dared with an unmarried woman. "Or a sweetheart."

Generally, such a gift would include a small inscription placed out of the way. One inscribed the inside of a ring in such a manner or put a few heartfelt words on the back of an item. One did not brand one's initial on the front. Then again...

The letter *B* was her mother's first initial. And her mother was just the sort of woman to brand a gift. She caught Mr. Thornhill's questioning gaze. "Oh, my uncle once mentioned that Mr. Smith was briefly engaged to a Miss Brines. She passed away before the wedding."

"How tragic. Perhaps he engraved the watch himself, in memory of her." Mr. Thornhill shook his head sadly. "It must have torn his heart to have lost it."

"Yes, I imagine it did. Mr. Thornhill, if you would allow me to purchase this from—"

"Purchase? I won't hear of it. It's not mine to sell, is it? You take it. Give it to Mr. Smith when you find him. Better yet, have your uncle return it to him." He nodded, pleased with the idea. "There's a fine start to a renewed friendship, eh?"

"I can't. It may not even belong to Mr. Smith."

"Then send it back, if you like. Mind you, it won't be doing me and the wife a spot of good, sitting on the cupboard shelf."

"But it has value. Let me pay—"

"I mean no offense, Mrs. Ellison, but that watch isn't worth the time it would take out of my day to sell it. It's not of the highest quality." He reached over to lightly pat her hand. "You take it for now. If you can't find your Mr. Smith, maybe it'll bring your uncle a bit of comfort to have something of his friend's to keep."

She couldn't claim to be an expert on men's watches, but she'd helped her father steal and fence a few, and she was fairly certain the old man was deliberately understating its value. The watch had a bit of wear and tear, but it could be pawned for a few pounds at least. But Mr. Thornhill was determined to be generous, refusing several more offers of payment, until Esther was finally forced to accept the watch as a gift.

"Thank you. This means a great deal to me. To my family. Thank you."

"It is my pleasure."

Once inside the carriage again, Esther pulled the watch from her bag and handed it to Samuel. "He had this. I think it may have been a gift from my mother." She tapped the enormous engraved *B*. "Beatrice. My mother didn't like to be forgotten."

Samuel let out a low whistle. "That is a bold reminder."

"She was a bold woman."

He took the watch from her and studied it carefully, turning it over in his hands. "It's too old."

"What? What do you mean? How do you know?"

"The case is fifty years old at least."

"Is it?" She snatched the watch back as disappointment set in. "How can you tell?"

"The design mostly. The wear as well. Although it is possible she bought it secondhand and had it inscribed."

"Oh, yes, of course. It may have already been inscribed, for that matter." Her mother would have appreciated the convenience of a ready-made gift. "Realistically, there's every possibility that it's not connected to my family at all. Still…" She fiddled with the watch a moment longer, then opened her bag and dropped it inside.

"Do you feel better for having come back?" Samuel asked.

"I do." She felt a tremendous sense of relief. "Thank you for bringing me."

"It was no trouble." He regarded her with an inscrutable expression. "I was thinking about something whilst you were inside."

"Oh?" She felt a thrill of excitement, and her blood warmed with a sudden awareness of his closeness in the carriage. Was he thinking of the way he'd been staring at her at breakfast, his piercing eyes so full of wicked interest? She certainly hoped so.

Just in case his thoughts ran in that direction, she tugged the corner of the drapes firmly closed. Carriages were such wonderfully confined contraptions, and so conveniently private.

She leaned forward a little, and caught the subtle spice of his soap. "What were you thinking?"

"Do you remember when we found the diamonds Will had stolen from the duchess?"

She sat back again, deflated. This was not the

direction she'd been hoping his thoughts had taken. "Difficult to forget."

"You were upset that Will had broken the tiara so it would fit behind the picture frame," Samuel said. "You wanted it repaired before it was returned to the family, and you insisted on paying for the repairs yourself."

Rightfully so. She'd played a role in stealing the tiara, and then her father had destroyed it, wholly unconcerned with the skill and talent that had gone into creating such a magnificent piece of art. The philistine. "I remember. What of it?"

"Sweetheart," he said, his voice low and tender. "You can't hope to repay every shilling you helped your father steal."

Esther blinked once at the endearment.

To the best of her recollection, no one had ever called her sweetheart before. Nor darling, pet, poppet, love, or any of the countless little terms of affection she'd heard other men offer their wives and daughters. She'd simply never been any of those things to a man. Any man.

She had the most extraordinary reaction to Samuel calling her sweetheart. Her lips curved involuntarily, her heart sped up, and a swell of pleasure built in her chest. She suddenly felt more important, special, singled out in the best possible way.

It was a silly response to what was likely an offhand comment, but that didn't seem to matter. She very much liked being Samuel's sweetheart.

She wished she could take the time to savor the feeling, but Samuel was looking at her expectantly, waiting for a response.

"I know I can't repay every shilling," she replied. "I don't even know the names of anyone else I helped swindle. But I know his. I can repay him. I have to try." She shrugged. "It isn't always enough to be sorry. There is something to be said for putting a bit of effort into atonement."

"So there is. There is something else I didn't ask before we left. Why did you lie about how you came to know Mr. Smith was your natural father? Why didn't you tell me about the six pounds?"

"For the same reason you didn't want me to shave your beard."

Samuel nodded, then regarded her thoughtfully. "Renderwell once described you as wounded."

"Did he?" She made a face at that. "Can't say I care for the description."

"I thought it apt at the time. But not now," Samuel said softly. "Mending. That's a better description for you, I think. You're mending." He reached for her hand and pressed a soft kiss into her palm. "It's not an ugly scar, Esther. Not anymore."

The sun was setting by the time Samuel returned Esther to the house. He left immediately after seeing her settled, claiming a need to follow up on inquiries he'd made into recent attacks in Hyde Park. And, of course, he had other, *paying* clients who demanded at least some of his attention.

Remembering their kisses, and that wonderful look over the kitchen table that morning, Esther waited for his return with excited expectation. Perhaps that evening he would turn his wicked interest into wicked intent.

She took dinner later than she would have liked, hoping he might be back to join her. Afterward, she read in the parlor until her eyelids began to droop. She might have fallen asleep right there, but Sarah's voice pulled her from her half slumber.

"Mrs. Ellison?" Sarah looked over from where she was holding back the edge of one parlor drape. "Mum, come here and have a look at this."

"What is it?"

Esther set down her book and rose just as Sarah turned to the window again and frowned.

"Oh, it's gone now."

"What's gone?" Esther joined her and peered into the lighted street and deep shadows beyond. "What did you see?"

"I don't know. A dark figure just there at the edge of the Ginley house." She pointed at a home across the way and one door down.

A dark figure? The hair on the back of Esther's neck stood on end. "One of their staff?"

Sarah shook her head. "Awful short to be a body. I thought it was one of the bushes until it moved."

"Maybe it was a dog."

"Bit tall for a dog." She glanced over her shoulder at Harry, who was sprawled out in the middle of the floor. "Most dogs." Her gaze shot back to Esther. "Do you think it might be someone skulking about the place?" She hunched her shoulders and bent her knees. "Crouched down all sneaky?"

"I don't know."

She thought of the men in the park. There was no reason to believe they'd followed after the attack. But the bushes down the street would be a fine place to hide and watch Samuel's house.

Tension pulled across her shoulders, and her heart began to beat a little faster. She leaned closer to the glass, and Sarah followed suit. For several long seconds, they stood there, shoulder to shoulder, staring silently into the darkness.

Suddenly, the drapes on one of the Ginley windows shifted, and a weak beam of light escaped to illuminate a long, thin figure in the grass.

The women leaped back simultaneously. Esther gasped. Sarah let out a little yelp.

The curtains moved again, and the shadow with it. The dark figure bent and curved up the nearby bushes, creating a short, squat shape.

"Oh, for *God's sake.*" Esther exhaled heavily and patted her chest twice to coax her heart out of her throat. "It's just shadows from inside the house." She looked to Sarah. "That is what you saw, isn't it?"

"Aye." Sarah swallowed hard. "I think so. *Blimey*, that gave me a fright."

"And me." She blew out another hard breath and managed a choppy laugh, amused at their silly overreaction. "The pair of us, jumpy as field mice." She thought about that as she inhaled deeply once more and let it out slowly. "Don't mention this to Sir Samuel."

"No, mum."

Esther nodded. "Right. Right. Cup of tea for both of us, then?"

"Oh, yes, please."

In the kitchen, Sarah made up a light brew that did an excellent job of soothing nerves. Esther lingered over her cup, then poured herself a second after Sarah left. Halfway through, her lids grew heavy again. She tried blinking the sleepiness away, but it was no use. She gave up the effort to wait for Samuel's return and sought out her bed.

Thirteen

THE NEXT DAY, ESTHER DECIDED THAT THE BEST thing she could say about searching through records at the General Register Office was that Samuel had no objection to her participation provided she kept her veil down.

The process itself was slow and tedious, but after much hard work, and a little bribery, they were able to obtain the location of Mr. Brumly, the former owner of 23 Rostrime Lane. They also discovered that 58 Commercial Street had, indeed, once belonged to a Mr. George Smith. It had been a grocer's before it burned down. The property had then been sold to a Mr. Jonas Wheaton, who had built the structure currently on the premises before willing it, and a number of other properties, to a nephew two years ago.

To Esther, it felt as if they were finally getting somewhere. At least, it did until Samuel returned to the carriage from calling on the nephew, Mr. Gregory Wheaton, at his grand town house on Arlington Street.

"He claims not only to have never heard of George Smith but to be unaware that he has any interests in

Spitalfields." Samuel pounded on the roof of the carriage with a bit more force than Esther felt was warranted.

"Could the records be wrong?" she asked, a little wary of Samuel's mood.

"Always a possibility, but I suspect his denial stems from fear for his reputation. He was very quick to see me out."

"He doesn't want to admit to having any association with a place like Spitalfields," she guessed.

Samuel nodded and Esther made a face at Mr. Wheaton's elegant home. "And I thought my determination to win the good opinions of others was foolish."

"It is."

She rolled her eyes at the small jab. "Thank you."

"The difference is that his is shameful. You're not the sort of woman who would degrade others to elevate yourself."

She was stunned by the comment, unable to respond in any way but to produce a half smile, pull down her veil, and pretend a sudden interest in the passing neighborhood. She didn't know what to do with a compliment that was at once enormously flattering and at the same time...terribly wrong.

She *had* hurt others. She was *exactly* that sort of woman. Time and time again she had stolen from people, turned them into victims, all in an effort to raise her father's opinion of her.

Her shame was no different than Mr. Wheaton's. How could Samuel believe otherwise? She slanted a covert look at him. Had he managed to justify her past transgressions in his own mind somehow? Had he turned her into a better woman than she really was? She didn't care for the idea, but neither had she the courage to set him straight. The need to be liked, perhaps to be loved, certainly to be a *sweetheart*, was as strong as ever, and the notion of reminding Samuel that she was capable of being despicable held little appeal.

It was probably unnecessary at any rate. He was clumsy with words, wasn't he? He'd likely meant to acknowledge that she *no longer* hurt others for her own gain.

This was, after all, the same man who believed he'd made a declaration of affection by announcing she could no longer go to her hotel.

Lord only knew how the man went about choosing his words.

She kept her thoughts to herself as they made their way to Mr. Brumly's house, which turned out to be situated in a slightly less fashionable neighborhood than Mr. Wheaton's. Though its size was somewhat imposing, its brick exterior had a comfortably weathered appearance, and the multitude of brightly colored flowers blooming in its small front garden lent a welcoming air.

"I would like to go inside with you," she said to Samuel.

She expected him to refuse, to invent some ridiculous argument wherein their deal had been satisfied at Rostrime Lane. To her surprise, however, he hesitated only a moment before offering his hand to assist her from the carriage.

Five minutes later, she was settled on a settee in Mr. Brumly's parlor, trying her hardest not to appear ill at ease when the man himself walked into the room.

Mr. Brumly was a tall and remarkably handsome older gentleman with a full head of silver hair, a pair of warm brown eyes behind round spectacles, and a friendly, if somewhat distracted, smile. He greeted them politely and listened with interest as Samuel related their fictitious quest to find the long lost friend of Esther's uncle, Mr. Smith.

"I remember your Mr. Smith," Mr. Brumly said with a thoughtful nod. "Odd duck, that one. Good sort, but odd."

"As is my uncle," Esther replied. He'd have to be, to send his widowed niece out on a ridiculous quest on his behalf.

"In that case, if your uncle has need to let a town house, he need only come to me. I'll take his friendship with Mr. Smith as a reference."

"He was a good tenant, then?" Esther asked.

"Quite. He let the house for a year and paid the annual sum in advance. Then he left the house as immaculate as he'd found it less than three months later without asking for a coin of rent returned. All very advantageous for me, of course. But most odd."

Esther exchanged a look with Samuel. If her father had already paid for his rent, it was unlikely he'd left for financial reasons. At least she could cease wondering if she'd played a part in sending him to the workhouse.

"Did he have family? Staff?" Samuel inquired.

"Oh, let me see." Mr. Brumly briefly tipped his head back in thought. "He had a housekeeper. Mrs. Fowler. And there was a young woman named Lydia. She was..." He gave Samuel a knowing, amused look. "A maid, I'm sure."

Esther took that to mean Lydia had likely been her father's mistress. "Anyone else?"

"There was a young lad about." He shot another look at Samuel. "Possibly related to the aforementioned maid. I don't recall his name. And there were two other young women employed as day maids. Their names also escape me, I'm afraid."

"Do you know where we might find any of these individuals?" Samuel inquired.

"I'm sorry." Mr. Brumly shook his head. "Mrs. Fowler went to work for another family of my acquaintance after Mr. Smith's departure and passed on not long after. God rest her soul. She was the only individual from that household with whom I had any contact after Mr. Smith's departure. Aside from Mr. Smith, I met the other residents only once or twice in passing."

"Might you have any sense of where Mr. Smith was headed after he left?" Esther asked.

"None at all. I had nothing from him but a hand-delivered letter encouraging me to let the house to someone else at my earliest convenience."

Samuel leaned forward in interest. "Do you recall who delivered it?"

"A young lad I'd not seen before or since."

"Do you still have the letter?"

Mr. Brumly adjusted his spectacles, his lips turned down in thought. "I suspect my man filed it away somewhere. I'll have him dig it out and send it to your office if you think it might be of use in your search."

"Thank you," Samuel replied, getting to his feet. "We're grateful for your assistance."

"I'm only sorry I could not be of more help."

Esther wasn't sorry. She returned to the carriage in a light mood despite their lack of progress. They may not have been any closer to finding her father, but the visit had been far from fruitless. Her fear that her actions eleven years ago had caused irreparable harm had been laid to rest, and the letter her father had delivered to Mr. Brumly might yet prove useful.

She could no longer ignore the possibility, however, that it might take longer to find her father than she had planned. The time to leave London was drawing ever closer. Her meeting at Paddington station was only three days away. Whether or not she found her father and discovered the identity of the mystery man, she would need to return to Derbyshire before Lottie and Renderwell returned.

The thought brought on a new worry. If necessary, she could continue her search for George Smith from Derbyshire. She could hire Samuel in earnest, or Gabriel, or some other private investigator. It wasn't ideal, but at least she would know she had first done what she could herself.

But what of the rest?

Once she left London, what would become of her relationship with Samuel? Would they remain friends? More than friends? Or would everything be set aside and forgotten the moment she left?

She didn't want to set it aside. She most certainly did not want to be forgotten.

"Will you call on me in Derbyshire?" she asked suddenly and winced at her choice of words. They sounded rather like a request to be courted. "That is... will you visit?"

He often came to see Renderwell at Greenly House, and her own cottage was nearby. That had been part of the compromise she'd made with her sister. She could have the funds to set up her own home, but she couldn't move out of reach of Renderwell's protection.

Samuel gave her a wry smile. "I'm not sure your sister and Renderwell would appreciate my attentions to you."

"Probably not." She wouldn't mind their disapproval particularly, except that much of it would stem from concern for Renderwell's sisters, some of whom were still unmarried. If she caused gossip in the village, the young ladies would suffer for it. "It is fortunate, then, that I am so often at Greenly House to visit my sister."

They both knew that statement was nothing short of a blatant request to see him again. And a request, Esther realized, was probably as bold as she got. She never would have been able to seduce him in the parlor. She felt terribly exposed and vulnerable. It would be so easy for him to hurt her now. So easy to humiliate her.

She was on the verge of making light of her statement, twisting it into an offhand comment when he leaned over and lifted her veil. "I had planned on visiting in a fortnight myself."

"Oh." She licked lips gone dry. "What a happy coincidence."

"Indeed."

Carrying on a romance under Renderwell's roof seemed far more scandalous to her, but there was nothing else for it. If she wanted to see Samuel in the future, it would have to be at Greenly House.

And she *did* want to see him again. She wanted more games of badminton, more quiet afternoons in the parlor, more stolen kisses and secret moments of passion. She wanted more of everything, for as long as she could have it.

A future without Samuel was not something she cared to imagine.

You'll have to eventually.

There was no ignoring the little voice this time. There was no getting around the fact that, someday, Samuel would want a family, a wife and children.

She remembered his visits to the Walker home years ago. He used to carry her very young brother about on his shoulders and surprise him with sweets and listen with endless patience to the boy's nearly nonsensical babbling about toys and bugs and scraped knees and elbows.

Samuel would make a wonderful father. And, no doubt, he would one day make an exemplary husband for the right woman.

She was not that woman.

Esther had no interest in taking an oath to honor and obey. The prospect of relinquishing her independence to a man, any man, did not appeal to her in the slightest. And yet, when she imagined Samuel setting her aside for someone else, a terrible sense of dread settled over her.

What would that day be like? The day Samuel Brass replaced her. Would she be ready to let him go by then? Or would she argue with him? Plead with him?

Would she try to change herself in an effort to keep him?

The old memory of pitiful desperation layered over the dread. And she thought… *No.* Never again. If and when that fateful day arose, she would face it with grace and dignity, and she would face it as herself.

⁂

The woman was incapable of sitting still in a room for more than fifteen minutes at a time. From his seat in the parlor, Samuel watched Esther inspect a candelabra on the fireplace mantel, then wander over to peek out a window into the night, then stroll over to fiddle with one of the lamps.

In a few moments, she would resume her seat in the delicate green wing chair across from him. He liked seeing her there, liked watching her frown in concentration over her book and steal furtive glances at him when she thought he wouldn't notice.

And then, fourteen and a half minutes later, she would be up again to meander about the room.

He liked that too—the gentle sway of her hips, the soft swish of her skirts, the faint hint of roses when she wandered near.

Earlier, she had wandered near enough to touch, and he'd been sorely tempted to reach out, snag her, and pull her onto his lap. But Mrs. Lanchor and Sarah had been in and out of the parlor twice in the last half hour, and while he wasn't particularly concerned about shocking his staff, he had no interest in embarrassing Esther.

So he contented himself with the simple, tortuous pleasure of having her near and wanting her closer.

He had, perhaps, been letting himself enjoy it a bit too long. There was a discussion that needed to occur, one he'd been putting off since they'd left Mr. Thornhill's house.

"Esther?"

She turned from flicking her fingers over the tassels on the drapes. "Hmm?"

"I know you don't want to hear this, but given what we've learned so far"—what little they had learned—"it appears unlikely we will find your father in the next few days."

She sighed and gave a small, resigned shrug. "Yes, I know."

"I'm sorry."

"It's all right." She wandered back to her chair again and sat down heavily. "I'd always known it was a possibility. A fairly good one, considering. But one doesn't begin a challenge with the hope and expectation of failing."

"You've not failed."

"No, I don't believe I have, either. I'm doing all that I can whilst I'm here, and I will continue to do all I can from Derbyshire if I must. I'll have failed when I give up."

It was a relief to hear her approach the dilemma so rationally, but the necessity of it bothered him. He hated the thought of her returning to Derbyshire and putting those six pounds back in her hope chest. She needed to be rid of them.

"There are still avenues left to us," he assured her. If he couldn't promise her success while she was in London, he could at least help her retain the hope of it for as long as possible. "The family who took on George Smith's old housekeeper might know what happened to the other staff. With a little more time, I might be able to track down this Lydia woman."

"I've no doubt you're capable, and I thank you in advance of your success. In the meantime, perhaps we should concentrate on the mystery man I am to meet on Wednesday."

The chill of fear darted up his spine. "You can't possibly still think to meet with this man after what happened in the park."

She shook her head. "Why should one have anything to do with the other? It wasn't the same man. Those were large, fully grown men. The boy at the station was just that, a boy."

"He was a young man."

"He wasn't one of *those* men," she countered and pointed one delicate finger at him. "You *know* he wasn't one of those men. You remember everything and everyone. If that young man had been one of *those* men, you would have recognized him."

"I am not infallible. And it was nearly dark. I make mistakes."

"Yes, you do," she agreed, her voice laced with amusement. "Telling me of your extraordinary memory, for example."

"Esther—"

"I'd wager you're regretting that just now."

"Bitterly," he grumbled and bit back an oath when her lips twitched.

He needed to take a different approach. Appealing to her sense of fear would get him nowhere. Esther wasn't fearless, exactly—only small children and idiots were truly fearless—but she did have what he considered an underdeveloped sense of caution and an overdeveloped love of adventure. The combination was dangerous.

"Tell me this," he tried. "Did you come to London to find this man?"

"Of course not, but now that he has found me, it is my responsibility to see that any threat he might pose is removed, for my family's sake."

"It is your responsibility to see the task done as quickly and efficiently as possible. Rather than wait until Wednesday, let me look for him tomorrow."

"On your own?"

"It's the wisest course of action, Esther. You know it is." He held up a hand before she could argue. "You've some past experience working with criminals, but you've no experience tracking and capturing them. I do. You have other strengths. Why not put them to use?"

"Which others?"

"You're clever, to start, and we need to organize the information we've learned thus far. We need a clear record of events and movements of all the players. Write everything down. When your mother left and when she returned. When your father lived in, then moved out of, the house on Rostrime Lane. When the grocer's burned down, when it sold, and to whom. That sort of thing. Seeing it laid out might help us make a connection we've missed."

Her eyes lit with interest. "You're the one with the fine memory. Shouldn't you do it?"

"I remember details, but I'm not the most adept at seeing patterns or connections. Which is why, when I work with Gabriel, I might construct the record, but I leave the interpretation of it to him. He's like you; his perspective is more"—he paused, searching for the right word—"creative. We could work the same way, if you like. Or you may take the entire task on yourself."

"I could see to it," she replied after a moment's consideration. "I could also *learn* to track and capture criminals, just as you did."

"You could," he agreed, and he meant it. He had an instinctual aversion to the notion of Esther chasing men down dark alleys, but there was no denying she was more than capable of learning the job. "I suspect you'd be a quick study, as you've half the necessary skills already. But you can't acquire the other half overnight."

She considered that for a long time. "No, not overnight," she finally conceded and sighed. "I don't like this sitting about whilst you go off."

"I know. I'm sorry."

She sighed again and slumped a little in her seat. "But you're right. My work with Will was criminal, not investigative. They're not the same thing."

Damn it, she looked crestfallen. That wasn't what he was after. He wanted to keep her safe, not render her miserable. "Why don't we make a deal? Give me tomorrow to look for him, and when this is all over, I'll teach you anything you want to know about being a private investigator." The offer felt rather like an encouragement for her to pursue dangerous activities, but he pushed aside the initial uneasiness it brought him. Maybe there was something to her assertion that he could stand to be a little less stodgy, particularly where she was concerned. It was just a lesson, after all. Well…it was *another* lesson. But why shouldn't Esther have all the lessons she wanted? Learn any skills she liked?

Why shouldn't he be the one to offer them? Might be a bit fun, really. "Perhaps we could start with proper interrogation techniques," he suggested.

"What's wrong with my techniques?" she asked, straightening up.

He ran his tongue over his teeth. "When we captured your brother's kidnapper last year, the first thing you did was stick a knife in his arm."

"It was his shoulder," she said primly. To his delight, a small, albeit slightly embarrassed, smile played at her lips. "And he deserved it."

"Without question, but we needed him to talk, not faint."

"Fair point."

"Give me tomorrow to look for him, Esther. Please." There was a good chance he'd need more than one day, but he'd cross that bridge if he came to it. "Do that, and I'll show you how to get information out of a man without potentially killing him."

"Look for him where? How?"

"In Spitalfields. In the usual manner."

"But you've already looked in Spitalfields in the usual manner," she pointed out. "You don't even have a name. What do you hope to accomplish by asking after a young man with fair hair and ragged clothes, twice?"

"A young man of fifteen or sixteen, five feet six inches tall, nine stone. Long face, thin nose, small scar above the left eyebrow—"

"You *do* have an eye for detail."

"I have experience looking for people who don't care to be found. Do we have a deal, Esther?"

"Very well. I suppose a day wouldn't hurt. And if you're not successful, I still know where to find him on Wednesday." She eyed him speculatively. "What else can you tell about how he looked?"

"Pointed chin, narrow jaw, high cheekbones—"

"Wait." Her eyes lit with excitement. "Wait, I have an idea. I can sketch him."

"You said you can't sketch well from memory."

"I can't sketch well from mine. But maybe I can sketch from yours. Wait right here," she repeated and leaped from her chair. "I'll fetch some paper."

Esther dashed from the room, through the library, and into the small office she'd noticed earlier. Unlike much of the rest of the house, this room suited Samuel. It was full of dark, rich colors, lovely old millwork, and comfortably oversize furniture. It was also surprisingly cluttered, with books and strange odds and ends piled haphazardly along the shelves and stacks of papers strewn across the desk. There was a light powdering of dust on some of the artwork and the fireplace mantel, leading her to wonder if the staff were not permitted in to clean.

Maybe she should have asked before coming in herself. She didn't wish to intrude on his sanctuary.

She took two steps back and stopped, feeling ridiculous. Samuel hadn't forbidden her entry to any part of the house. And she was already in the room. She might as well grab her paper before she left.

Feeling unaccountably guilty, she hurried to the desk and began quickly opening and closing drawers. Writing utensils, ledgers and bills, more odds and ends. When she reached a deep drawer on the bottom, she opened it fully expecting to find paper, but what she discovered was an enormous pile of letters.

She shut the drawer. Hard. Then she just stood there, bent over and with her hand still on the drawer handle.

Leave it alone. It is not your concern.

But she couldn't leave it alone. In that split second the drawer had been open, she'd seen too much.

Slowly, she opened the drawer again and stared, dumbfounded, at the contents.

The letters, dozens of them, were all unopened, and every one of them was from the same individual.

Mrs. Rebecca Brass.

She picked up a letter from the top of the stack and ran her thumb over the name.

Unless she was living in a Brontë novel, and Samuel had a wife hidden away somewhere, Mrs. Rebecca Brass had to be his mother. Could be an aunt, she supposed. He'd never mentioned having an aunt. He'd certainly never mentioned having an aunt who sent him letters which he kept but never opened.

"What are you doing?"

She nearly jumped out of her skin at the sound of Samuel's low voice in the doorway.

"I wasn't snooping," she said quickly. "I was looking for paper."

He jerked his chin at the other side of the desk. "Second drawer on the left."

"Oh. Right. Thank you." She looked down at the letter in her hand. There was absolutely no way to pretend it wasn't there. And, frankly, she didn't want to pretend. "Are these from your mother?" she asked, holding up the letter.

"Yes."

"You've not opened them." She looked down at the open drawer. "Any of them."

A hardness settled over his features. "No."

"Why not?"

"There is nothing she could possibly say that I care to hear."

"I don't understand." Not the sentiment, and certainly not the frighteningly icy tone of his voice. It was so unlike him.

"It isn't necessary for you to understand."

It felt necessary to her. "Do you not speak with her at all?"

"No."

"Will you tell me why not?"

His expression didn't change, but Esther could sense the battle going on inside him. He stood unnaturally stiff and still, and his gray eyes alternated between searching her face and staring at the letter in her hand with such intense hatred it was a wonder it didn't burst into flames.

At long last, he spoke and drew his finger down the scar on his face. "I told you how I acquired this."

"Yes. Your father..." A terrible thought occurred to her. "Did she help him?"

"No. And, yes. She blamed me," he said flatly. "In her considered opinion, a boy had no business interfering with a husband's right to discipline his wife. When questions were raised regarding my injury, she concocted some preposterous story about my father and me having trouble with a horse."

"And people believed her?" Her experience with horses was limited, but even she could tell the difference between a kick or bite from a horse and the wounds sustained in a beating from another human being.

"Of course not. Everyone knew what my father was. But people pretended to believe it. At her urging, I was sent to Flintwood to avoid further trouble. No doubt my father went back to drinking, and my mother went back to inventing stories to explain her injuries."

"I'm so sorry," she whispered, her heart breaking for a little boy, wounded and betrayed by those who should have loved and protected him.

He moved out of the doorway at last, crossing the room to take the letter from her hands. "I didn't hear a word from her. Not one word until news of my knighthood reached the village and the truth about my childhood began to appear in the papers. The sanctity of marriage, it seems, is no match for public humiliation. Or maybe just a son with a fortune."

"She might have seen the error of her ways." Some part of Mrs. Brass might have been aware of her terrible mistakes even as she made them. It was shocking, the appalling things a person could say and do when they were afraid.

"She betrayed me," he said, his voice giving away no emotion.

"Yes." Unforgivably, to Esther's mind. Afraid or not, one did not blame a child for the abuse suffered at the hands of his father. But she didn't know the woman. Mrs. Brass was nothing but a name to her. She was Samuel's mother. He'd loved her once. Loved her enough to stand between her and a violent man. Wasn't he at least curious about what she might have to say? "She might be sorry."

"Or she might not be. I don't care either way." He tossed the letter back with the others. "Second drawer on the left. Get the paper and let's find your young man."

He didn't wait for a reply. He just turned his back and strode away.

Esther watched him leave while a strange knot formed in the pit of her stomach. She didn't understand the cause of it. Samuel had every right to refuse contact with Mrs. Brass. He had every reason.

Why, then, did his decision to ignore his mother leave her feeling ill at ease?

She didn't mention the letters again as they worked on the sketch of the young man. Samuel remained stiff and withdrawn from her, even after they'd finished making a likeness of the mystery man and tried to replicate their success with their attackers in the park.

Troubled by his dark mood, she tried distracting him with random, irrelevant bits of conversation as they worked. Hoping he might take comfort from touch, she took every opportunity to make a physical connection—a hand on his arm, a brush of shoulders, a graze of fingertips. In an attempt to elicit a smile, she teased him when their efforts to re-create an attacker produced little more than a nondescript blob of a human face. Even Samuel's memory, wonder that it was, could not see through near darkness.

An hour later, an urgent summons arrived from another client, and as Esther watched Samuel shrug into his coat in the foyer, she couldn't help but feel as if she'd failed him. He'd not be looking so glum and distant if she hadn't gone snooping through his desk.

"May I be of help?" she asked tentatively.

"No, it's a private matter between a man, his wife, her lover, and her lover's husband." He gave a terse sigh. "This could take a while."

"Is it absolutely necessary that you go? Couldn't they all just draw lots for each other?"

He looked up quickly from straightening his neck-tie. He blinked once and then finally, *finally*, his lips curled in a smile. "I'll suggest it. Come here."

He didn't wait for her to comply. Instead, he closed the distance between them in two long strides. Slipping his big hand behind her neck, he bent his head and took her mouth in a long, lush kiss that left her deliciously weak in the knees.

"I can't believe I'm going to say this," he muttered against her lips between rough breaths. "But don't wait up for me, sweetheart."

Fourteen

Samuel didn't find the man the next day. He worked well into the night, showing the sketch Esther had created to everyone in a three-block radius of the old clothes shop on Commercial Street. The only information he was able to garner was that the young man might, or might not, be Ronald Wainsberth, or possibly Phineas Brown, or Edmund, surname unknown.

This last he'd bribed out of little Henry Causer. The boy now had possession of a small fortune, enough to move his entire family out of London and their squalid set of rooms in Peerpoint Alley.

"Edmund, sir," Henry had said. "That's all I know. It's what I heard him called."

"Where can I find him?"

"I don't know. I ain't seen him since I gave him the note."

"And his friends?"

"I don't know 'em. I seen 'em round, is all, but not in a while. There's a big one what gives me the evil eye sometimes..." The boy had demonstrated by squeezing one eye shut and bulging out the other.

"Mean as a snake, he is. I heard him call out once to the man what gave me the note."

"And you're sure he said Edmund?"

The boy had shuffled his bare feet. His gaze flicked to the money Samuel had put on his mother's table.

"There's no right or wrong answer, Henry. The money is yours provided you give me the truth as you remember it."

Henry ducked his chin and mumbled into his chest. "They were drunk, sir. Hard to hear 'em."

Which meant the boy might have mistaken any number of slurred comments for the name Edmund.

Still, it was information, and under other circumstances, Samuel would consider two and a half names an encouraging start. Under normal circumstances, he'd have time to follow up on the leads. But Esther was going to Paddington station the day after tomorrow, and short of tying her up in the hotel room, there was nothing he could do to stop her.

He was giving some real thought to tying her up as he stepped from his carriage and climbed the steps to his house.

Maybe she would be safe at the station. Maybe she wasn't afraid. But he damned well was. Things could go wrong so quickly. He'd seen it a dozen times—a simple arrest, a well-laid plan, an ordinary search, even something as benign as an interview could turn violent and deadly in a heartbeat. All it took was one mistake, one short-fused or panicked man with a gun. Then everything changed.

He couldn't stand the thought of it. Of Esther in danger or injured. Or gone.

She wasn't just important to him. Not anymore. She was *essential*. Everything about her was necessary. That captivating laughter. Her sharp tongue and clever mind. The sweet and bite and surprise. He needed all of it. All of her.

He couldn't let her go. He would find a way to convince her to let him go in her stead. Determined, he went inside, tossed his hat and coat on the side table in the foyer, and headed into the parlor.

The *empty* parlor.

He scowled into the room. Why wasn't Esther there?

There was no particular reason she should be there, he supposed. It was just…he'd been picturing her there all day. He'd imagined her reading in the delicate green chair and wandering about the room, fiddling with this and that. The image had been sitting in the back of his mind almost since he'd left the house. He'd liked it there. He liked the idea of coming home and finding Esther in his ridiculous, too-feminine parlor.

"Sarah!"

The young maid popped into the room almost immediately. "Sir?"

"Where the devil is everyone?"

"Oh, well." Sarah began ticking off the occupants of the house on her fingers. "The beast is in the garden. Mrs. Lanchor is abed with a sore head. Tom has gone to visit his ailing mum. Jeb has the day—"

"Where is Mrs. Ellison?"

"Upstairs, sir. She took an early meal and asked not to be disturbed."

"Why? Is she ill?"

Uneasy, he didn't bother waiting for a reply. He

strode from the room, took the steps two at a time, and, finding the door to Esther's bedchamber ajar, pushed it open without bothering to knock.

The room was dark but for a single lamp on the mantle and what little light filtered in from the street. Esther was leaning over a small table in front of a window. Propped up on her elbows, she held her chin in her hands as she watched guests arrive for a dinner party across the street.

She stood in the shadows, in her blue tea gown, but he could still make out the subtle movement of her hips as she swayed to the music floating in through the open window.

Immediately, all thoughts of illness, and parlors, and dangerous meetings with mysterious men disappeared like so much smoke. In their place, the most deliciously wicked images filled his mind. The loose gown, the hips, the table.

God, the things he wanted to do to her.

Without realizing what he was about, he reached behind him and closed the door.

Esther's head whipped around at the sound. "Oh, it's you. You startled me." She smiled at him, lifting her brows. "Did you find him?"

He shook his head, still mesmerized by the sight of her. The way she peered over her shoulder, her lips curved up just so…as if issuing an invitation. "What are you doing?"

His voice sounded rough and strained to his own ears.

"Your neighbors are having a soiree. Or a small ball. I suppose most of society is in the country."

"Yes, I know. Why are you watching in the dark?"

"I didn't want them to see me staring," she replied with a light shrug. "It's rude."

"It's not rude if they can't see you?"

She scrunched up her face a little, then leaned farther over the table to close the window and pull the drapes shut. "You're right."

"You didn't have to do that. You can watch if you like."

"It doesn't matter." She straightened and leaned back against the table. "I think most of the guests have arrived now. Weren't you invited?"

"I made my excuses this morning."

"You shouldn't have done that. I'm perfectly safe here with your staff and Harry."

"Goliath."

"Harry." She reached for a finger lamp on the desk and set about lighting it. "I still have work to do on that record of events you asked for. You might as well go and enjoy yourself for a few hours."

"I wouldn't enjoy myself."

"Why not? What's not to love about a ball? The music. The conversation." She sighed wistfully. "The dancing."

"The noise. The smells. The crowd. The heat."

"A small gathering wouldn't pose those difficulties. I should dearly love to attend a London ball. As a guest, not a thief," she qualified. "I should like to dance at a London ball. That's something else I've never done. I have never danced in London."

Something else she would never do, he thought. Unless... "You can't go, Esther—"

"I know." She turned the lamp to a soft glow. "I wasn't hinting that I should."

"If I may finish? You can't go. However..." He

walked to a cabinet and retrieved a large rosewood music box. He set it atop the table and wound the small brass handle. "You can still dance in London."

He held out his hand as the tinkling refrain of a waltz he couldn't hope to name floated from the old box. "May I have this dance, Miss Bales?"

"Miss Bales is a fiction," she said softly. "But I would love to dance with you, Samuel."

There wasn't sufficient room between the furniture for a proper waltz. Instead, Samuel moved chairs out of the way and turned Esther in a slow, small circle in front of the fireplace.

It occurred to Esther that they must look rather silly. Certainly, they were out of step with music that slowed with every passing minute. But it mattered not a jot. She was dancing in London with Samuel. If nothing else about her trip turned out as it should, this alone would make it all worthwhile.

She felt graceful as a swan. She was the most elegant woman at the ball, and she was dancing with the most desired man in the room. Quite literally in both cases, she thought with a smile.

"Is something amusing?"

She shook her head, amused by her own whimsy. "You don't strike me as the sort of man to purchase a music box for himself."

"It was a gift."

"From a woman?"

He pulled her closer, much closer than would be allowed on a proper dance floor. "Are you jealous?"

Not at the moment. It wasn't another woman in Samuel's arms. It was just her. "Should I be?"

"No. It was given to me by Mrs. Bethram, an elderly lady who hired me to find a lost ruby bracelet."

"Had it been stolen?"

"So she suspected." He pulled her into a subtle turn, and his arm slipped farther around her waist. "But no. She'd taken it off in the library and it had slipped beneath the settee. I found it in under an hour. Along with several earrings, a fan, two sets of gloves, and a pair of spectacles. She was forgetful with her things, and her staff was remiss in cleaning under the furniture."

Her hand slid across his broad shoulder and her fingers found the back of his collar. "Do your clients often pay you in music boxes?"

"She sent it as a gift after I refused payment."

Of course he had refused payment. She smiled at him, and the dance took on a dreamlike quality, like that first kiss before everything had gone astray. There was only Samuel, leading her through the moves, his arms wrapped tight around her, his scent tickling her nose.

They swayed and turned and drew ever closer. They danced even as the box wound down, the tempo slowing, slowing…

When the music stopped, Samuel only pulled her closer and bent his head to whisper in her ear. "If we were at a proper ball, I would have to return you to your chaperone."

"I'm too old for a chaperone. And we're not at a proper ball."

"No, we are not." His lips brushed against her jaw. "There are benefits to dancing in the dark, you know."

The tingle of anticipation danced over her skin. "What sort of—?"

Before she could finish, his mouth found hers in the semidarkness.

There was the stillness again, that singular moment before the knife left the hand. She expected it to slip away, but it only intensified as Samuel gently coaxed her lips apart under his own.

The slide of his tongue against hers sent a delicious wave of longing coursing through her blood. He broke away to drag his mouth down her neck in scorching kisses that wrenched a breathless moan from her lips.

She could feel his hands moving over her, molding her hips, brushing her breasts. Heat gathered in her belly, then spread out through every nerve. She felt flushed to the tips of her toes. He ran his palms up her back, bringing her closer still, until their bodies were pressed together, hardness against softness. The stillness shifted, giving way to a thrilling impatience that had her shoving aside the lapels of his coat. There was still too much space between them. She'd waited so long to discover what lay beyond his wicked intent. She'd waited so long for *him*.

She wanted to be closer.

Samuel pulled back a little, his chest rising and falling hard beneath her hands. "Esther—"

Before he could say another word, she went up on her toes, gently clasped his face, and kissed him for all she was worth.

She was rewarded with a deep, masculine groan. His hands fisted into the fabric at the back of her gown

a second before his mouth tore away from hers again. "I don't mean to push—"

"I do." She meant to push for more of him, for all of him. For everything she wanted for as long as she could have it. "Don't stop."

Bending closer, he moved his lips along her cheek. She could feel him smiling. "Is that an order, Esther?"

"Yes." Absolutely, yes. "And for once, Samuel..." She turned her head, leaning into him. "Do as you're told."

His breath broke against her skin in a choppy laugh. The sound created an extraordinary sensation inside of her, a heady mix of power, humor, affection, and terrible need.

She nearly sighed with relief when his fingers moved to the buttons of her gown. He wasn't stopping. She could have what she wanted.

The taffeta loosened at the shoulders, then the waist, then finally slid away to pool out at her feet.

She followed his lead, divesting him of his coat, tie, and waistcoat.

Apprehension warred briefly with desire when he removed his shirt. Even clothed, Samuel's size could be intimidating. Now she saw the raw masculine power that lay beneath the veneer of his gentleman's wardrobe—the muscled torso, the hard planes of his abdomen, the broad expanse of his shoulders.

And the terrible scars. Her fingers found the injuries, tracing the jagged lines, lingering at the damaged skin at his shoulder where he'd taken a bullet protecting her family.

He stood still under her ministrations, and her

momentary flicker of unease was forgotten. Samuel might be clumsy with words and overbearing with his high-handed orders, but his touch was gentle and sure. He was always careful.

Emboldened, she pressed her lips to the healed wound at his shoulder. His powerful body shuddered a second before he slipped his hand around the nape of her neck and pulled her into a kiss that left them both breathless.

This is what Samuel had wanted, what he'd been waiting to offer Esther. Moonlight and dancing, soft words and romance.

Releasing her mouth, he began stripping away the remainder of her clothes, stopping to taste and touch each newly exposed inch of skin. She was soft everywhere—the slope of her shoulder, the hollow of her neck, the gentle swell of her breasts. He reveled in the feel of her against his hands and tongue, and in the delicate scent of roses, in her every gasp and shiver.

He helped her undress him, and soon only the flickering glow of lamplight played over their skin. Lifting her into his arms, he carried her across the room, but he hesitated at the edge of the bed, reluctant to break contact as she pressed soft, fleeting kisses along his neck and torso.

Then she stretched up and nibbled at his ear.

Every muscle in his body went taut with need. "God, Esther."

He had her arranged under him on the bed before she took her next breath. For a moment, he simply closed his eyes and savored the stunning pleasure of feeling Esther's soft naked form pressed fully against his own.

Her arms came up to encircle him, and her fingers danced lightly at the base of his spine.

Suddenly, the need to touch, to move became undeniable. He gave in, exploring the curves and planes of her body without hurry or direction, running his hands up the tight muscles of her calves, the sensitive skin behind her knee, the inside of her thighs.

His gaze tracked down to where his big hand was splayed over her fragile rib cage. It was hard and calloused. The tanned and scarred skin stood out in stark contrast against her pale, smooth skin. Was he holding her too tightly, being too rough?

He'd always been mindful of his size, of how easily his strength could bruise or break. But the need to take care had never felt more important than it did now.

Murmuring to her softly, he eased his grip and lowered his head to her breasts. He kissed one tempting peak as his hand wandered lower to tease the soft curls between her legs. He hid a smile against her damp skin when she instinctively squeezed her legs shut.

"Let me." He flicked his tongue over the taut nipple at his mouth, then gently sucked it between his teeth before releasing her. "Let me, sweetheart."

She relaxed against him with a tremulous sigh, and he slipped a finger inside the soft heat of her, exploring the new territory with a patience designed to torment them both. He withdrew and pressed again, and her hips lifted beneath him in subtle encouragement.

"Sweet," he crooned, adding a second finger. So sweet, his Esther.

She arched again, stronger this time, and her fingernails dug into his back. The bite was every bit as welcome as the sweet.

He set a gentle rhythm, sinking in and retreating, and lifted his head to watch the signs of passion play across her lovely face. Her eyes were closed, her brow furrowed in concentration, long blond lashes fanned out above her flushed cheeks. Breathy sighs broke into long moans as he increased the tempo and his thumb moved to rub the sensitive nub above his fingers. She cried out in wonder, and he did it again, and again, until she was bucking and twisting beneath him, her hands clutching at his back convulsively.

Leaning down, he whispered in her ear. "Let go, Esther."

"I can't… I don't…"

"You can."

She came apart in his arms, her entire body going impossibly tense before she sagged against him with a long, ragged exhale.

He rose above her then, shaking with the effort to be gentle. Coaxing her knees up to his hips, he pressed into her, swallowing her gasp with his mouth. He whispered her name, trailed kisses along her neck, and moved in careful, shallow strokes. Slowly, relentlessly, he courted her into accepting the full length of him.

And then he waited, petting and stroking, until she softened beneath him, the tension draining from her limbs.

Gaze fixed on her face, he withdrew and sank back in slowly, carefully gauging her reaction. When he saw no pain, only pleasure, he shut his eyes and let instinct take over.

Little by little, his control slipped away, until there was nothing left but the driving need to please her and find his own release.

Dimly, he was aware of whispering in her ear as he thrust into her welcoming heat, broken, rasping words he'd never offered another woman—promises, praise, demands.

He listened to her breathing quicken, her moans growing louder and higher in pitch. He gritted his teeth against the sharp pleasure of hearing his name spill from her lips as she tightened around him a second time. He wanted to hear it again, needed to feel it again, but he was too close to the edge. There was no turning back.

At the last second, he forced himself to withdraw and spend his passion on the white cotton sheets. The strength of his release left him shuddering for long moments after. Small tremors raced through his muscles even as he gathered Esther into his arms and tucked her head under his chin.

His last coherent thought before sleep overtook him was that she was his now, and he was hers.

And he wasn't letting her go.

She was having an affair.

Esther smiled to herself and lightly ran her hand up Samuel's bare chest as he slept. His heart beat strong and steady beneath her ear.

She hadn't known it would be like this. She'd never

imagined it could be like this. Years ago, Will Walker had paid a courtesan to explain the sexual act to Lottie in detail. Lottie had then passed the information on to Esther. Being eleven and eight years of age, respectively, the sisters had privately agreed that adults were quite vile. No one in their right mind would want to engage in such dreadful activity.

Time and age may have tempered Esther's opinion on the matter, but she had still only expected the act to be…pleasantly exciting. Nothing more and nothing less.

She'd been undone. And, she could admit, a little overwhelmed. Perhaps even a bit frightened. Such intimacy demanded an inordinate amount of trust. More than she had expected, and far more than she would have imagined herself capable of offering.

She tipped her head up to study Samuel's profile, and a warm sense of contentment filled her. She'd trusted Samuel because she could. He was so honorable. So clever and brave and kind. He was everything a woman could possibly want.

A fairy-tale prince. A knight in shining armor.

At the thought, her sense of contentment reshaped into a heavy, uncomfortable weight in her chest. Suddenly, she felt a bit like a thief, as if she'd taken something she hadn't fully earned. Something she didn't deserve and would never be able to keep. She tried to shove the feeling aside, determined not to ruin such a perfect moment. But in the still, silent night, the old doubts and fears returned unchecked.

She saw her mother, abandoning her family at every opportunity, only to return when she had nothing better to do and nowhere else to go. She remembered her father, spending time with her simply because the daughter he loved wasn't available. She thought of every young man she'd ever flirted with in her old village and how they had walked away without a backward glance once she stopped flattering their vanity with coy smiles and pretty words.

She imagined Samuel with his future wife, that well-bred, well-behaved lady who would gladly sit at home with her needlework while Samuel went off to work. For some reason, Esther pictured the lady with dark hair curled into ringlets about a pretty, wholesome face. She'd be patient and soft spoken. Naturally, she'd be obedient. And when Samuel returned at the end of the day, she'd smile at him demurely from her seat in the lovely green chair Esther thought of as her own.

Esther was second-best. She was filler, a stand-in until something better came along, or came back. She wasn't good enough to keep. She wasn't worth fighting for. And whatever approval and acceptance she might garner were undeserved, and temporary.

She could and would be replaced at the earliest opportunity.

Cold from the inside out, she shifted closer to Samuel. He grumbled something in his sleep, turned over on his side, and wrapped both arms and one leg around her, dragging her to his chest.

The warmth and scent of him enveloped her, chasing away the chill and fear.

With a sigh, she closed her eyes. This was different. Samuel was different. He wasn't her father, or mother, or a silly young lad who needed his vanity stroked.

He was his own man. And that man liked her. Not

someone she was pretending to be, not a fictional woman created to hide a secret past. He liked *her.* The former criminal. The knife thrower. The woman who argued with him and irritated him, laughed and danced with him. The woman who hadn't the foggiest notion how to stitch a sampler and wouldn't be content to wait at home with needle and thread even if she did.

He liked her just as she was.

Feeling better, she worked her arm under his so she could clasp his back and hold him close.

Devil take his would-be future bride. The useless ninny couldn't have him.

Earned or not, deserved or not, Samuel was hers. And she was keeping him.

Esther was not a morning person. Samuel had thought that might be the case, but his suspicions were confirmed when he rose just before dawn and tried to rouse her with a kiss before he left. Half awake, she batted him away like a sleepy, ill-tempered kitten.

Laughter rumbled in his chest. He caught her hands in his own and kissed her softly until her eyes fluttered open. She offered a drowsy smile, mumbled something incoherent, and tugged one of her hands free so she could brush her fingertips along his jaw. Then she fell right back asleep.

Four hours later, Samuel was still fighting back a grin at the memory as he climbed the front steps to his house. He'd managed to keep the smile in check while he'd gone about his business in town, but he gave up the fight the moment he stepped inside and found Esther waiting for him in the parlor.

There she was, sitting in that ridiculous green chair. God she was beautiful. Even in her severe black widow's weeds, she was perfect.

She glanced up from the book in her hands and blushed as their eyes met from across the room. Ah, he liked that. He could get used to watching Esther color at the memory of a night spent in his arms.

"Good morning, Esther." He could get used to saying that.

The blush faded, and she twisted her lips in mild irritation. "You went out without me. Again."

"You were sleeping."

"I've been up for over an hour," she replied, rising. "And now—"

"And now I'm back," he cut in and held up the hatbox he'd carried in from the carriage. "With this."

"Another present?" She softened a little. "That wasn't necessary."

A new and unwelcome thought occurred to him. "I intended to purchase this yesterday. I want you to know that. It's not because we..." He motioned in the general direction of the stairs. "It's not for... That is..."

Laughing, she rose from her chair. "Duly noted."

Relieved she'd not mistaken the purpose of his gift, he closed the distance between them and handed her the box. "Strictly speaking, it's not an appropriate item for a gentleman to gift a lady."

"I won't tell if you won't." After a brief inspection of the box, she untied the twine and lifted the lid. She pulled out a small green bonnet he'd purchased at the shop down the street from where Esther had found the badminton set. "Oh, it's lovely."

He thought it a bit dark for her coloring, but what did he know of fashion?

"Green with velvet ribbons. That is what you said?" He hated to think he'd made yet another error after the debacle with the rope. "It's the right one?"

"It is. You remembered." She laughed a little at her comment. "You always remember. Oh, it's perfect. Isn't it perfect? It was made for her, really."

"...I beg your pardon?"

She turned the bonnet in her hands to study the back. "Lottie's hair is so silky, it slips out of its pins and the perch hats that are so fashionable, but see how this one comes down a bit farther in the back? It won't give her nearly as much trouble. And the color will flatter her tremendously. I wish I could wear this shade of green."

Lottie. The damned bonnet was for Esther's sister. "I see."

"Pity I can't give it to her straightaway. But I don't want her to think I'm trying to bribe her for forgiveness. I want her to enjoy... Where are you going?"

He was headed for the door. "Shopping."

"Whatever for? Samuel, stop." She chased after him and pulled on his arm. "I want to go to speak to the family who employed my father's old housekeeper. I know it's unlikely they can help, but—"

They both came to an abrupt stop as a high-pitched scream rent the air.

Samuel recognized it as Sarah's, coming from the direction of the kitchen.

He spun on his heel, even as he pushed Esther toward the parlor. "Stay in there. Lock the doors."

She didn't of course—she followed his dash through the house and down the stairs. He shoved her behind him as they entered the kitchen.

Sarah stood in front of an open door that led to a shallow set of steps into the garden. She held a pair of boots in one hand and struggled to keep hold of the beast's collar with the other.

"Sarah? What is it?" Samuel demanded. "Are you hurt?"

"No, sir. I'm sorry, sir. I didn't mean to make such a fuss. Startled, that's all." Her cheeks bloomed pink with embarrassment. "I was going outside to clean me boots and..." She jerked her chin at the doorstep. "Just a dead rat, sir."

As Sarah backed away from the door with the dog, Samuel and Esther stepped closer to investigate the admittedly rather large, but definitely very dead, rodent.

Samuel glanced over his shoulder. "You screamed because of a dead rat?" The girl was a Londoner. This couldn't possibly be the first one she'd come across.

She wrinkled her nose in distaste. "I stepped on it a bit. In me bare feet."

Next to him, Esther gave a little shudder. "Ew."

"Aye, mum."

Samuel sighed at the dead rodent, then took a small step back as the stench of death hit him. "The beast's doing, I presume?"

"I imagine so, sir. Third one in as many days. I don't know where he's finding them."

Esther leaned a little closer, then reared back and

threw her hand over her mouth and nose. "Good Lord," she said through her fingers. "That rat has been dead for a while."

Sarah nodded in agreement. "I think he hides them for a bit first. Then leaves 'em by the kitchen door for me to find." She slanted the dog a look. "You're worse'n me grannie's cat, you are."

The beast thumped his massive tail against the floor.

Ignoring the stench, Samuel studied the dead animal. No bite marks were discernible. The beast must have simply grabbed hold once and snapped its neck with a good shake. It made sense that the dog was the culprit, and yet...

He stepped over the rat and looked up into the garden. He'd never had problems with rats before. There'd never been any sign of them in the garden. And the signs would not have gone unnoticed in such a small space.

It was possible that a few rodents had begun working their way in from the alleyway behind the house. The garden was walled, but there was a small wooden gate in the corner. They could be digging their way under it.

It was possible. But the explanation felt wrong somehow. He preferred logic over gut feelings, but he wasn't one to discount instinct out of hand. It had served him well a time or two in the past.

"Stay here," he ordered Sarah and Esther.

He turned the problem over in his mind while he disposed of the rat himself. He considered all the possibilities, all the variables, and the nagging instinct that something was off.

By the time he returned to the kitchen, he'd made up his mind.

"You'll stay inside whilst I'm out," he told the women. "All of you. Everyone in the house. The beast can be put out in the garden when necessary, but I want you to keep an eye on him from the windows upstairs. Keep the doors locked at all times."

His orders issued, he strode from the room.

He wasn't particularly surprised when Esther followed him, demanding an explanation. He was a little surprised Sarah followed suit.

"Sir? I don't understand."

"It's only a rat, Samuel. Where are you going?"

He flicked a glance over his shoulder. "I said stay inside."

The two women began talking at once, trailing him through the house. "But the beast needs his walk," Sarah insisted, "and Mrs. Lanchor needs flour and eggs—"

"I stayed inside yesterday," Esther reminded him. "If you think for one moment—"

"—and I promised Mary she could come to the market with me. And Tom—"

"—that I'll sit about twiddling my thumbs for another, you are woefully—"

"—wants to bring a basket to his mum."

"—*woefully* mistaken."

He stopped in the foyer, turned, and gave each of them a look designed to quell the struggles of violent, uncooperative criminals.

"Inside," he bit off. "All of you. Until I return. Am I understood?"

Sarah snapped her mouth shut, then opened it again for a very quick, "Yes, sir."

Esther planted her hands on her hips. "Not the least bit."

He counted to five for patience. "Sarah, inform Mrs. Lanchor of my instructions."

"Yes, sir. Right away, sir." Eyes wide, she bobbed a quick curtsey and dashed away.

Esther watched her go, then gave him a withering look. "Was it absolutely necessary to scare the girl?"

"To keep her safe? Yes."

She dropped her hands, blond brows drawing together. "I don't understand. It's a rat."

"It's three rats in three days."

"You have a dog—"

"I've had a dog for nearly three weeks. And he only now begins hunting rodents and leaving them on the doorstep?"

He saw the first flash of misgiving cross her features. "It must be a new habit."

"One he adopted just days after you're recognized in Spitalfields and after we were attacked in the park?"

"You think someone left them there?"

"I'll not take chances." Stepping close, he cupped her face in his hands. "Not with you." He leaned down and gave her a soft kiss. "Stay inside, Esther. Promise me."

"Where are you going?"

"To check on a few things."

"I'll come with you."

"You can't. I need to speak with Inspector Jeffries." There weren't many in Scotland Yard who knew the

Walker children even existed. But most of those who did believed the family had left the country nine years ago. "You know he can't see you. Besides, I need you to look after the staff. Where are your daggers?"

She looked a little surprised at the question. "You want me to protect your staff?"

"If it comes to it, yes." And he expected his staff to watch over her in return. As long as they all stayed inside and stayed together, however, the danger would remain limited. "Do you have them on you?"

"Yes, but it's just the one, remember?"

One wasn't good enough. Twelve wouldn't be good enough as far as he was concerned. "Do you know how to shoot?" He waited for her nod. "Then have Mrs. Lanchor show you where the rifles are kept. Make certain she passes them out to the footmen as well."

Her eyes went wide. "Do you want us to march about your house like soldiers on patrol?"

"No, just stay alert." He had fine servants, but he'd wager Esther would spot someone tampering with a door or window before any of them. "I'll be back as quickly as I can."

"You know this is likely for nothing." She pointed in the general direction of the kitchen. "Harry killed that rat."

"Goliath," he corrected and felt a bit of anxiety slip away when her lips twitched. "And you're right. It is likely nothing. Humor me, anyway. Keep your eyes open and your dagger ready. And promise you'll stay inside until I return."

She pressed her lips together in obvious annoyance. "Oh, very well. I promise."

Fifteen

"What do you want with my boy?" Mr. Phineas Brown squinted at Samuel over the rim of his mug. Though the tavern light was dim, and the air hazy with smoke, Samuel could see the man's eyes were both brimming with hatred and glazed with copious amounts of ale.

Standing next to the table, Samuel took care to keep his voice calm and even. "I just want to ask him a few questions."

Mr. Brown slammed his tankard on the table. "One mistake. The boy made one mistake and he paid the price. Now any nob in London turns up without his purse, and you bastards come looking for him. You won't give him a moment's peace." His fingers tightened on the mug until his knuckles turned white. "Rabid dogs, that's what you are. Someone ought to put the lot of you down."

Though Mr. Brown was clearly hoping to be that someone, Samuel wasn't particularly worried about him. The man was too drunk to pose a threat.

The men sharing his table, however, were another matter. Those two seemed sober enough.

A tall, reedy man with thick muttonchop sideburns looked to the ceiling with a resigned sigh. Samuel guessed this wasn't the first time Mr. Brown had over-indulged and caused a scene. The stout man sitting next to him didn't seem surprised either, but he did look pleased. His fat lips were curled in a grim smile. He was every bit as eager for a fight as Mr. Brown.

Samuel was a little tempted to oblige the both of them. It had taken him the entire day and nearly four pounds in bribes to track down the Brown family.

Quickly as I can had turned into *possibly before the end of the night.*

That hadn't been his aim. He'd met with Jeffries to discuss the attack in the park, and to learn if there had been any recent reports of pranks involving rats in Belgravia or the surrounding neighborhoods. Jeffries had been unable to help with either matter. But he did have the name of a new informant in Whitechapel who might know something about the Phineas Brown Samuel had been asking after. That informant had pointed Samuel in the direction of another man in another dangerous area of the city. And *that* man had sent Samuel off in search of yet another man. On and on it had gone, until Samuel had finally learned that Phineas Brown could be found at the White Loom Tavern every evening.

It had taken Samuel all damned day to learn the young man's whereabouts, but when he'd asked one of the barmaids for the boy, he'd been pointed in the direction of Mr. Phineas Brown, the elder.

He was running out of time and patience. A good brawl might be just what he needed to dull his mounting frustration. But he didn't like the look of the eager friend. One armed man with a fuse, he thought. That's all it took.

"I'm not the police," he said, subtly shifting to widen his stance. "I just want to know where your son was last Wednesday evening."

"If you ain't police, then I don't have to talk to you, do I?" Mr. Brown shoved back his chair and took a few stumbling steps forward. "Bugger you."

The tall man swiped a grab for his drunk friend, but missed. "Don't be an idiot, Phineas. Sit down."

Samuel held up a hand. "I only want a word, Mr. Brown. There's no need—"

"I gave you two words." He retracted his arm, then swung out in a loose, drunken arc. "*Bugger you.*"

Samuel took a step back, letting Mr. Brown's fist fly harmlessly by. He caught the back of the man's arm as it sailed past and gave it a quick yank to the side. Under normal circumstances, the tug would do little but send a man stumbling a couple of feet, but the drunken Mr. Brown stumbled four, then tripped, then caught the edge of a chair and crashed to the ground.

Damn it.

The tall man with the muttonchops set down his ale and pushed back from the table with another beleaguered sigh. "Hell. Now you've done it."

Indeed he had.

The eager friend launched himself from his chair with a wild cry and swung his mug at Samuel's head. Samuel blocked the blow, threw an elbow into the man's nose, then grabbed him by the shirtfront and tossed him onto the table.

The tall man used the moment of distraction to charge, but Samuel was faster, and he had a longer reach. He swung once, but not nearly as hard as he might. The man was only defending his friends, and reluctantly at that. Still, the blow was sufficient to knock the man to the ground, where he had the good sense to remain.

His eager friend was not as prudent. He pushed off from the table and rushed again, ramming a shoulder into Samuel's chest in an attempt to shove him off-balance. When Samuel didn't budge, he leaped back and tried again. Then again. Then finally he put his head down, let out a roar of anger, and charged like a bull. He caught Samuel around the waist, but he lacked both the momentum and the weight to make an impact.

Samuel stood his ground.

It would have been easy for him to bring his knee up into the man's gut, but he didn't have the heart for it. These men weren't thugs or fighters by trade.

They were just idiots.

Besides, what satisfaction he lost in forgoing a proper fight, he gained in seeing his attacker finally give up and jump back to goggle at Samuel with baffled fury. "You're a bloody mountain."

Samuel shrugged. "Maybe you'd like to take a run-up." He flexed his fist and gave the man a second to imagine the damage it could do to a man running toward it full-tilt. "Or maybe you'd like to take your seat."

The man ran the back of his hand under his bleeding nose. He studied the blood on his fingers a moment, then studied Samuel's fist. He took his seat.

Several feet away, Mr. Brown was still struggling to regain his feet. Samuel grabbed him by the back of his collar and shoved him into an empty chair.

"Where is your boy?"

"I ain't tell—"

A third voice chimed in. "Leave him alone."

Samuel looked over his shoulder and studied the young newcomer standing in the open door to the kitchen. Blond hair, slight of build, narrow face. "Are you Phineas Brown?"

The boy tipped his chin up even as he nervously wiped his hands over his apron. "I am."

Son of a bitch. He was the wrong man. "You're not who I'm looking for." Releasing Mr. Brown, he pulled out the sketch Esther had made and held it up. "Do you recognize this man?"

Phineas crossed the room cautiously, then frowned at the sketch. "Looks a bit like me."

"It's not you." He shoved the sketch back in his pocket, then shoved Mr. Brown back into his chair before he toppled to the floor. "Get your father home. Put him to bed."

Without waiting for a reply, he turned and strode for the door.

Outside, he cleared the smoke and sour scent of spilled ale from his lungs with the marginally cleaner air of Whitechapel.

Bloody hell, he'd *needed* Phineas Brown to be the right man.

Esther was set on going to Paddington station tomorrow. Only an early capture of the mystery man would put the idea out of her head. There was still a chance Samuel might find the right man in the few hours he'd have to search tomorrow, but he wasn't counting on it.

That left him with only two possible plans of action. Persuasion or force.

He absently slipped his hand into his pocket to touch the jeweler's box he'd picked up between his visits to Scotland Yard and Whitechapel.

He'd try persuasion first.

Plan in place, he returned to his town house and was greeted by Esther almost immediately upon his entrance.

"Where the devil have you been?" she demanded.

This was, perhaps, not the homecoming he'd hoped for, but it wasn't far from what he'd expected.

At least he'd found her waiting in the parlor, sitting in her little green chair, quite like he'd envisioned. The scowl marring her pretty features, however, was not from his daydreams.

He removed his gloves as he stepped into the room. "I "

"Quickly as you can? Twelve hours is *quickly as you can*?"

Technically, yes. He'd finished the job and returned as quickly as he could. Noting this, however, was probably not the wisest course of action. "I was delayed."

"Were you *really*?" she marveled. "I vow, I had not noticed."

"Esther—"

"Where did you go?" she snapped.

"I spent the day chasing down informants," he replied and crossed the room to his own seat.

"I could have helped."

"No, not with this." He held up a hand. "I swear, Esther, not with this. The men I met with today would have refused to speak a word in your presence. You would have spent the day sitting in the carriage." In bloody Whitechapel. "The night ended in a tavern brawl." He lifted a brow. "How well can you aim your blades with your veil down?"

"Quite well. I practiced," she replied, but her voice now lacked the sharpest edge of anger. She leaned toward him. "Were you injured?"

"No." And since the possibility of bodily harm seemed to soften her, he was a little sorry now that he'd blocked every blow. "Shoved about a bit." Or very nearly.

Her eyes tracked from his head to his feet, taking careful inventory. Apparently satisfied he wasn't bleeding anywhere, she sat back again with a huff. "I did not come to London to sit in your carriage or guard your parlor. I'll accept that I could not have accompanied you today, but you shouldn't have made me promise to stay here until you returned unless you were certain you would be back at a reasonable hour." She gestured at the front door. "I could have been out searching on my own. I've wasted another day."

"It wasn't wasted. You were needed here. But if the lost time bothers you, stay an extra day to make up for it."

Once the immediate danger to her was eliminated, there was no reason she couldn't spend an additional day, or even two, in London. Hell, she could stay another week, now that he thought about it. Renderwell and her sister wouldn't be back for another fortnight.

She looked genuinely surprised by his comment. "That's not a suggestion I expected from you."

"Why not?" Pleased with this new idea, he rose from his chair and took her hands to draw her to her feet. "I'm not exactly eager to be rid of you."

"Neither were you eager to find me here in the first place."

"That was before," he said and slipped his arms around her waist and breathed in the clean scent of her.

She didn't return the embrace. Instead, she placed the palms of her hands against his chest and tilted her head at him, her gaze speculative. "Before you liked me?"

"No." He dipped his head for a quick kiss. She tasted like tea liberally sweetened, and for one fleeting second, he considered putting off the discussion about Paddington station until tomorrow. "Before you liked me."

Before he'd realized he didn't want to spend a day without her. Before he'd realized he would do whatever it took to make her happy.

Before he realized he would do whatever it took to keep her *safe*.

Her mouth curved in begrudging amusement. "Were you looking for the young man from the station? Or the mysterious gifter of dead rodents?"

"I suspect they are one and the same."

She relaxed a little in his hold but still wouldn't put her arms around him. "If he knows I am here, then why would he bother meeting me at the station?"

"Because he imagines you'll be alone." Only she wasn't going to be alone. With any luck, she wasn't going to be there at all. "Esther..." He released her reluctantly and produced a small box from his pocket. To cover a sudden and inexplicable case of nerves, he shoved it at her with less finesse than he intended. "Here."

Esther accepted it but looked somewhat less excited than she had with the other gifts.

Still angry, he thought. And she was only going to get angrier.

Lifting the velvet lid, she revealed the sapphire pendant necklace he'd purchased between his visits to Scotland Yard and Whitechapel.

She ran her finger over the deep blue gem and finely wrought gold chain. "It's beautiful, Samuel. It is. But you could have just said you were sorry."

He hadn't really thought of it as an apology. "To be honest, I was hoping it might put you in an agreeable frame of mind."

"And why do you need me to be agreeable?" she inquired, slipping the necklace from its box and lifting it to her neck.

Anything to keep her safe, he reminded himself. "Esther, I'm sorry. You *cannot* go to Paddington station tomorrow."

Esther paused briefly with her hands behind her neck, then lowered her arms, the necklace still in her fingers. When she'd accepted it, she'd also accepted the fact that it was part of an apology. It wasn't the sort of apology she wanted. It certainly didn't make up for having been left to wait all day, but she'd been willing to consider the necklace as a kind of peace offering.

But now… It didn't feel like a gift. It felt like manipulation. She carefully laid the necklace back in its velvet lined box. "That is not your decision to make."

He scowled at the box as she set it aside on the chair. "What are you doing?"

"I am declining the necklace, thank you."

"Why?"

"Because you bought it to ensure my cooperation," she replied calmly, "and I am not going to cooperate. You shouldn't have to pay for something you'll not receive. You… No, I'll not take it," she insisted when he retrieved the box and tried to hand it to her again.

"It's not a bribe." He took her hand and pressed the box into her palm. "I bought it because it suits you, and I hoped it might please you."

"You thought to gain my compliance." She put the gift right back on the chair. "I am not a twit to be distracted with a pretty bauble, Samuel."

"I don't think you're…" He scowled at the box again, then dismissed it with an impatient gesture of his hand. "Fine. Don't accept the necklace, if it displeases you. It changes nothing. I know you want to outwit the man at the station, Esther. God knows, you're capable of it, but I am asking you to let me do it. I have the experience, the training—"

"This isn't a matter of tracking and capturing someone," she cut in. "All I want is to meet with him."

"Meet with a potentially dangerous criminal."

"Well, I have some experience with that, haven't I?"

He sucked in a breath as if to argue, then snapped his mouth shut, effectively ceding the point.

"I can do this, Samuel."

"How?" he demanded. "What, exactly, do you intend to say to this man?"

She calmly brushed her hands down her skirts, determined to remain composed in the face of his mounting temper. "As I see it, I've three options. First, I could meet him as myself and ask him what he wants. If it's ten pence, or even ten pounds, he's after, I'll pay it and inform him that if he wishes to collect more in the future, he'll need to follow me out of the country to obtain it."

"And if he wants more on the spot?"

"That brings us to the second option. You apprehend him for blackmail and turn him over to the police." If the young man thought to threaten the Walkers, he could lament his error in prison. "We can tell the authorities my visit to England is temporary."

"And the third option?"

She sucked in the corner of her lip, hesitant to share an idea she knew would not impress him. "I considered pretending to be someone else. I might convince him that he is mistaken in my identity."

He looked at her like she'd spouted complete gibberish. "Why the devil would another woman agree to meet him at the station?"

"The Walker daughters can't be the only women in London with secrets to keep. I might be Mrs. Winslow, hiding from my brute of a husband and willing to pay to keep my existence in London a secret."

"And you just happen to resemble another woman he's looking for? For God's sake, no one would believe such a preposterous coincidence."

The hint of ridicule in his voice set her teeth on

edge. "He has asked for ten pence. How astute do you imagine him to be?" She planted her hands on her hips. "And don't speak to me as if I'm a fool. I know the third option is flawed. That's why it's the *third* option. And it is no less preposterous than the idea that this young man recognized me in a shop after so great a time. He can't be more than sixteen, which means he could not have been more than seven years of age the last time I was in London. How well could he possibly remember me? Do you really think a seven-year-old who caught a glimpse of me nine years ago would recognize me in the few minutes I lifted my veil?"

Clearly aggravated, Samuel dragged a hand down his face. "You think he is mistaken."

"He might very well be. But if he is not, it is because someone has described me to him or..."

"Or there is a picture of you somewhere," he finished for her.

"Father didn't allow portraits." There were no photographs of the Walker children and, to the best of her knowledge, the only sketch of her in existence was in one of her father's old journals, safely locked away in Derbyshire.

"People can sketch from memory," Samuel reminded her. "You worked with your father. People saw you."

"Yes, I know." Will had never introduced her as his daughter, but it was likely that some people guessed or suspected the truth. "If this man has a sketch of me, I need to know it. We need to find it."

"*I* can find it," Samuel pressed. "I can go to Paddington station and bring the man out. Let me—"

She cut him off with a shake of her head. "He is unlikely to show himself to you. He is expecting me."

"Then disappoint him," he snapped, his agitation all but palpable now. "It's too dangerous."

"But only for me?"

"For any number of people. Including you." He stabbed his fingers through his hair. "Damn it, *especially* you."

Especially her? Insult warred with disbelief. When she managed to speak again, it was through a jaw clenched tight with anger. "I am clever. I am quick. And I am capable of defending myself from one man in a crowded railway station." One man in broad daylight, for pity's sake. Not a bloodthirsty pack of murderers in a dark alley. "The only reason, the *only* reason, you'll not agree to my going is because I am a woman."

"That is not… We don't know there will only be one. We don't know anything about this man, what he knows, or what he has planned. And you're not just *any* woman," he bit off. "You're…important. You're…" He made a sound that was half snarl, half-frustrated groan as he clearly struggled to find the words he wanted. He swore viciously, then spun about to stalk to the window and back again. When he stood before her once more, his features were hard as stone, and his voice was lowered with barely restrained fury. "What sort of man would allow his woman to put herself in danger whilst he hides away?"

Esther took a steadying breath in an attempt to rein in her anger. It mostly failed.

Allow his woman, indeed.

"The sort of man who does not mistake his woman for his child," she replied in the coolest tone she could manage. "Allow me to be perfectly clear, Samuel, as you appear to have trouble grasping the concept. You do not *allow* me anything. I make my own choices. I choose my own actions."

"Your own mistakes."

"Those as well. And when I am in error, I will take responsibility for the consequences."

"Is that what this is about?" he demanded, throwing an arm up. "Your quest for atonement? This man isn't your father, and you cannot make up for one mistake by throwing yourself into another."

"It is not a mistake!"

He dragged his hand through his hair again and looked for a moment as if he might stalk to the window and back again as well, but he stepped closer instead, looking over her like a wrathful bear. "Do you honestly not realize how selfish you are being? Can you not trouble yourself with one thought for the people who care about what might happen to you? Who worry about you?"

It was an accusation, not a question, and it infuriated her. "Oh, you *hypocrite*. You've been a soldier and a police officer and now you are here, telling me you should go to Paddington station and meet this man alone whilst I wait here and worry. But that's not the least bit selfish, is it?"

"I was a police officer when you met me," he returned, "and I have been a private investigator for nine years. You knew what you were taking on before any of this began."

"I was Will Walker's daughter when you met me," she shot back. "You knew what you were taking on."

"I thought you were trying to be someone else, someone *other* than Will Walker's daughter. I *thought* you had left that woman behind."

That woman? She gaped at him, shocked beyond anger. Someone else? "That is not what I am trying to do." That was the exact opposite of what she was trying to do. "I *am* Will Walker's daughter. I've never claimed otherwise. Not to you."

She was Esther Walker. Not Esther Bales. Not Esther Smith. Not Mrs. Ellison. *Walker.* She had learned to pick a lock when she was six and escape a set of manacles at eight. She'd had a dagger strapped to her ankle since the age of twelve. She had accidently kidnapped a duchess at nineteen. And she had learned from Will Walker the consequences of allowing a man to bend her will to his own.

For better or for worse, she was a Walker. She could be more than the name. She could be better than what she once was. But she could not pretend to be someone *else*. Not even for Samuel.

He stared at her, looking every bit as stunned as she felt.

The silence between them stretched out for so long that the very air around her felt strained. She was on the verge of saying something, anything to break the tension so they might move past it to an understanding, but then his eyes narrowed and his mouth set in a hard line.

And she realized in that terrible moment that someone *else* was exactly who Samuel had imaged her to be.

He had never liked her just as she was. He had liked a version of her that never existed.

He wanted Miss Bales. The woman who had never degraded others to elevate herself. The woman who would meekly follow his order to wait at home.

The woman who was not *that woman.*

Disappointment, confusion, shame, and fury all washed over her so quickly, she couldn't hope to sort one out from the other. A terrible ball of pain settled in her chest, and humiliating tears pressed against the back of her eyes.

"It would seem you were mistaken in your impression," she choked out. "Excuse me."

She spun on her heel and left the room quickly, desperate to reach the privacy of her guest room before she embarrassed herself further.

Even as she rushed down the hall, a part of her hoped he would call out to her, or follow her. He would apologize. He would explain that he'd been clumsy. He hadn't meant to be insulting, to look at her as if she were a complete stranger, as if he'd never known her at all and didn't care to know her now.

He liked her just as she was. She was exactly what he wanted.

She heard nothing but the muffled thump of her heels striking the hall runner.

Samuel left the house at first light the next day and returned at two in the afternoon with a pounding head and a knot between his shoulder blades. He was close. He was so damned close. He'd marked the second name off the list of suspects. Ronald Wainsberth had set sail aboard the merchant ship *Good Tidings* ten days ago. He could not have been the man from the station.

That left only Edmund.

Samuel had a name, a detailed sketch, and a good idea of where in London to look for answers. There was even another informant he'd yet to track down—an elusive old man known as Chaunting Charlie for his eagerness to sing to the police. With a little more time, he could find them both.

He might have taken a little more time today. He'd considered searching for Edmund, surname unknown, until the last possible minute. But Samuel hadn't been able to shake the worry that Esther might try to leave for the station without him.

She'd said she wanted him to accompany her, but he couldn't be certain the contrary woman wouldn't change her mind.

I am trying to be more.

I am *Will Walker's daughter.*

Samuel had stewed over Esther's words the whole of the evening. He'd gnawed on the bitter end of their argument until his jaw had ached from grinding. In the end, he'd been forced to concede that the two statements weren't mutually exclusive. Esther could be Will's daughter, and *more* than Will's daughter. Considering the brittleness he'd seen in Esther a year ago and the more self-assured woman she was now, it was fair to say she'd succeeded in her efforts.

But she was still reckless and unpredictable. And, damn it, she was still selfish. For God's sake, she wanted him to sit at Paddington station… No, not *sit*, he corrected with growing anger…*hide*. She wanted him to *hide* at the station while she confronted a dangerous man.

How could she ask it of him? How the bloody hell could she ask him to stand aside like a coward, like a milksop, like…a useless little boy.

But hiding behind Esther at Paddington station was preferable to not being there at all. So he'd come home early just to be safe and spent the next four hours nursing cups of tea he didn't want, in a parlor that had never suited him, in a house that suddenly felt very empty. Not peaceful, mind. It was as active as ever, with the beast crashing into furniture, and Mrs. Lanchor barking out orders, and pots and pans banging about in the kitchen, and maids and footmen darting to and fro. Everything was exactly as it had been a week ago. And that was all wrong. Esther's voice was missing from the mix. Her laughter was gone. Her smile, her scent, her swish of skirts. All missing.

The house felt empty because, for all intents and purposes, Esther wasn't in it. He hadn't seen her since their argument the night before. She was holed up in her chambers like a recluse.

She might as well be back in Derbyshire. What did it matter that they were under the same roof if he couldn't speak with her, or touch her? Or bellow at her until she saw reason?

She was gone, and it ate at him.

She was a five-second walk away and he *missed* her.

He was overthinking the matter, of course. He'd gone long periods of time without seeing her in the past. Her absence hadn't troubled him then. Why should it trouble him now after only a few hours? It was ludicrous.

And yet, when she appeared at a quarter to five, a part of him settled, even as a heavy tension fell over the room.

She stood just inside the doorway and watched him through guarded eyes.

"His name is Edmund," he announced. "Probably."

"You found him?"

"Not yet. I need another day or two." Or six. However bloody long it took.

"To find one particular Edmund in all of London?" She clasped her small gloved hands at her waist. "We don't have the time."

"We can make time."

"Perhaps if you had let me help you look instead of—" She snapped her mouth shut and a furrow appeared between her brows. "I apologize. That isn't fair. I did agree to your looking alone at least some of the time."

He needed her to agree to it *now*, when it mattered most.

And he didn't want her damned apology. He wanted her to be furious so *he* could be furious. He wanted an anger so consuming it left no room for hurt or fear. And he wanted another row. A proper one with lots of shouting. Because at least then he would be *doing* something.

Instead he just sat there feeling every bit as helpless and ineffectual as he had at the age of twelve.

"I am asking you not to go to Paddington station," he said softly. "Please."

It wasn't begging. One *please* did not a grovel make. Still, he found it easier to stare out the window rather than look at her as he waited for a reply.

He heard her take a small, shallow breath. When she spoke, her voice was small and a little sad, but unmistakably resolute. "I am asking you to please come with me."

And that was that. There would be no more argument, no more discussion. If very nearly begging wouldn't convince her to stay, nothing would—short of using bodily force.

He could do that. He could pick her up, carry her upstairs, and lock her in her room until morning. God knew, he'd imagined it two dozen times over. It was the next logical plan of action. Finding the mystery man had failed. Persuasion had failed. *He* had failed. Brute force remained.

He could do it.

He wouldn't.

It wasn't just that she would hate him for it. He could live with her hate if it meant she'd be safe. He wouldn't do it because it was wrong.

Her decision to go to Paddington station was also wrong, if for no other reason than that it bloody well hurt him. But forcing her compliance through brute force would be worse.

He dug his fingers into the arms of his chair. "I'll have the carriage brought around."

It was the longest carriage ride of Esther's life.

Samuel wouldn't look at her. He'd pushed his side

of the curtains back an inch and had been staring through the small crack since they'd left the house.

Esther watched him through her veil. It didn't seem to bother him that she was staring. She wasn't even certain he noticed. His eyes never left the window. It was like she didn't exist.

Perhaps, in a way, she no longer did to him. He'd imagined her to be someone else, and now that woman was gone.

It was monstrously unfair. Why should he be angry with her, think less of her, for taking a risk he'd not think twice to take himself? Why should she feel guilty for not playing the helpless ninny simply because he asked it of her? Why should she still want him, even knowing she would never be what he wanted?

Suddenly, she found it impossible to look at him. She fixed her gaze on the wall of the carriage and spoke without thinking. "It seems we are more incompatible than we realized."

She regretted the words almost immediately. They were too final, too absolute. She sought a way to take some part of them back. "I think we could be friends. I should like to be friends."

He didn't reply. He didn't say a word to her for the whole of the trip.

It was too late. Unfair or not, Samuel wanted nothing more to do with her.

Sixteen

It would be a simple matter for Samuel to stay out of view at the station. The general offices opened directly onto platform one. He merely introduced himself to a gentleman inside and immediately gained permission to access the office.

But he hesitated on the platform, unwilling to leave Esther alone to wait.

"I will be right behind that wall," he told her. "Right on the other side of that window. If I see him make one wrong move—"

"I understand."

"It doesn't have to go that far," he pressed on. "He doesn't have to make that first move. If you want the meeting to end, if you become frightened or uncertain…hell, if you become bored, call for me."

"I will."

"Promise me."

"I promise." She gave a jerky, nervous nod. "I do. I will call."

And still he hesitated to walk away. He took her hand instead, heedless of the curious eyes of the passing travelers.

He'd never experienced such a host of incongruent emotions—anger and fear, longing and frustration. He itched to put them all into words. But the right ones eluded him. So he simply stood there, her small hand grasped in his, until the cool fabric of her glove warmed in his palm.

She stared down at their joined hands as if confused. "He'll be here soon. You have to go."

And still he hesitated.

She looked up at him then and gave her hand a little tug. "Samuel—"

"Right."

He released her hand and strode into the office, taking up position next to an open window.

Esther stood not ten feet away, but with a wall between them, it felt like miles. She was too far away from the window for him to touch, and though he might be able to sneak a look, he couldn't really watch her without being seen.

His hands clenched and unclenched at his sides. The warmth of her touch still lingered in his palm.

God, he felt bloody useless.

He told himself that this was no different than the countless times he had stood in the shadows while Renderwell and Gabriel put themselves in the line of fire. He had been nervous then, too. Just as they were when it was his turn to face danger. There was always risk, always the possibility that something could go wrong. His friends were constantly turning up with scrapes and bruises. They laughed them off, teased each other over black eyes, bite marks, and, in his case, bullet holes. It was part of the job.

Today was different. He couldn't brush off the fear. He could scarcely stop himself from marching back out the door and dragging Esther out of the station. He hadn't found the red marks around her neck the least bit amusing. The very idea of her injured, of someone laying hands on her, made his hands shake and his blood boil.

This was nothing like working with his friends.

Esther wasn't his damned friend.

The young man arrived five minutes early. Esther watched him weave his way through the crowd, her belly tight with nerves. He was dreadfully pale and gaunt, and the circles beneath his eyes were so dark they could be mistaken for bruising. He didn't look particularly threatening, she thought. But looks could be deceiving. He might be armed. He might have friends about. There was no telling.

She inclined her head in recognition when he drew near.

To her surprise, he plucked the cap off his head as if he'd just stepped into her parlor. "Miss."

She touched the bag at her waist. "I brought the ten pence."

"Right. About that... You don't happen to have a full shilling, do you?"

"I... Yes, I suppose." He was terribly polite for a blackmailer. "Why do you want a shilling from me?"

"I thought we'd ride to Bower Street station. Thing is, I ain't got the full fare. I had an extra two pence last Wednesday. I could pay my own one-way fare for third class, but I figured first class'd give us a spot of privacy. You'd have to make up the difference, if you don't mind. I ain't but six pennies today."

"You want to ride the rail?" One of the underground rails. Absolutely not.

His gaze jumped nervously at a rambunctious group of travelers. "Give us a fair bit of privacy, like I said. And I'd get off at Bower Street. You'd only have to pay for me one way. I'll pay you back when I can."

"I'm sorry. I can't ride with you."

His brows drew together in confusion. "You ain't scared of me, are you, Miss Walker? I don't mean you no harm."

"Miss Walker? I'm sorry, I don't know that name. I am Mrs. Peterson." Good Lord, she had an alias for her alias.

"Aye, the other's not a name you'd want bandied about, I suppose. Thing is, Mrs. Peterson, I thought… I thought maybe I could call you Esther, seeing as how we're in the way of being family."

"I'm sorry? Family?"

"Well, I'm Edmund," he said, as if certain that should mean something to her. The frown of confusion deepened when she didn't immediately reply. "I'm Edmund Smith. George Smith's son. I'm your brother."

"I…" For several long seconds, she was struck mute. She'd considered the possibility of half siblings before. Of course she had. She'd even wondered if she might learn of one or two once she met her father. But she'd never imagined she might meet one like this. "You… I… Could we sit down, please?"

She didn't wait for his reply. She stumbled back to

a bench directly beneath the window where Samuel was listening and sat down hard.

Then she stared at him, simply stared at him.

He was family. *Might* be family, she corrected. He claimed the connection, but could she believe him? She didn't see much of herself in him. The color of the eyes, maybe, and a similarity about the chin. But physical comparison meant little, particularly when one party was so obviously ill.

"You all right, Esther?" A faint blush crept into his pale cheeks. "That is, miss, if you prefer." He seemed to reconsider this as well. "Or missus."

"I…don't know. Yes?" Good God, why was she asking him?

"It's a shock to you, my being here, isn't it? I can see it." He ducked his head, but not before she saw a terrible sadness fill his eyes. "Didn't know about me, did you?"

She heard the tremor in his voice, and she knew in that moment that she couldn't pretend to be someone else. She couldn't possibly tell this young man she was not the sister he sought. He might be a confidence man. He might be acting the part of the lost and wounded boy for her benefit. But she couldn't risk the assumption. The cost of being wrong would be too high.

"I'm sorry, Edmund. I'm so sorry. No one told me."

"Right. Well." He sniffled a bit and shrugged the way Peter did sometimes when he didn't want anyone to know he was upset. "Not your fault, is it? Nor mine. And what's done is done, I suppose." He gave her a wobbly smile. "And now we've met properly, you and me. I knew it were you, you know. In the shop. Well, I thought as much. You look just like the picture."

"The picture?"

"'Ere." He dug in his pocket and pulled out a leaf of paper, creased down the center and yellowed by age. "See? It's a fair likeness of you."

It was an incredible likeness of her as a very young woman. "Where did you get this?"

"Da made it. He saw you now and then, when you was working with Walker. I recognized you at the old clothes shop in Spitalfields. You're a bit different. Older and such. But I knew for certain it was you when I heard you asking after mean old man Smith."

"He's mean?" Oddly, that hadn't occurred to her either. That her father might be indifferent to her, or even unhappy to see her, had both seemed reasonable expectations. She'd not considered outright meanness.

"Mean as they come, our grandda. If you've a mind t'meet him, I'd change it quick. He won't be welcoming the likes of you or me."

"Oh. Oh, our *grandfather.*"

"He won't admit to it. Being family, that is. I went to see him once at his fancy house in Bethnal Green." A meager hint of pink stained the very tips of his ears. "Kicked me out on me ear."

"I'm sorry," she murmured, feeling stunned. The fancy house in Bethnal Green. The haughty old George Smith on Apton Street. "Our father was named after him," she guessed.

Edmund nodded. "Aye, George Arnold Smith. But his mates called him Arnie. He said I weren't to seek you out either. That you was living like a real lady and didn't need me giving you trouble."

A real lady. Well, that answered the question of how much George Arnold Smith knew about the Walker family. "I'm glad you sought me out. But why the secrecy? Why did you run from me the last time?"

He shifted nervously in his seat. "You was with Brass."

"You know Sir Samuel?"

"I know who he is. Brass the Almighty. He was police."

"He's not a policeman now." She watched him twist the hat in his hands. "Are you in trouble, Edmund?"

"Might be I am a little," he mumbled, his gaze jumping around the crowded station. "I had a proper job working the docks, but I lost it seven months back. I fell in with what you might call unsavory sorts. I want to be rid of 'em, but it's not that easy."

No, it wasn't easy to walk away from that life. "Can't your father help?"

"Our da?" He gave her a curious look. "He's gone, miss."

"Gone? He…he's dead?"

"These six years. That's why he gave me the picture. He knew he was going." He rubbed the back of his neck. "I'm sorry. I thought you knew."

"No." Her voice sounded small to her own ears. All this time she'd been looking for her natural father, making plans, imagining what he might be like, what she would say to him when they met…and he was gone.

She'd never had the courage to tell Will Walker to go to the devil, and she'd lost the chance to give George Smith his six pounds. She'd waited too long for both.

"Me mum's passed, too," Edmund said quietly. "You're the only family I got."

His admission pulled her from her own sense of loss and disappointment. "There's no one else? We've no other siblings? Aunts or uncles? Distant cousins?"

"Just our grandda."

"I see. How old are you, Edmund?"

"I'll be seventeen in three weeks."

She was afraid to ask her next question. "And how long ago did your mother die?"

"Four years back."

On his own since the age of twelve. Oh, she had waited far, *far* too long. "I'm very sorry," she said quietly. Sorry for so many reasons. Feeling sick, she reached for her bag and the coins inside.

Edmund shook his head at her. "You keep what's in there to yourself. That's not why I came here. That's not why I sought you out. Wanted to meet you, was all."

Wanted or not, he'd have her help, but she set the money aside for now. "Then why the note? Why didn't you speak with me that first day in Spitalfields?"

"Right. Well. The thing is..." His expression turned sheepish. "The thing is, I might have shown your picture to a few of the lads, now and then. I didn't mean no harm by it. I was proud, was all. Pretty lady for a sister. I didn't..." He made the face again. "I thought you was out of the country."

"I'm only in London on a visit," she replied evasively.

"Might be a couple of the lads were with me when I saw you in Spitalfields."

There were a great many *might bes* in Edmund's

world. "Did they recognize me?" she asked carefully. "Did they know me, Edmund?"

"I don't know. I pretended like I didn't. And they pretended like they didn't. But then John made excuses to be off right quick, and Victor and Danny followed. That's why I sent the note instead of introducing myself proper. In case someone was watching. I think you should get out of London. Just in case. John's older brother, Clarence, was hanged next to Horatio Gage, and some people say Will Walker had something to do with it. That he brought the police to Gage's door."

"Gage kidnapped a duchess. That's what brought the police to his door."

"Aye, no arguing it. But Gage paid his men well. When Clarence hanged, John lost a brother and the money to feed his ma and sisters. His mum took to the streets. He's got to blame someone."

"And he blames me?"

Edmund scratched behind his ear and shifted in his seat again. "Your da more. But he weren't taken by the picture of you, I can tell you that. Sorry. I didn't know his way of thinking just then."

"How long ago did he see the picture?"

"Few months back. Maybe two? Said you looked familiar, but I told him you couldn't. Then I told him who you were." He cringed a little. "He tried to spit on the picture."

Esther thought of the rats. The men in the park. Three men. It might not be a coincidence.

She hoped Samuel was able to hear through the window. She briefly considered calling for him now so they could ask Edmund questions about his friends together. There was no way of knowing, however, if Edmund would stay or run the moment he learned they weren't alone. He was growing more fidgety by the second. She couldn't take the chance he would bolt before she had answers, and before she convinced him to accept her help.

"Tell me about them," she pressed Edmund. "John and his friends. What are their full names? What do they look like?"

"John Porter, Victor Norby, and Danny Mapp. They've some years on me, and some size. That's why I took up with them. It helps having big friends in Spitalfields. Or so I thought. John and Victor are dark. Brown hair and eyes. Danny's like me." He tugged on a lock of blond hair. "And a bit skinnier than the others. John got a few teeth knocked out of him in a brawl last year. Some people took to calling him Gaping John. Victor's got pockmarks."

Esther couldn't recall if any of the men from the park had spots—the dim light hadn't allowed for a clear look at all of them. But the one with his hands around her throat had leaned in close and bared his teeth. There had been several missing. "Where do they live?"

"Here and there. Move about a fair bit. I don't know where they are now."

"Do you know how to find them? Do they have other friends, or employers? Do you know where their families are?"

"I couldn't find John if I wanted to. I hardly know any of 'em, really, just the story John told me about his brother after he saw your picture. But none of 'em got proper work. I know that." He threw another nervous glance over his shoulder. "I can't stay long. Out in the open like this. It ain't safe."

He was in more trouble than he was letting on. "Edmund, answer me honestly. Are you wanted for a crime?"

"No. It ain't that. I done some things…but no one's looking for me. Except maybe Victor and John, and some of their ilk. I owe 'em favors. They can't collect if they can't find me." He rubbed the heels of his hands up and down his thighs in agitation. "I should go."

"If you would agree to meet with me and Sir Samuel somewhere—"

"Maybe 'nother time," he replied in a tone that clearly said *probably not ever.* "Wouldn't mind seeing you again, though."

He stopped rubbing his hands to resettle the cap on his head.

"I should like to see you again, too." She'd like to see more of him right now. Their meeting was too quick. She still had so many questions. But he was sixteen, frightened, and determined to leave. There was nothing she could say that would convince him to stay. She could, however, make certain he was safe. She reached into her bag again and grabbed her coins. "I want you to take this."

"I told you, I don't want your help. I'll take care of my own troubles."

She took his hand and pressed the money into it. "I have another little brother, very near your own age. Right now, he is at a very fine school acquiring a very fine education, whilst wearing very fine clothes and eating very fine food. This coin comes from the same coffers that pay for all his finery. You are also my brother, Edmund. Please, let me help you."

He stared at their joined hands a long time, his brow furrowed. At last, he nodded and curled his fingers around the coins. "All right."

"I do have some conditions. I want you to go to Brighton. Alone." The cleaner air would do him good, and the distance from London would keep him safe. "Take rooms there and write to me as soon as you are settled. We'll decide together what is to be done next."

"I don't know where to find you."

"Send the letter to the offices of Sir Samuel Brass and Sir Gabriel Arkwright. They'll see it reaches me."

"The Thief Takers?"

"They're my friends. They'll not open your letter. I promise." She gave his arm a gentle squeeze. "I have trusted you. Now you must trust me."

"Aye. I suppose I can..." He opened his palm and glanced down at the coins. His eyes flared wide. "Jesus." He quickly closed his hand again. "I can't take this. It's too much. It'd take me years to pay you back."

"It's not meant to be paid back. You will take it, go to Brighton straightaway, and write me. Promise me."

"Aye." He nodded rapidly, shoved the coins in a pocket, then placed his palm over the pocket as if concerned the coins might jump out again. "Aye, I promise. I'll not disappoint you. I swear it."

"Good. Good. Now, I'm very sorry, but I have to ask for the picture."

"Right. Right." He gave her the folded image. "That's for the best, isn't it?"

"It is. I was—" She broke off at the loud grind and huff of an engine. The sound of it nearly scared Edmund off the bench.

He stood up, nervous eyes darting about the station. "I can't stay any longer. I can't. I'm sorry."

"It's all right. I understand. Wait." She reached out and snagged his arm when he tried to turn. "One more question. What was he like, our father?"

For a brief second, the fear and sadness left his face. "Oh, he was a good sort, he was. A proper da. Took care of me and my mum. I never went hungry, and I never felt the back of his hand. He even made an honest woman of her before he died. He was a good sort." He shrugged and smiled. "For a thief."

"For a thief? Wasn't he in shipping? Or a grocer?"

"Our da?" He shook his head. "Might have played the part of a tradesman now and then, but he were a trickster through and through. Old man Smith were the grocer. Had himself a place in Spitalfields for a time and another in Whapping and Shadwell. I have to go now." He slipped free of her grasp. "I'll write. I promise."

"But—" She reached for him again, but it was no use. He'd already turned his back. A few more steps and he disappeared into the crowd.

Samuel stepped out of the office and, for a full minute, did nothing but stare at Esther's profile. Slowly, the sick worry he'd carried since their argument the day before faded away. He wanted to sweep her up into his arms, run his hands over every inch of her, but watching her would have to do.

She was safe. She was completely, utterly unharmed.

Maybe not entirely unharmed, he corrected. One didn't come away from such an encounter wholly unscathed. She was sitting still as a statue, staring off into the throng of travelers. But she wasn't watching them. He could tell from the way she held herself that she was looking without seeing. She was lost in her own thoughts.

He approached her slowly, giving her plenty of time to notice him before he placed his hand on her shoulder.

She tipped her head back to look at him. "Samuel." Her voice sounded distant and a little hollow.

"Are you ready to leave?" he asked.

She turned to look in the direction Edmund had gone, then gave a little shake of her head, as if dragging herself back to the present. "Yes. Yes, of course. No point lingering about here, is there?"

When she stood, he took her hand and guided it to his elbow. He kept his peace as they walked from the station to his waiting carriage. He couldn't imagine what it would be like to learn of the existence of an adult sibling and the death of a parent in the course of a single conversation, but one could assume it was, at the very least, unsettling. Whatever needed to be said would wait until he was certain Esther was all right.

Expecting a silent carriage ride, he was surprised when Esther pulled up her veil the moment the door was closed. "How much did you hear?"

"All of it. I was on the other side of the window,

you'll recall." And nearly dove out of it when the young man had suggested the two of them board the train.

"I wasn't sure how well you could hear."

"I heard perfectly." He studied her a moment before continuing. She was paler than he'd like, but her eyes were clear and dry, and the hands in her lap were still and relaxed. He didn't need to wait. "You gave him the six pounds."

"Yes."

"Did it occur to you he might be lying?"

"I'm a Walker," she reminded him as the carriage jolted forward. "Of course it occurred to me."

"And still you gave him the six pounds."

"It was the best option at hand. At worst, he is a liar and I've allowed myself to be swindled out of six pounds. That would be galling, but hardly the stupidest thing I've done in my life. Had I not given him the six pounds, then the stupidest thing I will have ever done in my life is to turn my back on my own brother just so I could put my six pounds back in my chest."

"You'll investigate his claim, of course."

"Certainly I will." She looked down and began tugging off her gloves. "I'll ask Renderwell to hire a private investigator directly."

He cleared his throat. Ask Renderwell indeed.

She glanced up and made a face. "Well, not you."

"Not me? Why not me?"

A corner of her mouth curved up. "You've far too many scruples."

"Too many?" How the devil did a man have too many scruples? *Far* too many?

"Yes. I want a man who will look into the affairs

of my possible brother without passing judgment on him."

"What do you expect will be found?"

"I've no idea," she replied, tucking her gloves away into her bag. "He said only that he had lost his job and fallen in with a bad lot."

Which meant a gang of criminals, no doubt. "I'm not the police, you know."

"You were a police officer once."

"Yes, and a good one."

The half smile returned. "I daresay you were."

"Do you know what makes a man a good police officer, Esther?"

She thought about it, shrugged. "Courage, a strong sense of duty, and strict adherence to the law of the land."

"Sound judgment guided by compassion," he informed her. "That's all. If this young man is your brother, then it would be foolish, cruel, and a detriment to society to deny him the opportunity to become a productive citizen in favor of punishing him for a stolen trinket or crust of bread."

It occurred to him that he'd given more speeches in the last week than he had in the last decade. Esther did have a talent for...drawing him out, he supposed.

"But what if his crime was more severe than a stolen crust of bread?" she asked.

"I'll not turn a blind eye to murder, if that's what you're asking. Would you?"

"Of course not. But there is quite a bit in between."

"That's where the sound judgment comes in."

She cocked her head at him, her expression

thoughtful. "Is it important to you that I should ask you to see to this?"

He didn't know how to answer that. It damned well was important to him. But not because of the boy. And it had nothing to do with judgment and compassion. Everything he'd said about both was true, but it wasn't why he wanted the job.

He wanted it for one reason, and one reason only. Because it was important to *her*.

"Is it?" she asked again.

"Yes."

"I see..." Smiling a little for the first time since their argument, she stuck out her hand like a man of business. "Then you have the job."

Seventeen

Samuel sat at his desk in the study and stared at the glass of whiskey in his hand. He scarcely remembered pouring it. He didn't even remember wanting it. It had just been something to do, a mindless act to occupy his hands, when what he'd really wanted to do was grab Esther before she could dart upstairs and lock herself away in her chambers.

He'd wanted a word. Maybe more than a word. Instead he'd poured himself a drink.

He didn't understand it. For a moment or two in the station, and again in the carriage, he'd felt as if the gap between them had narrowed, the roughest edges of their argument had dulled. But the moment they'd arrived at the house, she'd withdrawn without a word, without so much as a backward glance.

It was as if she'd given up.

We are not compatible people.

I should like to be friends.

To hell with that. Twice. Ill-matched or not, they weren't going to be just friends.

He took a long swallow of his drink and reveled in the angry burn of liquid in his throat.

Why the devil had she given up? Because she was still angry? That was no excuse. *He* was still angry—furious in fact, and growing more agitated by the second. But he'd not given up. Surely she didn't believe that a single heated argument meant the end of them. She couldn't possibly imagine he would let her go so easily.

She had to be waiting for an apology. Probably she took the innocuous events at the station as proof that she'd been right to insist on going in the first place. She'd come home without a scratch, after all. Obviously he'd worried over nothing. To hell with that as well.

He took another sip before setting his drink aside and decided that, no, she wasn't getting an apology.

She was, however, going to talk to him. They didn't have to argue. Neither of them needed to apologize. All he wanted was a promise that she'd never again ask him to hide behind her damned skirts. And then they'd put the absurd business of being just friends behind them.

Samuel clung to his righteous anger for a solid six seconds. Which was exactly how long it took him to reach Esther's room…and discover the sound of her crying.

Her door was barely ajar, but he could hear her every sob, every hiccup. He could feel them, like sharp stabs to his chest.

Damn it. *Damn it.*

The door opened silently at the gentle nudge of his hand, and he saw her sitting on the foot of the bed with the dog, her legs curled into her chest and her forehead resting on her knees. She had a piece of paper gripped in her hand, and her other arm draped over the beast's hulking form. Her shoulders shook with every jagged breath. It tore at him.

As he crossed the room, he had to remind himself that he was good at this sort of thing. He had an inordinate amount of experience patting hands and offering condolences. He'd held Esther in the carriage after the attack in the park, hadn't he? He knew how to comfort.

And yet his hand was shaking a little as he reached for her shoulder. She hadn't been crying in the carriage.

As he leaned closer, he saw the paper she held was the record of events she'd been working on. It was half crumpled in her hand, but he could clearly make out where she'd marked her father's death.

"It's all right, Esther."

At the sound of his voice, she leaped to her feet like a scalded cat. Puffy, red eyes glared at him accusingly. "What are you doing in here?"

"I heard you crying. It's all right—"

"Of course it is." She swiped at her cheek with the back of her hand and frowned a little as Goliath hopped down from the bed and trotted from the room. "I'm perfectly fine. It's only residual nerves, I'm sure. Or I'm coming down with something. I'm prone to crying jags when I don't feel well—"

"That's not what I meant." And he was fairly certain she was lying about the crying jags. He reached for her hand, only to miss when she stepped away. "It's all right to...not be all right."

She sniffed, looked away, and said nothing.

"Why don't we sit down together?" he suggested.

"I'm fine, thank you."

He closed the bedroom door, then took a seat himself and patted the mattress beside him. "Sit down, Esther. Please."

"I said I'm quite all right," she snapped.

But she wasn't angry. He knew embarrassment when he saw it.

"You're rude is what you are," he returned. "If you won't sit down, I'll have to get up. And I only just sat down."

Her mouth set in a mulish line, but after a moment, she relented. To his surprise, she settled next to him rather than take a seat at the far edge of the bed. Her skirts brushed his legs and he caught her faint scent of roses.

"I'm sorry you'll not have the chance to meet your father," he said and wished he could put his arm around her, but he wasn't sure she'd allow it.

She was quiet for so long, he began to wonder if she intended to simply bite her tongue until he gave up and went away. But then she pulled her legs up again, sighed heavily, and rested her cheek on her knees.

"It's not that," she said quietly. "Not entirely. It's only..." She looked down at the paper still in her hand. "All this time I've had a brother. I imagined it possible, even likely George Smith had other children, but... I don't know. I suppose I imagined that they had all been cared for as I was. These past few years, I've been comfortably settled in the country, and he was suffering in poverty. He lost his father, then his mother. Our grandfather wanted nothing to do with him. He was all alone. If someone had just told me. If I hadn't waited so long… He shouldn't have been alone."

There was still the chance that Edmund was a swindler, but he rather doubted the possibility would cheer her up. "It's unfair, but that's not your fault."

"I know." She squeezed her eyes shut. "But so many other things are."

And with that, she let the paper fall to the floor, put her forehead back on her knees, and wept.

He did put his arm around her now. He couldn't have stopped himself if he wanted to. The sound of her weeping made him want to…break something. And then maybe fix it. Which clearly made no sense, but he couldn't shake the feeling that if Esther was crying, then surely he should be fighting and/or fixing something.

He needed a dragon to slay, or a broken wing to mend. And he had neither.

Instead, he rubbed her arm, stroked her hair, and murmured soothing nonsense against her temple until, at last, her sobs quieted to sniffles.

"There now," he crooned and wedged his finger under her chin so he could lift her face. "There now. That's better, isn't it?"

She looked at him with mild disgust. "No." Her nose sounded a bit stuffy. "It's humiliating."

"Nothing shameful in tears." He pulled out a handkerchief and handed it to her.

"Oh, yes," she drawled, leaning away a little to wipe her face. "I'm sure you indulge regularly."

"Not regularly."

She slid him a skeptical look. "You cry?"

Pure masculine pride compelled him to repeat, "Not regularly."

"Crying as an infant doesn't count," she muttered, looking away again.

He gave into the urge to tuck a loose lock of blond hair behind her ear. It felt like silk between his fingers. "You know I met Renderwell on the Crimean Peninsula."

"Yes." She sniffled again and frowned a little at the sudden change in subject. "He was your commanding officer."

He nodded and, because she didn't protest his touch, brushed his thumb along the soft curve of her jaw. "There was a dog that used to come into our camp," he said, reluctantly withdrawing his hand. "He would beg scraps from every soldier he could find, but at night, he'd come in my tent and sleep at my feet. Damned uncomfortable. But I liked him. I liked that, for whatever reason, I was his favorite companion."

"If something bad is going to happen to the dog, I don't want to hear about it."

"Nothing bad happened to Richard."

"Richard?" She gave him a pitying look and balled up the now very damp handkerchief in her hand. "Dreadful name for a dog."

"Fair sight better than Harry. He was Richard the Lionheart."

"Oh." She smiled a little. "I take it back. That's a fine name. What happened to him?"

"He returned home with me and—"

"You brought him back with you?" She used her fingers to wipe away a tear she missed on her chin. "To England?"

"I did. He lived a long and happy life. Spent every night at my feet and never failed to greet me at the door. Fine dog, Richard." He dug into his pocket, pulled out his extra handkerchief, and held it out to her. "I wasn't an infant when he passed away at a ripe old age."

Her hand paused in midreach for the offered linen. "You wept over your dog?"

"I did. And I'm not ashamed of it." He pressed the handkerchief into her hand. "But if you tell anyone else, I'll call you a filthy liar."

She produced a small, wet laugh. The sound of it made him feel as if at least a few dragons lay dead at his feet.

Esther used the new handkerchief to finish drying her face—her no doubt exceedingly puffy face. It wasn't often that she cried. It had been years, in fact. But if memory served, it wasn't a pretty sight. There was blotching involved.

She should make some excuse to gain her privacy. Samuel would probably welcome the opportunity to escape. Then again, he'd come in of his own accord.

And she didn't want him to leave. Not yet. She'd been so certain during their carriage ride to the station that he'd washed his hands of her. But then he had held her hand. Afterward, he had insisted on investigating Edmund for her. He had sought her out in her room and held her as she cried.

She wasn't sure what to make of that. Those weren't apologies or declarations. But they spoke of affection and engendered a hope that, quite frankly, baffled her. She didn't know what to do with it.

Samuel didn't want *that woman*. She wasn't good enough.

So what was she hoping for? Friendship? She'd snatched at that possibility earlier, but it had been an act of desperation. And now that desperation made her feel small and pitiful, like she was begging for scraps of him.

I'll be whatever you want me to be. Even if it's only a friend.

She hated the way that made her feel. Hated that she hoped for it even now after he'd rejected the offer. But she still didn't want him to leave. Not yet.

She fished about for some suitably neutral topic to keep him with her and landed on, "Edmund didn't leave those rats on the doorstep." Which was something of a clumsy transition from the Crimean War and a loyal dog, but Samuel didn't seem to mind.

"Likely not," he replied. "But it might have been John Porter or his friends."

"Or Harry."

"Goliath."

She smiled a little when he did, but it seemed only an echo of the comfortable teasing they'd known before their argument. "Do you think they were the men at the park? John and his friends? There were three of them."

"Possibly."

"Could they have followed us here?"

"They wouldn't need to if they recognized me," he said with a shake of his head. "It's no secret where I live."

"Perhaps I should have stayed at the hotel." The idea that she might have led violent thugs to Samuel's home made her feel ill.

"I can't control who comes and goes from a hotel," Samuel replied. "You're safer here."

She might be, but the same could not be said for the rest of the house. "But if—"

"As long as you're in London, you'll stay here."

The steely tone of his voice offered no room for discussion. Another time she might have argued anyway, but she just didn't have the heart for it today. "I suppose. I won't be here for much longer at any rate."

"You still have your extra day. Why not use it to meet with your grandfather?" he suggested. "He must have been the one who wrote the letter you found."

The grocer in Spitalfields, she thought. Yes, the letter must have come from mean old Mr. Smith. "Why would he send a letter if he wanted nothing to do with his grandchildren?" she wondered aloud. "I might need more than a single day if he's not quickly found."

"Your sister won't be back from Scotland for a while yet." There was a slight hesitation before he spoke again. "Are you in a hurry to leave?"

"No." Oh, that had come out much too quickly. She felt the heat of embarrassment at the back of her neck. She didn't want him to know how desperately she longed to stay with him. "This John needs to be found as well," she said hastily.

Samuel rubbed his jaw thoughtfully. "We have his name and the names of his friends. Provided he has not gone to ground, it should be relatively easy to find him."

And then what, she wondered. Could they convince him he was mistaken in thinking she was Esther Walker? Could they trap him in blackmail? "Maybe you were right. Maybe I should not have come to London. I've put my family in danger."

"Your family? Is that one of the other things you believe is your fault?" he asked tenderly. When she remained silent, he dipped his head to catch her gaze. "You haven't put your family in danger. Not directly. Your presence in London doesn't offer any clues as to their whereabouts."

She gave him a wry look. "I believe I made a similar observation during our argument in the parlor. You didn't appear convinced at the time."

"At the time, I was trying to dissuade you from going to Paddington station."

"Dissuade," she murmured, remembering the raging fury in his eyes. She unfolded her legs to hang them over the bed. "Not quite how I would put it. You keep your temper well hidden, Samuel."

His eyes tracked down to the big hand resting between them on the mattress. "I keep it under control."

Because his father had not? "Are you afraid of becoming like your father?" she asked before she could think better of it.

He frowned a little at the question but didn't seem to take offense. "I was for a time. When I was much younger. And you're afraid you'll become like yours," he guessed. "Like Will Walker. Something we have in common."

She stifled a sigh. He still didn't understand, still only saw what he wanted to see. "It's not something we have in common, Samuel. You were never like your father. I am still like mine."

Less now than she'd once been, but only because she now chose to use her skills differently.

Samuel watched her for a moment, his gaze speculative. "Were you lying when you told me you wanted to be more?"

"No, of course not," she replied quickly. "I do want to be more. I think I am more. But I can't be someone else."

"You are a different woman than you were when you worked with your father. Doesn't that make you someone else?"

"No, it makes me a different *me*."

He muttered something under his breath, something that sounded rather like *barrister*. "We're arguing over semantics."

"We're not. You're just missing the salient point," she replied and ignored his grumble of dissent. "I am still a Walker. In many ways, I am still *that woman*."

Bafflement briefly crossed his features before he seemed to recall his words from the night before. "I spoke out of anger," he said with a grimace. He shifted closer to her and rubbed the back of his fingers along her cheek. "You're not that woman, Esther. Not anymore."

It would be so easy, she thought, so incredibly easy to simply agree with him, to accept the reconciliation he was offering. She could lean into his touch then. She could twine her arms around his neck and pull him close. Yesterday's terrible fight could be forgotten. Tomorrow they would go on as if nothing had come between them.

She could keep him.

But for how long? How long would it be before she did something, or said something, that reminded him that part of her was *that woman*? How long before she hated herself for pretending to be someone she wasn't?

She felt as if she were standing on the brink of a great precipice, her toes already dangling over the side. And she wanted to jump. She longed to throw herself into the air with a shout of laughter and with her arms flung wide. But she was terrified that at the end of the long, tumbling fall, she would find herself all alone at the bottom of a chasm. She was afraid she would look up and see Samuel still standing on the edge or, worse, halfway to climbing his way out again.

She needed him to jump with her. And she needed him to do it with his eyes wide open.

Drawing away from his touch, she turned to fix her gaze on the carpet at her toes. "A part of me is, Samuel. As a Walker, lying comes easily and naturally to me. I'm not ashamed of that, any more than I am ashamed of my knives, or my ability to cheat you out of a fortune in a card game, or the fact that I am not put off by a bit of danger. I regret how I utilized the skills I learned from Will. I do not regret the skills themselves. Nor do I—"

"I see no reason you should be ashamed," he cut in.

She threw him a cautious glance. "You had little patience with my unique capabilities today."

"I had little patience with how you chose to apply them," he corrected.

"My skills are mine to use as I see fit." She shook her head when he made an aggravated noise in the back of his throat. "And I don't think you'll ever approve of the way I choose to apply them."

"That's not—"

"Someday," she cut in, eager to explain herself. "I will do more than dream of traveling to Paris. I'll see it for myself. Maybe someday, when Peter is grown, I truly will move to America. Perhaps I'll set up a shop. Or apply myself in some other trade. I heard Renderwell say the Pinkerton Detective Agency in Chicago is rumored to employ female investigators. Who knows, maybe… Good Lord, you've gone pale at the very mention of it."

"Well, for God's sake," he snapped and rose from the bed. "Should I relish the thought of you jumping from one danger to the next? Do you expect me to apologize for wanting to protect you this morning? For being afraid for you?"

"No." She didn't mean to dismiss his concerns, only make him understand that she'd not bend her will to match his own. "I wasn't serious about the Pinkerton Agency, merely making a point. And I do know that it was every bit as difficult for you to take me to the station as it was for me to sit at home whilst you searched for Edmund on your own. I—"

He swore savagely and moved to stand in front of her, his enormous frame filling her vision. "No, Esther, it *wasn't*. I have significantly more experience and training, and I am twice your damned size. An injury that inconvenienced me could kill you. I know it was hard for you to wait, to set aside your desire to act, and I'm sorry for that. Maybe I should have…" He dragged a hand through his hair and shook his head. "Maybe I could have bent more there. I will try to bend more in the future." He dropped his hand. "But let us be honest, you weren't terrified for me when I went out, and you weren't bloody ashamed of yourself."

The amount of anger in his voice surprised her, but the raw pain she heard buried beneath absolutely shocked her. She chose her next words with extraordinary care, and still she managed to trip over her tongue. "I didn't want… That is… It was not my intention to hurt you. I am sorry that I did. Truly. But you're wrong if you think I wasn't afraid for you."

He sucked in a breath to speak, then pressed his lips together and shook his head again. After a moment, he visibly relaxed. The harsh lines of anger eased from his features, and he blew out a long breath of air. "I'm sorry as well. I shouldn't have lost my temper, and I didn't mean to belittle your own fears, nor—"

Before he could finish, she rose from the bed, brushing past him to take up position in front of the cold hearth. His forgiveness and apology only served to make her feel worse, only cementing her belief that they were hopelessly ill-matched. She had wounded him without meaning to, without even realizing what she'd done.

"Hurting you is the last thing I want to do. But…" She brought her hands up in a helpless gesture, one facing palm up and the other bunched around the wet handkerchief. They both trembled slightly. "I can't promise I'll not do it again."

She couldn't promise to be what he needed. What he wanted.

He looked as if he meant to argue, but she rushed ahead, her words spilling out in a great tumble. "Because I'm sorry that I hurt you, but I'm not sorry that I went to the station. I'll never be content to let someone else make that sort of decision for me. I don't want somebody else to decide where I am to go, or how much I am to risk, or what dangers I am allowed to face. I won't be made to feel as if I've no control over my own life. I can't pretend to be something, or someone, I'm not, and..." Her voice was growing oddly strained, and she couldn't seem to stop twisting the handkerchief in her hands. "And that's exactly want you want me to be. It's what you need me to be—an obedient, biddable lady who will be happy to do as she's told. I'm not a biddable woman. I'm not even a particularly *good* woman. Certainly I'm not the thieving Esther Walker of old, but neither am I the deadly dull Esther Bales. I'm trying to be the best of both, really, but you seem to have willfully forgotten I was the former in the hopes I'll be the latter."

"Esther—"

She shook her head when he stepped toward her. "We really *are* incompatible. I'd thought perhaps our differences would prove an interesting challenge, but clearly there isn't enough understanding between us to bridge the gap—"

"Esther. Stop. Good God." He reached for her, but she dodged away.

"No, there's no point in—" She sidestepped him again, narrowly avoiding his grasp. "You'll never want..."

"Come *here*, damn it." He lunged and caught her around the waist. A choppy laugh broke from his throat.

He was amused? She was a hair's breadth from tears and he was *laughing*? She struggled in his implacable hold. "Why are you laughing?"

"Because you're bloody hard to catch, for one thing." Adjusting his grip, he pulled her even closer. "Esther, listen to me. It's only an argument. We've had them before. There's no—"

"Of course we have." She ceased her attempts to break free but remained rigid in his arms. "But this is different."

"Why is it different?"

"Because it's important!"

Because I am afraid.

God, she was positively *drowning* in fear. She was scared she'd already gone over the edge of that cliff. She was afraid she'd jumped over with a man who thought she was someone else. She was worried that one day she would look at Samuel and find him staring at her just as he had in the parlor, his steely gray eyes brimming with anger and contempt. That would break her heart as nothing else ever had or ever could.

All humor fled from Samuel's face. "Sweetheart," he said softly, and his hand came up to gently cup the side of her jaw. "It's important to me as well."

"But you aren't listening. You don't understand."

"I'm trying to," he said carefully. "You believe we don't suit because I want a biddable woman and you are, most assuredly, *not* biddable. Do I have it right?"

"That is part of it," she said and watched him warily. "You were of a similar mind yesterday, and again this morning." He hadn't been willing to consider even a friendship with her.

A furrow formed across his brow as he considered her words. "I was angry," he replied after a time. "I resented being reminded of a time when I felt helpless and unnecessary."

Reminded…? Oh, God, *of course*. His mother. Another wave of remorse washed over her. She should have thought of that. She should have taken better care. "I'm sorry. I—"

"No more apologies," he cut in and bent his head to press a kiss to her brow before brushing his thumb along the edge of her cheekbone. "As for the rest—you're wrong."

"I beg your pardon?"

"I don't want a biddable woman, Esther. I want you."

"No, you don't. You want—"

"Stop presuming to tell me what I want," he ordered with a hint of impatience. "I'm not a child to be told what's best for me any more than you are."

"I'm not…" She wasn't getting through to him. "Why won't you open your mother's letters?" she tried instead.

He drew back in surprise. "What does that have to do with anything?"

"I think it's because you're afraid she might be sorry," she pressed. "And you'd never be able to reconcile that with the woman who betrayed you all those years ago. I think, with you, it must be one or the other."

"One or other what?"

"One sort of person. Good or bad. Honest or a liar. Trustworthy or untrustworthy. Your world is so black-and-white." And she was decidedly gray.

"My views are slightly more nuanced than that," he muttered. "You think I should forgive my mother?"

"Not unless that's what you want. But shouldn't you make certain she is still a villainess before consigning her to a lifetime of your hatred? Perhaps she is..." She struggled to find the right word. "Imperfect. Perhaps she is imperfect and still worth knowing."

Hope flickered when he didn't immediately argue against the idea. "I don't keep—"

Whatever he'd been about to say was lost when a hesitant knock sounded on the door.

"Come in," Samuel called out as Esther quickly slipped from his arms and backed away a respectable distance.

Sarah stepped inside, studiously avoiding eye contact with either of them. "Begging your pardon, sir, but this come for you. I was told to bring it to you straightaway." She handed Samuel a letter and quickly disappeared again.

Esther knew she should be embarrassed to have been caught in a closed bedchamber with Samuel, but she just couldn't work up the energy for anything more substantial than a resigned sigh.

Samuel read the contents of the note and swore under his breath. "That's it," he growled in disgust. "I'm retiring. End of the year."

"You're what? Why? What's happened?"

She reached for the note just as Samuel crumpled it up and shoved it in his pocket. "Our erstwhile lovers were arrested for a four-way brawl on Bond Street."

"*No*," she breathed, fascinated despite herself. "Even the ladies?"

"Evidently," he muttered. "I have to go." He reached for her again, catching her chin in his hand and holding her gaze. "I know what I want. You. Only you. Understood?"

Before she could respond, he took her mouth in a brief but hard kiss, then strode to the door.

For a long time after, she stood in the middle of the room staring after him as his words played in her mind over and over again.

I know what I want. You. Only you.

She wanted to believe him. She wanted to go back to envisioning a future with him. And yet she couldn't shake the fear that someday he would change his mind. That there would be more fights like the one yesterday. They would add up over time, she thought, like letters piling up in a drawer, waiting to remind him of a woman he didn't much like and would be better off without.

Samuel eyed the desk drawer containing his mother's letters in the same manner Sarah had eyed the dead rat at her feet—warily, with no small amount of disgust and perhaps a begrudging sense of pity.

He shouldn't have kept them. He wasn't even sure why he had. He certainly wanted to be rid of them now.

Briefly, he considered tossing them out as rubbish. Then he thought about burning them. Finally, he imagined opening the drawer, inviting Goliath into the room, and letting nature take its course.

But even as he sat there in the silent, sleeping house, picturing all the ways he could be rid of the damned letters, he knew, in the end, he would open them.

"Damn it."

It had been well past midnight when he'd finally been able to come home, and his first impulse upon walking through the front door had been to seek out Esther. He could wake her with a slow kiss, watch her eyes flutter open, her lips curve into a soft, dreamy smile. He ached to hold her, to have her skin under his hands, to feel her body move beneath his own.

He wasn't sure he'd be welcome.

To his mind, their fight was over. They had reconciled, and it was time to move on. He wasn't confident she shared his opinion, however. He'd sensed a distance between them even after he'd made it clear he wanted her. He'd sensed it even as he'd kissed her good-bye.

And so tonight, instead of holding a warm and willing Esther in his arms, he was sitting in his study, glowering at his desk.

Your world is so black-and-white.

Esther's words echoed in his head. It was an odd accusation for her to have made. He could be stubborn in his views, yes. He could be harsh in his opinions. But she knew he was neither narrow-minded nor willfully blind. She had been the one to insist he wasn't a hard man.

Except that now she appeared to have changed her mind, and he suspected he knew the reason.

As he stared at the desk drawer, he absently rubbed his scar with the back of his hand. Old scars were tricky things. They made themselves known in unpredictable ways...pinching and itching when you least expected.

He was well aware that his need to guard and

protect stemmed from his experiences as a child. It was like a pain he couldn't fully soothe, a nagging itch he couldn't quite reach. It would always give him trouble.

Esther had her own scars—the work she'd done with her father and the years she'd spent twisting her personality to fit the ideals of the people around her. What was it she had told him earlier? That she had acted out roles to please others, because she didn't know who she really was, but if people liked her, then surely whoever she was couldn't be all bad.

He should have paid more attention to that last bit, that quick acknowledgment that she did, in fact, have some opinion on the sort of woman she was.

All bad, he thought. The old Esther. The one who'd been inferior in her own father's eyes. The one Samuel had called a selfish imbecile only a year ago.

That woman. Christ, he owed her a proper apology for that. Not for the words, but for the damning way he'd said them. With one careless, insulting tone, he'd managed to both shame her for the past and insinuate that no portion of the woman she'd once been was worth preserving. It had been so easy for her to hear in those words an opinion he didn't share—that for the first twenty-seven years of her life, Esther Walker had been *all bad*.

Good or bad. Honest or a liar. Black or white.

No wonder she'd changed her mind. No wonder she'd been so insistent that he didn't understand her, didn't really want her.

At the very notion of not wanting her, Samuel gave a harsh laugh and dragged a hand down his face.

Hell, he *ached* from wanting her. All of her—her sharp tongue, her wind-chime laugh, her passion, her trust, even her stubbornness and terrifying sense of adventure. He wanted every bit of her, every moment of her time. Her past, present, and future.

But he'd been clumsy. She'd prodded at his old scars and, without realizing it, he'd responded in kind.

The error couldn't be undone. And, God knew, he lacked the eloquence to win her back with pretty words.

He could, however, make a symbolic gesture.

Once more, his eyes tracked to the drawer.

He could prove to her that his opinions were not so black-and-white. That he did believe a person might be imperfect and still worth knowing, worth loving.

Eighteen

To Esther's surprise, it took Samuel less than half a day to track down Mr. Smith. Her grandfather had moved only once since leaving Apton Street. His new home was a tiny, weathered house in a neighborhood that looked to have just slipped off the edge of shabby-genteel and was now rapidly descending into full dilapidation.

"I should like to do this alone," she told Samuel as they sat in the carriage outside Mr. Smith's residence.

Samuel released the grip he'd had on the carriage door. "I don't think that's wise."

Please, not this argument again. "Mr. Smith is more than seventy years old, and I've knives strapped to my ankles. I suspect I'll return unscathed."

"We don't know who else is in that house. I don't know anything about his staff."

She glanced at her grandfather's home. It was smaller than her cottage. "He can't have more than one or two. I'd wager neither are assassins."

He slanted her a decidedly unamused look. "If he insults you—"

"Then I will wish him to the devil and take my leave."

A muscle worked in his jaw. "I don't want you to be hurt."

She stifled the sudden urge to lean across the carriage and brush her hands across that grinding jaw.

It truly was harder for him to wait.

Samuel had been right—when he had gone off in search of their mystery man alone, she had worried about him, but she had not been terrified for him. He was just so capable. Her confidence in his abilities left no room for something as uncomfortable as raw fear.

She was capable as well, but her abilities were admittedly less honed than Samuel's. There was room for fear there. And he had such a terrible need to protect.

She glanced at the waiting house and back at Samuel. She felt guilty for not fully appreciating how difficult it had been for him to take her to Paddington station. But she wasn't facing anything more dangerous here than a spot of disappointment. And for God's sake, he didn't need to follow her everywhere.

"I don't know him, Samuel. I've no attachment to him at all. He might insult me. He might toss me out of his home, but it won't hurt me." It would, however, add a painful layer of humiliation to have Samuel bear witness to whatever insults or accusations her grandfather might care to hurl at her. "I need to do this alone."

She watched him struggle with her decision for a moment before giving one curt nod. "All right."

The concession, and the knowledge of what it cost him, warmed her from the inside out.

Maybe they weren't so incompatible, she thought

as she hopped down from the carriage. Maybe they could always find their way to an agreement, so long as they didn't give up trying.

Maybe, in time, he'll replace you with a lady who won't ask him to subjugate his needs to her own.

She was nearly to the house when this unwelcome thought intruded on her newfound hope. It angered her, even as it pricked at her conscience.

Maybe I'll replace him with a gentleman who doesn't ask the same of me, she thought tartly, but that idea only made her feel worse.

She shook her head, setting those fears aside for now, and knocked on her grandfather's door. A young maid in skirts that were visibly patched promptly answered.

"Mrs. Ellison to see Mr. Smith, please. I am come about his son."

She was shown into a miniature parlor crammed with furniture that had been out of fashion for at least fifty years.

Esther had barely taken a seat on the threadbare chair before the parlor doors opened again, and the maid returned with her grandfather.

As she rose from her seat, all Esther could think was that Mr. Smith looked even older than his seventy years. He shuffled into the room with the aid of a cane, his back bowed forward and his knuckles white from supporting his weight. A sparse patch of white hair crowned a narrow face heavily lined with wrinkles.

He blinked at her once, then waved a gnarled hand at the maid. "Leave us."

"Yes, sir."

"Who are you?" he rasped to Esther. "What do you know of my son?"

"I am..." She swallowed hard and glanced at the parlor door to make certain the maid was no longer in earshot. "I am Miss Esther Walker. I believe your son was my father."

Mr. Smith went very, very still. "You are Esther Walker?"

At least he appeared to have heard of her. "I am."

He moved toward her slowly, until they were standing nearly cane to toe. Clouded blue eyes searched her face for a long, long time, then, to her astonishment, filled with tears. "You are real, then. You are real."

He lifted his free hand and she thought for a moment he might touch her face, but he hesitated and patted her shoulder weakly. "My granddaughter."

Esther nodded, thrown off-balance by his reaction. She had braced herself for insults, recriminations. At best, she had hoped for mild interest. She had not expected tears.

"You are just as she described," Mr. Smith breathed. "Just as beautiful as she described."

"I beg your pardon?" Who had described her?

He closed his eyes briefly, as if remembering an old pain. But when he opened them again, the tears had dried. "How did you find me, child? Your mother, I presume?"

"I..." She shook her head to clear it. She had so many questions, she wasn't quite sure where to begin. "I found a letter. Or part of one. I thought it was from your son, but—"

"It was from me. Your mother and I kept up a

regular correspondence for a time. Did she send you here?"

Regular correspondence? With a woman who would disappear for months at a time and not bother to write her own children? "No, I'm sorry. My mother has been gone a very long time." Years before the letter she'd found in the desk had been written.

"Ah. I am sorry to hear it." His gaze turned pensive. "I did wonder if that was the way of things." He gave his head a little shake, sending the puff of hair wafting. "Well, there is no good to come from wallowing in old grief. Or so I have found. Come. Come. Take your seat."

He carefully lowered himself to the edge of the settee across from her chair. Both hands braced on his cane, he leaned forward and regarded her with avid interest. "Now then, Esther Walker. Tell me of yourself."

For the next ten minutes, Esther drew a very faint sketch of her life, offering only the most basic, harmless details. Her parents were gone. She had no children. She enjoyed her art, gardening, and the new game of badminton.

Though it pained her, she also lied. Right through her teeth. She was widowed. She had traveled from Boston to find her father's family.

Another act, another role to play. But it couldn't be helped. She didn't know this man. She couldn't trust him with the truth. And there was something amiss with his story.

Mr. Smith listened intently, almost raptly, as if every word out of her mouth was fascinating. To her relief, he did not pose probing questions about her late husband and life in Boston, and with a little encouragement, he began offering information of his own.

"You have a younger half brother, you know," he told her.

"Yes. Edmund." She considered her next comment carefully before speaking. "He is under the impression you dislike him." Immensely.

"And no wonder, as I did for a time." He sighed heavily, the sound a wheeze in his chest. "I am a very old man, Miss Walker. I've had a great many years to make a great many mistakes. I have amassed a fortune in regret. But none weigh so heavily as the loss of my family."

"We are not all gone."

"Indeed not." He tapped his cane once in emphasis. "Indeed not. You are of noble stock. Did you know?"

She shook her head and smiled a little at the very idea. "Am I?"

He waggled a hand at an enormous book lying atop a small table. "There. There. The Bible. Bring it here."

She retrieved the tome and laid it in his lap. It looked to be at least a century old. Its binding was cracked, the pages thin and frail. Inside, the names and dates of births went back three hundred years, the earlier entries obviously copied from older records.

"Do you see?" He tapped his finger at the top of the page and she took a seat beside him. "Second Earl of Silsbury."

"In the year of our Lord 1531."

"The title reverted to the crown many years ago. But it was ours for a time. You are a blue blood, Miss Walker."

The very palest of pale, pale blues. The second earl

appeared to have had only daughters. There was a long line of titleless entries after that, spanning several pages, and with the surname changing every so often when the male line ran out again. The last few entries carried the decidedly undistinguished surname of Smith. Her father's name was the final entry.

Mr. Smith pointed to one of the entries. "Your great-great-grandfather was a naval captain of some renown. He dined with some of England's finest families. Even King George, himself."

"I see." She didn't really. It was almost impossible to imagine a blood relative of hers keeping company with royalty. Unless it was to steal from them.

"It costs a fair amount of coin to keep up with royalty and nobility," Mr. Smith continued. "There was little left over for his son, my father. And he left even less to me. I had a decent education, and when my father passed, sufficient funds to go into business for myself."

"You were a grocer."

"Yes. A common grocer." He trailed his fingers down the list of names. "We were a mighty family once."

"So it would seem."

"We took pride in it. I sold my goods in Spitalfields, and elsewhere, but I refused to live in rooms above a shop. Like my grandfather and father before me, I spent on my vanity what I should have saved for my boy."

"I doubt it did my father harm to have been raised in a better neighborhood," she ventured.

He didn't seem to hear her. "Even the mighty fall," he murmured. He tapped the page gently, almost reverently. "But we do not care to admit it." He sighed again. "George and I had a terrible row. A falling out."

"I'm sorry."

"He took a path I could not condone. He dishonored the family." With great care, he closed the Bible. "But I am not blameless in our estrangement. He came to me one day and told me he was to marry a Miss Thatchum. Edmund's mother. I knew who she was, and I knew of the boy they'd had out of wedlock. Just as I knew he'd sired a daughter as well. Miss Thatchum was a seamstress. Her mother had been a woman of ill repute."

She didn't know what to say to that. Did one express sympathy for having a prostitute attached to the family tree?

"A doxy in the family," Mr. Smith continued. "It was not to be borne. But you..." He wagged a finger at her. "I heard a rumor that your mother came from good family."

"Oh. Er..." Her mother had been the only child of tenant farmers somewhere in the north. At least that was the story she'd been told. "They were respectable, I believe."

He bobbed his head. "I thought, if I could arrange a reconciliation between my son and your mother, he might throw off the other woman."

"Mr. Smith, my mother was married."

"At the time, I believed that a dalliance with a married woman of respectable stock was preferable to a permanent alliance with Miss Thatchum. To that end, I hired a man to find your family."

A man? "What man?"

"A private investigator. He gave me an address in Kent. I wrote your mother introducing myself and indicating my intent to see her reconciled to my son."

"In Kent?" The Walker family had never lived in Kent "How long ago was this?"

"Oh, ten years or so."

"I'm afraid you must be mistaken, Mr. Smith. My mother passed away sixteen years ago."

His mouth hooked down thoughtfully, then he made an impatient sound. "Bah. I am an old man. Dates and details occasionally escape me. At any rate, we wrote for several years. Though she would not agree to renew contact with my son, she did keep me apprised of your accomplishments. And I kept her informed of my son's current residence, should she be interested."

"You told her where to find your son?"

"It would have been near impossible for her to do so otherwise. The boy was constantly moving about, never staying in one spot for more than a year at a time. Often no more than a month or two."

"My family was much the same." Criminals were like that, she thought. Terribly jumpy.

He nodded absently, not really seeming to hear her. "I have never seen my boy so angry as the day he discovered those letters in my desk. He left London shortly after and refused to speak another word to me for the rest of his life. I was so angry with him. And so bitter at the loss of him. When Edmund arrived at my door four years ago, I blamed him." He gave that terrible wheezing sigh again. "I alienated my own son and discarded my own grandchild out of pride. I have long wished to make amends, but I have lacked the courage."

"But now I am here," she offered quietly.

"Yes." His face brightened. "Yes, you are here. Like an unexpected and undeserved present. And a pretty little present you are, as well. You've a bit of your grandmother about the mouth, I think."

"Have I? I should like to know all about her. But first…" She retrieved the engraved pocket watch from her bag. "Do you recognize this?"

Mr. Smith's face brightened at the sight of it. "I do, indeed. It was my father's. Benjamin Smith. I gifted it to George on the occasion of his twenty-first birthday." He patted her hand. "Keep it. A child should have something to remember her father."

"A father's watch should go to his son. Were you aware your son married Miss Thatchum?"

He absorbed that information quietly for moment. "I have often wondered," he murmured to himself. Then his gaze fell to the Bible in his lap and his pale lips curved up in a slow smile. "Would you be so kind as to fetch a pen and ink, my dear?"

She did as he requested and watched as Mr. Smith painstakingly added Edmund's name to the list of entries.

When he'd finished, Mr. Smith blotted the ink and nodded approvingly at his work. "Ah. The mighty may fall, but the resilient will always rise up again."

She returned the smile he offered, genuinely happy for him, but she inwardly winced when he set the pen aside.

Her name would not be recorded in the family Bible. Mr. George Smith might be happy to receive her, even acknowledge her as his granddaughter, but she was not a true Smith. Not a legitimate member of the family. She was…not quite good enough.

She shook off the sense of disappointment. There was no point in dwelling on it. And she still had so many questions. There were pieces to his story that didn't quite fit, even if he had managed to remember exact dates incorrectly.

"Mr. Smith, may I inquire how long you continued to write to my mother without receiving a reply?"

"I wrote twice without answer as I recall. Three months, I suppose?"

"Is that all? Are you certain?"

"More or less."

That couldn't be right. That couldn't *possibly* be right. The letter in the desk had been written five years after her mother's death. "You didn't attempt to write her again some years later?"

"Certainly not. I'm not one to press a lady. And I had my pride, of course."

"Of course," she murmured, careful to hide her astonishment. If Mr. Smith's final attempt to contact her mother had been made only months after he'd received her last letter, then that meant… Mr. Smith had been corresponding with a dead woman for *years*.

Esther's mind whirled with all the possible explanations, but it kept returning back to one. "Did you happen to tell her of your falling out with your son?"

"I did."

And then the letters from her dead mother had ceased. Will Walker had taken her to burglarize the house on Rostrime Lane at nearly the same time.

She swallowed around a lump in her throat. "Who was the private investigator you hired to find my mother in the beginning?"

Mr. Smith absently rubbed the handle of his cane. "I don't recall. I only remember that he came highly recommended and that he did not earn his commission. It was an upstart competitor of his who found your mother for me. He approached me with the promise to deliver your mother's address within a week in exchange for a moderate reward and letter of reference. I agreed and he delivered."

"What was his name? The upstart?"

"Ah, yes. *His* name I remember." He smiled a little in memory. "Hernando Gutierrez. Quite the charming young Spaniard. And exceedingly obliging. He saw to the delivery of the letters himself."

Hernando Gutierrez. Uncle Hernan. Her father's favorite alias.

Oh, Will Walker, you tremendous bastard.

Nineteen

"Will Walker used my grandfather to keep track of my father." Esther relayed this bit of information to Samuel the second she stepped back in the carriage and shut the door. "He wrote to Mr. Smith pretending to be my *dead mother*."

It was probably a testament to how often Samuel encountered the truly bizarre in his line of work that he met this revelation with just one raised brow. "Sounds like something Will might have done."

"It's appalling." Which, *yes*, meant it was something Will would have done.

He made a prompting motion with his hand. "Tell me what all was said."

As the carriage rolled toward Belgravia, Esther provided Samuel with a detailed recounting of her conversation with her grandfather. She pulled the timeline she had created from her bag and used it as a visual guide in her explanation. She told him about Uncle Hernan and her grandfather's correspondence with her long-dead mother. She mentioned the fictional residence in Kent and pointed out that the burglary on Rostrime Lane had occurred near the same time Will Walker would have received news that no more information about the younger George Smith would be forthcoming. But she didn't mention the Bible. She had her own pride.

Samuel rubbed his chin thoughtfully at the end of the telling. "Will must have heard that Mr. Smith was searching for the Walker family and decided to take matters into his own hands, introducing himself as a private investigator." A corner of his mouth hooked up. "He must have relished being paid to find himself."

"And paid to deliver letters to himself." That was the only part of the story that made sense to Esther. "Pretending to be a private investigator to throw off a search, I understand. But why not simply inform my grandfather that my mother was dead? Why continue to write to him for years? Merely to keep track of my father? Was he *routinely* burglarizing the young Mr. Smith? Did he seek revenge against all my mother's lovers in such a manner?"

"Will wasn't above getting back a little of his own."

"Will wasn't above much of anything," she muttered, remembering the way he had laughed in the tavern while she'd stared at her coins. She folded up her paper and put it back in her bag. "I suppose it was all just a game to him."

The man had loved his games, the more challenging and sordid, the better.

"I'm sorry. But yes, I imagine it was." Samuel reached out to slide his hand over hers. "Are you all right?"

She stared down at their hands, just as she had in the station, with a confusing mix of fear and longing.

"Yes," she replied quietly. "It all worked out for my benefit in the end. If Will hadn't written my grandfather, I wouldn't have found the letter in the desk. I wouldn't have come to London and met my brother and grandfather." And she wouldn't have had this time with Samuel. She turned to him, shifting her feet a little as the carriage rolled to a stop in front of his house. "Events may not have played out exactly as I imagined, but I'm glad I came."

Whatever happened between them going forward, she would never regret the week she'd spent with him here.

Samuel's assessing gaze tracked over her face. "I've an errand to run. And there's a man I want to try to find this evening. Someone who might be able to tell me where to find John Porter and his friends. We'll talk when I return."

As evening fell, Esther wandered Samuel's house, checking windows and door locks. In the past, she had often sought solitude when her thoughts troubled her. She preferred the privacy of her bedchamber, where she could work through her problems without distraction. Tonight, however, her body felt as restless as her mind, and she was glad for the excuse to stroll about. She drifted from room to room, absently smiling at staff and silently cataloging every inch of the house. She wasn't aware she was doing the latter until she caught herself scrutinizing the faint signature on an uninspired watercolor in the downstairs hall.

Shaking her head, she moved on, meandering into

the parlor. Why on earth did she feel compelled to memorize every detail of the house? Was it because she would leave tomorrow and never return?

Was she leaving tomorrow?

She'd taken her extra day and found her grandfather. Was she *supposed* to leave now? Expected to leave?

Everything was still undecided. It all felt so uncertain. Only days ago, she'd been happily dreaming of a future with Samuel. Now that future seemed hazy, ill-defined, and a little frightening. She didn't know what came next. She didn't know what *should* come next. Their argument had been smoothed over, but the doubts it had produced remained entrenched.

She felt as if she was standing on that precipice, still waiting on Samuel for…something. A clearer indication that he'd been listening, perhaps. A sign or reassurance. Maybe if he decided she could stay one more day, or promised he still meant to see her in Derbyshire in a fortnight, or told her…

Suddenly aware of the appalling tenor of her thoughts, she came to a clumsy stop, her slippers catching against the parlor carpet.

Good Lord, she was doing it *again*. She was waiting for someone else to make decisions for her.

For all her grand talk of taking control of her own life, in the end, she was waiting for Samuel to decide their fate. No, not just decide, she realized. *Insist upon*. She was waiting for him to take complete charge of their future. She wanted him to talk her over the edge of that precipice so she wouldn't have to take the risk for herself. She wanted him to cajole and persuade, and make promises. And she wanted all that, she realized, because then only Samuel would be responsible for what came after. If he changed his mind later, she could always comfort herself with the knowledge that she wasn't at fault for his disappointment. She'd warned him. The affair had been his idea. He'd *insisted.*

And that was rubbish, expecting Samuel to soothe her insecurities as if she were a child, expecting him to make all the decisions, take all the risks, accept all the responsibility. And she would just...let herself be dragged along.

That was *cowardice.*

She needed to make her own choices. She would decide for herself what to risk and how much.

And for Samuel, she thought with growing determination, she would risk everything.

Hands clenched at her sides, she resumed her directionless walk, heading into the library.

Perhaps Samuel did see her differently than she saw herself. Maybe his life *would* be simpler, calmer with an obedient wife at his side. But neither of those possibilities altered the fact that life would be *better* if they were together.

Nothing changed the fact that she loved him.

She was hopelessly, irrevocably in love with Samuel Brass. The man who had chased her all the way to London out of concern for a friend. The man who had played a silly game with her in the park. The man who argued with her, laughed with her, teased her, and tempted her. How could she not love his wicked hands and his kind, crinkle-at-the-eyes smile? God help her, she even loved his arrogance and overbearing protectiveness, his gruffness and clumsiness with words. She *adored* him.

And she would fight to keep him. That was her choice.

And as soon as he…

Passing the open door to his study, her gaze flicked over a scattering of papers on his desk.

She froze, then slowly turned her head for a better look.

Not papers. The letters from his mother. And they had been opened.

She walked into the room slowly and stood over the desk to stare at the stacks of correspondence. Without thought, her fingers came up to lightly brush the edge of one envelope.

Several emotions assailed her at once. There was fear for Samuel, because there was no telling what the missives contained, no telling how much it might have hurt him to read them. And there was humbling wonder, because he had read them for *her*. He *had* been listening.

And all the while, she had not been. He had told her he didn't want a biddable woman. He had said he wanted *her*, and still she'd kept her distance, waiting for him to convince her.

All so she wouldn't have to take the risk of telling him the truth.

He was everything she wanted. He was the only thing she needed. He was the best person she'd ever known. She loved him. And if he would only give her the chance, she knew she could make him happy.

And if he wouldn't give her the chance, she'd take it anyway.

She wasn't going back to Derbyshire without the promise he would follow. She wasn't going to toss away a future with Samuel out of fear.

She bloody well *would* fight to keep him.

And she was going to tell him all of this. As soon as he came home.

She glanced at the clock on the mantel, wondering how much longer he would stay away. It was immensely frustrating to be brimming with a sense of purpose and have nowhere to direct it.

Turning from the study, she took a few steps into the library before spying Sarah near the parlor doors. The young woman was dragging her feet, staring at the floor ahead of her and muttering something under her breath.

Worried, Esther waved her hand to gain the maid's attention. "Sarah?" She hurried to her side. "Something the matter?"

Sarah gave a little start, her head whipping up. "Oh. No. Sorry, mum. Nothing the matter. Just going to let the beastie inside." She made a half-hearted gesture in the general direction of the kitchen as she resumed her walk. "Been watching him from the sitting room windows."

Esther fell into step beside her. Watching a dog play in the garden wasn't what had brought on the slumped shoulders and glum countenance. "I'll join you, if you don't mind," she decided, selfishly grateful for the chance to distract herself with someone else's troubles.

"Of course not, mum."

When they reached the front hall, Esther touched her arm to stop their progress. "Just a moment." She dashed over and snatched up her black parasol from the hall stand. "Here we are."

Sarah's features twisted in comical bemusement. "What's that for then?"

"Rats," she supplied. "Harry might find them a lark, but I'd just as soon not shoo one away with my foot."

"Oh. Aye. I wouldn't recommend it," Sarah replied. She smiled a little, but she grew quiet again as they headed downstairs.

Dipping her head, Esther tried to catch the maid's eyes. "Won't you tell me what's troubling you? I can keep a confidence."

The girl let out a tired sigh. "It's Mrs. Lanchor. She's put out with me because someone left the kitchen door unlocked."

Esther's heart leaped into her throat. She grabbed Sarah's arm, bringing them both to an abrupt halt just inside the kitchen. Visions of three men picking the lock on the kitchen door and creeping into the house danced in her head. "What? When?"

It hadn't been but a half hour since she'd checked the kitchen door herself.

"Just a bit ago. Ten minutes, maybe," Sarah replied. "She went to let the beast out and found the door unlocked. She said it was me, but—"

"Why did no one tell me?"

"There's nothing nefarious in it, mum. Honest." She grimaced and cast a quick glance over her shoulder before whispering, "It was just Tom. I know he come down here five minutes before Mrs. Lanchor."

"You're certain? Absolutely certain?"

Sarah gave a quick nod. "Said he wanted a quick

spot of air in the garden. I saw him come this way, and I heard him open the door. He must have come back in straightaway. Mrs. Lanchor only just missed him."

Relieved, she released Sarah's arm. The door shouldn't have been left unlocked out of carelessness, but at least it hadn't been pried open by John Porter and his friends. "Mrs. Lanchor doesn't believe you about Tom?"

"I didn't mention it," Sarah confessed. "He's a good sort. Been a bit daft lately, is all, what with his mum taking so sick. He's been making mistakes all month."

Esther's annoyance with Tom's negligence dimmed. It would be easy to forget something simple like locking a door when the mind was crowded with worry for an ill parent. "And you don't want to add to his troubles, is that it?"

"Sir Samuel's a fine master. Good as they come." Sarah grimaced again, a little dramatically this time. "But he won't be pleased to know his orders weren't followed."

"I see… Would it help if I talked to Sir Samuel?"

Sarah blinked at her, then smiled brightly. "It might at that. Thank you, mum."

Looking a little more like her chipper self, Sarah stood back while Esther went to open the door. Thankfully, there were no rats to be found on the other side. Still, she waited until Harry dashed inside, and she shut and locked the door behind him before tucking the handle of her parasol into her belt.

All clumsy paws and swatting tail, the dog bounded to Sarah for a rub, then Esther, then back to Sarah, then did an abrupt turnabout and bolted out of the kitchen.

"Beastie!" Sarah called out after him. "Oh, Mrs. Lanchor will have my hide if he breaks another vase," she grumbled. She picked up her skirts and gave chase, leaving Esther standing alone in the kitchen.

Well, she thought with a flicker of amusement, the trip to the kitchen had succeeded in taking her mind off Samuel for all of three and a half, possibly four, minutes.

With a small huff, she sat down on a nearby stool and wished he would hurry home. Then again, it might be best if she worked out what she meant to say to him before he returned. Love and strength of purpose were all well and good, but she needed to convince him she was in the right…

Later, Esther would think that had she not been so lost in her own thoughts and worries, she would have realized she was not alone in the room. If she'd been paying proper attention, she would have heard the footsteps approaching from behind.

She was unaware of the danger, however, until a beefy arm snaked around her neck and yanked her backward off the stool into a hard wall of muscle and bone. A hand clamped over her mouth.

"Been waiting for you." The voice in her ear was low and harsh. "Nice of the boy to forget to lock the door."

Terror bloomed in her chest. She bit down on the hand and opened her mouth to scream, but got no further than an indrawn breath before something hard crashed against the side of her head.

The world revolved in a slow, sick circle. A wad of cloth was shoved in her mouth. It smelled of sweat and smoke. She threw an arm up, but it was a clumsy and useless gesture. Her arms and legs wouldn't work properly. She nearly toppled over when she tried to kick backward. Something thick and rough slid over her head, blinding her, and then she was being dragged backward, out the door and into the garden.

⁂

Samuel piled coins on the scarred table at the Brook's End tavern. Across from him, Chaunting Charlie sniffed through a nose that had been broken and left unset at least half a dozen times over the course of his fifty years. If the bruising under his eyes was any indication, the latest injury had occurred less than a week ago.

"I ain't talking, Brass." But of course he would. The refusal was merely a formality. His gaze was already locked on the money, adding up every coin.

Charlie wasn't a professional informant, as such. His long-standing habit of talking to the authorities for a few coins meant no criminal in his right mind would trust the old man with a secret of any import. Charlie fell more along the lines of professional gossip. He was good for names, personal histories, and, if the coin was right, the occasional address.

One could always count on Charlie for the basics. Provided one could track the man down.

"I've been looking for you," Samuel said. "Could have used your services two days ago."

"I got my own troubles, don't I?"

Samuel looked over the healing bruises across the man's face. Professional gossips might not be worth the bother of murder, but neither were they popular. Men of Charlie's ilk were often obliged to disappear for days or weeks at a time.

"Looks that way," Samuel said. "Blown over, has it?"

"Aye. Well enough." He threw a nervous glance over his shoulder. "Unless I'm seen here with you. What are you after?"

Samuel pushed one of the coins across the table into Charlie's reach. "What do you know of a man named John Porter?"

"That's a common enough name. What do you want with this fellow?"

Samuel offered another coin. "Runs with a Victor Norby and Danny Mapp. All I want is to talk to him."

The older man eyed the money and scratched the underside of his chin with the back of his hands. "Well now, might be John could do with a discussion. His mum would be turning over in her grave to know he took up the resurrection business."

Samuel slid another coin across the table for the information. "He didn't take it up alone."

Stealing bodies from their graves was a hard, nasty, filthy, and entirely nocturnal line of work. Edmund's pale skin and sunken cheeks could easily mark him as a resurrection man.

"Got a few lads with him. Your Victor and Danny. But Edmund Smith as well."

Samuel slid another coin. "What do you know of them?"

Charlie pocketed it with the others. "Victor's a bludger. Nasty piece of work. His da's doing a stretch for a pannie. Danny's a quiet one, but they say he'll do what needs doing. If he's got family, I ain't heard of 'em."

"And Edmund?"

"Edmund's a good lad, but gulpy. And a sap. Tell the boy a sad tale and he'll lend you his arse and shite through his ribs, he will."

"He's gullible."

Charlie waggled his fingers. "That's what I said. Gulpy."

Samuel passed over another coin. "What do you know of his parents?"

"George Smith were a gentleman sharper. None better from what I hears. His mum was a soft touch like her son. She worked at what she could find. If you're looking to find him, I can't help you. He stopped running with John and his friends a while back."

Which meant finding Charlie earlier may have linked their mystery man to Esther's father, but it wouldn't have led Samuel to Edmund himself. Esther still would have gone to the station. "Where can I find John and his friends?"

"Can't tell you where Edmund's gone. The rest of that lot..." He jerked his chin at the remainder of the money. When Samuel shoved it across the table, Charlie grinned and gave up an address in the Old Nichol.

Deciding it would be wiser to visit the rookery tomorrow in the light of day, Samuel left Charlie to his earnings and rode home.

He was eager to see Esther. He had a gift for her, and this one was perfect. It was made just for her. And he wanted to tell her about the letters. He'd opened them and read every damn word. He still wasn't sure he cared for his mother. Her letters contained a shrewish, judgmental quality that set his teeth on edge. But she had apologized. She asked for a reconciliation, and she was sufficiently dedicated to have written three times a year despite Samuel's silence.

He'd give it some thought.

Sarah was waiting for him in the foyer. The moment he stepped inside, the young girl rushed at him. "She's gone, sir. Mrs. Ellison is gone."

"Gone?" His heart made a quick, painful revolution in his chest. "What do you mean gone? She left?"

"I don't know, sir. Her things are all upstairs. But... I'm sorry, sir, but someone left the kitchen door unlocked, and that's where I saw her last. There was a stool tipped over and the door was wide open. The garden gate too—"

He didn't hear anything else. He was already running for the door.

He thought he'd known fear before. In battle. At the park. When he'd taken Esther to Paddington station.

This was different. This was fear that teetered perilously close to panic. It tasted like acid in his mouth, cut his insides like razors, and ignited a fury unlike any he'd ever known.

~

Esther's dizziness passed in stages. She was vaguely aware of being in some sort of conveyance, a carriage or cart. The rag in her mouth was loose. She spit it out and took in a deep breath to scream, but the sound died in her throat when she felt something the size and shape of a gun muzzle press against her temple.

"Behave."

The next thing she knew she was being hauled outside, her hands tied behind her back. She couldn't remember having her hands tied. Her legs were free, but it was difficult to keep her feet under her as she was dragged up a short set of steps. She heard a door open in front of her. Her captor shoved her forward a few feet, and the door shut behind her. More stumbling, down a hall or through rooms, up a long, long flight of steps.

The journey seemed endless, and she was grateful for it. With every step, every second that passed, her mind cleared, her coordination returned. But with that clarity came increased fear. Her heart raced wildly in her chest. Her lungs struggled to suck in air that felt scarce. She was shaking now, and she hated that, hated giving her captor the satisfaction of seeing her afraid.

At last they reached a landing, then a short walk, and finally a door opened in front of her. A few more steps, and then she was abruptly shoved to the floor.

Expecting her captor to immediately fall on top of her, she tensed and shifted, ready to roll away. But he moved off without a word.

She tried to follow his movements in the room, but it was difficult to make out sounds over the roar of blood in her ears. The mingled scents of dust, damp wood, and parlor matches filtered through the cloth over her face.

Her mind raced with questions, plans, and frantic grasps at hope. Did he really have a gun? Had he been bluffing? Could she reach the dagger under her skirts with her hands tied behind her back? Would it be better to scream and invite a swift death, or hold out and hope she could fight him off? Maybe she could talk to him, reason with him. Maybe she could scream and fight him off. Maybe Samuel would find her. Maybe…

Calm down. Calm down.

Forcing several hard breaths through her nose, she willed her mind away from the present and pictured herself holding her dagger in front of a target. She lifted it, aimed… And there it was. That moment of calm, of peace. She held on to it as long as she could, let it wash over her.

The roaring receded. The shaking eased into trembling, then shivers. Her thoughts quieted. Terror remained, but it no longer controlled her.

She was a Walker. She was *Esther Walker.* All she needed was her dagger, and she would show this man the meaning of fear.

She felt rather than heard the man come to stand behind her head. His hands were on her neck, and suddenly the cloth over her head was ripped away. She blinked up at a vaulted ceiling with exposed wood beams that looked half-rotted.

Her gaze darted about the room, quickly taking stock of every detail. She was in a large attic devoid of furniture except for a rickety old table and chair set in front of a dormered window. She saw no fireplace, no rugs, and no artwork, but there was plenty of light. A pair of wall lamps blazed brightly. Her parasol lay against the wall near the only door in the room.

Finally, the need to know who stood behind outrode the fear of tipping her head back and exposing her throat. She looked back and immediately recognized the blunt features, shaggy black hair, and sinister, nearly toothless grin.

"It's you," she gasped. "From the park." The man who'd wrapped his hands around her neck and squeezed.

He sketched out a mocking bow. "John Porter, at your service."

Still smiling, he walked around her to squat at her feet. Elbows resting on his knees, he absently twisted the gun in his hand while he studied her. "I've been trailing you for days," he said conversationally. "Ever since Spitalfields."

He waited then, as if expecting her to say something.

"No," she ventured. If conversation kept him distracted from whatever plans he had for the gun, she would gladly talk all night. "Not this whole time. Not everywhere." She'd been alone in the carriage while Samuel had gone house to house, seeking information about her father. John could have easily shot the driver and hauled her away.

"Can't trail a man like Brass for long distances," John replied with a small shrug. "He'll notice. But I got close enough to take money right from your fingers, didn't I?"

"Money?"

He dug his hand into a pocket and pulled out a single coin. "Don't you recognize your own charity?"

Her eyes darted from the coin to his chin and landed on a small, indented scar. "Outside the tavern." The false beggar. "That was you too."

"I wanted to see if I could do it. Wanted to see just how close I could get to you." He tossed the coin up a couple of inches, caught it midair, then shoved it back in his pocket. "And I trailed you to the park from your hotel. You lost me for a bit. Me and my friends. But then we saw your carriage and heard you laughing. Knew Brass would take you home after that. All I had to do then was wait." He tapped the muzzle of the gun against her foot. "Did you like the presents I left you?"

"I don't..." She shook her head, at a loss.

"I know you found 'em. Left 'em right at the door for you."

It took her another moment to realize what he was talking about. "The rats?"

"Diseased rats. You weren't worth the effort of a fresh one." He tapped the gun again. Twice. "Diseased." *Tap.* "Rats." *Tap.* "Did they remind you of your friend Will? Did you recognize him?"

Friend. Not father. John Porter didn't know who she was. Not really.

"Will who?" She knew she'd made a mistake playing innocent when his jovial facade slipped. "Will Walker, do you mean? I scarcely knew the man."

"Ain't she a pretty liar?" He moved the gun muzzle under the hem of her skirts and lifted. "What's under here then, lovey?"

She kicked out at him, but her movements were hampered by the heavy material and fear of his gun.

Ignoring her struggles, he shoved his hand under her skirts and began pawing at her legs with his free hand. "Where is it? Eh? Where is it? Ah, here we are." She felt the dagger at her ankle slide free of its sheath.

Clutching the knife in one hand and the gun in the other, he crawled over her on all fours, then leaned down close and held the dagger up to her face.

"Got your claws, Kitten." He grinned at his own

joke. "That's what Walker called you, isn't it? His kitten? Aye, you bloody well knew him. Me brother told me all about you. Pointed you out a time or two. Told me all about how you and him did work for Gage." He leaned in even closer, forcing her to turn her head to escape his fetid breath. He didn't seem to mind. He pressed the flat of her blade to her cheek and whispered into her ear. "So you tell me. You tell me why it were my brother Clarence what swung with Gage, and not Walker. You tell me where the son of a whore is hiding."

"Hiding?" Because her voice shook, she covered it with a small laugh. "He's dead. Will Walker has been dead for years. Gage killed him."

"That's what they says, all right. So how come ain't no one ever saw a body? How come ain't one person in London what knows where he's buried?"

"The police saw. They know where he's buried."

"And they ain't talking?" He snorted and pulled back a little. "Peelers see a man like Walker put down, they crow about it. Take credit for it, if they can."

Unless Walker were working for those peelers, of course. Then they kept their mouths shut. But she couldn't tell him that. Because if Walker had been working for the police, then *she* had been working for the police.

"I had nothing to do with your brother's death." She didn't even remember a man named Clarence. Gage had dozens of men. "I'm not sure I ever met—"

"Shut your mouth. You—"

A door slammed shut somewhere downstairs, and masculine voices floated in through the open door.

John gained his feet and aimed the gun at her. "Not a word. Not one peep or it'll be worse for you. You understand?"

She nodded and expelled a ragged breath of relief when he turned and left the room, closing the door behind him.

Now was her chance.

She eyed the chair in front of the table, then her parasol. If she could wedge the chair under the door before John returned, it might buy her enough time to get her hands free and possibly escape out of a window. But she'd have to move the chair without making a sound, an unlikely feat with her hands caught behind her back.

The parasol first, then.

She scrambled up awkwardly and made her way to the parasol as quickly and quietly as she could. Praying her movements couldn't be heard downstairs, she pressed her back against the wall and slid down until she could reach the handle of the parasol with her bound hands. Once she had a proper grip, she gave the handle a twist and pulled the hidden dagger inside free of the case.

The blade was short and thin, but it was sharp. Used well, it could be lethal.

She maneuvered the blade to cut through the ropes, but it was an awkward business. Her fingers were half-numb already, and the rope was thick. She nicked herself twice just trying to make a notch in the rope.

Hurry. Hurry.

Outside, the wind howled. The old house groaned, the windows rattled, and the door popped open a few inches.

Angry voices floated up the stairs. She strained to listen even as she sawed at the ropes, wincing when the blade sliced her skin.

"Have you lost your mind, kidnapping Almighty's woman?"

She didn't recognize that voice, but she heard John reply, "I told you, she's Walker's girl."

"I don't bloody care. I wouldn't bloody care if she were made of solid gold. You'll bring Brass down on us."

"You weren't squalling when we was following them to the park, were you?"

"I didn't know who he was then, did I?"

"Aye." A third disgruntled voice piped in. "Bit of quick coin, you said. And what'd I get for it? A bleeding knife in me leg."

The other men from the park, she realized. Not likely allies, but they were angry with John. There might be a chance…

"It was her that done that," John said. "Don't you want a taste of revenge?"

"I ain't beating on a woman. I never agreed to that. I never agreed to a blessed thing 'cept to help with a nob in the park whilst you nicked a lady's jewelry. You never said it'd be Brass, and you never said a damned thing about beating on a woman. I sure as spit didn't agree to kidnapping."

"You want to take her back to Brass?" John demanded. "You think he won't know you from the park?"

"We ain't needing to bring her to him. Just take her out a ways and let her go."

Like an unwanted dog, Esther thought, and she prayed with all her might that her captor would agree to the plan. She was sawing at her bindings as best she could, but she suspected she was doing more damage to her skin than the rope. She could feel the warm trickle of blood sliding down her fingers.

"I can't, can I?" John said. "She's seen me. She knows my name."

There was a round of low, vicious cursing.

"You're a fucking idiot," the second man growled. "Give me your gun. You can't shoot her here where half the bloody street can hear it."

"Don't want to shoot her, do I? Bitch can't talk from the grave." There was a dull thud of metal against wood. "Take it then. You can have her little blade too." Another thud, softer this time. "There's your quick coin, Danny. You'll get a pretty penny for that."

"It ain't bad."

"Aye. She's been living like a damned duchess all these years. *All these years*. You think about that... Now, are you with me or not?"

There was a short pause.

Say not. Please, please say not.

"Ain't never been against you," Danny grumbled. "Thick and thin, right? As always."

The glimmer of hope she'd had of gaining allies died. She hacked at the ropes like a mad woman.

Hurry.

"Aye," she heard John say. "As always."

Seconds later, the stairs creaked under the weight of John's boots.

Momentarily forced to still her blade, she hurried back to her spot in the middle of the room. By the time John stepped back inside, she was sitting just where he left her.

He closed the door behind him without taking his eyes off of her. His eager gaze slid over her from head to toe. She didn't bother hiding her shiver of revulsion.

"Ready to play, Kitten?"

She scooted away from him, letting her movements disguise her renewed struggles with the rope. Was she leaving a trail of blood on the floor? She was afraid to look, terrified he might follow her gaze and figure out what she was about. "Don't do this, John."

He crept toward her slowly, like a predator toying with his prey. He didn't actually draw any closer to her, but neither did he let her get farther away. "Where you running to? Ain't nowhere for you to go."

When she hit the far wall, she leveraged herself up to her feet. Couldn't he hear her sawing at the ropes behind her back? It seemed so loud to her. Too loud. But she couldn't stop. She was so close. She felt the bindings loosen, but it wasn't enough to pull herself free.

John began to close the distance between them. Six feet... Five feet...

"No point in fighting me, Kitten. All I want is Walker. Just tell me where he is."

"He's dead."

His gaping grin returned. His hands fisted at his side. "I was hoping you'd make this difficult."

Four feet...

Too late. It was too late. She'd failed to get through the ropes in time. There was only one option left.

She stepped forward from the wall to give herself room to maneuver, then turned the knife in her hands to face the blade out. At the last second, just as John reached for her, she lunged left and spun at the same time, drawing the blade in a broad, awkward arc behind her back.

John stumbled back with a grunt of pain. The injury was minimal, just a small gash in his hip, but it held him off long enough for her to dash away to the other end of the room.

With an oath, he lunged forward a half step, then came to an abrupt stop, seeming to think better of charging her again. "What was that? What the bleeding hell do you have?!"

"Why don't you come over here and I'll oblige you with a proper look," she suggested. She took two threatening steps toward him.

He stepped back, which was immensely gratifying. But then he reached under his coat and pulled out an enormous knife of his own, destroying her brief boost of confidence.

She turned her own blade again and sawed at the ropes.

Eyes narrowed, John looked her over from head to toe. "You think to fight me with your hands behind your back? Are you mad?"

"Oh, quite," she assured him with as much menace as she could muster around the ball of terror in her throat. "There's something you might have considered before taking me on. Ever fought a madwoman before, John?"

"They bleed, same as others."

"Not if they're quick."

She was nowhere near that quick. His reach was longer, his blade was bigger, and she no longer had the element of surprise on her side. If he rushed her now, he'd have her.

If only the ropes would give. She was so close. So close.

John gave the knife in his hand a quick twirl. "You think you're quicker'n this?"

Her rope slipped away. At last.

"No." She held up her free hands and the blade, ignoring the coating of blood over both. "Just quicker than you. Put your weapon down, John."

His features twisted in anger. "Right." He twirled the blade again, licked his lips, and widened his stance. "Right. A proper fight, then."

"I am not going to fight you." She used her skirts to quickly scrub the blood from the fingers of her right hand, then gripped the knife by the tip of the blade and brought it up to throw. "You take one step toward me. One step, and I will kill you. If you call for your friends, I will kill you."

"You won't throw it. What if you miss? Then you got nothing."

She gave him a cold smile. "I don't miss."

Please, please don't make me throw it. Don't take that step.

He took a step, but not toward her. He moved to the side. She did the same. They began a slow, silent circling of each other.

She let him lead, only moving when he did, giving him no reason to start the attack.

When she reached the side of the room where her parasol lay against the wall, she bent down and scooped it up, never taking her eyes off of her opponent.

John's brow furrowed in confusion, then lifted as

he gave a short bark of mocking laughter. He gestured with the tip of his blade. "What do you mean to do with that?"

"Where do you imagine I hid the blade?" She gave the parasol a little shake. "Can you guess what else might be inside?"

Not a damned thing. The parasol base was hollow. But it was sturdy enough to fend off a few swings of his knife if need be. And the possibility of an additional weapon worried him. He stopped laughing, and his eyes darted back and forth between her knife and the parasol. A film of sweat formed on his brow.

"Put your weapon down, John." If he would just put it down, she could tie him up, bolt the door, and climb out the window, or call for help at least.

He shook his head. "I ain't letting you go." He gripped his blade with both hands. "I didn't come this far to swing for kidnapping. And I want Walker."

"You don't have to swing. Just put the—"

"Bugger this." He charged her.

She hurled the knife and hit her mark. The blade sunk into John's chest just below the collarbone.

Howling, he stumbled back into the corner of the table. Its spindly legs buckled beneath his weight, and man and wood crashed to the ground.

Even before the wreckage settled, she heard the sound of boots charging up the stairs.

She lunged for the chair with the vague idea of using it to wedge the door shut, but she hadn't made it more than two steps before a giant of a man barreled into the room.

Standing half a foot taller than John, his chest was

as broad as a blacksmith's. He had two black eyes, a swollen nose, and his right arm was bound against his chest. In his left hand, he carried a thick wooden club that was scarred and stained from use.

The man she'd stabbed in the leg in the park was only seconds behind. He was notably smaller than his friend. She might have had a chance to fight him off long enough to get away, if he hadn't been holding John's gun.

The parasol suddenly felt as flimsy and useless in her hands as a handkerchief. What good would it do against a club? Against a bullet?

The small man stumbled to John, who, somehow, was still alive, still conscious, and writhing on the ground. He'd retained his grip on his knife, the other hand wrapped around the dagger in his chest.

"What the bloody..." The limping man gasped. "Jesus God, John."

The giant's head swung from his fallen friend to Esther. "I'll kill you meself."

"She's mine!" John's voice was thick with pain and rage. "Help me up. Help me up, damn you."

With the aid of his friend, John gained his feet. His face was ashen, his shirt soaked with blood. Her dagger remained in his chest, and Esther realized that she had killed him—it was only a matter of time before he succumbed to the injury. She just hadn't killed him fast enough.

Shoving away from his friend, John stumbled toward her.

Her eyes darted to the door and windows. There was nowhere to run, nowhere to hide, but she backed away out of reflex and swung the parasol at him when he closed in. She made a desperate grab for the dagger sticking out of his chest.

John pivoted, took the hit on his shoulder, and snatched the parasol out of her hand. He turned it about and swung it back at her. The base caught her on the side of the head, in the same spot where he'd hit her in the kitchen.

She stumbled sideways, then felt the hard impact of the floor against her knees.

His fingers dug into her shoulder, grabbing fabric and skin alike. He hauled her back to her feet, and the world revolved as it had before, in a long, sick roll.

She swayed, then tensed for the next blow, but John backed away.

"Give me that." John snatched the gun out of the smaller man's hands and aimed at her.

The small man, Esther thought, trying to focus around the pain and dizziness. The one who didn't want to beat on a woman. He was her one chance. What was his name? What had John called him downstairs?

"Danny!" That was it! "You don't have to do this. You don't have to—"

"Shut up." All three men spoke in unison.

Danny flicked her a glance, then turned away. "Make it quick, then."

John lifted the gun an inch higher, aiming for her chest. "Can't have Walker," he spat, a bubble of blood forming at the corner of his mouth. "I'll take you."

Oh, God. Oh, God. She was going to die.

The world seemed to shrink and narrow, growing smaller and smaller until it was only a pinprick of light stretching between her and the barrel of the gun. She wanted to face her death with dignity, with her chin up and her eyes open, but her shoulders curved in involuntarily as if she could make herself a smaller target. Her skin felt oversensitive, crawling in horrible anticipation of the tear of the bullet. She squeezed her eyes shut when John cocked the gun. She couldn't help it.

I'm sorry, Samuel. I'm sorry. I'm sorry. I'm...

The blast reverberated off the walls. She dropped back down to her knees with a cry, waiting for an explosion of pain that didn't come.

There was a thud, a grunt, a pounding and scraping of feet, a clattering of metal against wood.

Her eyes flew open.

"Samuel." She whispered his name, or thought she did. Dizzy, she blinked and tried to focus again, tried to make sense of the chaos around her.

Samuel had come. He was fighting the men. John was on the ground, his eyes open and unblinking at the ceiling. That was the shot. Samuel had shot him.

She saw two guns. One at John's side. Another lying on the ground by the open door. She didn't understand how it had come to be there.

Her eyes tracked back to Samuel.

It had been too dark to see him fight their attackers in the park. She'd thought him a graceful man before, but she saw now that there was nothing elegant in the way Samuel fought. He was simply...efficient. Blunt and brutal. He wasted no movements and gave no quarter.

She watched in a kind of mesmerized stupor as he wrested the giant's club away and swung it in a powerful arc. It connected with the side of the big man's head with a sick crack that made her flinch.

Danny launched himself onto Samuel's back.

She should help, she thought. She needed to help. She could sneak past them and reach one of the guns.

She pushed off the floor, her bloodied hands slipping out from under her twice before she managed to gain her feet. But she'd not taken a step before Samuel flicked Danny off his back like a gnat, then threw a punch that sent the man flying into the wall. Danny slid down to the floor and stayed there.

It was done. All three men lay unmoving.

Samuel crouched in front of the biggest man, tying his hands. His gaze, cold and hard, flicked to John, then back to her. Blood trickled from a gash in his bottom lip. He swiped it away with the back of his hand. "Are you injured? Did they hurt you?"

"No. No, but—"

"Go wait in the hall."

"But I—"

"In the hall. Now."

His tone brooked no argument, and for once, she was happy to follow his orders. Only... "Come with me."

She didn't want to go alone. She didn't want to leave him alone.

Something passed over his features, softening the hard lines. "I won't be long, sweetheart. Go on."

She nodded once and stumbled into the hall on unsteady legs. A single lamp lit the narrow corridor. Leaning her head against the wall, she took deep breaths to clear her mind and steady her racing heart. It didn't help. She began to shake, just as she had in the carriage after the attack in the park. But there was no wild desire to laugh now.

Maybe it would come later, once Samuel was with her.

God, how she wanted Samuel.

And then he was there, striding toward her purposefully. She rushed to meet him, and his arms wrapped around her with bruising force. She burrowed into the warmth of him, breathing in his scent.

He pressed his face to the side of her neck to mutter nonsense she didn't understand, strings of curses and half-finished promises.

A tremor went through him, then another. "Never again, Esther. Never again."

"I didn't want… This isn't the adventure I wanted."

"That's not what I meant. God, he took you from the house."

Pulling back, he reached for her face with hands that were scraped and bloody. The pinky on his right hand was bent at an unnatural angle. The club, she thought. The giant must have hit him with the club to dislodge the gun.

Horrified, she moved to grab him. "Your finger."

"Your *hands*." He snagged her forearms, seemingly oblivious to his own injuries. "My God, your hands."

"They're all right." They weren't of course. They were still bleeding a bit, but the cuts were not deep, and the pain was lost to the overwhelming relief of being safe with Samuel. "It's all right."

"That son of a whore," he snarled.

"No. It's all right. I did it. I had to cut the ropes."

He brought her hands up and pressed a kiss to her wrist. Steely gray eyes held hers. "He did this."

"Yes." She gave a shaky nod and winced at the pain in her skull. "Yes, I suppose he did."

"Your head? Did he—?" His fingers delved into her hair, gently probing her scalp. A fresh string of curses spilled from his lips when he found the painful knot. "This will never happen again. I swear it. Never again."

Her heart turned over at the hint of vulnerability beneath his anger and fear. Lifting a hand to his face, she brushed her fingers lightly across the scar. "Samuel, I'm sorry—" She broke off at the sound of pounding footsteps and shouts below.

His arm curved around her shoulders, pulling her close again. "It's all right. It's only the police. I had Mrs. Lanchor send for them."

"They'll know. They'll know I'm in England. My family—"

"They'll know you made the trip from Boston," he said calmly. "Alone. Nothing more."

She turned her face into his chest, as much for comfort as to keep her features hidden. She was so tired now. As fear drained away, it took the blessing of numbness with it, and a thousand aches and pains began to make themselves known.

Samuel's large hand curved protectively around her head as men poured into the room. She listened to the scuffling of feet. Voices floated over her. Samuel was talking to someone, answering questions, promising to fill in the details later.

"It will have to wait." He slipped an arm behind her knees and scooped her into his arms. "I'm taking Miss Walker home."

An hour later, Esther sat in her room with her bandaged hands curved around a lukewarm cup of tea. She didn't want the tea especially, nor the brandy Sarah had all but dumped in with it, but it gave her something to do while she waited for Samuel to finish with the inspector who had insisted on following them home.

There was a soft knock on her door, and as she set aside her drink and rose from her chair, Samuel stepped inside.

She'd not had a chance to really speak with him since they'd left John's house. Exhausted and hurting, she'd slipped in and out of a light doze in the carriage. The moment he had carried her inside and set her down in the front hall, she'd been swept away by a tutting Mrs. Lanchor and weeping Sarah.

Now he was standing before her, and suddenly she wasn't sure what to say to him.

There was too much that *needed* to be said, too much she wanted him to understand, and she didn't know where to begin.

Samuel appeared to be suffering from a similar dilemma. He'd taken two steps into the room before coming to an abrupt halt.

They just stood there, staring at each other as the tension between them grew palpable.

And then…

"I have something for you," Samuel said.

At the same time she blurted out, "Will you marry me, Samuel?"

His brows lifted and his eyes went wide. "I beg your pardon?"

"Oh." *Oh, dear.* "I didn't mean to skip so far ahead."

"I imagine not. Care to continue?"

Not really, but she rather doubted he'd be willing to say his piece first now. Wishing that she'd taken the time to work out what she wanted to say beforehand, she swallowed convulsively and pressed ahead in a rush. "I thought to never marry. I didn't want to be under a man's thumb. I want control over my own life."

A muscle worked in his jaw. "You are not under my thumb."

"No. I realize that now. You issue orders, and you demand, and you presume all manner of authority, but I've not been made to do anything I didn't want to do. Well, I've compromised some," she amended after a moment's consideration. "Quite a lot, actually. But that's only natural, isn't it? Everyone must compromise now and then. You've compromised as well."

"Some." He frowned a little. "Not as much as I could, or should have."

"The same could be said of me." She shook her head when he looked to argue. A debate over who had been the least flexible was not what she wanted. "I am not my father—either of my fathers—nor my mother or my grandfather. And I refuse to be the young woman I once was—making mistakes and amassing regrets out of fear."

"Fear of what?" He took a step toward her, his expression troubled.

"Fear that you would one day want someone else. Someone better." She winced at the embarrassing words but didn't seek to retract the confession. He deserved the truth. All of it. "You said you do not want a biddable woman, but I thought you might *prefer* one. I thought you might be happier with a woman content to always be at home. I can't be that woman, and I don't want to be that woman. Clearly, it wouldn't guarantee my safety anyway. But I can still make you happy. I *know* I can. We can be happy together. I think I've always known that, I just… I was afraid. I needed to argue with myself for a bit."

"I don't want—"

"I love you, Samuel." She said the words quickly, afraid that whatever he'd been about to say would steal her courage away. Ultimately, he might reject her offer, but she'd be damned if she didn't have her say first. "I love you more than…" She couldn't think of something sufficiently large. "Anything. Everything. I want to marry you. I want to watch you become a better man. I want you to watch me become a better woman. I want to argue with you until we come to an understanding. I want—"

"Yes."

"—to see you…" She trailed off awkwardly. "I'm sorry?"

His lips curled in humor and something else, something warm and hopeful. "I said yes. I will marry you."

"You will?"

"I will. I have something for you."

"You do?" She sounded foolish, but she couldn't help it. She couldn't quite grasp the idea that he was agreeing with her. She had gathered all her courage for a fight. Not with him, but *for* him. She was ready to do battle for the man she loved, ready to swallow all her fears and lay her pride at his feet. She didn't know what to do now that he'd said yes.

Hope bloomed, bright but still unsteady, as he pulled a small rectangular box from his coat.

She accepted it with hands that shook. "You don't have to keep buying me gifts."

"I know," he said simply. "Before you open it, I want you to know that I read my mother's letters."

"Yes, I saw them," she replied carefully.

"I'd like to make two things clear before we continue. First, the reason I did not open them was not because I was afraid she might be sorry. It was..." He cleared his throat, looking a little uncomfortable. "It was because I was afraid she might not be. Unopened, they offered the hope of one day reconnecting with the mother I once loved. I was afraid of losing that hope."

"Oh." She bit her lip, worried for him. "And have you?"

"No. The years apart from my father have been good for her. As for the second thing..." He took her face in his hands and lowered his head until they were looking eye to eye. "I meant what I said. I do not want a biddable wife. Understood?" He waited for her nod before releasing her face. "Good. Now open the box."

Obliging him, she lifted the lid and gasped at the small dagger nestled inside. Careful of her injuries, she took it out and turned it over. The silver handle was simple and elegant and the perfect size and shape for her hands.

"It's exquisite."

And it was a dagger. A gift fit for a Walker.

Etched along the handle were the small, delicate letters *ESWBB*. She felt a welling up of emotion when she realized what they stood for. "Esther Smith-Walker-Bales-Brass." She laughed breathlessly. "That is quite a mouthful."

"I had it engraved yesterday." He put his finger beneath the initials. "The woman you were. The woman you are. And the woman I'd hoped you would become. All of them together. One and the same. There's more on the other side."

She gave another nervous laugh. "Heavens, you've scribbled all over the thing." She flipped the blade over and read the inscription aloud as tears pressed against the backs of her eyes. "Just as you are."

Samuel reached up again to cup her face in his hands. "I know who you are, Esther. I am in love with all that you are."

The nerves drained away, replaced by an overwhelming sense of joy and peace. Like that second before the dagger left her hand. Only so much better, infinitely better, because this wasn't a single moment that would slip away. This was the rest of her life. An entire lifetime with the man she loved.

"I'll give you the devil's own time," she warned him with a smile.

Samuel ran his thumbs across her cheekbones. "And you'll have it right back. I know you need more than a quiet life in Derbyshire to be happy. We can travel the world together. Let me take you to see Paris and the Louvre. Let me talk you out of climbing atop an elephant in India." As she laughed, he bent down and pressed his forehead to hers. "I don't want someone else, Esther, and I never will. I want you. Only you. It will *always* be you."

"I want *us*," she whispered and slipped her arms around him. "Just as we are."

Epilogue

Three Months Later

"What do you mean retire?" Gabriel bolted upright in his seat. "You can't retire."

Feeling relaxed in the respectably sized chair in his parlor in Cheshire, Samuel merely shrugged at his friend's outrage. "Esther can't live in London. And I can't live without Esther."

"God," Gabriel groaned with a grimace. "You're worse than Renderwell."

"Worse than me at what?" a new voice inquired. Renderwell, looking rather disgruntled, entered the room with his wife. "Be specific."

"Ignore him," Lottie ordered, nudging him onto the sofa. "He wants his vanity stroked."

Gabriel smirked at their former leader. "Are you still cross because Esther took fifteen pounds from you at cards? Again."

"She cheats," Renderwell grumbled.

Lottie settled next to him, and her lips curved up in a small, mischievous smile. "You can't prove it."

"She cheats *really well.*"

Samuel made a mental note to keep Esther away from card tables on their upcoming honeymoon.

Then he promptly erased it.

Esther could do as she damn well pleased.

Lottie shook her head at her husband, dislodging a loose strand of dark hair from its pins. "If it troubles you to lose so often, stop agreeing to play with her."

A calculating gleam entered Renderwell's eyes. "I'm going to figure out how she does it."

"She'll beggar you first," Gabriel warned.

A flash of movement outside caught Samuel's attention. Not for the first time, his gaze was drawn to the parlor windows. Esther was on the front lawn engaged in a sort of three-way game of badminton between herself, Peter, and the dog. They'd lost nearly a dozen shuttlecocks and one racquet to Harry's massive jaws so far, but at least he'd stopped jumping on visitors.

He smiled as Esther lunged and swung, her pink skirts swirling around her. He'd been right that day in Hyde Park—the country suited her. She looked happy and carefree playing on the green grass in the sunlight.

But freedom alone wouldn't be enough for her. Nor for him. Eventually, they would both need more. Which was why he'd told Gabriel he'd *been* considering retirement.

"Are you listening, Samuel?" Gabriel's voice and an impatient snap of fingers drew Samuel back to the conversation in the parlor. "We're discussing you, man. Pay attention."

"Snap your fingers at me again and I'll break them," Samuel said without heat.

"You're welcome to try," Gabriel returned.

Lottie rolled her eyes at the easy exchange of threats. "Gabriel says you mean to retire, Samuel."

"He *can't* retire."

"Why not?" Samuel asked, mostly out of curiosity.

"Because we're the Thief *Takers*. Plural." Gabriel held up two fingers and took on the tone of a patronizing schoolteacher. "Plural means more than one."

"Thank you."

"Besides," he added, dropping his hand, "you'll be bored."

"Renderwell seems happy enough."

The man in question casually tucked his wife's hair behind his ear. "Very," he assured the room.

Gabriel waved that argument away. "He has estates, sisters, and a mother to care for. What will you do with all your time?"

"Honeymoon," Samuel replied.

"And there's Edmund to consider," Lottie added.

Yes, there was Edmund. True to his word, the young man had left town the day after he'd met Esther at the station and had written as soon as he'd taken rooms in Brighton. A quick search had turned up a birth record listing George Smith as his father. Samuel had also been able to determine that Edmund had been employed at the docks for a time, just as he'd said, and though he was suspected of having worked with John and his friends as a grave robber for a time, he wasn't officially wanted for any crime. He was free to build a new life as a member of Esther's family, if that was what he wanted.

"He's been on his own a long time," Lottie pointed

out. "It might take some work to convince him to come here."

Samuel nodded. "I doubt he'll agree to live with us, but he might be persuaded to live nearby."

"And then what?" Gabriel inquired. "After the honeymoon and after Edmund is settled—what will you do?" He shook his head. "I know you. You won't be happy leading the life of a country gentleman. Not for long."

Samuel let his gaze track back to the windows. Harry was charging full-tilt toward the front doors, shuttlecock caught firmly between his teeth. A laughing Peter chased after him. The game, it would seem, was over.

"No," he admitted. "It won't keep me content for long."

"There now, you see?" Gabriel relaxed back into his chair, clearly pleased with the small victory. "You're starting to sound almost reasonable."

Renderwell's face turned hard in an instant. "You can't be in London with Esther."

"No," Samuel agreed. "But there's plenty that might be done outside of town." There were always lost wills on the continent and ne'er-do-well sons to track down in Scotland.

"Have you discussed this with Esther?" Lottie asked.

He rose from his seat as he saw his wife nearing the house. "I'm about to. Excuse me."

As Samuel strode into the front hall, he was greeted by the sound of a scuffle and Peter's laughing voice on the other side of the door. "Give it here you great, bloody beast of a—Ha! Got it!"

The door swung open and Peter tumbled inside, his young face flushed from a combination of exertion and his sensitivity to the dog. He sneezed once as Harry pushed past him and bounded into the parlor. "He got another one, I'm afraid. Sorry, Sir Samuel."

"Not your fault." Samuel gestured toward the parlor. "You know where to find the others."

What was left of them. He'd purchased a small fortune of replacements the last time he was in town. At the rate Harry was going, however, Samuel would need to either replenish the supply on a monthly basis or learn how to make the damn things himself.

Peter grinned, sneezed again, and followed Harry into the parlor just as Esther stepped inside.

And there she is, he thought. Esther Brass. His wife. Someday, he would grow accustomed to the idea, to his tremendous good fortune. But not today.

Without waiting for her to close the door, he slipped an arm around her waist and pulled her close for a long, searing kiss that'd torment him for the rest of the day.

She smiled at him when he pulled away. "Kissing a lady in broad daylight where anyone could walk in and see," she admonished and tsked at him.

"Too indecent for you?" he asked.

Laughing, she slipped out of his arms to close the door, then returned to give him a quick kiss of her own. "Were you on your way somewhere?"

"To find you."

A light blush of pleasure colored her cheeks. "I'm glad you did. Oh, did you tell Gabriel about your decision to retire then?" She shot a look toward the parlor and winced sympathetically. "Is he very upset?"

"No, because I've reconsidered."

"Have you?" Her eyes darted to him. "When? Why?"

"He made a strong argument against it. He pointed out that if the Thief Takers are to continue, there needs to be at least two."

A small, baffled laugh escaped her. "You're not serious."

"I am, but I was thinking..." He took a deep, calming breath. Last chance, he thought. There would be no turning back after this. "I was thinking...perhaps the Thief Takers function best when there are three."

"Renderwell, do you mean? Does Lottie know he—?"

"No, not Renderwell," he cut in with a chuckle. "You."

She stared at him, eyes wide and lips parted for a full five seconds. "Are you in earnest?"

"I am. We'll start slow. You can't—"

"Learn everything overnight," she finished for him in an excited rush. "Of course not."

"We'll pick and choose our cases. Nothing in London or Edinburgh." Nothing that might lead to chasing dangerous men down dark alleyways. Not yet. "You'll have to work behind the scenes quite a bit, particularly if the police or press are involved." He wasn't surprised by her eager nod of agreement. "And you'll have to wear your widow's weeds again. Probably quite a lot."

"I can do that." She tipped her head at him, concerned blue eyes searching his face. "Is this what you want, Samuel, or is this only for me?"

"It's for both of us." He couldn't stop himself from

reaching up and toying with the sapphire pendant at her throat. "If you're amenable to the idea. The idle life is not for us, I think. We can travel for a time, but you'll miss your family before long, and I imagine you'll want a greater sense of purpose at some point. We both will."

"You've been thinking about this for a while."

"I have." He nodded once. "I had to be certain I could follow through with the idea before I proposed it."

"It won't be easy for you," she said quietly.

"No, but it won't always be easy for you either."

She would be more reckless than he liked. He would be more stodgy than she preferred. They would argue and debate, fight and apologize. He would be clumsy with his words. She would take offense where none was intended. And they would keep doing it until she agreed to be a little more careful, and he agreed to be a little less overbearing. One way or another, they would reach a compromise. They would find a way to make each other happy.

She placed her hand over his own and held it there. "I'll remember that. I'll make concessions of my own. I promise."

"Are we agreed then? Once Edmund is settled and we've tired of traveling, we'll work together?"

"Well..." The eager pleasure returned to her face, along with a sly tilt of the lips. It was the Walker smile. God help him. "I suppose the Thief Takers *could* do with a proper leader."

About the Author

Alissa Johnson is a RITA-nominated author of historical romance. She grew up on Air Force bases and attended St. Olaf College in Minnesota. She currently resides in the Arkansan Ozarks, where she spends her free time keeping her Aussie dog busy, visiting with family, and dabbling in archery. Visit her at www.alissajohnson.com.

Luck Is No Lady

Fallen Ladies

by Amy Sandas

"You should not have kissed me," she replied breathlessly.

"I do a lot of things I shouldn't. It does not mean I won't do them again."

Gently bred Emma Chadwick always assumed she'd live and die the daughter of a gentleman. But when her father's death reveals a world of staggering debt and dangerous moneylenders, she must risk her good name and put her talent for mathematics to use, taking a position as bookkeeper at London's most notorious gambling hell. Surrounded by vice and corruption on all sides, it is imperative no one discovers Emma's shameful secret, or her reputation—and her life—will be ruined.

But Roderick Bentley, the hell's sinfully wealthy owner, draws Emma deep into an underworld of high-stakes gambling and reckless overindulgence. She soon discovers that in order to win the love of a ruthless scoundrel, she will have to play the game...and give in to the pleasure of falling from grace.

Praise for *Reckless Viscount*:

"An engaging and unusual historical romance. Beautifully sensual love scenes are woven into this intriguing romance." —*Night Owl Romance* Top Pick

For more Amy Sandas, visit:
www.sourcebooks.com

A Talent for Trickery

The Thief-takers

by Alissa Johnson

The lady is a thief

Years ago, Owen Renderwell earned acclaim—and a title—for the dashing rescue of a kidnapped duchess. But only a select few knew that Scotland Yard's most famous detective was working alongside London's most infamous thief…and his criminally brilliant daughter, Charlotte Walker.

Lottie was like no other woman in Victorian England. She challenged him. She dazzled him. She questioned everything he believed and everything he was, and he has never wanted anyone more. And then he lost her.

Now a private detective on the trail of a murderer, Owen has stormed back into Lottie's life. She knows that no matter what they may pretend, he will always be a man of the law and she a criminal. Yet whenever he's near, Owen has a way of making things complicated…and making her long for a future that can never be theirs.

The Infamous Heir

The Spare Heirs

by Elizabeth Michels

The Spare Heirs Society Cordially Invites You to Meet Ethan Moore: The Scoundrel

Lady Roselyn Grey's debut has finally arrived, and of course, she has every flounce and flutter planned. She'll wear the perfect gowns and marry the perfect gentleman…that is, if the formerly disinherited brother of the man she intends to marry doesn't ruin everything first.

Ethan Moore is a prizefighting second son and proud founding member of the Spare Heirs Society—and that's all he ever should have been. But in an instant, his brother's noble title is his, the eyes of the *ton* are upon him, and the lady he's loved for years would rather meet him in the boxing ring than the ballroom.

He's faced worse. With the help of his Spare Heirs brotherhood, Ethan's certain he can get to the bottom of his brother's unexpected demise and win the impossible lady who has haunted his dreams for as long as he can remember…